the BURNING man

ALSO BY MARK CHADBOURN
FROM GOLLANCZ

The Dark Age:
The Devil In Green
The Queen of Sinister
The Hounds of Avalon

The Age of Misrule:
World's End
Darkest Hour
Always Forever

Kingdom of the Serpent
Jack of Ravens

Underground
Nocturne
The Eternal
Testimony
Scissorman

the BURNING man

kingdom of the serpent: book 2

MARK
CHADBOURN

GOLLANCZ

LONDON

The right of Mark Chadbourn to be identified as the author
of this work has been asserted by him in accordance with
the Copyright, Designs and Patents Act 1988.

First published in Great Britain in 2008 by
Gollancz

An imprint of the Orion Publishing Group
Orion House, 5 Upper St Martin's Lane,
London WC2H 9EA

A CIP catalogue record for this book is available
from the British Library

ISBN 978 0 57507 6 778 (cased)
ISBN 978 0 57507 9 496 (trade paperback)

1 3 5 7 9 10 8 6 4 2

Typeset at The Spartan Press Ltd,
Lymington, Hants

Printed and bound at Mackays of Chatham plc,
Chatham, Kent

The Orion Publishing Group's policy is to use papers that
are natural, renewable and recyclable products and made
from wood grown in sustainable forests. The logging and
manufacturing processes are expected to conform to the
environmental regulations of the country of origin.

For Liz, Betsy, Joe and Eve

Acknowledgements

Jessica Lazar for her excursion into deepest China. Lisa Rogers for her dedication to her work, and her appreciation of New York bars. Lizzy Hill for keeping the archives. Jo Fletcher for always excellent advice and guidance. And to the members of the Mark Chadbourn messageboard for constant support.

contents

the final age *1*

prologue Semi-Charmed Life *9*

chapter one An Unkindness of Ravens *24*

chapter two The Last Train *45*

chapter three Haunted *59*

chapter four Two Minutes to Midnight *77*

chapter five Some Kind of Karmic-Chi Love Thing *110*

chapter six The Bull, The Serpent, The Ivy and the Wine *126*

chapter seven Cult of Souls *148*

chapter eight The Victorious City *170*

chapter nine The Lone and Level Sands *199*

chapter ten The Way *224*

chapter eleven Forbidden *247*

chapter twelve The Burning Man *269*

chapter thirteen Waking Up in the Sleepless City *295*

chapter fourteen Clutching at Straws *317*

the final age

My name is Jack Churchill, known to my friends as Church, and I am only a man. This is a story of gods, and powers higher than gods. I write these words in my head, and thus on a page, and thus throughout all Existence, as I stand here, at the end of the world.

From the first day that I accepted my role as a Brother of Dragons, I have struggled long and hard. At the time I didn't understand the full nature of the responsibility thrust upon my shoulders. Now I do.

Looking back, I can at least begin to glimpse the great, hidden pattern and how apparently random events came together, all the mysteries and secrets gradually emerging into plain sight.

But at the start I had no idea of the bigger scheme.

In my past life, what I used to call my 'real' life, I was an archaeologist, but my days had been blighted by the death of my girlfriend, Marianne. I'd lost all hope. And then magic and wonder and terror returned to the world. The ancient gods of Celtic mythology – the Tuatha Dé Danann, who called themselves Golden Ones – invaded an Age of Reason unable to cope with their irrationality. Society creaked and groaned and collapsed in the face of such a supernatural force.

For more than two thousand years, Existence had always brought together five champions of Life to battle such threats, the Brothers and Sisters of Dragons. I was chosen to be one of the latest group, bound together by the Pendragon Spirit, the powerful spiritual force that runs through the earth in lines of Blue Fire, and through all humanity. As a war broke out between the Golden Ones and their ancient race enemy, the demonic, shape-shifting Fomorii, I was joined by four others: Ruth Gallagher, gifted in the ways of the Craft; Shavi, a seer; Ryan Veitch, a warrior; and Laura DuSantiago, who was radically changed by the god Cernunnos to become a powerful force for nature.

We overcame great hardship to win a significant battle against Balor, the terrible god of the Fomorii, but we paid an awful price. Ryan Veitch was manipulated by the gods to betray us and we thought him dead. And I was flung back through the ages, separated from Ruth, the woman I loved.

As society attempted to recover from that Age of Misrule, five new Brothers and Sisters of Dragons took up the struggle. There was Mallory, who trained in the art of warfare in the new order of Knights Templar in Salisbury; his lover Sophie Tallent, who also learned the powers of the Craft; Caitlin Shepherd, a doctor devastated by the deaths of her husband and son; Hunter, a Special Forces operative employed by the Government; and Hal, a clerk working for the same Government.

But their struggle was even greater than ours had been. Beyond the edge of the universe, a devastating force had woken and turned its attention towards Earth. Known in ancient myths as the Devourer of All Things, or the Void, it was the opposite of Existence, of life itself, and it wielded the unlimited powers of the ultimate creator. It could even alter reality itself, twisting it into new shapes that would help maintain its rule.

The new Brothers and Sisters of Dragons could not vanquish such a force, even when aided by Ruth, Shavi and Laura. At the point of defeat, Hal chose to sacrifice himself and become part of the Blue Fire so that he could seek me out in time, and guide me back for the final battle.

Secure in its victory, the Void changed reality to a very familiar construct: the age-old prison of money and power, devoid of magic and wonder; and it locked the remaining Brothers and Sisters of Dragons into fake lives, denying them their memories so they would never again attain their true potential and threaten its rule.

At the time, I knew nothing of these events. I walked out of the morning mists into an unspoiled world more than two thousand years ago, a huge part of my memory missing. Members of a Celtic tribe adopted me in their village at Carn Euny, in what would become Cornwall, and I lived a simple life with new friends. But the simplicity and beauty of that rural existence did not last long, for the Void still saw me as a threat. It despatched through time its supernatural agents, the Army of the Ten Billion Spiders, to prevent me and the Brothers and Sisters of Dragons from challenging it again.

Existence, however, had other ideas.

At the great stone circle of Boskawen-Un, I encountered Hal in the Blue Fire, who set me off on a quest across two millennia to return to my own time. And in a brain-twisting paradox, I became the first Brother of

Dragons, initiating the heritage that would welcome me into its ranks two thousand years in the future. My new friends Etain, Branwen, Tannis and Owein became the other four members of the first group.

Establishing the first of the Watchmen, a brotherhood that would grow over time into a network of spies who could help my cause, I felt ready to take on the challenge of the Void. But in that moment of initial success, tragedy struck. Etain and the others were slaughtered by a mysterious assassin, and I fell under the control of Niamh, one of the Tuatha Dé Danann, who took me back a prisoner to the Celtic Otherworld, known as T'ir n'a n'Og or the Far Lands.

Niamh was the cruel, capricious queen of the Court of the Soaring Spirit, and saw me as little more than entertainment. I became friends with another of her prisoners, Jerzy, the Mocker, who had been surgically altered at the grim Court of the Final Word to become Niamh's jester.

Yet during my imprisonment I discovered the route back to my own time. T'ir n'a n'Og was essentially timeless. I could while away my days there while centuries passed in the real world, and eventually return when my own age rolled around again.

But the Void was not about to let me go without a fight. First I was attacked by Etain, dead yet alive, now a Sister of Spiders. And then I encountered the Void's most lethal agent: the Libertarian, a sardonic, brutal killer with lidless red eyes who threatened to kill Ruth in the twenty-first century if I interfered with the Void's plans.

There was nothing I could do to warn Ruth, but I found a way to see her during a visit to another of the twenty great courts of the Tuatha Dé Danann, the Court of Peaceful Days. A mystical object called a Wish-Post allowed me to see into the future, where I observed Ruth, Shavi and Laura, all living their miserable fake lives, lost without me.

When I returned to the Court of the Soaring Spirit, I discovered that Niamh's brother, the god Lugh, had gone missing. I accompanied her in a search to the last place he had been seen – Roman York in AD 306. There I encountered the Brothers and Sisters of Dragons of that era: Marcus Aelius Aquila of the Sixth Legion; Decebalus, a Dacian barbarian; Lucia Aeternia Constans, a practitioner of the Craft; the North African seer Secullian; and Aula Fabricia Candida, an agent of the powers of the natural world. And in that encounter I began to understand the strange, repeating patterns that underpinned all reality.

As Niamh introduced me to her set of Tarot cards with its mysterious fifth suit, ravens, only available to the gods and used to contact higher powers, another mystery was unfolding. The long-lost Ninth Legion had returned under the control of the Army of the Ten Billion Spiders. As I rallied the Brothers and Sisters of Dragons to defend the city, I was captured by the Libertarian and Marcus was killed. In an attempt to instil despair, the Libertarian revealed that many powerful human leaders were now being controlled by a single spider embedded somewhere in their skin.

I escaped, but during the battle with the Ninth Legion Secullian was also killed, this time by Etain and her fellow undead Brothers and Sisters of Spiders. There were only four of them – I should have guessed one more would be necessary to achieve the magical number. It was Ryan Veitch, resurrected by the Void and filled with bitterness over what he perceived as his betrayal. Veitch had loved Ruth, too, and in his twisted perception, I had allowed him to be sacrificed so I could get Ruth to myself. He was wrong, completely wrong, but he'd been corrupted by the Void – manipulated once again. Now all he wanted was revenge. He was the stranger who had murdered Etain and the others, but now, in their afterlife, he had struck up some strange, perverse relationship with Etain, both of them united in their hatred of me.

The extent of Veitch's desire for revenge was driven home when he vowed to move across the years slaughtering every Brother and Sister of Dragons he could find. He was going to strike a blow at the very heart of Existence for abandoning him.

Veitch captured me and took me to Rome where I was to be sacrificed to the god Janus, one of the great architects behind the mysterious unfolding struggle. But I was rescued by the remaining Roman Brothers and Sisters of Dragons, who accompanied me back to the Far Lands where I recovered from my ordeal. Though Lugh still hadn't been found, my relationship with Niamh had started to change. I didn't recognise it at the time, but she was beginning to fall in love with me.

Meanwhile, the Void had been establishing a fortress for its growing army on the edge of the Far Lands. The remnants of the spider-controlled Ninth Legion marched there along with an array of foul creatures – Redcaps, the Lament-Brood, the vampiric Baobhan Sith and more. The Void wanted to keep control of the universe, and the army and the spiders would ensure that any hope and resistance generated by Existence would be crushed.

Meanwhile, there was a new arrival at the Court of the Soaring Spirit: a human, Thomas Learmont, who had been transformed into the mythic hero Thomas the Rhymer by the prophetic powers given to him at the Court of the Final Word. Tom had become a great friend to me, but that was far in the future, when I had first become a Brother of Dragons. Here, in the distant past, Tom didn't know me at all, but his prophetic abilities knew I was vital in the coming war with the Void.

Using his visions of the future, Tom guided me, Niamh, Decebalus, Aula and Lucia back to Earth, to Venice in 1586, to locate a magical item that Tom knew was required by the Void's agents – the Anubis Box.

While retrieving the box, I encountered Will Swyfte, Elizabethan England's greatest spy, who took me to meet the court's mystic, John Dee. He directed me to a secret Templar store beneath London Bridge where another magical item was hidden away – a crystal skull that had to be used in conjunction with the Anubis Box.

But the skull and the box were stolen by the Void's agents, Lucia was murdered and I gave pursuit across the Atlantic to the new English settlement at Roanoke Island, in what would come to be America.

In a ritual in the new colony, Janus and the Army of the Ten Billion Spiders utilised the Anubis Box and the crystal skull to attempt to bind two gods – Apollo and the missing Lugh. Apollo was corrupted by the power of the Anubis Box and joined the Void's forces in the Far Lands, but with Will Swyfte's help I saved Lugh.

The colonists were not so lucky. The small group, including Virginia Dare, the first child to be born in the New World, were stolen from Roanoke and transported to the Void's Otherworldly fortress.

Back in the Court of the Soaring Spirit, while Niamh celebrated the return of her brother, I saved Jerzy from committing suicide. He was terrified he would betray me. During his surgery at the Court of the Final Word, a Caraprix had been inserted into his head so that he could, at any time, be manipulated by the gods. The Caraprix, I had discovered, were mysterious, shape-changing creatures that all the gods carried with them in some kind of symbiotic relationship. No one appeared to know their origins – they were simply *there*.

I was determined to seize an advantage in the ongoing fight and petitioned Niamh to allow me to move back and forth between the worlds at will. My plan was simple: to locate as many Brothers and Sisters of Dragons as possible before Veitch found and killed them, and to bring them back to safety at the Court of the Soaring Spirit where they would form the basis of an army that could challenge the Void's own forces.

In 1851 at Stonehenge, Jerzy mysteriously disappeared from our group. Unable to find him, we proceeded to the Crystal Palace Exhibition at Hyde Park where I encountered the Seelie Court, a travelling group of Tuatha Dé Danann who were very friendly with 'Fragile Creatures', as the gods call us. Veitch, in the grip of his desire for revenge, tried to kill me, but I was saved by an uncanny creature who called himself Spring-Heeled Jack.

It was not until 1940, when London was in the throes of the Blitz, that I discovered his true identity – the shape-shifting trickster Puck, also known as Robin Goodfellow, 'the oldest thing in the land'. It was he who had kidnapped Jerzy, for reasons I didn't discover, and who had been manipulating me for his own undisclosed ends. In the middle of the Blitz, I fought Loki, another god corrupted and controlled by the powers of the Anubis Box. Janus was drawing gods from a variety of pantheons to the Void's cause, creating what would eventually become an unbeatable force. More by luck than skill, I forced Loki to flee and managed to retrieve the Anubis Box – only for the Puck to steal it for his own devices.

Back in the Far Lands, I journeyed to the sinister Court of the Final Word, which appeared to be behind so much of the misery I had seen – the place where Tom, Jerzy and even Veitch had been so altered. What I discovered there was beyond any horrors I could have imagined. The court squatted on a river of blood, and in its secret confines the god Dian Cecht conducted sickening experiments on humans stolen from our world. Through his studies, he believed he could divine the true nature of Existence and thereby give his people complete control over all that was, guaranteeing their survival in the face of the Void, while at the same time ensuring that they would not be supplanted by Fragile Creatures.

Dian Cecht also revealed that reality was fluid, and that it could be altered by someone in whom 'the Pendragon Spirit burns brightly'. At the time, I didn't understand what he was really saying. He also allowed me to look into my own time through another Wish-Post – more from cruelty than kindness, I think. And there I saw Veitch terrorising Shavi, Ruth and Laura, who had all started to awaken from their fake lives. But, separated from them by time, there was nothing I could do to help them.

Devastated by what I'd witnessed in the court, I fled to Earth with Niamh and Tom, shirking my responsibilities for a nomadic life in America during the sixties. There I discovered that the spider-controlled people were attempting to destroy a resurgent hope that had gripped the world, through a series of political assassinations, repressive actions and war in the Far East. The Void was creating the kind of world in which it felt most comfortable.

Some of the secrets of the Void were revealed to me by an unlikely source – the LSD prophet Timothy Leary, the so-called 'most dangerous man in America'. We talked about the Gnostic secrets John Dee had first hinted at three hundred years before – that when the universe was created, the organising force split into two parts – the Light, or Life, and the Dark, or Anti-Life – the Void. And the Void had been running the show ever since, causing all the suffering in the world – for how could a benign god allow such terrible things to happen?

But the Light had planted the seeds of the Void's destruction: shards of itself embedded in all humans – the Pendragon Spirit. And the aim of all Gnostic teaching was to awaken that Spirit so that Fragile Creatures could rise up to achieve their true potential.

Much of what I'd experienced suddenly became clear, and the true mountain I had to climb was revealed – to overthrow the dark god that ruled the universe! How could I, or any mortal, achieve that?

In 1967, on the West Coast of America, events were escalating to a climax. Veitch and the Libertarian were working together, and the Army of the Ten Billion Spiders was searching for the insanely powerful Extinction Shears, a tool that could cut through all reality. The spiders wanted to use the Shears to sever the Blue Fire from Existence, and thus cut off the power of the Brothers and Sisters of Dragons.

And once the Shears had been recovered from the Tuatha Dé Danann's travelling Market of Wishful Spirit, that's just what they did. In a cavern beneath the jungles of Vietnam where the Blue Fire poured into our world, the Shears were activated and the flow stopped. The Fabulous Beasts that lived in the Fire were threatened with extinction. Though the Shears were once again lost, all hope was vanishing fast.

At the Woodstock Festival in 1969, the Libertarian came to me and offered me a deal – if I gave myself up to the Sleep Like Death, locked for ever in a casket in the Far Lands, Ruth, Shavi and Laura would not be killed. I'd reached my lowest ebb – I could see no other option, and at least this sacrifice would allow me to hold on to the hope that Ruth and the others might find some way to continue the rebellion. I agreed.

But the Libertarian had one final surprise for me. When he locked me in the casket in the Far Lands, he filled it with spiders.

The potion I had taken threw me instantly into the Sleep Like Death, and I was unaware that both Tom and Niamh visited me to offer their respects – and each left me a vital gift: Tom a sacrament from Timothy Leary, and Niamh the Tarot cards she used to contact the higher powers.

The power of the two gifts combined to transport me, in reality or in my mind, to another place. In that dreamlike state, I encountered a past or future version of myself, and then met the Caretaker, an intermediary between humans and the higher powers. He led me to a cavern where two more intermediaries waited – a strange, frightening man and woman looking into a bubbling cauldron.

In the cauldron, I watched events unfolding in the real world – the return of the Celtic gods and the Fomorii during the Age of Misrule that my younger self had experienced; the deaths of Niamh and Tom, sacrificing themselves for the greater good; and the events that had awoken the Void.

Afterwards, the Caretaker led me past a cavern where the three Daughters of the Night unravelled, measured and cut the threads of human life, and then to another cave containing the Axis of Existence. By shifting what I perceived to be a lever, but which was truly something incomprehensible, I could alter reality, as Dian Cecht had hinted. Still believing it to be a dream, I moved the lever and thus saved Tom, Niamh and the Tuatha Dé Danann, unaware that there would be repercussions for my action.

While I slept my restless sleep, Ruth, Laura and Shavi escaped Veitch and made their way to the Far Lands, where Ruth woke me with a kiss. After more than two thousand years, I was finally reunited with the woman I loved, and with my friends and comrades. The reunion kindled the embers of hope I needed to pick up the fight.

I knew we had to relocate the Extinction Shears, the only thing with enough power to destroy the Void. But first we paid a visit to the Eden Project, the environmental site in Cornwall, where the Seelie Court waited, and where I knew a great Fabulous Beast was hidden. If we could awaken it, we could release into the land what meagre Blue Fire still existed.

The Army of the Ten Billion Spiders did everything in its power to stop us reaching the Eden Project. Once there, we faced one final battle with Veitch and the Brothers and Sisters of Spiders. At the last, Veitch threw himself onto his sword, which he'd thrust into my hands. It looked like a last, desperate act of suicide when he knew he was beaten, but at the moment he died, mysterious black lightning flashed between him, me and Ruth, all of us joined in one moment of searing cold.

I had no idea what that had done to us, if anything, and in the midst of victory gave it little thought. The Fabulous Beast was awakened. Magic returned to the land. As Veitch's body was reclaimed by Etain, Hal manifested in the resurgent Blue Fire, my own genie in a bottle, offering me guidance regarding the way forward. The first thing he suggested was that we free Mallory, Sophie, Caitlin and Hunter from their fake lives so that we would have a strong force of Brothers and Sisters of Dragons.

And after that? A long, hard road lay ahead . . .

SEMI-CHARMED LIFE

1

London sleeps, London dreams.

In the quiet hour before dawn, the city breathes steadily. The river drifts, dark and slow. The trains have stopped, the traffic has slowed. Listen. You can almost hear each exhalation, and the whispers rising from the subterranean unconscious.

In Ealing and Richmond and Clapham, children wake, crying about a fire, a terrible fire, and their parents cannot calm them. In Battersea, a disconsolate mother sits alone in a dark lounge, sobbing.

Along the Strand, a policeman stops, troubled. Every night an old homeless man everyone knows as Glasgow Tom sits on his patch and babbles relentlessly from dusk till dawn. Tonight, for the first night the policeman can remember in three years, Glasgow Tom is silent. He sits against the wall, reeking of strong, cheap beer and urine, and traces an outline of a man against the dark sky, over and over again.

In the zoo, to the north, beyond the green expanse of Regent's Park, the silence is shattered as animals howl and chatter and scream in a way their keepers have never heard before. The beasts look to the sky as if seeing things no human can see. In every cage and pen, animals looking to the sky. With jokes and shrugs, the keepers try to believe there is some rational explanation. There is not.

At the insect house, in the glass case of *Solenopsis invicta*, sixty-five million years of order have fallen. In their nest, the fire ants have turned on each other, killing their own kind wantonly. In the glass cases beyond, the arachnids are still and watchful.

The city dreams strange dreams.

9

To the east, in the commercial district bleeding out of the City and into the old Docklands, the rich and privileged dream of hard things, of their monumental buildings, and expensive cars, and well-tailored suits: of money and what money makes. Sleep here is easy.

But there are those who do not have the luxury of rest. High up in the tallest tower in Canary Wharf are the offices of Steelguard Securities, which prides itself on being the hardest, most driven, most morally ambivalent – and therefore most successful – company in the quarter. Here two employees still toil despite the lateness of the hour.

Mallory is beneath notice, in his blue overalls, his dark hair fastened back with an elastic band, with his vacuum and his cleaning products, maintaining his ironic disposition despite the relentless routine of emptying bins and cleaning phones night after night after night. When he is asleep, Mallory is not allowed to dream. His dreams come when he is awake, in flashes that are almost like memories, rich in detail and clarity of purpose. Yet they could not be real in any way, and so he is troubled by them. In his dreams, he is a hero with a magical sword, battling in a fallen world. One of five great heroes struggling to prevent life from slipping into endless shadow.

Yet here he is with his vacuum and cleaning products. No sword; no hero by any measure.

In the main dealing room, beyond the glass partition wall that Mallory cleans every night, sits another employee. Like Mallory, she is in her late twenties, with an intelligent and knowing face that Mallory finds intriguing. Sophie Tallent is not allowed to dream while she sleeps either. She watches the figures on her screen as the Nikkei 225 index rises and falls in minute increments. Like Mallory, Sophie has lucid flashes of another life that she fervently wishes was real. A life filled with meaning, the soothing pulse of nature, swelling emotions and deeds that help make the world a better place. In contrast, her existence at Steelguard is a ghost-life, where the dead perpetuate the meaningless rituals they followed when they were alive.

Sometimes she glances at Mallory, and sometimes he casts a furtive glance at her, but their eyes never meet. It has been that way for as long as they have worked there, which feels like for ever. Occasionally they wonder what they would see in those depths if their gazes did coincide.

On this particular night, Mallory was so engrossed in the woman that he did not hear any footsteps approach through the echoing annexe. Perhaps there had not been any. Startled by a cough, he turned to find the kind of man who could appear in any situation and leave no impression whatsoever: bland features, neither handsome nor unattractive;

dark hair, cut short but not too severely; dark suit, not too expensive, not too cheap. Mallory even had difficulty estimating his age.

'I'm Mr Rourke, the night manager,' he said. 'Haven't you finished here yet? Stop dragging your feet.'

Mallory thought he knew everyone on the night staff, but he had never seen Rourke before. 'Nearly done.' Sullenly, he returned to his cleaning products. Something about the manager set his teeth on edge.

When he had retrieved the window cleaner, he was surprised to see that another person had arrived silently behind Rourke. Mallory had a second to take in the man's determined face before a fiery crackle severed Rourke's head from his shoulders.

At first Mallory had difficulty perceiving the assassin's weapon. His mind told him it was some kind of clockwork machine, much too large for him to hold, then a crystal glowing a brilliant white. Finally he realised it was an ancient sword with a thin blue flame flickering along its edges.

And suddenly he was no longer the Mallory who cleaned the toilets five times a day. Instinctively, he whisked his mop handle to the stranger's throat like a sword. The stranger simply smiled.

'You killed him,' Mallory said incredulously.

'I've been looking for you for a long time. They hid you well,' the stranger said. 'My name's Church. I'm here to take you back to your real life.'

Mallory's thoughts were already racing ahead, evaluating numerous strategies for disarming the assassin, defensive positions to protect the woman in the next room.

Church appeared to know exactly what Mallory was thinking. He wagged one cautionary finger, then pointed down.

Where Mallory had expected to see Rourke's corpse and severed head, there were now spiders, lots of them, some small, some as big as his fist. Rourke's body was also disintegrating rapidly as more spiders poured from its depths. With a single mind, they surged towards Church, and where they passed it looked as if the very fabric of the building was being scoured away to reveal a hole into space.

'Don't ask questions now,' Church said. 'If the spiders get you, you'll be gone from this world in an instant.' He grabbed Mallory's arm and hauled him away from the black stream. 'To the stairs. I'll explain everything once we're safe.'

Mallory half-resisted, but in the same instinctive way he had wielded his mop like a weapon, he knew Church could be trusted. 'There's a woman—'

'She's being taken care of.'

Through the glass, Mallory saw an unfamiliar woman who reminded him of a Pre-Raphaelite painting, dark, curly hair framing a pale, attractive face. She was talking intently to the woman he had been watching work at the terminal.

'Her name's Ruth,' Church said. 'She's one of us. She'll get your friend out.'

Mallory had no time to question Church's use of the word 'friend' for the spiders were now flooding in pursuit. Mallory flipped over a desk to block their path, but they cut through it with such ease it appeared illusory.

'What the hell are they?' he hissed.

'The things that really rule this world. Now move.'

Ruth and the other woman emerged from another door into the lobby near the lifts.

'Two for two,' Church said to Ruth. 'Result.'

'We're not out of here yet.' Ruth flashed a smile at Mallory. 'This is Sophie Tallent,' she announced. 'She feels as if she knows me from somewhere.'

Sophie. Mallory turned the name over in his mind. He was oddly pleased to see a determination in her face, somehow familiar. Her eyes met his for the first time: an instant connection, deep and puzzling and exhilarating.

Casting a glance at the spiders flooding into the lobby, Church threw open the door to the stairwell. 'We're not risking getting trapped in the lifts. You're the one with the power,' he said to Ruth. 'Can't you do something?'

'It's not like turning on a light switch,' she snapped. 'I really need a ritual—'

'Just do what you can.'

Cursing under her breath, Ruth turned to face the spiders, half-bowed her head and closed her eyes. Mallory heard her whisper a word he didn't recognise, but which made his stomach turn. An instant later the lights went out.

'Brilliant,' Church said.

'I told you I needed a ritual!'

Mallory felt himself being propelled into the inky stairwell and heard the door slam behind him.

'That won't hold them at all,' Ruth said.

Church sighed, said nothing.

A cool hand fumbled into Mallory's and he realised it was Sophie's.

'If we can get down three floors there are windows,' she said. 'The spotlights aimed at the outside of the building will give us enough illumination to see what we're doing.'

'If we haven't all broken our necks by then,' Ruth said sourly.

Clutching onto the handrails, they moved down the stairs as quickly as they could in the pitch darkness. An intense rustling came from the door at their backs.

'Moan, moan, moan,' Church said. A faint blue light began to glow. Mallory realised it was coming from the sword that Church was now holding aloft like a lantern.

Down two flights they hurried, stumbling and cursing, until small objects began to fall on Mallory's head and shoulders, each igniting a burning sensation that made him yell. Church brought the sword closer. In its glow, Mallory was horrified to see spiders clinging to him, eating through his thick overalls and into his flesh. More were raining from above.

'Get them off!' he shouted. 'I hate spiders!'

The others helped tear them off him as they stumbled down the stairs. The spiders felt hard, almost metallic, and they writhed sickeningly under Mallory's fingertips. His overalls sticky with blood, he hurled the spiders away as fast as he could pull them loose. Some burst against the walls, but the majority merely bounced and renewed their attack.

They were only a few steps ahead of the cascading spiders when they reached the windows that looked out over London's glittering cityscape.

'Is this supposed to be some kind of rescue?' Mallory snapped. 'Because if it is, it's the worst one ever.'

They made it down three more floors, their injuries mounting with each level. Finally they could go no further. The volume of spiders behind them was so great that the stairwell was covered – floor, walls and ceiling – apart from a small semicircle where the four of them had been backed against the window.

'How many of them are there?' Sophie said, aghast.

'About ten billion,' Church replied. 'Give or take.'

'You're pretty blasé about this,' Mallory said, tension hardening his tone.

'You're taking it in your stride, too.'

Mallory was surprised to realise this was true.

'Give me your hand,' Ruth said to Sophie. 'If everything's right, you should still have some vestige of ability to manipulate the Craft.'

'I have no idea what you're talking about.' Sophie bristled, unable to take her eyes off the advancing black line. Ruth took her hand nonetheless.

'Try not to make things worse this time,' Church said.

Ruth mouthed some insult, but she was already focusing her attention internally.

'What am I supposed to do?' Sophie asked.

'Don't think. Just feel.'

Mallory was surprised to see that Church was now oblivious to the threat of the spiders. He had returned the sword to a scabbard strapped across his back and was standing with his hands pressed against the glass, looking out over the Thames and the lights of the City.

Mallory kicked out at the nearest spiders. The toe of his boot soon hung ragged where it had made contact with them. 'A little help here, maybe?'

'I am helping,' Church said quietly. 'You need to lighten up.'

Behind the skyscrapers of the financial quarter, lightning illuminated the clouds. 'Okay,' Church said to Ruth. 'Do your stuff.'

Ruth bowed her head, her hair falling across her face. The stale air of the stairwell suddenly took on the freshness of the seaside and the advancing spiders came to a hesitant stop. All movement in the stairwell ceased. Outside, a distant rumble of thunder; another flash of lightning.

Sophie stiffened, her eyelids fluttering as a flush coloured her cheeks. The hand Mallory still held was limp and unresponsive.

'Now would be good,' Church said.

Ruth threw her head back and said a single word. Mallory was brought to his knees by a force that came from nowhere. In an eerie silence, the windows blew out, glass shards glittering as they fell to the railway far below. Standing on the brink, Church was oblivious to the powerfully gusting wind that raged inside, threatening to pluck them all out.

Sophie staggered, shook her head. 'What the hell happened there?' As she came to her senses, she noticed a curious thing: the spiders had moved back several feet. 'They're scared,' she said, puzzled. 'Of us.'

'It'll pass.' Ruth grasped Church's shoulder and he slid his arm around her waist; automatic, familiar gestures in which Mallory recognised tenderness. 'This would not be a good time to screw up.'

'Don't worry. Look.'

Mallory followed Church's pointing arm to a strange motion in the sky far away over the City. The lights of the Lloyd's Building were briefly obscured before reappearing.

'The spiders are moving again,' Sophie warned.

Mallory was fascinated by the shifting patterns of shadow and light outside. Gold and red flared briefly against the towering structures. Deep in the dark at the back of his head, where his true self had been locked away for too long, memories stirred: feelings of danger, awe and wonder.

Church saw the thoughts play across Mallory's face. 'The world doesn't have to be like this,' he said.

'Church, we can't wait any longer.' The urgency in Ruth's voice jolted them both from their reflection.

The spiders inched forward, gaining confidence.

'Whatever you did . . . can't you do it again?' Mallory asked.

'It doesn't work like that.' An edge of weariness sharpened Ruth's words. She pressed Sophie back towards Mallory and Church at the window.

Another strong gust. Mallory grabbed the window jamb to stop himself being pulled out. He had a brief, head-spinning view down the vast expanse of the tower to the railway line so far below it was barely visible.

'Okay, out there,' Church said decisively. He motioned to a thin ledge that ran around the outside of the tower just below the window.

'You're joking!' Mallory saw that Church wasn't.

'Come up with a better plan, you get to be king.' Steeling himself, Church stepped out of the window, pressing his back against the smooth wall of the tower. Mallory could see the strain in his face as he forced himself not to look down. The wind gusted, a deafening roar.

A surge of spiders drove Mallory, Sophie and Ruth out after him. Sophie gave a small cry, her face drained of blood, and Mallory grabbed her and pressed her back as she almost lurched over the edge.

'What's wrong with you?' Mallory yelled to Church over the wind. 'There's nowhere to go from here! Why did I ever come with you?'

'Because you chose life.'

Mallory's ironic laugh was stolen from his lips by the raging wind. He could barely hold on. Closing his eyes, he thought he was going to be sick.

'Keep moving,' Ruth shouted. 'The spiders are still coming.'

'This is pointless!' Mallory yelled. 'We're all dead!'

'I'm trying to buy us some time.' Church edged further along the ledge.

Eyes screwed shut, Sophie was paralysed, barely even breathing. Closing his own eyes so he didn't have to see the drop, Mallory squeezed her hand and urged her to match him step for step along the ledge. The wind tugged at his feet, slipped behind his back and lifted him away from the wall. He forced himself against it, gasping. 'Nowhere to go,' he said to himself.

'Yes, there is,' Church shouted. 'Look!'

Above the Thames, whatever Mallory had spied earlier was moving closer. Occasionally it was caught in the spotlights illuminating the new buildings that lined the river, and then it gleamed like something jewel-encrusted. It was still a silhouette against the city's lights, but Mallory could tell it was the size of an airliner. A burst of fire erupted from the front with a roar, and in its glare Mallory saw burning eyes and a serpentine tail, and the billowing wings that carried it on the currents that surged amongst the skyscrapers.

Gaping, he almost forgot where he was. It was a dream, of the city, of his own troubled, imprisoned mind. Behind him, the spiders swarmed along the side of the building, many plucked off by the wind and sent spiralling into the dark gulf, forgotten now in the face of approaching wonder.

'Is that . . . ?' Sophie had opened her eyes as though she had sensed what was coming.

'Yes,' Mallory said, 'it is.' He was puzzled why he wasn't more surprised. He saw Church smiling and that didn't surprise him either.

The Fabulous Beast caught the thermals and soared over the Thames.

'Come on!' Ruth urged. 'I've got spiders nibbling at my fingers!'

'You're summoning it?' Mallory asked.

His eyes glassy, Church didn't respond.

The Beast glided languorously around the towers of Docklands, the beat of its enormous wings echoing louder than the wind.

As it neared, Church came alive. 'When it passes beneath us, jump.'

Mallory and Sophie looked at him with horror.

Before they could protest, Ruth placed one hand in the small of Sophie's back and propelled her off the ledge. Church did the same with Mallory.

The wind tore at Mallory as he fell, kicking. Two seconds of plummeting stretched to an age, and then he hit the back of the Beast, winding himself. He slid, grabbed a bony tine along its spine, felt the others land nearby. The wings thundered with a steady, deafening beat and they rose higher, and higher still. Mallory watched the lights of the towers fall away as he clung on for dear life.

He realised he must have been wearing an odd expression, for Church was looking at him curiously. 'Scared?' Church asked.

'No,' Mallory replied, baffled. 'I just had the strangest feeling of déjà vu.'

2

England sleeps, England dreams. Across the rolling landscape beyond the capital, chill in the late spring, there is no peaceful darkness. Sodium lights burn brightly everywhere. There is no silence. The arterial roads still throb with traffic.

In the north-west of England, on the edge of the wild but beautiful country that runs down to the Lake District, Caitlin Shepherd sits in her car outside the Tebay motorway service station. The lights are bright, but all is still. Soon it will open for the first visitors of the day, the lonely few for whom travel is life. But not travel in the sense of mind-altering, character-enriching experience. Back and forth travel, mundane travel, a relentless round with no final destination. Perpetual motion with no meaning is Caitlin's lot, shipping samples of beauty products to shops that will consider stocking them, or perhaps not, and, like Caitlin, will not give it a second thought the moment the decision has been made.

Another dawn approached relentlessly. She craved sleep for escape, even though she was not allowed the luxury of dreams, but sleep would not come.

She was not alone. Several container lorries were parked nearby, their cabs dark. Yet Caitlin felt that in one of them someone was watching her. She always felt she was being observed, tracked, hunted, wherever she was, whatever she was doing. Paranoia, she thought wearily, another mental illness to add to the constant buzzing voices in her head. Her doctor had prescribed pills, several different types, in fact, and for a while she'd taken them; the voices stilled, the unease dulled, and with it went any sense, however slight, of being engaged in life. Eventually she threw them all out and consigned herself to a future of never being happy.

She closed her eyes. Sleep still did not come.

Wake up, Caitlin.

One of the voices, the little girl. She fought against the urge, then gave in and looked around, hating herself for it. It always made her feel queasy when the voices told her things her unconscious could not possibly know.

An attractive, charismatic Asian man loomed up next to the passenger window, his black hair gleaming in the car park lights. A leather eye patch covered one eye, but it did not make him look the least bit menacing. He smiled and tapped gently on the glass. Yet Caitlin could see he was on edge, his eyes flickering from side to side, searching the dark.

'Go away,' she said.

'We need to talk.' His voice was calm, yet insistent.

'No, we don't. If you're not away from here in ten seconds, I'm going to turn on the ignition and drive over you.'

The sound of a lorry door opening echoed across the quiet car park. The Asian man glanced in its direction, his voice and body language becoming a touch more urgent.

'My name is Shavi,' he said. 'I am a Brother of Dragons—'

'I'm not interested in your little cult.'

'You are a Sister of Dragons. We share a heritage—'

'Six, seven, eight . . .'

'Forgive me,' Shavi said.

Shattering the window with a tyre iron, he yanked open the door. Caitlin yelled and leaned on the horn. Barely one short blast echoed across the car park before Caitlin went woozy from the fumes from a small wooden box that Shavi had thrust under her nose.

'Just herbs,' he whispered. 'Do not worry.'

Dreamily, she saw herself being hauled out of the car as if she was watching a stranger. Shavi carried her effortlessly away from the bright lights to the dark of the moorland that pressed up hard against the service station. Behind them, Caitlin was vaguely aware of movement; rescuers responding to her cries, she thought obliquely.

She was aware of the stars and the moon, the lush smell of vegetation, but she couldn't muster either fear for herself or any desire to fight back.

It was only when they lay behind a scrubby bush on cool grass with the lights of the service station a distant glow that she began to think coherently once more. Her attacker, she realised, didn't seem violent; in fact, there was a benign, gentle air about him. Yet she struggled as soon as she was able.

He placed a hand firmly over her mouth and said quietly, 'Hush. Look.'

Responding to something in his tone, she peered past the bush towards the car park. Shadows shifted across the moorland. People searching for her? Shavi released his grip on her mouth, and it was that action which convinced her to trust him.

'What is it?' she hissed. Some quality of the quickly moving silhouettes did not appear right.

'Keep watching,' he said. 'But if they come too close, be prepared to move quickly into the wilderness. If they see us, we will not be able to outpace them.'

His words unnerved her. *What's out there?* she thought.

Before she could voice the question, a shape loomed up on the other side of the bush and she almost cried out. It had approached from a different direction, moving quickly. Shavi pressed her down, holding her still. His heart thundered against her back. Their chance of escape gone, they could only hope against discovery.

Caitlin could smell a foul farmyard odour. Breathing like the scraping of rusty iron echoed loudly. Whatever was on the other side of the bush had stopped. It sniffed the air.

Its bestial qualities increased her heartbeat another step, and she became afraid that her body would betray her with some random muscle spasm. Yet she had to see. Twisting her head slowly, she looked through the branches of the bush.

There was not a hint of humanity in the brutish thing that waited beyond. Eyes gleamed with a yellowish light in a face that combined the qualities of hog and gorilla. The body was thick-set and powerfully muscled. From its posture, Caitlin couldn't be sure whether it moved on two legs or all four. She noticed it was clothed, and with a second, chill glance realised the nature of those clothes: flayed human skin, scalps and internal organs had been stitched together in some sickening amalgam of uniform and war trophy. An eyeless face stared back at her blankly from the side of the creature's head.

It waited for a full thirty seconds that felt like as many minutes and then moved off rapidly, keeping low.

When she was sure it was gone, Caitlin asked shakily, 'What *was* that?'

Shavi searched the moorland until he was satisfied they were safe. 'A Redcap,' he said. 'They are the shock troops of the Enemy.' He returned his attention to Caitlin and a look of sympathy crossed his face. 'I am so sorry. The world is not the way you believe it to be.'

3

London sleeps, London dreams. Hyde Park is quiet. The tourists will not return until the fumes and the roar of constant traffic fill Lancaster Gate. Moonlight catches the still pools in the Italian Gardens. The statue of Peter Pan watches over the boundary between the magical and the real, conjuring dreams of stolen children and other worlds.

Hunter brought his knife away from the gaping throat and stepped back to avoid the arterial flow. Another job well done, more peaceful sleep for the country. On the surface his flamboyant, piratical appearance – long black hair tied back with a black ribbon, single gold earring, devilish goatee – belied the nature of the work he did; underneath, it illuminated it perfectly: a new age cut-throat.

Dragging the body into the cover of the trees, he meticulously wiped his blade on his target's jacket. He needed to sleep; his weariness had built up brick by brick over the relentless weeks and months, in Bosnia and Fallujah, Tehran and Priština, and a score of other places that all merged into one. Only the faces remained distinct. Superficially they were similar, glassy-eyed and bloodless, but he could never forget the telling details: a frozen, accusing stare; the faint impression of contempt or betrayal on the lips. Every one the same, every one different.

'Nice job.' A woman's voice, laced with sarcasm.

Hunter started; no one ever crept up on him unawares. His shock was quickly brought under control, the knife palmed, ready for use. He didn't speak. Instead, he rapidly scanned his surroundings and was surprised once more that he couldn't locate the intruder.

'What are you? Some kind of psycho? Existence chose well this time.' A pause. 'Actually, situation normal.'

Now he had a lock on her position. He shifted his body weight, ready.

The woman recognised his subtle movement. 'If you're thinking of using that knife on me, it won't do any good. I've had worse things than that stuck in me.' Her tone highlighted the double entendre.

The branches of an overgrown bush parted and the woman stepped brazenly out. She had white-blonde hair and an expression that fell somewhere between challenging and seductive. Her smile suggested that Hunter's coldly efficient brutality had not scared her in the slightest.

Hunter weighed his options. He couldn't leave any witnesses behind. His superiors in Vauxhall would instantly shift him into the box marked 'Liability', with all the repercussions that entailed. Nor was he prepared to hurt an 'innocent' (and the one thing that kept him going was that none of his victims were 'innocent').

He lunged quickly, hoping to find a way to resolve his dilemma once he had her in a position where she couldn't raise the alarm. As he shifted his weight, he found his ankles mysteriously constricted and he pitched forward to the ground. Long grass was inexplicably wrapped tightly around his feet.

'That's how I like my men,' the woman mocked. 'On their knees before me.' She tapped his arm lightly with her motorcycle boot, then skipped out of the way when he lunged for her again. 'So, did you see what I did there?' She nodded towards his feet.

'You did that?'

'Yes, I'm a beautiful wood nymph.'

'You have a very high opinion of yourself.'

'I like to call it realistic.' She sat cross-legged just out of reach.

Hunter began to saw through the strong, fibrous grass with his knife. 'You should start running now,' he said.

'I never run. Besides, I can do much worse than that. You know how painful it is when you get a thorn stuck in your thumb? Now imagine one going through your eye and into your brain.'

Her statement held such utter conviction that Hunter had to believe she thought she could do it. 'Who are you?'

'My name is Laura DuSantiago and I am here to save the world,' she said archly. 'And you go by the name of Hunter when you're not using one of your many aliases.'

'Who do you work for?'

'Existence.' She lay down and stared flirtatiously into his face. 'I'm not interested in the stupid little-boy games you've been playing. I've got a bigger agenda.'

'Which is?' Hunter freed himself, then balanced the knife on the palm of his hand before thrusting it into the ground.

Laura appeared quietly impressed by his choice. 'Ever felt this life you're leading is wrong? Made up? That you've got another life you can't quite remember?'

Hunter's practised non-committal expression gave nothing away.

'Do certain places give you a real buzz, like there's electricity in the ground? Do you get creeped out by a man called Rourke?'

His bland, ever-friendly line manager. 'How do you know about Rourke?'

'Oh, he gets around. Have we had sex?' she added with a hint of puzzlement that did not appear manufactured.

'I think I'd remember.' Yet even after he'd said the words, he realised that, strangely, he wasn't sure. 'But we could get it out of the way now if you like.'

'I think you ought to be disposing of that body first.' She teased him with her eyes. 'But before that I've got a little fairy story to tell you, about five great heroes, a magical quest and a threat that could destroy everything we hold dear.'

'Okay.' Hunter lounged back with his hands behind his head. 'Then can we have sex?'

4

England sleeps, England dreams.

In one of the few areas of unspoiled landscape within the shadow of the capital, Church breathes deeply, enjoying the soothing night air and the aromas of grass and tree. Here there is an abiding sense of peace that is difficult to find in the cluttered, busy nation. It comes not from the confluence of natural elements, but from something intangible deep within the land itself, a force that is both there and not there, physical and spiritual, earthly and otherworldly. It refreshes him and renews his purpose, but that is not the reason he is there.

Overhead, the Fabulous Beast swoops on the night winds. While Church stands on the rolling parkland looking up, he is also in the Beast's head looking down at himself. Its thoughts, if it has such things, are unknowable. Church is not even sure it can be characterised as alive, in any sense he understands. It is an idea, a manifestation of the power in the land, a terrible force of nature, a symbol and a Beast all at the same time. It is also the last one.

It must be protected in the same way that the Earth must be protected, for once the symbol is gone, the thing it symbolises withers and dies, too. It is the last one, and the last hope for a better world.

The ground shudders and a section of turf tears itself upwards to reveal a gaping hole that disappears into the earth. The Fabulous Beast circles one final time and then plunges into the dark tunnel. The turf closes behind it.

The Enemy won't find it there. It can rest until it is needed again.

Satisfied, Church turns away and prepares for the struggle to come.

5

The Grim Lands, where there is no sleep and no dreams.

Mists blanket the rocky, depressing landscape. Through the folds of grey, the dead move slowly, their whispering tread converging on a subterranean temple as desolate and heartless as anything in that place, but filled with a deep, tidal power.

Why is there a temple in the Land of the Dead? What could they worship there?

The dead do not enter, but instead gather at the entrance to the long, stone-lined tunnel that leads to the heart of the complex, in their tens and twenties, hundreds and thousands, all of the dead, from all over the Grim Lands, converging on that one place, where they wait, as silent as ever.

Why do they wait?

At the far end of the stone-lined tunnel is a great hall, carved from bedrock and lined with stone blocks. The ceiling is lost in the shadows. Wall paintings soar up into the gloom, their inhuman scale as disturbing as the images they depict. Grotesque effigies without any human char-acteristics stand grimly. Everywhere is still.

In the centre of the hall, on a stone plinth, lies a long marble box. Standing around it at the four cardinal points are the Brothers and Sisters of Spiders – Etain, Owein, Tannis and Branwen – as silent as their true brothers and sisters beyond the temple.

They wait, though time has no meaning to them, for an alignment of ritual and word long since put into effect. They watch the box. They listen. And as the vast army of the dead draws to a halt, the atmosphere becomes infused with dread. A hiss of sparks heralds a discharge of black energy.

In the lull that follows, a moan rises up, becoming a chant, low and somnolent. It is the dead cheering. There may be words hidden in the unearthly sound, and if there are they would be these: *He is risen.*

The stone lid of the box slides aside and crashes to the floor. It is the loudest noise ever heard in this hall, and its echoes reverberate for almost a minute. A hand rises from the box, followed by another, but this one is silver and mechanical. Heavily tattooed and muscular, Ryan Veitch levers himself up. He is pleased that his plan has worked and that he has not yet joined the ranks of the Grim Lands, and pleased at the response from his vast army of followers outside the temple. He is pleased also that more subtle strands are now creeping out from the spell to which he had reluctantly committed himself.

He looks around at the faces of the Brothers and Sisters of Spiders and finally settles on Etain. Her gaze is as empty as her companions', but Veitch sees something.

'Come on, darlin',' he says with a grin. 'Did you really doubt that I'd be back?'

6

England sleeps, England dreams.
But not for long.

23

chapter one

an unkindness of ravens

1

Early morning sun reflecting off glass and steel gave London a brassy newness. The city was awake and ready. Exhaust fumes and noise rose up from the clogged streets, and the offices and stores were filling with people preparing for slow, uninspiring toil. This was the modern age.

From the highest viewing point atop St Paul's Cathedral, Church watched the humdrum ritual of a sleepwalking world. He'd cut his hair, shaved cleanly, in the hope that he'd be able to merge into the somnolent mass, but every time he looked in the mirror he could see the scars of two thousand years of struggle. It made him an outsider, and if it was visible to him, it would be visible to the Enemy, too.

Drawing himself out of his reverie, he made his way down the wrought-iron steps to the quiet seclusion of the Whispering Gallery. Inside the dome, the atmosphere was charged, protective. He was relieved he had chosen the right meeting place. Safe locations were few and far between in an enemy landscape.

Ruth waited amidst the susurration. 'Shavi's just arrived with the last one. They're ready for you.'

'They're cooperating?'

'I've not heard any arguments so far. I think they felt it instinctively, like we all did.'

'They don't know what we're going to ask of them yet.'

'They'll live up to it, you know they will. That's why they were chosen.'

She kissed him. After so long yearning for her, and fighting to get back to her, he still couldn't believe they were reunited. Her memory of their previous life together still hadn't returned, so everything had the freshness of new love as she explored him, finding little details and quiet touches that cemented their feelings for each other.

They made their way down into the vast body of the cathedral, and then down further into the crypt. At the eastern end stood the Church of St Faith-below-St Paul, a chapel that had been established in the crypt of a church pulled down in the thirteenth century when the cathedral was enlarged. The atmosphere of sanctity that infused the whole building was even more potent there. To one side, Shavi and Laura waited with Mallory, Sophie, Caitlin and Hunter.

After introductions had been made, Hunter said, 'Congratulations. Very clandestine. I could find you lot a job. I'd have preferred somewhere with more alcohol and women, though.'

'We're safe here,' Church said.

'Speak for yourself. I'm normally run out of this kind of place with a pitchfork.' Hunter leaned against the wall, arms folded. He was grinning, but his eyes searched Church's face for any hint of weakness.

'He's right. Can't you feel it?' Sophie pressed one hand against the cool flags. 'There's something here . . . some kind of power.'

'That's it exactly,' Ruth said. 'A power that runs through the land. It's focused at certain nodes, in places that have been considered sacred for hundreds, sometimes thousands of years. Cathedrals and churches, yes, but also stone circles, wells, lakes, hilltops—'

Hunter snorted. Ruth flashed him a glare, and grew more annoyed when he only laughed out loud.

'You have to see it—' she began.

A lick of blue flames across the floor cut her short. Within seconds they had risen up into a wall of fire that separated the chapel from the rest of the crypt.

'I wish I could claim credit for that,' Ruth said.

Hunter reached out tentatively, then plunged his hand into the fire. 'Cold,' he said. Withdrawing his hand, he looked puzzled. 'I feel kind of . . . good?'

'I remember this,' Caitlin said dreamily. 'But long ago. Was I a child?'

In the flames, the figure of a man gradually formed. His features were indistinct but, strangely, they could all tell he was smiling.

'Hal,' Church said.

'Yes, it's me, your favourite genie,' Hal said wryly. 'Don't worry – nobody will see the Blue Fire if they come into the crypt, but they won't approach the chapel either. It'll give us a few minutes of privacy.'

'Who the hell are you?' Hunter said. 'The Human Torch?'

Hal laughed. 'I'm one of you, Hunter. You'd know exactly who I was if

25

your memory hadn't been wiped. Existence chooses groups of five to fight for Life. The four of you, and me . . . we're the last Brothers and Sisters of Dragons.'

'The last?' Church echoed.

'After this group is gone, there won't be any more.' An odd note in Hal's voice made Church uneasy.

Hal turned to Mallory, Sophie, Caitlin and Hunter. 'The Void made you live false lives so you wouldn't remember who you are and what you're capable of. I escaped into the Blue Fire.'

'Where you . . . what? Get to chip in with gnomic comments from time to time?' Hunter said.

'Something like that. But I'm here now because you're at the start of the next phase of your journey.'

'And this journey,' Hunter pressed, 'is to usurp the god who really rules the world?'

'The Void,' Shavi said. 'Although it has many other names.'

'Everyone on the planet is held by the Mundane Spell,' Hal said. 'It makes them think the things they do are normal and reasonable, however ridiculous they might be.'

'Like striving for money and power,' Shavi added wryly.

'They'll never be able to break the spell because they can't contemplate anything beyond what they see around them,' Hal continued. 'You can change that. You can make them open their eyes.'

'But how are we supposed to destroy a god?' Caitlin asked.

'There are two forces at work in this world – two polarities, if you like,' Hal replied, 'but they've been out of balance for a long time. The Void isn't omnipotent. It's aware of the force you all represent. It respects it . . . it's wary of it. If you want to unseat the Void, you need three things. The Extinction Shears, which can cut through the warp and weft of reality. They can untether the Void, and reshape everything. But to get the chance to use the Shears, you need two Keys. Two people hidden by Existence, somewhere in the world. One has the power of destruction, the other the power of creation.'

'Hidden somewhere in the world,' Hunter said sardonically. 'Amongst six billion plus people.'

'You'll find them,' Hal said.

'An optimist. I like that. Or maybe you're a fantasist. I'm not entirely sure.'

'Can't you help us?' Sophie asked.

'You need to do this yourselves,' Hal said.

'Oh, yeah.' Laura snorted. 'We haven't told you about the whole learn-while-you-burn thing.'

'The act of finding shapes us into the people we need to be to use the things we find,' Church said. 'Which is a mouthful, but that's the rule we're stuck with. We may get a push here and a prod there, but basically it's down to us. We can't do it on our own—'

'Especially with our number depleted,' Ruth said.

Church eyed her, but didn't explain. 'We need you. Will you help us?'

'Hang on,' Mallory said. 'You've obviously elected yourself leader—'

'That's not how it is.'

Mallory shrugged. 'If the Void controls the whole world, how can we move around without being seen?'

'Not easily,' Church admitted, 'but the Blue Fire offers us some protection in the places where it's strongest – which, frankly, at the moment isn't very many. But when we're on the lines of force that link the nodes, the Blue Fire pretty much blinds the Void to us.'

'So it's cathedrals from now on?' Mallory said. 'I'm with him.' He jerked a thumb towards Hunter. 'Cathedrals and me don't go together very well.'

Sophie silenced him with an insistent wave of her hand. She appeared to grasp what Church was saying. 'We stick to the lines of force and the nodes of power as much as we can. But apart from that we just have to keep moving, right?'

'That's about it,' Church said. 'I'll be honest, we're always going to be at risk—'

'From the spiders,' Hunter mocked.

'Trust me, they're not like any bugs you've seen before,' Mallory said.

'We all get that you're a cynical smart-mouth, Hunter,' Laura said. 'But this is the point where you need to lever that massive ego to one side for a while.'

'Well, you're a woman of hidden depths, aren't you? Selflessness now, is it?'

'If I can do it, anyone can. Even you.'

'We've got an obligation here,' Church said.

'The only obligation I've got is to myself,' Hunter snapped, 'and frankly I've not heard anything here that makes me think this is going to turn out anything other than disastrous.'

'We have a plan—'

'No, you haven't. You've got half a notion, a little bit of an idea concocted from a brew of rumours, innuendos and hints. Even if I laughably consider that there's the vaguest glimmer of truth in what I've heard, the possibility that we could do something about it is beyond my comprehension.'

'Don't you *feel* it?' Caitlin persisted. 'You know in your heart there's something bigger going on. Why don't you trust them?'

'I don't trust anybody. And I don't feel anything. I can see you're all doing the evangelical bit, and you give a good sermon, really. But this doesn't work for me. I wish you well, but I'll be honest, I'm not going to lose any sleep over leaving you to it.' He nodded decisively and glanced at Laura, who returned his look haughtily, and then walked through the wall of Blue Fire and away.

'You're not going to let him go?' Ruth said to Church. 'We need him.'

'We can't force him to help us.'

'We could try,' Mallory said hopefully.

'We need all the Brothers and Sisters of Dragons we can muster if we're going to stand a chance,' Ruth continued. 'What are we going to do now, Church?'

Church looked to Hal, but he shook his head. The flames had begun to die down, retreating towards the ground. 'I'm sorry,' he said. 'I can't help. You're on your own.'

2

Hunter spent the rest of the day in a brothel just off Wimpole Street. The girls came and went, but nothing could take his mind off everything he had seen and heard since he had first encountered Laura in Hyde Park. He felt troubled, and then angry that he felt troubled. He took great care to order his life so it would be bearable. The last thing he needed was to have it all shaken up, more responsibility thrust on him, more obligation.

When he emerged into a light rain as dusk was falling, he was in a bad mood and in need of some serious drinking. He made his way down to Soho where he could lose himself in the backstreet pubs without bumping into anyone he knew. He drank Jack Daniel's and Coke at a rapid clip and only became more irritated when drunkenness didn't come quickly enough.

It was past midnight and the rain was still falling when he finally gave up. The weather had driven the stragglers home or to clubs and the streets were deserted. As he made his way along Wardour Street, the instinct that had served him so well over the years came alive. It was the kind of unease he had felt moving through Belgrade at night with the Serbian security forces close behind. Slipping into an alley, he waited.

For several moments there was only the rain-slick street gleaming in the sodium lights and the drumming of droplets on fire escapes and parked cars. Then, at the far end of the street, a shimmer like the reflection of light from a moving car. Patches of mist emerged from doorways and alleys, rose up from manholes, gradually taking on greater substance before moving rapidly around. *Searching*, he thought. From a distance, the shapes resembled rags caught in the wind, but as they drew closer the faces of beautiful women became visible within the coalescing mist.

Entranced, Hunter believed they were the most attractive women he had ever seen; any doubts were unnaturally silenced, even the dim realisation that they were searching for him as they quickly moved into every available space.

Closer and closer, the pale figures whirled through the rain. A cat darted out of one of the alleys where it had been scavenging in a bin and froze in the middle of the road, its hackles raised. Three of the women spun around, arms raised, swaying on the spot. They looked like cobras, hissing and drawing back their lips to reveal needle teeth. In the hollows of their eyes lay something corrupt and terrifying.

Hands grabbed Hunter's shoulders and pulled him roughly back into the alley. It was the second time he had been surprised in as many days, and the shock of it broke the spell. He whirled to confront an ageing hippie, his grey hair pulled back in a ponytail, wire-rimmed spectacles, faded combat jacket, peace symbol T-shirt.

'I thought you people were supposed to be better than this,' he hissed. 'Come on.' He hurried into the shadows further along the alley. Hunter glanced back at the rapidly nearing feral women and chose to follow.

'Who are you?' Hunter asked when he caught up with the man, who was now staring up into the dark.

'Quiet. The Baobhan Sith can hear the movement of an insect.'

'The what?'

'There's a fire escape up there. If you boost me up, I can pull it down and we can get up onto the roof.'

'Remind me why I'm listening to you?'

The stranger's eyes were filled with a power belied by his shabby appearance. 'Because in two short minutes, those things on the street will be tearing you limb from limb. Thirty seconds after that you'll be nothing but a fine spray of blood and a few shards of bone.'

'Okay, you've convinced me.' Hunter cupped his hands and propelled the man up to the ladder, which slid down noisily. Within a minute they were on the wet roof. Hunter grabbed the man's arm and said, 'What do I call you?'

'Tom. And despite what you might be thinking, I am a friend.'

Still suspicious, Hunter crawled to the edge of the roof and peered over the parapet. The Baobhan Sith flitted across the street with mounting frenzy. They reminded Hunter of hounds scenting their unseen prey. 'Can they follow us up here?'

'They could, but they're not the sharpest knives in the box.' Tom eased next to him.

'Why are they after me?'

'When you lived a life of dull ignorance, you weren't a threat. Now you can no longer be contained or condoned. The alarms have gone off. You need to be removed from the field.'

'Oh, I get it. You're with the other lot. The mad Dragon Family.' Hunter ducked as one of the Baobhan Sith scanned the rooftops. 'They sent you to get me back.'

'No. I have yet to join up with them. In these dangerous times, a touch of subtlety is required. Frankly, I think they're flailing around like idiots. Dragging you in from your fake lives without any thought for how much fuss they're making. Where's the finesse? They're going to bring all hell down on their shoulders, mark my words.'

'If you're not working with them, how do you know what's going on?'

'I've been watching.'

A high-pitched shriek rose up from the street, setting Hunter's teeth on edge. It was joined by another and another.

Tom blanched. 'They have found us.'

Hunter drew a carbon-steel knife from the sheath strapped to his calf. 'Shall we see if they're any good?'

'You've got a death wish.' Tom tried to grab Hunter's arm, but he was already scrambling to the top of the fire escape. In the alley below, the Baobhan Sith looked like a mass of billowing sheets.

Before they could rise up the ladder, there was a disturbance at the entrance to the alley. A drunken couple were engaging in an argument en route home from the pub. She was shouting, 'You didn't have to keep looking at her!'

The Baobhan Sith stopped their relentless approach and turned as one. The couple were ripped to pieces in seconds. Hunter gaped at the speed and brutality of the attack; of all the many atrocities he had seen in his life, that was the worst.

'If you'd run when I said, they might not have died,' Tom said cruelly. 'The Baobhan Sith are attack dogs. Anything that wanders into their vicinity is a target.'

Hunter felt a real weight descend on him as he led the way across the rooftops, and became increasingly uncomfortable when it refused to dissipate. Climbing down another fire escape, they emerged into the crowds around Piccadilly Circus as the rain stopped. Hunter propelled Tom into an all-night café, where they sat at the back, drinking espresso in the steamy atmosphere.

'What were those things?' Hunter was angry, and in two minds about giving the irritating old hippie a pasting just to make himself feel better.

'They come from another place, a world that's only a step away from our own.' Tom removed his glasses to clean the raindrops from the lenses. 'The things there have populated our myths for millennia as they crossed back and forth between worlds, and the Baobhan Sith are one of the worst nightmares to crawl out of that place. Any time you read a tale about some blood-sucking woman drifting out of a cemetery in a shroud, you can trace it back to them.'

'This wasn't some random attack—'

'The Enemy controls them. The Enemy controls everything monstrous and frightening and unpleasant because its currency – its entire ethos – is despair. The Baobhan Sith spread poison in this sad and miserable reality, but on this occasion they were directed to eliminate you.'

Hunter tapped his spoon on the Formica table. 'So essentially I no longer have any choice about getting involved in this madness.'

'Correct. The Hunter has become the hunted.'

'Nice joke. You know I can actually kill a man with this spoon?'

'The smell of testosterone is overpowering.'

'Where do you come into this? Are you the Grandpa of Dragons?'

Tom eyed Hunter over the rim of his coffee cup. 'I have an interest in your success, shall we say. I accompanied Master Churchill for several hundred years—'

'You wear it well.'

'—most of it spent in the timeless Otherworld. The war has affected everything. It has destroyed lives, changed the course of time, shifted reality once, perhaps on many occasions. The stakes are the highest imaginable—'

'Survival? That's what it usually comes down to.'

'On one level. The survival of our dreams for a better world, for meaning, for humanity finally to attain its true potential.'

'So why am I so special?'

'Yes, hard to believe, isn't it?' Tom sipped his coffee and smacked his lips. 'The story goes that at the start of everything, two powerful opposing forces were created. Call them Good and Evil, if you want to be stupid. Dark and Light, in symbolic terms. The Dark got the upper hand and

31

decided how the universe should be, and it got to rule it. That explains why there's Evil in the world, because if the universe was ruled by Good, Evil would not be tolerated. That's the essence of Gnostic thinking.'

'Okay – Good, Evil, Light, Dark. I think I can get my head round that.'

Tom kept one eye on the door. 'When the Light and the Dark were formed, slivers of Light were embedded in all humanity. It's the key to our salvation – if we use that Light we can oppose the Dark, and turn things around for the universe. And those slivers of Light go by another name around these parts. The Pendragon Spirit.'

'And that's what links the Brothers and Sisters of Dragons.'

'You lot get to access what everyone has hidden within them. That's what makes you champions of Life, whether you want to be or not.'

'Not a very good story, is it?' Hunter finished his espresso and ordered another.

'I'm just repeating what I've been told. Who knows what the truth is?'

'So there's a little group of us – a few plucky guerrillas – hoping to overthrow the evil god of the universe.' Hunter considered that for a moment. 'I like those odds.'

'You'll fit right in.'

'You're saying the Enemy won't let me walk away. That I don't have a choice about getting involved in this.'

'You always have a choice. You just have to be prepared to live with the consequences.'

'Basically, it's suicide whichever way I turn.'

'Death's not all it's cracked up to be.'

Hunter saw a shift in the impassive edifice of Tom's face. 'What?'

Tom looked into the black depths of his coffee and mused, almost to himself, 'Sometimes I dream of my death. I remember the details of it as clearly as if it really happened. Yet here I am.' Absently, he stirred in another sugar. 'I feel out of joint and I don't know why.'

Hunter watched cars pass the window in a wet haze of reflected light. Piccadilly Circus throbbed with the comfortable rhythms of steady life, red, amber, green, red, amber, green. Yet now he found his attention drawn beyond the surface to details he had never found a need to recognise before: the movement of mysterious shadows across the upper storeys of a building; the sudden, frightened expression on the face of a passer-by, as if a terrible secret had been whispered into their ear; vibrations permeating the walls and floor that felt like a distant heartbeat. He knew then and there that no good would come.

Church held Ruth's sweat-slick body tightly to him. Through the thin walls of the rooming house they could hear Laura singing a Basement Jaxx song loudly, with scant regard for any other occupants.

'How long do you think we can keep doing this?' Ruth asked sleepily.

'What, having sex?'

She looked up at him through heavy-lidded eyes. 'Running. Hiding. Trying to stay one step ahead of the Enemy.'

'We're not doing so badly.'

'We've been lucky. Sticking to ley lines, staying at any vaguely safe place we can find en route. Church, it's not sustainable. Sooner or later we're going to get caught out.' She nuzzled into his neck. 'I'm just being pragmatic. The Blue Fire can hide us from the Enemy's view, but it doesn't make us indestructible. It's not just the Void, or the Army of the Ten Billion Spiders, or any of the supernatural things lined up against us. There's plenty of normal people working for the Enemy, too. We don't know who we can trust. We only need to get flagged up on some CCTV camera, or pulled over for jumping a red light . . .' Her voice trailed away wearily, but then she surprised him with a long, deep kiss. 'I still wouldn't trade this for the world, though,' she added softly.

'You're sure?'

'I was so lonely in that fake life the Void gave me. I knew I was missing something really important, but I just didn't know what it was. I suppose that was all part of the punishment.'

'You still can't remember anything from before it all changed? Us together?'

'Not the detail. But the emotional memory is getting stronger all the time. If I wanted to get all girly I'd say I feel love, that real aching need to be together, just not the reasons how or why that love came about. Does that make sense?'

It did. 'Maybe the memories will come back once the Void's illusion fades completely.'

'I hope so.' She pulled the duvet around her shoulders and receded into it. 'Church, do you think Veitch did something to us?'

He knew what she meant: that moment when Ryan Veitch had impaled himself on his own sword in Cornwall and a bolt of black lightning burst through all three of them. 'If he did, it hasn't worked. Don't worry about it.'

She smiled, nodded, but Church could see she was still worrying. 'I'm going to get a shower.' She gave him another kiss and skipped to the bathroom.

Church turned to the pack of tarot cards on the bedside cabinet. They were a unique set left for him by Niamh, his long-time companion from the Tuatha Dé Danann, who had been worshipped as gods by the Celtic people. This pack had a fifth suit beyond the familiar cups, wands, swords and coins – ravens. 'Eaters of the dead, messengers of the gods,' Niamh had told him. The fifth suit was usually denied to humans because it had the ability to contact higher powers. To examine the workings of Existence.

The cards had helped save his life. In the moment of his greatest need, they had allowed a point of contact with mysterious beings far higher up the scale than the Tuatha Dé Danann who had hinted at a great role for Church in some sprawling, mysterious scheme.

Since then he had repeatedly tried to use the cards to contact those higher powers without even a glimmer of success, but somehow, he was sure there was a trick he was missing. He laid them out on the bed in the spread he had seen Niamh using. Three cards in and he knew the situation had changed. Each of the cards was a raven. He continued to turn over the cards. All ravens. An involuntary shiver rippled through him, the uneasy sensation of brushing against the unknown. As he laid the final card, a jolt of energy leaped from the image of the raven into his fingers and he recoiled sharply. With anticipation, he waited for something else to happen, but there was nothing beyond an odd feeling permeating the room.

A knock at the door made him start. Shavi came in, looking exhausted.

'I have conducted three consecutive rituals. The residents of the Invisible World can be unpleasant, troublesome, and will not give out even the smallest and most inconsequential piece of information unless they are backed into a corner.' Shavi sat on the end of the bed and ran his fingers through his long hair. The rituals of contact took so much out of him sometimes that he could not even stand afterwards, yet he never complained. 'Yet I truly believe they do not know where our two mysterious targets are, and that troubles me.'

'Stands to reason that if they're a threat to the Void, they're going to be well hidden.'

'There has to be a way of locating them. We just have not found it yet.'

'We could cross over to the Otherworld. Try to find someone there who could help.'

'Yes. Perhaps your friend Niamh.'

The mention of her name flushed Church with hope. Niamh had

helped him in his darkest moment, and he had repaid her by saving her life. He wondered if he should tell the others about his near-hallucinatory experience when he had shifted the Axis of Existence, changing the course of history. Niamh and Tom now lived when they should have died. Yet it felt too monumental to express, and so unreal that the facts of what had truly happened were elusive. Perhaps it had all been a dream and Tom and Niamh were still dead. But if they had survived, he had achieved something remarkable, and perhaps paid Niamh back for the centuries of love she had offered him that he had never returned.

Shavi went to the window and looked over the wet rooftops of North London. 'I wonder where Hunter is. I hope he is safe,' he mused.

As he turned the matter over in his mind, Church decided on a compromise. 'We send Mallory, Sophie and Caitlin to Otherworld. They can ask Niamh to help – she'll understand if I'm not there. The Extinction Shears are with the Market of Wishful Spirit over there, the Keys are over here. It makes sense for us to split up. And they can hook up with all the other Brothers and Sisters of Dragons in T'ir n'a n'Og.'

'The ones you saved from this world?'

'The ones I saved from Veitch.'

'I still do not understand how he could go from being one of us . . . one of the Five, a champion of Life . . . to causing slaughter on such a grand scale.'

'We were all screwed up to some degree, but Veitch was worse. Some-how the Void twisted his own insecurities into something awful.'

'And he always loved Ruth.'

Church flinched; there it was.

Shavi read Church's thoughts. 'Veitch is dead now. We do not have to worry about him any more.'

'He made sure his legacy would stick around for ever,' Church said bitterly.

Shavi clapped an arm around Church's shoulders. 'We are together now. Stronger than we ever were alone. We must not forget that. I will tell the others of your plan.'

As Shavi left, Ruth returned from her shower, naturally attractive with a scrubbed face and her hair pulled back. Church opened the window and they kneeled before it. The clouds had started to clear and the moon illuminated a silvery path across the wet rooftops.

Ruth rested an arm across his shoulders. 'It's a grim world out there. You really think we can make a difference?'

'We did once. We brought the magic back when the world needed it.

That was one battle in a much bigger war, and there will be victories and set-backs, but—'

'We can do it again.'

A shooting star blazed across the quadrant of sky visible between the clouds. Church had a vague impression of seeing one before in a similar situation, but it was lost in his fractured memory.

'I think we need to make the most of what we've got here and now,' he said. 'We'll deal with what's to come when we get there.'

4

'You feel it, too. That sense of being disconnected.' Sophie sat cross-legged on the bed.

Mallory couldn't take his eyes off her. She had an entrancing, ethereal quality that was completely mysterious to him, yet at the same time strangely familiar. After so long being denied contact with her in the Steelguard offices, the mix was heady and compelling.

'What are you smiling at?' she asked.

'Nothing. We've just been dragged out of our lives and told we're the ultimate sleeper agents. "Disconnected" doesn't even begin to cover it.'

Caitlin turned from the window where she had been keeping watch. Her eyes gleamed. 'Isn't this better?' She gave an excited laugh. 'I think there's something wrong with me. All this danger, and I'm just buzzing! This beats repping beauty products up and down the country.'

'When I was cleaning toilets I used to dream of repping beauty products.' Mallory studied Caitlin's face. Behind the sparkle of her excitement, there was a shadow of abiding sadness.

'Oh, you two have had it so hard,' Sophie said. 'Try living with several million pounds of someone else's money hanging over your conscience.'

Shavi interrupted them. 'Church has decided on a plan of action,' he said, 'but it will mean the three of you operating alone.'

'Seriously, who put him in charge?' Mallory asked.

'Existence.' Shavi smiled. 'Besides, he has earned it.'

Shavi carefully explained about the Far Lands and how it was possible to cross over at certain points, before fielding their incredulous questions. Once acceptance had set in, he detailed what was expected of them. 'Are you ready to take on the responsibility?' he asked.

'You might think your little group has the monopoly on the hero thing,' Mallory said, 'but we're going to be better.'

'Ah, a competitive spirit. That should add an edge to the proceedings,' Shavi said, without even a hint of competition in return.

'Hang on.' Caitlin had returned to the window. 'Something's happening outside.'

5

With her iPod on, Laura sang out loudly. All the others were worried about what lay ahead. Not her. Going out in a blaze of glory was better than spending her days flipping burgers and filling her nights with drugs and sex in a futile attempt to find some kind of meaning in her life.

Her bouncing on the bed came to a gradual halt as she noticed a flock of black birds framed in the skylight. There were more of them than she had ever seen in one place before, and they appeared to be circling the building.

Clambering onto a chair, she opened the skylight and peered out. Ravens, and they were everywhere, perched on chimneys, the pitch of roofs, in gutters, and flying in that enormous black cloud. But not one of them made a single sound.

The sight unnerved her and she slammed the skylight shut, but her fear was quickly forgotten in the shock of seeing her room transformed. Vegetation obscured the walls, window and door. Clusters of acorns hung from oak branches. Holly grew across the cheap dressing table, and the bed was now a bower of ivy and mistletoe.

'Daughter.' The voice rolled out like a summer tide hitting the beach.

Laura fought the hammering of her heart and scanned the room. And there it was, in one corner, given away only by its red eyes. The figure was constructed of the same dense vegetation and merged perfectly into the background. Yet for all the wild strangeness, the leaf-face was unmistakably benign. It was the face carved into the stone and wood of medieval churches, the echo of the greenwood and the magical power of fertility.

'Who are you?' she asked with as much bravura as she could muster.

'In your heart, you know, daughter.'

Laura felt the ghost of that knowledge at the back of her mind, infuriatingly just out of reach. 'The Green Man?' she ventured.

'That is one of my names. Fragile Creatures have known me by many others. I have long watched over your people from the depths of the great forests, and I have guided and helped where I could. The Brothers and Sisters of Dragons have always been close to me. And you, daughter, have been closest of all.'

Laura felt a burning on her hand. The circle of interlocking leaves etched on her skin glowed a faint green. She had presumed it was a discreet tattoo, though she didn't recall getting it.

'The memory is lost to you, daughter, but you gave yourself to me and I changed you, to better prepare you for the arduous road ahead.'

Conflicting emotions threatened to tear Laura apart: fear and comfort, the desire to flee and to fall into the green embrace. This was the source of her unique ability to control plants and trees. 'What do you want?'

'Know this: the Devourer of All Things is aware of you, daughter, and of what you plan. It cannot abide the Blue Fire being returned to the land. My people flee – it will not allow them to remain in case they aid you. Soon, I too must slip into the long winter-sleep to preserve my power. But there may be other allies in the Great Dominions. Seek them out.'

'I don't know what you mean.'

The Green Man became tense, his leaves and branches shuddering. 'You must leave this place quickly, daughter. Danger approaches.' He motioned towards the skylight where the ravens pecked against the glass. 'See. The *Morvren* know. They have come to accompany the Giant-Killer on his final journey. From now on, he will be known as Raven King.'

'Church?' Laura looked from the Green Man to the ravens, not comprehending.

'Run, daughter,' he said insistently. 'Run!'

6

Church looked out of the window at the ravens, remembering a time more than a thousand years earlier when he had been told that the ravens and their premonition of death would follow him.

'I'm scared,' he realised as he watched the birds fly. 'I never was before.'

'Scared of what?' Ruth asked.

'When it was just me on my own, I'd take risks, do whatever needed to be done, even if it meant putting myself in danger. Now I've got something to lose. You.'

Ruth fell silent for a moment. 'That's bad.'

'That's bad. That's good. That's bad.' Church shook his head, confused.

Mallory burst in, startling them. 'We've got to get out of here. Now.'

'What is it?'

'Police. They've closed off the street, doing house-to-house.'

Church noticed a flash of blue and white lights further down the street.

'Looking for us?' Ruth asked as she stuffed her meagre possessions into a hold-all.

'Got to be,' Church said. 'Get the others. We'll go out the back, over the rear fence into the next garden. I checked the route earlier.'

As Mallory ran out, Laura was already emerging from her room, and Church could hear Shavi, Sophie and Caitlin talking insistently as they made their way down the stairs.

The hall still smelled of the landlord's fry-up. Mallory checked the street through the small window at the side of the front door, then motioned to the others to move towards the back of the house. 'They'll be here any minute,' he whispered. 'There's an armed unit wearing flak jackets. We won't stand a chance if they get us in their cross-hairs.'

'The anti-terrorist squad?' Ruth said.

'Makes sense.' Church finished fastening the harness that held the sword hidden across his back. Ruth carried her spear in a long, customised, cylindrical map bag. 'The spiders will have people in the top positions everywhere, but they're still going to need some kind of cover story so they don't risk wrecking the Mundane Spell. Branding us terrorists will do the job nicely.'

Church pushed past the others into the darkened kitchen. His boots made a wet, sticky sound on the old linoleum. He had only a second to register the inert body of the landlord lying in a shaft of streetlight falling through the window by the door before a stool swung out of the shadows. He half-fended it off, but it clipped his temple and he went down, unconscious.

The others pressed into the kitchen before they even realised Church had fallen, and they were stunned when the light flashed on.

'Hmm. New faces, new blood.' Leaning against the cooker was a man who exuded a dangerous air of power and flamboyance. He was a pool of gloom, wearing sunglasses despite the dark; long, black hair, a black goatee, a black overcoat and black motorcycle boots: a studied cliché that still managed to summon up an air of menace while laughing at itself.

'The Libertarian,' Shavi noted.

The Libertarian removed his sunglasses to reveal lidless eyes the colour of blood. 'One name, amongst many. If Mr Churchill were awake he could not really claim to know me. Here at the source, I am a different person. At the height of my powers. I can touch you in a way I never could before. Touch you! Ah, euphemisms! I should have said "butcher you".'

Mallory kicked the kitchen table so that it pinned the Libertarian's legs against the cooker. At the same time, Caitlin snatched a carving knife from a block and threw it forcefully. It sank deep into the Libertarian's shoulder, but although he winced slightly his smile did not waver.

'Spirited. I like that.'

Caitlin followed up in rapid succession with the other five knives from the block. Shavi and Ruth helped up a groggy Church and dragged him out through the back door.

Mallory noticed that the Libertarian made no particular effort to pursue them, but he didn't have time to consider why. Kicking the table hard one more time against the Libertarian's legs, he snatched the key from inside the door and locked it behind him. Through the window, he saw the Libertarian pull out the knives one by one. The Libertarian saw Mallory watching and gave a little wave.

'Well, you're a vicious bitch,' Laura said to Caitlin as they raced by the broken-paned greenhouse towards the thick bushes and tall fence at the bottom of the garden.

Caitlin looked dazed. 'I just saw the knives and knew what to do.'

'I had my doubts before, but you're definitely on the first team.'

Four streets away, they paused to catch their breath. 'We obviously can't stay in one place for any length of time,' Mallory said. He eyed Church. 'Didn't you think of that?'

Ruth bristled. 'Don't criticise him—'

'It's okay.' Church looked Mallory in the eye. 'I thought it was a risk worth taking to get us some rest. We got out. What's your problem?'

'It's early days yet.'

Shavi stepped in between the two men. 'This is not helping. Where do we go now?'

'We split up, as planned.' Church glanced up and down the empty street. 'They'll be all over this place soon.'

'We go to the Far Lands?' Caitlin said uneasily. 'Mallory, Sophie and me?'

'It'll be all right.' Sophie gave her a reassuring smile. She was confident and calm and that helped Caitlin.

'Where do we cross over?' Mallory asked. 'Shit, *how* do we cross over?'

The flashing blue and white lights moved into the next street.

'Just find one of the old sites,' Church said. 'Best if you don't tell us which one you'll aim for – if we get caught, we won't be able to betray your location.'

'Use the Craft to help you cross over,' Ruth said to Sophie.

'I don't know how,' Sophie protested.

'It's inside you. It'll rise up when you need it, trust me.'

'How do we meet up?' Mallory asked.

'We'll find a way.' Church shook Mallory's hand. The others nodded to each other, silently and uneasily, and then they split into two groups and slipped into the night.

7

Church, Laura, Shavi and Ruth caught the last bus into the city centre, sitting apart to pretend they were not together. Against the moon-silvered sky, Church saw the billowing black cloud of the *Morvren* following the bus. At Euston Road, the ravens settled on the dome of the Planetarium and the surrounding buildings, a brooding infestation. It was long past one a.m., but the traffic still rumbled and the fast-food joints along Gower Street were doing a brisk trade.

Church and the others jumped off the bus and walked separately to the quiet of University Street where they congregated in a darkened doorway.

'Why didn't the Libertarian follow us?' Ruth asked.

'He knows we've got nowhere to go,' Church replied. 'He thinks it's just a matter of time until his lot catch us.'

'Isn't it?' Ruth said. She caught herself. 'I'm sorry. I'm just tired.'

'All right, where to now?' Laura said.

Before Church could answer, they were startled by the flapping wings of a large owl as it landed on a parked car. Ruth smiled to see her companion.

'Looks like you're wanted,' Laura said.

The owl was restless and didn't calm even when Ruth stood before it. In its large, unblinking eyes, she saw something that made her feel queasy. She turned to the others. 'Something's wrong.'

Church, Laura and Shavi were no longer looking at her. Over the rooftops, a crackling display of illumination was just visible, like the lightning heralding an approaching storm.

The owl soared away frantically. Ruth recoiled from the unexpected movement and when she looked back at the sky, the light display had been lost behind the towering buildings on Baker Street.

'What was that?' Laura asked.

Shavi's expression was grim. 'We should not remain here much longer.'

'Head into the centre,' Church said. 'We can lie low for a few hours, then get a train out of Paddington or hitch a lift west.'

Footsteps echoing noisily, they moved through the deserted streets that

41

ran between the main thoroughfares of Gower Street and Tottenham Court Road.

'Is it me or is it starting to smell like some blokes' locker room round here?' Laura said when they had finally given up all pretence of walking separately. She was right. It had grown unbearably warm and humid, and there was a mounting odour of stale sweat.

Shavi kept glancing up at the thin streak of sky visible between the tall buildings.

'Will you stop doing that?' Laura snapped. 'You're creeping me out.'

'Let's get into the crowds in Tottenham Court Road,' Church said. 'We might be safer there if we can blend in.'

'You might be able to blend in. I'm far too attractive,' Laura replied.

The traffic was heavy and the pavements thick with people, but if anything the atmosphere was even worse. Though there was nothing to see, passers-by regularly glanced up into the sky as though they were privy to some secret signal. Their expressions were uniformly worried, and after each skyward glance they would pick up their pace a little. Car horns blared as drivers peered upwards through their windscreens, missing the changing of the lights. Motorcyclists pulled over to the side to look, then drove off at speed through the gaps in the creeping traffic.

'I don't like this,' Ruth said.

'You're whining again.' For once, Laura's bravado sounded false.

A discharge of energy seared across the sky. People jumped, and a loud ripple of uneasy anticipation ran through the throng.

The crowds stopped to search the heavens. The car horns and the angry bellows of drivers were now deafening. Another golden energy discharge fizzed from behind the row of buildings at Church's back.

'Come on.' He grabbed Ruth's hand and pulled her into the jammed rows of traffic. Shavi and Laura followed close behind.

'It's coming for us, isn't it?' Laura said.

'The Libertarian did indeed know there was no point pursuing us himself,' Shavi said.

As they reached the middle of the road, a shadow fell across them. Huge, and moving forward quickly, it soon eclipsed the whole street. Church saw the expressions of the people packing the opposite pavement before he saw the shadow's source: at first disbelief, then confusion, then mounting fear.

The cacophony of voices was drowned by a thunderous crash as a mountain of brick and tile fell from the top of a building behind Church, crushing pedestrians and cars. As a cloud of dust enveloped the street, people abandoned their vehicles and ran screaming, but no one was quite sure which direction to go.

Church, Ruth, Shavi and Laura kept close together, scrambling over the bonnet of the final car before thrusting themselves into the swarming crowd.

Another crash of masonry, more sickening screams cut short. An energy discharge struck the ground and a car exploded. Shrapnel ripped across the street and the windows of all the shops blew out, killing more. Fire raged at the point of impact, spreading rapidly to all the cars stuck in the jam. A chain reaction of explosions as each tank ignited turned Tottenham Court Road into an inferno.

'We need to get away from the crowds,' Church yelled as they broke into Oxford Street. 'All these people are dying because of us.'

Laura came to a halt, transfixed by whatever loomed over them. Church followed her gaze.

Moving slowly over the rooftops was a monstrous echo of a Fabulous Beast. As big as a jet, it had two leonine heads, silently roaring, and a bulky big-cat body covered in fur, scales and feathers. A serpentine tail snaked out behind it. There were no wings or other visible means keeping it aloft, but still it flew, its clawed feet occasionally demolishing chunks of buildings as it passed. What disturbed Church the most was the way its four eyes rolled with idiocy, as if there was no sense in the creature at all. It was simply an engine of destruction, from which the energy discharges burst out at random.

'How can the Mundane Spell hold when something like this is tearing through the West End?' Ruth gasped as she ran. 'The Void must have given up trying to maintain the illusion.'

Church grabbed her hand as they ran. 'I don't believe that. The illusion is where its power lies.'

Shavi threw his arms around Laura and dragged her in the direction of the Virgin store as more masonry rained all around. They all raced in the direction of Oxford Circus amongst the scattering pedestrians, the pursuing creature crashing against the rooftops in its blind, stupid relentlessness. Crackling energy bolts sometimes missed them by only a few feet.

Together they stumbled down the steps to Oxford Circus Tube Station, hoping they could find shelter underground, but their way was blocked by a gate. Church shook it impotently; with the last train long gone it wouldn't be open again until the morning.

At the street entrance, the sizzling energy eased down the steps one at a time as the creature manoeuvred itself into position.

'We'll be fried if we go back up there!' Laura yelled above the din.

Church and Shavi threw themselves at the gate, though they both knew it was futile. Superheated air hit Church's back in waves, burning him through his clothes. Then, as he desperately examined the chain and padlock, he glimpsed a fleeting impression of a broad, disembodied grin in the dark of the Underground station, like the final fading smile of the Cheshire Cat. When he looked back at the chain, the padlock was open.

'What caused that?' Shavi murmured in disbelief as he helped Church wrench open the gate.

'Just accept it before it changes its mind.' Church herded them through into the dark ticket hub.

'I'm definitely sticking with you, Church-dude. The gods are on your side.' Laura helped Shavi drag the gate shut and refasten the padlock.

'I'm reserving judgment.' Ruth stared into the gloom. 'We might have just tumbled out of the frying pan.'

'That glass-half-empty attitude is going to wear thin pretty quickly,' Laura said. But as she turned, she realised Ruth might be right, for Church was nowhere to be seen, even though he had only been feet away from her a moment earlier.

chapter two

the last train

1

'Please help me. I don't want to be left on my own.' The little girl's voice echoed across the lonely expanse of Battersea Park, but it was Caitlin who spoke, hugging her knees on the steps of the Eastern-styled Peace Pagoda.

'What the hell's wrong with her?' Mallory had spent five minutes trying to quiet her, and had now diverted his energies to keeping watch across the park. His irritation was fuelled by mounting anxiety that the Enemy would be on them if they waited there much longer. A major disturbance was already taking place across the river in the West End, and though much of it was hidden by churning clouds and the constant wail of police and ambulance sirens, he feared the worst.

Sophie slipped an arm around Caitlin's shoulders. 'What's wrong?' she whispered.

'I'm scared.' Caitlin shivered into the crook of Sophie's arm. 'It's too dark here.'

Sophie listened thoughtfully to the tone of the little-girl voice, then asked, 'What's your name?'

'Why, it's Amy, thank you for asking.'

'Not Caitlin?'

'Oh, she's in here with Brigid and Briony. But I'm Amy.' Caitlin looked up at Sophie with a bright, innocent face. 'Will you look after me?'

'Of course I will. I'll be back in a minute.' Sophie pulled free from Caitlin's clinging embrace and joined Mallory.

'So? What's up with her?' he asked, tense.

'I think she's got some kind of mental illness. Multiple personality from the sound of it.'

'Why am I not surprised?' A flare illuminated the depths of Mallory's mind, gone in an instant. 'The Broken Woman,' he said dreamily.

'What?'

He shook his head. 'Sorry. Don't know where that came from. They call it Dissociative Disorder now,' he said, glancing at Caitlin who was rocking backwards and forwards, humming to herself.

'Stress-induced, yeah?'

'If she's going to start flipping personalities every few minutes, it's going to make things much more complicated for us.'

'We can't leave her behind.'

'I guess not.'

Sophie fixed a cold eye on Mallory.

'Just a passing thought.' He turned away, uncomfortable with any hint of reproof from her. 'So now what? I don't know anything about ancient sites and all that shite our self-appointed leader was banging on about. There's what . . . Avebury?'

'Stonehenge.'

'Too close to Salisbury.'

'What's wrong with Salisbury?' Sophie asked.

'I don't like the place. It's a prejudice. Unfounded, but it's there.'

'You're very irrational.'

'Yeah, but I've got a bad side, too.'

'Then it's Avebury.'

'No. It is too obvious.' The unfamiliar voice startled them.

His heart thundering, Mallory searched the dense shadows along the tree-line. Finally he identified the figure, standing so still it could have been a statue.

'Who are you?' Mallory weighed whether to escape or attack.

'It's okay.' Caitlin was at his side, one steadying hand on his arm. 'Brigid says, don't worry.'

'Fine. I always take advice from imaginary friends.'

The figure stepped into the glow of the lights running along the riverside path. It was a man in a smart 1940s-style suit. He wore a hat and kept his head slightly bowed so Mallory couldn't see his face. His hands were his most prominent feature, which were parchment white. As he slowly and theatrically raised his head, the light caught a mask: one half was the laughing face of comedy, the other the downturned features of tragedy.

'I'll ask one more time: who are you?' Mallory said.

'I have gone by many names in my long and wonderful life,' the new arrival said with a flourish. 'Max Masque, the Darling of the Music Hall. Jester. Tumbler. Juggler. Sage. But you may call me Jerzy, the Mocker.'

Mallory sensed no danger, but he wasn't in a mood to take anything at face value. Sophie was just as cautious, but Caitlin hugged the Mocker warmly. He appeared genuinely touched by her welcome, and tentatively returned her embrace.

'We must not tarry,' he said in hushed tones. He glanced around nervously.

'Of course we'll let you come with us,' Mallory said sarcastically.

'I have been sent to accompany you to the point of transition, and to give you whatever guidance I can.'

'Who sent you?' Sophie tried to read the eyes flickering behind the mask.

The Mocker shifted uncomfortably. 'These Fixed Lands are still a place of wildness. Not everything follows the rules of the Void . . . or the rules of Existence. And there are forces at play that would take great comfort in seeing you succeed in your quest.'

'Please, hurry,' Caitlin implored. 'Brigid says the spiders are drawing nearer. They're determined to stop us crossing over.'

Mallory looked to Sophie who nodded her agreement. 'All right,' he said. 'Let's get this ship of fools on its way. Where do you suggest we go?'

'We are humble pilgrims on a journey of enlightenment,' Jerzy said with a deep bow. 'And so we must to Canterbury.'

2

The Libertarian stood on the fifteenth floor of an office building just north of Euston Square and watched the black smoke rise up from the West End, fingers of crimson and gold licking the crumbling masonry. The vast shadow of the Riot-Beast moved across the face of the city towards the east.

Enough had been done to set the mice scurrying; the End was already in motion.

Behind him, every square inch of the room seethed with spiders. Everything was right with the world, finally, and that could not be allowed to change. There was order and cohesion and singularity of purpose. The debilitating terror of meaning and hope and yearning could not be allowed to spread, for that only caused chaos and uncertainty. He could not begin to comprehend the motivations of the Brothers and Sisters of Dragons. They were terrorists, trying to overthrow a system that worked, that made people happy. How could they justify the suffering they were inflicting on their own kind?

He vaguely remembered the time before he had been plucked out of the vast superstructure of reality to become an overseer of stability. Adrift from the ordered procession of events, it was often difficult to place memories in any consistent pattern that made sense, but he had a clear recall of emotions. Some images came back to him, of a kiss in the light of the setting sun, of a slow drive into the countryside with music playing, of his father pointing out his present next to the tree. He remembered the face of the girl who broke his heart, and his first dead body. In those days, when he was lesser, his existence had been shrouded with doubt, unease, depression. Now there was none of that, and he felt the better for it, as anyone would.

'This place,' he said to no one in particular, 'is characterised by two things: lights and the shadows they cast. Once the former is extinguished, there can be no darkness, no misery, no suffering, and so the work I do is right. I shall not rest until the last candle is snuffed out.'

Behind him a shiver ran through the corpus of spiders.

3

'Where is he?' Fighting to suppress her anxiety, Ruth roamed the circular ticket office, her spear drawn.

'It was a trap,' Laura said. 'That's why the gate opened so easily.'

'If that is the case, why were we not all taken the moment we set foot in this place?' Shavi remained calm. Turning slowly, he tried to read any subtle signals that might reveal Church's whereabouts.

'Because we're not important,' Laura snapped. 'It's always been about Church. He's the one with the big destiny thing going on. We're just here for target practice.'

'Will you shut up.' Ruth forced herself not to shout at Laura, who managed to irritate her even in stress-free moments.

'You don't get the monopoly on worry just because you've opened your legs for him,' Laura replied spitefully.

As Ruth bristled, Shavi stepped between the two women. 'The Enemy is undoubtedly on the way, perhaps even here already. We do not have the luxury of waiting here to search.'

'You're saying we should leave Church?' Ruth said.

'I'm with the Ice Princess,' Laura added. 'You don't abandon a friend.'

'I do not want to leave Church either. But if we allow ourselves to fall here, the price will be paid by all of humanity.'

Ruth considered Shavi's words, then nodded and headed towards the escalators. 'Church knows how to look after himself. He'll find his way back to us.'

Laura watched her coldly before following. 'You're such a weakling. I can't believe you've cut him loose.' Shavi reached out to calm her, but she threw him off.

'The difference between us,' Ruth called back, 'is that I have faith in him.'

They climbed over the ticket barriers and made their way quickly down the unmoving escalators. Dimly, they could hear the carnage above ground echoing through the walls.

As they made their way through the network of tunnels, Laura whispered to Shavi, 'Don't take this the wrong way, but I keep getting flashes of us doing the monkey-dance. Yeah, yeah, I know you dream about it every second, but it feels like it really happened.'

'I do not recall that, but I remember other things that are confusing. I think, perhaps, that our memories of our past time together are coming back. And that can only be a good thing. By all accounts, we achieved great things together. If we come to know each other as well as we did then, we can achieve great things again.'

'You're such a sucky optimist, Shavster, you're like a walking cheese machine,' she gently mocked.

On the platform, the head of Ruth's spear glowed gently, bringing out a beauty in her features that Shavi had not noticed before. She was still fighting to contain her worry over Church, and when she saw him looking she turned away.

A distant, insane shrieking brought them up hard. It echoed from the gaping tunnel mouth, and was intermingled with haunting string music. The hairs on Shavi's neck prickled; the sound was drawing closer.

'What in the name of Billy Bob Thornton is that?' Laura said, spooked, trying to hide it.

The shrieking rushed towards them, a raucous counterpoint to the music that grew more beautiful as it neared. The tracks began to sing in tune, and eventually a dim wash of light appeared on the walls in the far depths of the tunnel.

'There shouldn't be any trains running at this time of night,' Ruth said.

'Better recheck your timetable.' The apprehension in Laura's voice suggested they should all run, but they were transfixed by the sounds and the light, and by then it was too late.

When Church entered the ticket office, he was instantly aware of the cloying aroma of honeysuckle. He remarked on this to Shavi, and when he received no reply he turned to find himself alone in the echoing room.

His arms turned to gooseflesh. He caught a fleeting movement, a glimpse of sealskin and dangerous eyes, and that Cheshire Cat grin, and he knew.

'What do you want, Puck?' he asked loudly.

'Ho! No fool you, Master Churchill!' The voice echoed back, laced with mischief.

Emerging from the shadows far from where Church had seen him, the sprite appeared on the brink of breaking into dance, and though his mood was potent bonhomie, Church could sense the lethal nature behind it; he could turn as quickly as the weather.

'Many miles have fallen underfoot since we last met, hale and hearty, not far from this place.'

Church blinked, and Puck was only a foot away, staring deep into Church's eyes. 'You are a merry wanderer yourself these days, it seems.'

'What have you done with the Anubis Box?' Church was concerned that such a powerful object was in the hands of so unpredictable a force.

Puck held out his open palms and feigned an expression of puzzlement. It was pointless questioning him further.

'I'll ask you again: what do you want?'

'To light your way along a dark road. The Puck is a friend to the lost. If the lost are a friend to the Puck.' A hint of a threat shaded his comment.

Church tempered his tone; there was little point risking his life or his sanity. 'Any help would be gratefully received.'

'Then listen, Master Churchill. This world is a frightful place, and will grow more frightful still when the Devourer of All Things finds a home for his dark thoughts. They are building him a body of meat and cobwebs so he can more easily influence this mundane world he rules.'

'I thought a god could just snap his fingers and everything happened.'

'Can you snap your fingers and make a house of bricks and mortar crumble to dust? No, no, and thrice no. You would take a hammer to it. The Devourer of All Things is building his own hammer. There are gods, Master Jack, and gods and gods and gods. But each must follow rules, and not all of them are known. Not even to the Puck, who knows more than most.'

'Where is this happening?'

'Somewhere. But not here.'

'You don't know.'

Puck grinned. 'The finding is part of the solving.'

Church cursed under his breath.

'Follow the Burning Man. He will light your way.' The sprite vanished again, only to reappear at Church's shoulder. 'Light, light, and light. You carry a fire, too, that sears the Enemy and strips the darkness from its heart. It fears that light, like an imp feels good iron, for it cannot exist in its glare.'

'We know what we've got to do. We're not going to turn away from it.'

'What courage! What daring!' The Puck danced. 'But have you found your own hammer, Master Jack?'

'Three of us are heading to the Far Lands to find the Extinction Shears.'

Puck clapped his hands. 'Perhaps a fool should guide them? Yes, a Fool, indeed!' Another dance, another dark grin that hinted at unspoken things.

'If you really want to help, tell me how to find the two Keys.'

'And so to business.' The sprite bobbed up at Church's other shoulder. 'You will not find them along the quiet, winding lanes in the land of your fathers, Master Churchill.'

'Abroad, then.'

'One waits in a cold land where rainbows bring the gods to Earth. The other moves across a great nation, hiding in plain sight. But tarry not, Master Jack. Others would find these prizes first.'

'The Void?'

'That, and more.'

'Can't your kind ever give straight answers?'

'Aid is always on hand for those in need. Ask the wind and your voice shall be heard.' He mockingly cupped a hand to his ear. 'Hark! Is that help arriving now?'

Once the final word had left his mouth, he was gone.

The sound of an approaching train reverberated through the station. It was no normal train. Even in the ticket office the noise was deafening and the vibrations made the entire station shake. Plumes of dust fell from the ceiling.

Church ran for the escalators, knowing instinctively that he had to reach the platform before his last chance departed.

Ruth, Shavi and Laura were caught in the glare of the rapidly approaching lights. Whatever it was appeared to be travelling too fast to stop. The shrieking and the music now rang off the walls deafeningly.

Ruth pressed the other two back for fear they would be sucked under the wheels. All they saw was a blur of black and silver, and then there was a scream of brakes and the platform was filled with hissing, billowing steam. A ringing silence followed in its wake.

As the steam cleared, they were presented with a train like none they had ever seen or dreamed. Aspects reminded them of the Victorian royal coach, but there were echoes of an Egyptian funeral barge, with its curlicues and hawk-headed statues; of a Viking ship, with sleek lines and raven motifs; of a Chinese emperor's carriage; and of entirely alien modes of transport: wings and cupolas, scales and spikes. The body of the vehicle was an unreflecting sable, but the inlay and detail were silver.

All was silent. Ruth, Shavi and Laura strained to see into the darkened interior, but then candles flared into life along every carriage. Monstrous shapes were caught in the flickering half-light.

Slowly, a door swung open to reveal leather seats, brass fittings and an inordinate amount of foliage.

'They don't really think we're going to step in there,' Laura said.

A grinding came from the front of the train, followed by another hiss of steam. It was preparing to depart.

'Is it a trap?' Shavi asked. 'Or should we board?'

Ruth gripped her spear, unsure.

As the door began to close just as slowly as it had opened, Ruth, Laura and Shavi were propelled into the carriage, and a heavy weight fell on top of them. The door closed behind them with a click and the train began to move off.

'Get off me, you big, fat lump.' Laura threw off the weight and saw it was Church. 'And where've you been?'

'Somewhere near and far away. With Puck.' He helped Ruth to her feet.

She glanced at Laura. 'See. Bit of faith.'

Laura snorted.

'Friends,' Shavi said, looking down the corridor, 'we are not alone.'

The carriage was empty apart from a solemn figure. Long, pristine black robes shrouded a skeletal body, and the face, too, was skull-like, with just a few wisps of hair clinging to the desiccated skin that barely covered the bone. The eyes were heavy-lidded and the whites had a sickly yellow tinge. Ruth wrinkled her nose at the graveyard odour coming off him.

'Welcome,' he said in a crackling voice, 'to the Last Train.'

'That doesn't sound very good,' Ruth said.

'It's just a name,' Church replied.

The attendant's mouth broke into an enigmatic yellow-toothed smile. 'You may call me Ahken. I am master of this conveyance. All here is given freely and without obligation. Ask of me what you will.'

'Slight problem – no tickets,' Laura said. 'You going to throw us off at the next stop?'

Ahken took Laura's hand and turned it over. She shuddered at his touch: his bony fingers felt like dry wood. He pointed to the mark of Cernunnos. 'That will provide passage for all your group, to the end of the line.'

'What would have happened if that wasn't there?' Laura asked.

Ahken continued to smile, but his expression had changed ever so slightly and Laura wished she hadn't asked the question.

'I think we're supposed to be here. Isn't that right?' Church asked Ahken.

'You are here. You are alive,' Ahken replied, as if that should be answer enough. 'You may go anywhere within this train, except for the last carriage.'

'What's in there?' Ruth asked.

Ahken's smile faded, but he didn't answer. 'There are some here who are waiting to see you.'

'How could they know we'd be boarding?' Church asked. 'We didn't even know ourselves.'

'Your presence has always been expected on the Last Train.'

Laura cursed loudly. 'This is like trying to hold a conversation in an old people's home. Let's just find a seat and chill for a bit. I've had enough running around.'

'We need to know where we are going,' Shavi cautioned.

'Who cares as long as it's away from that hell-hole?' Laura replied.

'Shavi's right. Where's the end of the line?' Through the window, Church caught glimpses of distant flashes of light in the darkness that suggested they were no longer in the tunnel.

'The end of the line is far away in time and space,' Ahken said, 'but you will alight at the place where you need to be. And who knows, you may find your way back to the Last Train again, perhaps even for that final journey.'

'Okay, that's it. Conversation over,' Laura said. 'He's now reached maximum on the creepometer.'

Ahken bowed deeply. With a sickening twinge, Ruth thought she caught sight of things wriggling beneath his robe. 'I will take my leave,' he said. 'Should you require anything of me, please pull the gold cord at the end of the carriage.'

'Don't hold your breath,' Laura said under hers.

As he passed by them to the front of the train, an odour of loam and cleansing fluids followed in his wake.

'Looks like we're out of London,' Ruth said, 'but we can't keep running. Sooner or later we've got to get off the back foot.'

'That's the last thing the Army of the Ten Billion Spiders wants,' Church said. 'They're going to do anything they can to keep us off-balance.'

'We can take comfort from the knowledge that the Enemy considers us a sufficient threat to divert resources to destroy us,' Shavi noted.

'Oh yeah, lots of comfort,' Laura replied. 'They're aiming the big guns at us and Shavi wants to celebrate.' She gave Shavi's ear a painful but playful tweak, then eyed the end of the carriage. 'You reckon we can get a drink on here?'

'We ought to find out who wants to see us,' Church said.

As Ruth opened the door at the rear of the carriage, she felt a surge of vertigo. A small walkway constrained by low iron rails led to a short gap over which they would have to step to reach the walkway leading into the next carriage. An oppressive smell of iron hung in the air, and the wind buffeted them so wildly that it felt as if they were moving at five hundred miles per hour. The darkness on either side was so dense it was impossible to tell if they were in a tunnel or on a vast, night-blanketed plain.

The next carriage was a sensory rush of wild, fiddle-driven music and strange voices raised in song, of cloying, sweet incense and a mass of dancing bodies that were as colourful as they were inhuman: cloven hoofs and serpent tails, horns and wings and glowing eyes. Amongst them, achingly beautiful golden-skinned beings danced with a liquid grace that complemented their physical forms.

'The Seelie Court,' Church whispered in Ruth's ear. 'What are they doing here?' Church edged through the dancers, who recognised him and parted out of respect. The queen of the court smiled sweetly at Church, but in her eyes was a honeyed desire that Ruth had recognised at their last encounter in Cornwall. She felt a twinge of jealousy. Church was oblivious and that annoyed her even more.

'Brother of Dragons.' The queen allowed Church to kiss her hand. 'We meet again in these troubled times.'

'Your Highness. This is a surprise.'

'A pleasant one, I hope?' The king had a supercilious air, but clearly respected Church.

'You've been a great help to us. We won't forget that,' Church replied.

The queen's gaze fell briefly on Ruth, and then moved on to Shavi and Laura without even registering Ruth's presence. 'Sit with us awhile,' she said. 'There is much to discuss. Like you, we are dispossessed, forced to flee this land we love. The Devourer of All Things and its vast, unyielding army drive us out like rats, harrying and slaughtering those who fall behind. We, and all those like us, are being purged to make this a world without hope.'

'A new order has come,' the king added. 'The Devourer of All Things is building itself a body, and when it is complete, its legions will rule all that is, and has been, and evermore shall be.'

Courtiers cleared a space so Church, Ruth, Laura and Shavi could sit on the leather seats.

'What's changed since the last time we spoke?' Church asked.

'Why, you have, Brother of Dragons. The Quincunx has all but come together,' the king noted. 'Did you think the Devourer of All Things would sit idly by and watch while you organise a rebellion against its rule?'

'There was always a degree of tolerance in allowing beings like our-selves to move through this land,' the queen added, 'as long as the balance of power was not unduly affected.'

'So it *is* scared of us,' Ruth said.

The queen turned her full attention to Ruth for the first time and smiled patronisingly. 'Scared? The Devourer of All Things sees you as insects emerging from the fabric of its property. If the infestation is allowed to continue, then the foundations may be undermined. But still . . . insects.'

'As are we all,' the king said. 'Even the Golden Ones.'

'When the Brothers and Sisters of Dragons began to come together, ripples moved out across all Existence.' The queen's expression became grave. 'When the Fabulous Beast was awoken from its sleep. When the last remnants of the Blue Fire eased out into a land grown cold and still. All parts of a greater picture. For anyone who has the eyes to see, it is the final act in the story that began when this place sprang into being.'

'The end of the universe?' Ruth said. 'Are you serious?'

'Ragnarok,' Shavi explained. 'In Norse mythology, it is the twilight of the gods when the universe is torn apart. It will be preceded by the Fimbulwinter, the winter of winters; conflicts will break out and morality will disappear. There will be a final battle between the gods and the forces ranged against them, and in the end, death will come to all.'

Silence stretched between them for a moment. Then the king said, 'Everything that has happened to you has been leading to this. The Devourer of All Things knows it. It sought to subvert the ancient story by holding you Brothers and Sisters of Dragons in stasis. Now you are free, it rages, and seeks to hold back the end with the terrible power of its complete regard.'

'So basically it's not tolerating us any more,' Laura said. 'Or you.'

'Or any beings like us, born of wonder and magic and spirit,' the king replied. 'All things of greatness in this place are being harried. Those who fall are being taken to the dark camps in the Far Lands to be fed to the crushing engines of eradication. The Golden Ones who once walked this land with impunity now hide in the shadows, and run before the darkness that seeks to cleanse them. Even in the Far Lands, in the great courts, a debilitating fear has taken hold. Our long rule has been shaken. For the first time we know that we might fall.'

'Where are you going?' Shavi asked.

'Away,' the queen said simply. 'We seek safe haven, like many others on the Last Train.'

'You haven't found anywhere yet?' Church asked.

A shiver of sadness passed across the queen's normally implacable face, but she said no more.

'You are welcome to join us in our search for asylum, Brother of Dragons,' the king stated.

'We're not looking for a hiding place. We're finding a way to fight back.'

An awed whisper ran amongst the Seelie Court. The queen smiled. 'We recognised the potential in the Brothers and Sisters of Dragons long ago. This, then, is the moment when Fragile Creatures escape from the mire and start the long walk to their shining future.'

6

Laura was lost in the hallucinatory flicker of lights through the train window.

'Deep in thought?' Shavi slipped into the seat next to her. Apart from them, the carriage was empty. Church and Ruth were still locked in conversation with the king and queen of the Seelie Court in the adjoining carriage.

'I don't do deep thought,' she lied. 'Life's for feeling.' She could see from Shavi's face that she wasn't fooling him; she never did. Every time he would give his faint, knowing smile, but he would never challenge her. 'Got a question for you,' she said, deflecting the conversation. 'Those lives we all remember from before we came together. They were fake, right? So who are we really?'

Shavi's brow knitted; it was a question he had already considered. 'I know, in a way unsupported by memory, that we are all good friends. The very best, a friendship that can only have been forged by travelling through the hardest of times.'

'I only ask because since we all got together I've been getting flashes . . . images . . . snatches of conversation . . . things that don't fit anywhere into my life at all, but feel more real than anything I do remember properly. You get that?'

'I do. And it is growing stronger. We are throwing off the shackles of the Void. Moving closer to who we really are.'

'So, us having sex together, on a warm night, with the stars overhead . . .' She stopped, embarrassed at the dreamy tone that had materialised in her voice. 'What does that mean?'

'That you have excellent taste.' He gave a teasing grin.

'Did I mention it was a nightmare?'

'I recall one thing from my previous life: an emptiness,' Shavi said thoughtfully. 'I remember searching many spiritual paths for answers, finding none. Until I joined with you.'

His words echoed Laura's own thoughts.

They were interrupted by Church and Ruth returning from the adjoining carriage. 'This train isn't going anywhere we need to be,' Church said. 'We should get off as soon as we can.'

Laura glanced out into the dark. 'Don't want to burst your bubble, Chief, but no Railcard is getting us back home from here.'

'We're not going home.'

'Where, then?'

'Not sure exactly, but somewhere in Scandinavia.'

'That narrows it down,' Laura said sarcastically. 'Any particular reason for that destination, or do you just like cheap furniture with clean lines?'

'Puck told me we needed to look in a cold land where rainbows bring the gods to Earth. In Norse mythology, the Rainbow Bridge is the link between Earth and the gods.'

'You're putting all your trust in some mischievous imp that spends its time leading humans into swamps?'

'And saving them from them,' Church said. 'Don't forget the other side of the coin.'

'I have to agree with Laura,' Shavi said. 'At best the Puck's intentions are ambiguous. How do you know we can trust him? None of the Tuatha Dé Danann appears to hold him in high regard.'

'He's got his own agenda,' Church concurred, 'but my instinct says this time we need to follow his suggestion.'

'All right, so how do we get off this damn thing?' Ruth said.

'You ask. I exist only to serve.' Everyone started; Ahken was standing near the doors halfway down the carriage.

'Is that how people get off?' Laura snapped. 'You pop up like a rat from a drain and give them a heart attack?'

'Many have died on the Last Train.' Ahken clasped his hands in a gesture of deference that also appeared triumphal. He smiled and raised one hand. The train slowed. 'The Last Train is at your service whenever you might need it. One small thing will summon it: a spot of blood on the tracks.' Ahken bowed.

'You really think we're getting on this thing again?' Laura sneered.

Ahken smiled again, this time sly and cold. 'Everyone takes a scheduled trip on the Last Train once in their existence. Yours is still to come. A seat has been reserved.'

Laura felt a chill, resisted the urge to ask when that would be.

The doors slid open and they stepped onto the clean, modern platform of Heathrow Airport Underground Station.

'Shit. How did he know where we needed to be?' Laura turned to ask Ahken, but the Last Train had already departed, as silent as the grave.

chapter three

hunted

1

The last leg of the journey through the Kent countryside was illuminated by the silvery light of approaching day, and by the time Mallory drove the stolen rental transit across Canterbury's city limits, the sun was a pink and gold glow low in the eastern sky.

Sophie sat in the passenger seat, with Jerzy and Caitlin in the back. Now and then, she'd glance at Mallory, confused by emotions shifting deep inside her. Every day at Steelguard, she had watched him move around the office with his cleaning products, wishing she could talk to him, but with no rational explanation for why she would want that. He was always sullen, with a clipped politeness that undercut all his comments with contempt. Some of her colleagues, usually the braying, arrogant ones, were convinced their cleaner was a psychopath waiting to gut them in the lift one night. Sophie had never felt threatened by Mallory, though she had caught him looking at her on more than one occasion.

He was certainly good-looking, but a hardness shadowed his features that suggested his life experiences had not all been good. More troubling was that Sophie's feelings for him went beyond attraction to something deeper and more nuanced. It made no sense, and that left her frustrated and angry.

'I keep remembering something really sad, only I can't remember what it is,' Caitlin whined from the back in her little girl's voice.

'Can't you shut her up?' Mallory snapped.

'Have some compassion,' Sophie hissed harshly. 'She's not well.'

'Compassion is way down the list at the moment, behind anxiety and fear. I tell you, she's going to drop us in it big time.'

'Get a grip. You can deal with it.'

'I'll take that as a vote of confidence.' Mallory glanced at Jerzy in the back. The Mocker's mask gleamed above a voluminous blanket. 'All right, tell me now, you little weasel – why Canterbury? I don't know of any standing stones in this area.'

'Don't bully him,' Sophie said sharply.

'Get off my back, will you?'

'The Enemy will be observing the old stones where the Blue Fire is strongest,' Jerzy replied, 'but they are not the only places where it can be found. Anywhere with sufficient spiritual power will do if you know the right key to unlock the door. The ground in those places is like a battery, soaking up the energies of worship.'

'You know what worship gets you?' Mallory said. 'Sore knees and a sore throat.'

'Somebody died.' Caitlin began to cry quietly. Sophie watched a flicker of pity cross Mallory's face, but he hid it quickly.

'She shouldn't be with us. For her own sake,' he said firmly.

'We can't leave her behind.' Sophie softened her critical tone. She turned back to comfort Caitlin and was shocked to see that a new flintiness had replaced the little girl's innocence.

'I'm going with you. Nobody dumps me,' she said sharply.

'It's like having an acting class in the back,' Mallory muttered.

'Who are you now?' Sophie asked.

'I'm me – Caitlin, that is.' She softened. 'I know it's difficult for you both, but I'm asking you to make some concessions. I'm not going to let you down—' She paused. 'If I do, I'll make sure it's only me who pays the price. But I need to do this. I need to make things right.' She silenced Sophie's coming question and added, 'Don't ask me to explain. Memories are surfacing from a life I don't wholly remember. Upsetting things . . .' She choked back a sob.

'We all have different faces we put on when needs must,' Jerzy said. 'In this, Caitlin is no different—'

'Who kicked your box?' Mallory said harshly. 'Stop acting like you've got an opinion worth hearing.' He pulled the transit into a multi-storey car park and brought it to a halt in the first empty space. 'Okay, I'm sorry.' He turned back to Caitlin. 'We've all got our own big bag of rocks on our shoulders. Some are more obvious than others, but that doesn't give me a right to start mouthing off.'

Caitlin's touching, relieved smile made Sophie warm to Mallory, reminding her of the qualities that sometimes drew her to him so strongly.

Jerzy clapped his hands together. 'Oh, the band of heroes shapes before my eyes—'

Mallory jabbed a finger at him. 'You stay five paces ahead of us at all times. If I wanted a cheerleader I'd choose one who looks good in a skirt.'

Even though the streets were deserted, they kept away from the main thoroughfares as they made their way into the city centre.

'Everywhere I look I keep thinking I see spiders,' Sophie said. 'Is this how it's going to be? Never feeling at peace again?'

Mallory was distracted by a rack of newspapers outside a newsagent's. 'That thing we saw over the West End last night – the thing that shattered the Enemy's illusion of normalcy? All that fire and destruction?' He tossed Caitlin a copy of the *Daily Mail*. 'Think again.'

The headline read:

TERROR STRIKE ON LONDON
Fifty-Seven Dead in West End Attack

The rest of the front page showed firemen battling to put out a conflagration engulfing an Oxford Street store.

Uncomprehending, Caitlin flipped to the inside report. 'There's no truth here at all. It says all the devastation was caused by bombs in Tottenham Court Road and Oxford Street . . . and . . . and some kind of gas that made people hallucinate.'

'Clever,' Sophie said bitterly.

Mallory tore open a copy of the *Mirror*. ' "CCTV captured the terrorists fleeing from the scene. Photos have now been circulated to police, customs officials and security services." What's the betting they're nice little snapshots of us and the others?'

'It means we're not going to get much help from anyone,' Sophie said.

'Then come quickly,' Jerzy said. 'The Enemy has recruited many foul things and they will be attempting to prevent you from returning to the Far Lands.'

As they moved on, Jerzy drew a blanket over his head and shoulders and lowered his gaze to divert attention from his mask. Soon the cathedral was in sight, its gleaming stone incandescent in the morning sun. All was still around the remnants of the monastic buildings and grand old houses to the north. To the south, they lost themselves in the sprawl of streets and alleys of the medieval town that converged on Christ Church Gate, leading to the lawns surrounding the cathedral. Winged angels looked down at them from the gatehouse.

'That's us,' Caitlin said in her little girl's voice.

'That is our destination.' Jerzy indicated a circular tower on the eastern edge. 'Known as Becket's Crown, it is the oldest part of the site. The first church was built there, but before that there was another temple dating to the earliest days of your people. Thousands of years of unbroken worship empowering the ground.'

'How come you know so much about it?' Mallory asked.

'I came here for a while after the Blitz.' It sounded as though Jerzy was smiling beneath the mask. 'I was made more than welcome by the local people, despite my appearance. They all helped me with my mission.'

'What mission, Jerzy?' Sophie asked.

'Gathering any and all information that might help with the work that lies ahead. Your work.'

'You've been planning for this since the Second World War?' Sophie asked in disbelief.

'Oh, it has been planned for much longer than that.'

Mallory checked his watch. 'Still more than three hours till this place opens up. Let's find some breakfast.'

'Don't you think we should be staying out of sight?' Sophie asked.

'Got to eat.'

'What happens if our photos are on the morning news?'

'We fight our way back here.'

'You really are pig-headed.'

Mallory shrugged. 'I don't like hiding. It's not in my nature. You can stay here if you want. I'll cover you with branches.'

'No thanks,' Sophie replied. 'I think I'll come along just to hear whatever creative excuses you come up with when everything goes pear-shaped.'

'You're so negative.' Mallory wandered off, whistling. 'You need to enjoy life more.'

In the sizzling, hissing confines of a café patronised by early-morning workers, they ate their breakfast at a table with a clear view of the dawn-bright street.

'I don't understand you,' Sophie said. 'You actually seem happy to be doing this.'

'Whichever way you cut it, it's better than the life I had before. I suppose it boils down to slavery and freedom.' He sipped his tea thoughtfully. 'You can be a slave to all sorts of things – fear, guilt, self-loathing. You can be a slave by trying to keep yourself from feeling anything, trapped in a little world where you know all the boundaries. You throw yourself into everything the world has to offer without any fear, yeah, you suffer. You encounter a lot of bad things. But it's exhilarating.' He chose his words carefully. 'We were all made to experience. Good or bad. It's about learning. And by giving yourself up to that you become free.'

'A philosopher, too.' Sophie had intended the comment to be faintly sarcastic, but it came out tinged with admiration.

'I've experienced so many bad things.' Caitlin stared into Mallory's face as if he had given her some great revelation. 'My husband and son died, in that other life. That almost destroyed me. I want some of those other experiences. The good ones.'

Her words touched Mallory. 'We'll make sure you get some.'

'I think we should move from here soon.' Jerzy had been intently watching the street throughout the meal.

'You've seen something?' Sophie asked.

Jerzy lifted the edge of the blanket so that his mask caught the light. 'I think I see shapes . . . people . . . but they fade like the mist.'

'What's up with you, then?' A burly man with grey hair coiffured like a fifties movie star leaned across his fry-up to peer at Jerzy. 'You in a play or something?'

'That's right, mate.' Jerzy slipped into fluent cockney. 'Have to keep the image up when I'm off the stage.'

The burly man nodded. 'Your mask – it's the one that old music hall star used to wear, ain't it?'

'That's right. Max Masque.' A note of warm surprise was clear in Jerzy's voice.

'My old man loved him. Saw him up in the Smoke when he was a kid. He still remembers some of the old routines. Wears a bit thin when you've heard 'em a hundred times, but keeps him happy.'

'You can't beat the old stuff,' Jerzy said proudly.

Caitlin pointed past him through the window. 'Foxes!'

Ten russet forms darted across the street, investigating one shop, then another, and another, drawing closer all the time. The burly man and the other diners were drawn by the spectacle.

'Oh, that's beautiful,' Caitlin said.

'And weird,' Sophie added, frowning.

As the foxes crossed the street, they stepped into direct sunlight and disappeared. Sophie caught her breath. The animals reappeared in the shade on the other side of the road. 'Yes, definitely weird. Let's get out of here.'

The foxes' purposeful movement turned from mesmerising to unsettling. They shimmered as they ran and often appeared mistily insubstantial. Mallory's hand went instinctively to his side, reaching for a sword that wasn't there.

'Foxes,' Caitlin said distantly. The wonder faded from her face, and her eyes narrowed. She palmed a knife from the table.

'That won't do much good against a . . .' Mallory paused. 'What do you call a group of foxes?'

'Dead.' Caitlin was still and cold.

'You see what you get for banning hunting,' the burly man said. 'Bloody Labour.'

As the foxes neared the café, their eyes began to glow with emerald fire. They ran purposefully, their prey identified.

'Oh dear,' Jerzy said.

The foxes leaped as one towards the window, but instead of shattering the glass they passed through it, becoming smoke, fluidly changing shape again inside the café on the graceful downward arc of their leap. When they landed at the front of the café, they were foxes no more. Ten slim, strong, oriental men balanced athletically on their toes, poised to throw themselves forward. They wore loose-fitting brown silk, but their faces had a vulpine cast, their eyes still glowing green.

The one at the front scanned the café's occupants. When his gaze fell on Mallory, Sophie, Caitlin and Jerzy, he smiled slyly.

'Greeting,' he said with a heavy Chinese accent, 'from the Hu Hsien.'

To the surprise of the others, it was Jerzy who stepped forward. 'You serve the Devourer of All Things. Like all the foulest things in Existence, you have crawled over to its side.'

The leader's nostrils flared. 'You dishonour us with your tone. We demand respect.'

'Demand away,' Mallory said.

'Our master, the King of Foxes, received a request for aid. It was delivered with utmost respect to our Great Dominion, and so we have responded.' He gave a small bow. 'We know of your power and prestige in this world. We hold a great funeral once you are gone.'

'You're not going to stop us,' Caitlin said.

'Sadly, not true. You cannot be allowed to cross the boundary to the Far Lands. Your time has passed.' His left hand snaked out from his side and touched the chest of the bemused burly man, continued through his shirt, his flesh, his bone. When the leader withdrew it, he clutched the still-beating heart. The burly man stared at it in dopey bemusement before emitting a small whimper and keeling over.

Jerzy gave an anguished cry. A sales rep with a garish yellow tie lurched desperately towards the exit. The features of the shapeshifter closest to him fluidly transformed into those of a fox, though the body remained human. Lunging with snapping jaws, it tore the face clean off the sales rep. A shake of its snout and the flesh was swallowed, blood spraying from its whiskers. The leader gave a smile that was mockingly contrite, and then the Hu Hsien advanced as one, those at the rear eliminating the now-screaming diners with efficient brutality.

Sophie was only shaken from her shock when a kitchen knife flashed past her ear and embedded itself in the shoulder of one of the Hu Hsien. His expression registered disbelief, and before that thought had left his mind, Caitlin, who had thrown the knife, was upon him with a second knife. She rammed the blade upwards through his jaw and into his brain.

Sophie was astonished at the transformation that had come over her new friend. Caitlin moved with balletic grace and strength, her face now a warrior's, hard and focused. She had already slain another of the Hu Hsien before Jerzy's cry alerted them from the rear of the café. He had found the back door through which the kitchen staff had bolted. Mallory propelled Sophie towards it, and then grabbed Caitlin's arm as she prepared to confront the remaining snarling, now-wary Hu Hsien.

Out on the street, they ran for the cathedral as a wild barking rose up. The Hu Hsien gave pursuit, now fox, now human, now something of both.

'I seriously need a sword, like Church's,' Mallory snarled.

As they threw themselves inside the newly opened cathedral, blue sparks crackled from their feet.

'We're not going to outrun them,' Sophie gasped.

Jerzy stood in their path, arms outstretched. 'Wait, friends. We are safe. The Blue Fire in the ground, here in your own Great Dominion, makes this a place of sanctuary. Those loathsome things will not be able to set foot in here.'

Sophie saw that Jerzy was right. The Hu Hsien hovered along the cathedral's boundary in human form, their eyes glittering with malice.

'Next time there will be a reckoning,' the leader said. The group moved back, their bodies folding into fox-form, then shimmering into nothingness as they slipped into the morning sunlight.

'What were they?' Mallory leaned against the cool stone to catch his breath.

'There are many secrets in the vast spread of Existence,' Jerzy began hesitantly. 'Each of the races populating this wondrous place only sees a small fragment of all there is. None have the great view of the complete tapestry.'

'And you know more?' Mallory said suspiciously. 'What makes you so well informed?'

Jerzy's breath caught in his throat. He chewed a knuckle, unsure whether he had already said too much.

'Leave him, Mallory,' Sophie said.

'The Golden Ones – the Tuatha Dé Danann – believe they are the centre of Existence,' Jerzy continued hastily. 'They are not. There are many races of power, each overseeing their own Great Dominion, in this world and the Otherworld. And there were many greater powers before, and above, and beyond. The Hu Hsien serve the King of Foxes in the Great Dominion to the east. Most of these powers still slumber as they have done for an age, waiting to be awakened. Why the Hu Hsien are active, I do not know.'

'They were determined to stop us crossing to the Far Lands,' Caitlin noted, 'which suggests to me that we're doing the right thing.'

'What happened to you back there?' Sophie said. 'You were scary.'

Caitlin looked haunted. 'I just reacted. It was instinct.' Massaging her temples, she struggled to recall fleeting memories. 'Things I learned . . . that the person I used to be learned . . . Sorry, I'm not making any sense.'

'If you can do that again, I'll have you in the thick of it any time,' Mallory said.

Caitlin smiled with honest gratitude at the praise. Curiously, Sophie noted a faint, uncomfortable expression cross Mallory's face.

Jerzy urged them through the vast, ringing silence of the cathedral and behind the altar to a little chapel built in the memory of Thomas à Becket. Inside, the air was suffused with so much energy it felt like a storm was brewing.

'Wow,' Sophie said dreamily.

'What now?' Mallory ranged around the chapel, apparently oblivious to the euphoric atmosphere.

'Can't you see it?' Caitlin dropped to her knees to indicate a near-invisible filigree of Blue Fire running in a spiral pattern on the stone floor.

'Your true sight is returning,' Jerzy said. 'You are becoming who you were always meant to be.'

'Here, I think.' Caitlin traced the spiral to its nexus. She looked round at the others, hesitantly raised her hand, then plunged it into the focal point. There was a flash of the pure blue of a summer sky, and then the room was empty.

'These are the Last Days! This is the End-Time!' the wild-haired man roared as he pushed through the crowds traipsing through the hall of Heathrow Airport Terminal Three. He thrust badly scrawled leaflets into the hands of reluctant passers-by. Shavi requested one.

'Why do you encourage the nuts?' Laura sighed.

'The next great prophet will not be the person you imagine,' Shavi replied. 'They never have been. Visionaries will rise up from the great mass of the people in unforeseen places. I like to investigate all possibilities.' He gave his oddly peaceful smile. 'Who would wish to say they walked past the wisest person in the land without a second glance?'

'Yes, it's true. You are completely barking.'

Church's attention remained on the armed, black-flak-jacketed members of the Police Elite Firearms Unit who were patrolling the airport in response to what the media was describing as 'a major terrorist attack' in London's West End the previous night.

Ruth slipped an arm through his. 'There are seats on a flight to Oslo,' she said. 'Do you still want to do this? We're so exposed here. No Blue Fire to keep us safe.'

'It's the quickest route. If we can just stay off the radar long enough—'

Her dark eyes were fixed firmly on his, and he realised she wasn't listening to a word he was saying. 'What do the words "Always Forever" mean?' she asked.

'What kind of question is that?'

'They're echoing around in my head. I think I'm starting to remember . . .' Then, for no clear reason, she hugged him tightly. 'I'm so glad we found each other again,' she whispered.

As he held her, Church became aware of odd looks and sly glances, rising out of nowhere like the first wind of winter blowing through the crowd. A young boy was pointing at him, laughing with amazement. His mother's expression was a dark reflection of her child's, her eyes darting like an animal's as she attempted to haul the boy away.

Laura grabbed his arm. 'The balloon's gone up.' She nodded towards the large TV screens suspended over the terminal that had been showing BBC News 24 coverage of the deployment of more troops in the Middle East. It now featured grainy CCTV footage of four people breaking into Oxford Circus Tube Station. Around it were blown-up close-ups of himself, Ruth, Laura and Shavi, below which ran the legends 'FIRST

TERRORIST PICTURES' and 'SECURITY FORCES SEARCH FOR SUSPECTS'.

'I don't believe it. They're trying to blame *us* for what happened?' Ruth said.

'Come on.' Church urged the three of them into the crowd.

'To the check-in desk?' Laura asked.

Church felt responsible for the glimmer of fear in her eyes; he should have been smarter, faster. 'It's too late for that now. Get outside, find somewhere to lie low for a while.'

As they pushed past the cases and rucksacks, ripples of anxiety ran throughout the milling crowd. Overhead their faces looked down, frozen in the guilt of their horrific actions.

Soon space was opening up so they could run, but that made the situation even worse for it isolated and identified them, and brought even more pointing hands and shouts of alarm. When they were two hundred feet from the doors, ten members of the Elite Firearms Unit surged in, guns at the ready.

'Split up,' Church said. They scattered in different directions. The volume of travellers would have made it easy to fade into the background under normal circumstances, but the blue splashes of the armed police were moving in from all sides, their numbers swelling by the second. As Church hurried to the stairs to the upper floor he lost sight of Shavi and Ruth, but he saw Laura surrounded by four officers. She dodged, and when her way was blocked mouthed something clearly unpleasant. A gun butt came down hard on the back of her skull. Church wanted to rush to her aid, but knew there was nothing he could do.

On the upper floor, he slowed to a walk and tried to merge into the crowds, but he could see the CCTV cameras moving to follow his path. The police closed in on him not far from the open-plan bar. The crowds mysteriously evaporated and he was surrounded with seven guns trained on him.

'Kneel,' the police commander barked, 'or we shoot.'

Beyond the circle of police, the faces of the airport users watched him, filled with equal measures of hatred and fear.

3

The holding cell in the Heathrow Security Annexe was painted magnolia, even the reinforced steel blast door. There was one bench and no windows. The strip light glared, and there was a faint electronic hum that set the nerves on edge.

'Any other good plans, Church-dude?' Laura nursed the back of her head where blood caked her blonde hair.

'Stop whining. I don't hear you suggesting anything constructive,' Ruth snapped. A puffy bruise was growing just beneath her left eye.

'Ah, shut up. Let's face it – we never had a chance. A handful of people against the world? Like we were actually going to achieve anything.'

'Why don't you join Shavi? Do us all a favour.' Ruth nodded to Shavi who sat cross-legged in one corner, deep in meditation.

'Stop fighting,' Church ordered. 'If Mallory, Sophie and Caitlin did their job, we still have a chance of getting away.'

'You're expecting a last-minute rescue?' Laura said sullenly. 'I don't want to burst your bubble, but I wouldn't trust those three to find their own arses in a dark room.'

Ruth sat next to Church. 'This might be the last we see of each other,' she said quietly. 'They're going to split us up, ship us off to Belmarsh, the full terrorist route. It's not fair. We only just found each other again.'

Church took her hand. He was still searching for some meaningful words when the heavy lock rang out and the door swung open. Two armed and helmeted policemen flanked a senior officer. He still wore his flak jacket, but he had left his helmet behind. He was in his forties with silvery hair, and though his gaze was cold and steady, occasionally a tremor disturbed his features, an involuntary facial tic that Church had seen before. There was a faint disconnectedness about him, too, the result of his mind trying to process twin thought-tracks – his own and that of the spider that was doubtless embedded somewhere in his body.

'Get up,' he said. 'You're going on a short ride. We need to get you fitted for cuffs and leg-irons.' Though there was no obvious sign in the officer's words, Church was certain that none of them would be reaching their destination.

The men levelled their weapons for emphasis. Church and Ruth stood up. Laura gently stirred Shavi. When he stretched, he turned his good eye to Church and blinked slowly, a knowing sign that puzzled Church.

Ruth and Laura looked to Church. He nodded to them to proceed.

'That's right, be clever,' the officer said.

Behind the police, a figure loomed. 'All right, stand down. I don't know – give boys guns and there's always trouble.' Hunter flashed his credentials to the senior officer, who was clearly taken aback.

'Commander Hunter? This is a police operation—'

'Of course it is. That's why it's about to go pear-shaped.' He nodded to the two armed men. 'All right, clear off.'

The two men looked uncertainly at the senior officer. He was confused, but quickly tried to regain his authority.

Hunter cut him off. 'Let's not do this in front of your boys.'

The senior officer motioned for the men to leave and Hunter shut the door behind them.

'What's all this about?' the senior officer asked.

Hunter pressed a small black box against the senior officer's arm. There was a blue flash and the senior officer fell to the ground, unconscious. Hunter held up the box. 'Government-issue taser. Good for every occasion.'

'Found your conscience, then?' Laura said.

'Funny, when I pictured this in my head it involved you throwing your arms around my neck and smothering me with kisses of gratitude.'

'Get us out of here and I might just do that. But don't start thinking it actually means something.'

'Heaven forfend.' He dragged the senior officer into the corner, out of sight of the door. 'Do exactly what I say. We'll pick up those guards in the corridor and go out through security, where we'll collect your sword and spear. Then to the vehicle compound where there's an armoured prisoner transit waiting. Don't look at me. Don't talk to me. Act sullenly – should come natural to you lot. We've got to move fast. We won't have much time to cover the trail.'

'Okay,' Church said. 'And thanks.'

'It's a job. I always do things to the best of my ability.'

Hunter's credentials commanded surprising weight as they breezed through security. In the vehicle compound, the guards herded Church, Ruth, Shavi and Laura into the back of the armoured transit and Hunter drove it past the final security checkpoint towards the M4.

'I'll expect those kisses shortly,' Hunter shouted back through the wire mesh between the driver's cab and the back of the van.

'It'll be a life-altering experience. Hope you're up to it,' Laura replied.

'What changed your mind?' Church asked Hunter.

'The realisation that I really have no choice.'

'You are very cool under pressure,' Shavi said. 'To walk into the heart of the Enemy's territory . . . amazing.'

'I don't expect I'll be able to get away with that again. Next time my charismatic and sexy face will be alongside your mugshots.'

'Where are we going?' Ruth asked.

'To swap vehicles so we can't be traced. Take a breather, it's not far.'

Church settled back next to Shavi. 'You knew something like this was going to happen.'

'I feel myself awakening, like an orchid in the sun.' Shavi gave a faint, warming smile. 'Within me, there are vast depths. Once before I tapped them, and I will do so again.'

'Do what you can. You're our seer, Shavi. You can see things that we can't. We need that advantage.'

Soon after, Hunter pulled the transit into Heston Services where he abandoned it for a brand-new white van.

'I know they can still track us, but I'm not going to make it easy for them.' He urged Church to sit in the front with him. Once they were back on the motorway, he said, 'What's the strategy?'

'We need to get to Scandinavia.' Church described his encounter with Robin Goodfellow. 'But that's all I've got. Now that we're officially terrorists I don't see how we can even get out of the country.'

'Don't worry about that. Scandinavia, eh? Can we try to narrow it down to at least a thousand square miles?'

'I'm working on it.'

Hunter thought for a moment. 'Maybe we need to cause our own terrorist outrage. Blow somewhere up. Distract the security services.'

'That's not what we stand for,' Church said.

'I thought we stood for winning.' Hunter eyed Church with faint bemusement.

'We're symbols, too. You know that?'

A thoughtful pause; a nod.

'We have to be true to what we represent or we're nothing.'

Hunter didn't reply, but a faint smile teased his lips all the way to Membury Services where the early afternoon sun was starting to break through a bank of grey clouds. Hunter pulled in next to another identical white van. 'There's someone waiting to see you,' he said to Church.

In the restaurant, Tom was sitting in a corner drinking coffee. He was older than the last time Church had encountered him in the flesh, but he still had the same unmistakable aura of intensity.

Overcome with joy at seeing his old friend again, Church walked quickly to the table. But instead of an emotional reunion, Tom surveyed him with cold eyes flecked with tears.

'What's wrong?' Church asked, shocked.

'Sit down.'

As Church pulled up a chair, Tom leaned in, his voice trembling with restrained passion. 'What in heaven's name have you done?'

Deep in Tom's eyes there was a haunted intensity that shook Church. 'I don't understand—'

Tom gripped Church's wrist. 'I should be dead,' he hissed through clenched teeth. 'I know it . . . I can see it with the cursed vision that witch from under the hill gave me. I see two lives running parallel: one here, another where I'm moving across the Grim Lands and into the beyond. I ask you again: what have you done?'

'I changed reality. To save you, and Niamh and all of the Tuatha Dé Danann.'

'How?'

'I don't know if I can explain it. At the time it was like a dream. When I lay in the casket in the Far Lands in the Sleep Like Death, it felt as if I went to another place . . . where there was a Caretaker . . . and two other beings who claimed they were close to some higher power.' The memories were hazy, and the more Church tried to recall them, the more they slipped from his grasp. 'The Caretaker took me to something he called the Axis of Existence, and he told me that if I shifted it I could change what had happened—'

'You bloody idiot.' Tom covered his face, shaking silently. 'Do you know what it's like to feel alive and dead at the same time?'

'I'm sorry. I just didn't want you to sacrifice yourself—'

'It's not just me!' Tom snapped. 'You're not a god. To do such a thing, with no concept of the repercussions—' He caught himself. 'Nothing is created. Nothing is destroyed. There is only what is, all connected. To change one thing changes everything.'

Church weighed Tom's words, the burden of his distress. 'What have I done?'

'I don't know. That's just it! There is a puzzle on sale in the city – a glass ball encased in a network of string tied to wooden rods. The aim is to remove the glass ball by shifting the rods until a large enough hole appears in the network. But every time you move one rod, the string attached to it shifts another rod, and so on, so that the network continually shifts, confounding any attempts to create a hole. Do you see?'

'So by altering events to save your life—'

'The network shifted in other places. Perhaps someone lost their life who never should have. Perhaps something terrible has happened, or is happening now. Perhaps . . .' He flapped a weary hand and covered his face again.

'I only wanted to save you, Tom.'

'Good intentions in the hands of an idiot are a dangerous weapon.' He looked deep into Church's eyes. 'Nothing else to do now but deal with the situation you've given us. Are you up to it?'

'I've kept my head above water so far.'

'Just. Remarkable, considering you didn't have me to act as your common sense.'

Church was distracted by the sudden darkening of the sky through the window. The ravens descended on the service station, briefly blotting out the sun.

'The *Morvren*,' Tom said. 'They follow death and destruction, and supernatural terror.'

'They appear to be following me.' Church recalled what he had been told two thousand years earlier about the ravens, symbols of death, following in his wake.

'I think,' Tom said, 'we should not be sitting around debating any longer.'

4

Shavi was oblivious to the cacophonous bird calls that now drowned out the deep drone of the motorway traffic. He had left Hunter and Laura to their flirtatious insulting of each other, and Ruth to a quiet brooding that appeared to have been consuming her since she had left St Paul's, and made his way beyond the service station perimeter to where he had a view of the tranquil Berkshire countryside.

The struggle Church had set for them was vast and victory unimaginable, but he was convinced of its rightness. He was prepared to risk anything, even his own life, in pursuit of that victory.

At the bottom of a slope that hid him from the service station, he sat cross-legged, no longer feeling the warmth of the sun on his face, or hearing the wind in the copse nearby. Every part of him was focused internally.

A hint of fear, a remembrance of the price he had already paid, and then the familiar taste of iron filings in his mouth. Ahead of him, six feet above the ground, the air grew opaque and then began to steam and bubble. A hole opened up, and after a minute a figure forced its head and shoulders through, a mewling monstrosity being born. Its face was blank, but indentations revealed the location of its eyes and mouth; Shavi was convinced he could see the eyes moving just beneath the silvery caul.

'Who calls?' it said with wrenching jaw movements.

'I do. Shavi, Brother of Dragons.'

'Again you draw me from the Invisible World?'

'I need information.'

There was a short pause before it replied, 'You know the price, Brother of Dragons. A small thing. Only a small thing.'

Shavi remained calm, but inside he felt a ghost of the pain he had suffered the last time he had paid this being with 'a small thing'. Through his contact with the earth, he reached deeply within himself, feeling for the thin residue of the Blue Fire. It echoed in the darkness of his mind, spoke to him without words.

'A small thing?' he said.

'Just a small thing,' the construct said nonchalantly.

'No,' Shavi said. 'I am a Brother of Dragons. I am awakening to what that means, despite all the efforts of greater powers to keep me in a deep sleep.'

The construct shrank back. 'Then there can be no answers for you. The rules—'

'The rules have changed.'

Shavi quickly caught the construct at the back of its silvery head. The skin moved like mercury beneath his fingers.

'Stay back!' it said sharply. 'This cannot be—'

The words died in its throat as Shavi drove his fingers into one eye socket beneath the caul. The thing shrieked so loudly that Shavi's ears rang. Blood began to drip from his nose.

The skin split. Beneath it, an eye popped from the construct's socket. Shavi closed his hand around the gelatinous orb and tore it free.

The construct's shattering howl threw Shavi back several feet. 'Now,' he said, 'I will have answers. But first . . .'

He examined the eye, weighing up what the voice in the Blue Fire had told him. Then he tore off his eye patch and forced the shiny orb into his own gaping socket.

5

'Where's Shavi?' Church called as he ran to the van where Hunter and Laura were watching the flock of ravens settling on all the vehicles. So many flew overhead that it looked as if night was falling early.

From the perimeter of the car park, Shavi walked confidently towards them. They all stopped to stare, recognising a transformation that went beyond his missing eye patch. In the gathering gloom, a faint golden glow emanated from his new eye.

'What the fuck, Shavster?' Laura peered into his face and was relieved to see it was still her old friend.

'Oslo, Norway,' he said. 'That is our destination.'

'Look.' Ruth indicated steady movement in the fields that bounded the service station. Brutish figures moved close to the ground, approaching on all sides.

'Redcaps,' Tom said. 'They are only the first of many.'

In less than a minute, Hunter had the van racing onto the motorway. The birds followed, turning the sky into a cauldron of seething darkness.

'The whole bird thing – bit of a giveaway,' Laura said.

'The *Morvren* recognise the currents of reality,' Tom said. 'They see convergences that presage a maelstrom.'

Laura eyed him suspiciously. 'I know you somehow. Old guy, talking bollocks. Or was it just a bad dream?'

'This is all a bad dream.' Tom's glasses caught the light of approaching headlamps in the preternatural dark. 'Drive faster, now.' The calm in his voice was somehow more chilling.

'All right,' Hunter said as he searched the landscape for any sign of threat, 'starting to think I made the wrong decision listening to you back in London.'

Shavi began to recount what had happened to him, until his head suddenly rocked forward to his chest, then snapped back. His new eye shimmered a sickly green as he stared at things no one else could see. 'The air folds and spatters like liquid metal,' he said in a flat monotone. 'Shadows falling like rain . . .'

'He's having some kind of vision.' Ruth grasped Shavi's shoulders but he was rigid.

Hunter took the slip road for Swindon, then followed a circuitous route to avoid the most built-up areas. Eventually Shavi regained his composure.

'What were you thinking?' Laura said. 'You steal an eye from some supernatural tosser, and then stick it in your own head? There's a reason why the NHS doesn't do transplants like that.'

'I knew there would be a price to pay for the transaction,' Shavi said with a strained smile, 'but it is one I can bear.'

'We thought you were going to have a seizure.' Ruth brushed his sweat-matted hair away from his forehead.

'When I focus through that eye, I can see things in the Otherworld. I know things I would never have known otherwise. Things that can help us.'

'You can see two worlds at the same time?' Ruth asked.

Shavi nodded.

'No wonder you keep losing it.' Laura snorted. 'Shame. I was starting to like the eye-patch look. Still won't trust you behind the wheel, though.'

Hunter brought the van to a halt on a country lane. Beyond the hedge there was a high-security fence punctuated with Ministry of Defence warning signs.

'What are you planning?' Church asked.

'That's RAF Wroughton.' Hunter stretched, cracked his knuckles. 'I'm going to commandeer a Hercules Transporter to take us to Norway. It's a NATO ally. We can bypass all the civilian security clearances.'

'You can do that?'

'As long as they haven't already revoked my security clearance. In which case, I'll have to steal one.'

'Remember: you are not simply entering a new country,' Tom warned. 'It is a new Great Dominion. New rules, new dangers. The gods are very protective of their territories.'

chapter four

two minutes to midnight

1

The world was white. Sky and landscape merged into one horizonless snowy backdrop so that all there was felt enclosed in a glass ball and beyond existed only mystery. They exited down the ramp at the back of the plane where soldiers in parkas struggled to unload crates and military equipment.

The squaddies averted their eyes when Hunter walked by. Laura thought how lonely he looked, though he hid it well behind the cocky, rakish facade that irritated as many people as it charmed. She didn't like that; they were too much alike.

Stamping her boots in the snow, she half-considered folding a chunk of ice into snow to throw at Tom, but the cold was eating its way into her bones despite the Arctic gear Hunter had procured for them from the quartermaster.

'You know my flawless complexion is going to look as if someone's been at it with a wire brush in about five minutes,' she said. 'That's not a good look.'

'Better get used to it.' Hunter scanned the desolate airfield; no other planes were visible. 'With the wind-chill factor, temperatures drop to minus thirty. Touch any metal and you'll leave flesh behind.'

'I bet you like it. Prove what a big man you are by taking the pain.'

'Nothing to prove there.'

'Run along now. Catch us a caribou or whatever it is you do. I'm very hungry.'

'Can we get a move on?' Tom said irritably. 'While you two carry out your little dance of sexual attraction, the rest of us are slowly going numb.'

'We'd never be able to tell the difference with you, old man.' Laura looked past the small, run-down terminal buildings to the wall of white. 'You could have brought us somewhere where there was, you know, actual life.'

'We're in Oppland, north of Bergen and Oslo, south of Trondheim, about an hour outside Dombas.' Hunter struck out for the terminal, head bowed against the howling wind. 'Back during the Cold War, this was considered a major NATO line of defence against a possible Russian invasion. And, yeah, you're right, Tom – let's get somewhere warm to make plans.'

2

Night had fallen by the time they reached the hotel burning with light in the empty landscape. No other dwellings lay in sight, and even the road was lost beneath drifting snow. Stark black pines were the only contrast against the sweeping white plain.

The hotel was modern, glass and pine with roaring log fires for a traditional feel. It was clearly a venue for tourists exploring the high country, but it appeared to be almost deserted.

While Hunter ordered them food – reindeer steaks and rice and a vegetable stew for Laura – and bottles of beer, Shavi flirted briefly with the barman, a tall, muscular man in his early twenties with long brown hair and a shy demeanour. They made a connection that Shavi was determined to follow up later.

They consumed their meal at the comfy chairs in front of the fire, next to their unruly pile of parkas and boots.

'Couldn't we have stayed somewhere a bit more lively?' Laura complained.

'Depends if you want to still be alive in the morning,' Tom snapped. 'A ley line runs through here. It'll buy you a little more time.'

Church turned to Shavi, who was eyeing the barman. 'You got us here, but can you see the way forward?'

'Flashes, here and there. I am attempting to make sense of what they mean, but so far it has been too confusing.'

'What I don't get,' Ruth said to Church, 'is why your friend the Puck doesn't actually give you some help you can use. A hint here, half a clue there – it's all game-playing. Are you sure he's on our side?'

'Robin Goodfellow is on no one's side.' Tom removed a tin from his haversack and began to construct a roll-up. 'He moves things around to his own ends, whatever they may be. He cannot be trusted.'

'I don't trust him,' Church said, 'but I think at the moment his aims and ours coincide, and for now that's good enough for me.'

Shavi sipped his beer thoughtfully as he watched the flames leap up the chimney. 'It seems to me from what you have said that the Puck has been playing a long game, for millennia. There has always been purpose in his mischief.'

'What's that? Leading humanity off the edge of a cliff?' Laura finished her beer and took Tom's when he wasn't looking.

'A creature of wild magic like the Puck could not be content living in a universe ruled by the Void,' Shavi mused. 'Those other figures you saw, Church – the Caretaker, the man and woman with the cauldron – they appear to represent powers above and beyond gods like the Tuatha Dé Danann. An alliance, perhaps, against darkness and despair.'

'But we're just pawns to them,' Ruth said. 'They don't care if we live or die as long as we serve their ends.' The bitterness in her voice surprised them all.

'If there is one thing we have learned,' Shavi began soothingly, 'it is that there are currents of meaning all around us, shifting forces that we cannot comprehend but which guide us in a subtle way. I do not know what those forces are, but I do know we are not alone in this battle.'

'Listen to him,' Tom grunted. 'He's the only one of you lot that talks any sense.'

'None of it makes any sense to me!' Ruth's voice cracked and she stalked off in the direction of their rooms.

'Looks like Miss Frosty's got the painters and decorators in.' Laura sniffed. 'I'm going to have her beer.'

3

As midnight approached, Tom and Shavi went out to sit on the hotel porch. Gas heaters roared but did little to dispel the bitter cold. They braved the temperature for the view: the moon transformed the frozen landscape into a shimmering white dream.

Shavi took a deep breath that filled his lungs with ice. 'Do you know why I have such hope for us?' he said softly.

'Because you're deluded?'

'This world is too amazing to be ruled by the essence of despair. Everywhere I look I see wonder – resting beneath the gentle drift of snow, in a city street steaming in the summer sun, in October rain on a factory window. Magic, just waiting for us to release it.'

'Very poetic. Now, have you turned that incisive human eye on your own comrades?' The ember of Tom's roll-up glowed red as he inhaled.

'What do you mean?'

'I mean, you have two who are deranged by their own hormones, and two who are facing a rising obstacle between them, which they cannot yet see. If they don't sort themselves out and focus on what really matters, disaster will creep up like a thief in the night.'

'You can see that with your precog abilities?'

'I don't know what I see any more,' Tom replied bitterly. 'When the queen of the Court of the Yearning Heart arranged to torment me through the abilities I was given, I had centuries to adjust to the visions of the future that came to me. Yet there were none beyond a certain time because I was fated to die. Now everything has changed. I see new things all the time – flashes of terrible events – but I do not yet have a context for them. And so I am useless.'

Shavi was saddened to hear the raw emotion in Tom's voice. 'Yet you sense something bad is going to happen?'

'Oh, yes. Very bad indeed.'

Shavi's attention was caught by a flicker of movement far out across the snowy waste near the dark line of fir trees. He couldn't tell if it was man or beast, for it appeared to move first on two legs, then on four. With it came a palpable sense of apprehension.

'I think we should go in now,' he said.

4

Church followed Ruth back to their room where he found her staring disconsolately out of the window. Since they had landed in Norway she felt more distant than she ever had at any point during their two-thousand-year separation.

'Look at it,' she said without turning around. 'It's such a bleak, frozen place. I hate it here.'

Church rested a hand on her shoulder, but she remained rigid. 'Tell me what's on your mind.'

'No point,' she said. 'There's no space for you and me. We've got a job to do and that sucks every iota of energy out of everything.'

'What is it? You weren't like this when we first got back together.' With an aching clarity, he recalled her kiss that had woken him from the Sleep

Like Death, and the joy of their time together as they travelled to Cornwall for the confrontation with Veitch. And then, with a chill, it hit him: that was when it had all changed. So subtle at first that he hadn't noticed it, but now he could trace the lines of dislocation directly back to that point.

When Ruth turned, he could see she'd reached the same conclusion. 'He got his revenge in the end, didn't he? One last attempt to ruin something good.' She brushed away a stray tear. 'When Veitch leaped on his sword to kill himself, that bolt of black lightning burned through the three of us. What did it do? I feel it inside me now . . . drawing me away from you.'

'Fight it,' he said.

'For some reason, it's growing stronger.' She stared at her hands as if she would be able to see what had infected her. 'I feel cold, distant, tired, negative. I feel tearful, irritable and depressed. I can't see any good in anything any more, just at the point when I've finally found it.' There was a moment of silence before she added, 'If Veitch wasn't dead, I'd kill him with my own hands.'

5

By the fire, Hunter and Laura had moved on from the beer and were working their way through a bottle of tequila.

'You enjoy doing this?' Hunter lounged in his chair, boots on the table. 'Risking death. Fighting a war you can't win. Going up against things that would give most people nightmares.'

'Life's about living, dude. What's the point in inching forward just so you can arrive at death safely? Experience, that's what we all want.'

'If you want experience . . .' He held out his arms.

'What kind of women do you normally get, Hunter? Do they fall for that big-man act?'

'What do you fall for?'

'I'm class. I expect dedication, hard work, attention to detail and complete adoration. Because I deserve it.'

Hunter thought for a moment as he weighed his shot glass in one hand. 'I might be able to do that.'

'I'll get back to you.'

Laura shivered. It felt as if the door had been thrown open, but it was firmly shut and there was no discernible draught. She looked around the bar. 'Where is everyone?'

'It's just you and me—'

'Stop being a dick.' The hairs on her neck tingled. 'Something's up.' Her attention fell on a clock in the shape of a sunburst over the fire. It showed two minutes to midnight.

'And the clock's stopped.'

6

From the ruins of the ancient watchtower stretched a pastoral landscape of fields and woods, winding lanes, sparkling streams and small hamlets where wisps of smoke drifted up from thatched homesteads.

'I think I've been here before.' Caitlin shielded her eyes from the glare of the morning sun. 'Or was it a dream?'

After they had crossed over from the cathedral, Caitlin, Mallory and Sophie had taken a long time to come to terms with the delirious new world that had been presented to them. Every sight, sound and smell was heightened, rendering their own world a pale copy.

But Jerzy was insistent that they move on quickly, warning of the many dangers that lurked in the Far Lands. Stripping off his mask and coat, his true appearance shocked them all – a bone-white face with a permanent rictus grin – but he revelled in the freedom to be himself, performing tumbles and dances whenever the mood took him.

'I feel strange here, too,' Sophie said. 'Almost like coming home.'

Mallory was distracted by the odd shadows that clustered around trees, the unnatural way the grass moved when there wasn't a breeze. 'This place creeps me out. I feel as if someone's watching us all the time. Oi!' he called to Jerzy. 'Stop dancing like a loon. Are you sure we're going the right way?'

'Oh, yes. I could never forget the way to the Court of the Soaring Spirit.' The Mocker grinned. 'The home of my former mistress. For so long a prison. But now . . . sanctuary! We need a safe place in these troubled times.'

At the foot of the hill on which the ruined watchtower stood, they passed a small farmstead, the long, low building half-set into the hillside. A small man with berry-brown skin and dark, furtive eyes was tending the vegetable patch beside the house. When he saw them coming, he bolted inside, slamming the door and all the shutters.

'Brigid says everyone round here is scared,' Caitlin said in her little-girl voice. 'Now I'm scared, too.'

From a distance, the Court of the Soaring Spirit looked like a block of obsidian beneath the night sky. Against the foothills of the rising mountains, its monolithic bulk gave it an unpleasant gravity that set their teeth on edge. Fires blazed along the black walls that soared hundreds of feet above their heads, and occasional bursts of flame through the slit windows that dotted the walls suggested that a mighty foundry thundered within.

'Is this it?' Mallory said. 'Not what you'd call welcoming.'

Jerzy was filled with uncertainty, but gave a quick nod.

Fumes filled the air as they made their way to the gargantuan front gates. Everything was on a scale that made the individual feel insignificant.

The gates were opened by furtive guards in silver and ivory armour. None of them would engage Mallory and the others directly but a messenger was quickly despatched.

'They look very afraid, too,' Jerzy whispered to Mallory. 'The Army of the Ten Billion Spiders must have brought the threat right to the gates of the court.'

Within minutes Evgen, the captain of the guard, arrived, his hawk-helmet giving his face a raptor quality. 'The Mocker,' he said with dark amusement. 'We did not expect to see you here again.' He cast his cold eyes over Mallory, Sophie and Caitlin, opened his mouth to speak and then thought better of it. 'I am sure our queen will make you most welcome.'

'I've been to a city just like this before,' Sophie said to Mallory as they followed Evgen through the gates. 'I'm starting to remember. Except . . . it didn't look like this. That makes no sense, I know.'

The oppressive atmosphere grew more intense once they had left the outside world behind. Cobbled streets barely wide enough for two people to walk abreast wound steeply upwards between overhanging buildings that hid all but the slightest sliver of night sky. Constant twists and turns made it impossible to see far ahead or behind. Sewage ran in the gutters from emptied chamber-pots and the stench was only kept at bay by the greasy smoke of the flickering lanterns that barely illuminated their way.

The Palace of Glorious Light was in the centre of the sprawling city. It was a fortress, not a palace, and the name was rendered even more ironic by the roaring cauldrons of fire that lined the courtyard and were spaced out along the ramparts. They gave off thick, choking smoke and their scarlet flames added a hellish tint to the shining black walls.

Evgen led them into the palace and up numerous flights of claustrophobic stairs and along winding corridors. Eventually they came to a gloomy throne-room. It was unbearably hot, and filled with the constant hissing and crackling of the numerous braziers spaced around it.

From an antechamber emerged a beautiful, golden-skinned woman in a dress of such pure white that she glowed like a spectre.

Jerzy bowed. 'My queen.'

'You are always welcome here, faithful servant,' she replied in a gentle voice before turning to Mallory, Sophie and Caitlin. 'I am Niamh, queen of the Court of the Soaring Spirit. I bid you welcome.' She grew puzzled as she looked them up and down. 'You are Brother and Sisters of Dragons?'

Mallory was entranced. Sophie gave him an unnecessarily hard pinch. 'Ah . . . yes,' he stuttered. 'We . . . uh—'

'Your majesty, we are here to seek your help,' Sophie interjected forcefully. 'We're looking for a powerful weapon—'

'—that will help us defeat the Devourer of All Things,' Jerzy said. 'The object of power is known as the Extinction Shears.'

'I know of this thing,' Niamh said, 'but the Shears have been missing since they were encountered by my good friend Church, your Brother.'

'The Extinction Shears are held in the Market of Wishful Spirit. Find the market, you find the Shears.' Mallory had regained his composure.

'Then I will give you all the help you need to find the travelling market. Now tell me of Church,' she said brightly. 'Is he well?'

'He would have come with us, but he's needed back in our world,' Sophie replied. 'He is well. But it's a hard fight.'

Niamh nodded, and gave a smile shadowed by a fleeting sadness.

Chairs were brought and Niamh motioned for them to sit. She despatched Evgen to arrange for food to be brought from the kitchens.

'These are dark times in the Far Lands. War draws ever closer.' Niamh sat on a carved wooden throne between two braziers, oblivious to the heat. 'On the edge of this realm, the fortress of the Army of the Ten Billion Spiders sits brooding. Bigger than this court. Bigger than the twenty Great Courts. Its forces have swelled to an incalculable number. Lament Brood. Redcaps. Gehennis. The foulest things known to Existence. They march far and wide, leaving despair in their wake. Soon they will be upon us, and then . . .' She waved the thought away. 'It is not the numbers. It is the great powers they control. And in the sky above the fortress something is beginning to appear.'

'They have other gods working with them,' Mallory said. 'Janus. Loki. Apollo—'

'They may call themselves gods . . .' Once again she caught herself. 'Old habits die hard. The truth? The Golden Ones are driven back at every turn. Our power and influence wane. Sometimes, in my darker moments, I wonder if our time has passed.'

Caitlin sat with her legs tucked under her and her arms wrapped tightly around her. 'I'm still scared,' she said. 'Where's the Morrigan?'

'Don't worry about her,' Mallory said to Niamh. 'She's not . . . well.'

'The Morrigan helped me once.' Caitlin rocked in her chair. 'I need her to help me again.'

'The Morrigan is one of my dark sisters,' Niamh said. 'She has great power. She deals in blood and death.'

'And birth,' Caitlin added. 'And sex. New life.'

'She would be a great boon to us in the struggle ahead, but she has not been seen for a long time.' Niamh sighed. 'And she is not the only one. Over many generations, Church rescued Brothers and Sisters of Dragons from certain death and brought them here for sanctuary. One night they left as one, their mission unknown. They have not been seen since.'

'We were counting on them to help us,' Mallory said.

'There is something you should see.' Niamh whispered to an aide who hurried out of the throne-room, returning a moment later with a large case covered by a velvet cloth. He placed it on a table in front of Niamh and retreated.

Niamh hesitated, then plucked the cloth aside, uncovering a glass case edged with gold. Inside was a spider. Once revealed, it threw itself furiously at the glass, attempting to break free.

'This was placed inside my head to control me.' Niamh passed a hand across her eyes, troubled. 'I know not how it came to be there, but it took all the skills of my people to remove it. I keep it here to remind me that even the Golden Ones can succumb to the powers of the Army of the Ten Billion Spiders.'

'Have they tried to control any more of your people?' Mallory asked.

Niamh fell silent for a moment. 'Not that I know. But some Golden Ones have gone missing. My advisors suggest they may simply have fled the coming war, but I fear the worst.'

Promising to put all she had at their disposal, Niamh had Evgen provide rooms for the four of them.

'I like her,' Mallory said, once they were in their cramped, too-hot quarters.

'You would. You're a man.' Sophie examined Caitlin, who had already fallen into a deep sleep on the couch. 'I'm worried about her. She's retreated into her other personalities ever since we came here. And what was all that about the Morrigan?'

They were interrupted by a sound like distant thunder. The north window led onto a small balcony. Standing there they watched bursts of fire in the sky far to the north, punctuated by deep rumbles.

'This is a scary place,' Sophie said. 'I thought it was supposed to be Fairyland. It's more like hell.'

She edged closer to Mallory and he unconsciously slipped an arm around her waist. It surprised them both.

'I remember now,' she said. 'You and me.'

'My combat honey.' The words sprang from nowhere. Mallory gently traced his fingers across her face as the memories surfaced, slowly at first but then gaining intensity as if a barrier had been breached. 'We met in Salisbury. The Church was trying to establish a new order of Knights Templar. I signed up.'

Sophie giggled. 'You were such a lad!'

'The things you could do with the Craft. You were scary.'

'Still am.'

Another thunderous barrage of explosions lit the heavens, but now they were oblivious to it.

Another memory ignited on Sophie's face, sorrowful this time. 'That awful thing you went through . . . the one you killed . . . you poor baby.'

Mallory tried to brush it off, but a tremor ran through him. 'We can't become Brothers and Sisters of Dragons until we experience death.' His expression grew puzzled. 'But you . . . I'm still having trouble . . .'

The brief moment of anxiety was driven out by her smile. 'Forget about me! I was just a little rebel girl who hooked up with a bunch of travellers. Nothing compared to you.' She grabbed his head and kissed him with a desperate passion. 'We were both lost until we met each other. Getting together in Salisbury – that saved us, didn't it?'

He nodded, unable to take his eyes off her face.

'What the Void did to us with those fake lives . . . Seeing each other every day but never being able to talk, not knowing how much we meant to each other—'

Mallory kissed her again. It was soft and deep and their bodies folded together while fire roared across the sky. Gently, Mallory's hand moved up to her breast and his thumb circled her hardening nipple. Sophie kissed him more deeply, one hand caressing his erection before undoing his trousers and sliding her hand inside. Heat, delirious sensation and a torrent of emotion overwhelmed them, everything that had been denied them in recent months.

Not caring where they were or who might see them, Sophie pulled Mallory down onto the balcony floor. Hard and hot, he slid inside her, and then they kissed, and made love, and agreed a silent covenant that they would never be torn apart again.

8

Caitlin found Mallory and Sophie asleep on the balcony, wrapped in each other's arms. She was pleased for them, yet also, oddly, a little sad. If she could, she would have examined that feeling, but the voices of Amy, Brigid and Briony chattered continually in her head, warning her of terrible danger, trying to take control of what they called her 'day-mind' so they could drive her to hide or flee.

Yet the raw return of her own memories caused sufficient pain to keep her own personality in control. She recalled with a terrible surge of grief the deaths of her husband and son, a shattering event that had broken her mentally and rebuilt her as a Sister of Dragons. The memory of her possession by the Morrigan, too, was harsh and bathed in blood. It had turned her into a warrior who could overcome anything, but when the Morrigan had finally departed she had hoped she would finally be granted peace.

She crept out of the apartments without waking Mallory and Sophie and made her way into the dark jumble of stinking streets. Figures flickered in and out of the shadows, cut-throats and cut-purses, predators of all kinds. They circled Caitlin from a distance, watching from alleys and doorways, following then retreating.

Caitlin was oblivious. The chatter in her head was the sound of heavy machinery. Eventually, she gripped her temples and shook herself furiously, screaming, 'Stop it! Stop it!'

The figures all around paused in their secret machinations, then slowly melted into the darkness.

The sudden silence inside her mind was like the sea at night. Caitlin almost felt like crying. 'Now,' she said firmly, 'tell me where I need to go.'

The Hunter's Moon was an inn of gothic proportions, with over-hanging eaves and oddly pitched roofs, turrets and gargoyles. Through the diamond-pane windows, candlelight glimmered. It appeared to be the most welcoming place in the entire city.

Within, though, the mood was subdued. Small groups of drinkers indulged in whispered conversations, eyes flickering towards Caitlin before quickly moving away, scared and desperate. The clientele was a bizarre collection of grotesques, with horns and wings, scales and cloven hooves and hair that moved of its own accord. Caitlin saw none of the golden-skinned Tuatha Dé Danann, however.

'Tell me where,' she snapped out loud. The drinkers closed the ranks of their little groups for fear she would join them.

She found Jerzy in one of the tiny rooms in the rabbit-warren rear of the inn. He sat at a table with an unnaturally tall, thin man dressed in black with a stovepipe hat that appeared to be permanently on the brink of falling off. Two tankards of ale sat before them.

'The universe is going to hell and you're sitting here having a drink,' she said, not unkindly.

Jerzy jumped up, almost knocking over the table. His drinking partner snatched up the beer before it was spilled, adding flamboyantly, 'Dear me! Almost a catastrophe!'

'I was only catching up with an old friend,' Jerzy protested.

'It's all right, Jerzy.' Caitlin ruffled his green hair. 'Never forget to snatch the little moments of pleasure in the middle of all the misery.'

Jerzy gave her a puzzled look. 'Mistress Caitlin? Forgive me, but you seem . . . changed?'

'Waking up from a bad dream does that. Who is this?' She nodded towards Jerzy's drinking partner.

Shadow John, said Brigid in her head.

'Shadow John,' said Jerzy.

Unfurling his long frame, Shadow John bowed deeply, catching and tipping his hat in the process. 'I must say, it is a pleasure to meet a Sister of Dragons,' he said, beaming. 'I have been blessed to meet your kind before, and it is always a source of wonder.'

'Thank you.' Caitlin pulled up a stool. Shadow John hastily sought out the barman and returned with a goblet of red wine.

'Why is everyone here so scared?' she asked.

Shadow John flinched and looked away.

'No one here will say,' Jerzy explained. 'I have asked, but they are all sworn to secrecy. Even I, who was once one of them, am excluded.'

'Spies are everywhere,' Shadow John said through a fixed grin.

'You can talk to me,' Caitlin said sweetly. 'I won't tell a soul.'

Only us, Amy, Brigid and Briony said together.

Shadow John shook his head slowly, barely able to form the words: 'All is seen and heard.'

'By whom? The Enemy has infiltrated the court?'

But Shadow John would say no more.

'All right, those are questions for another time,' Caitlin continued. 'What I need to know now is, where is the Morrigan?'

Shadow John cried out and ran from the room.

A gust of wind down the chimney made the fire roar. 'I don't think we're safe here at all,' Caitlin said.

9

'Are you sure we should be doing this, master?' Jerzy's chalk-white face was hidden in the folds of his sodden cowl as he bowed his head against the torrential rain. The white horse he had borrowed from Niamh's stables made its way slowly through the treacly mud of the lane. 'This land is dangerous now. We are at risk of attack anywhere outside the court's walls.'

The rain reminded Mallory of trekking on horseback across Salisbury Plain. It had been a similarly difficult time with threats on every side, yet the simple fact that he could recall it filled him with elation. His love-making with Sophie the previous night had unleashed a flood of memories, and it was a struggle to assimilate them into the life he thought he had. It had affected Sophie the same way. Unsettled, she'd been sad to see him go, but they both knew there was no choice in the matter.

'I'd be an idiot to be sure about anything in these times,' he said, 'but I do know we're going to need all the help we can get.'

'There are swords in the court—'

'Not like this one. There are three great swords of Existence, filled with the power of the Pendragon Spirit. This one is Llyrwyn. I carried it for a while before the Void took everything away from me. Church has another of the swords, Caledfwlch. And it sounds like that bastard Veitch has the third, only somewhere down the line that one has become corrupted.'

'But you don't know where the sword is now. It was lost when the Devourer of All Things made its changes.'

'I'm making an educated guess. The sword had a keeper. I'm betting she found it and brought it back here until it was needed again.'

The landscape was suffused with rain, dripping from the trees, pooling in the meadows where the grass glistened a damp October green, spattering off the brown hedgerows. They came over a ridge to find the Court of Peaceful Days, still and brooding. The martial banners hung limply and the gates were shattered. The once well-tended grounds were overgrown

89

with long grass and willow herb pressing hard against the sprawling low buildings. An oppressive air of desolation lay upon it.

'The Enemy must have struck!' Jerzy whined. 'Oh, how this court has fallen! Once it rang with war drums and the clash of metal, with songs for the lives given to battle for the sake of glory and honour. But then its forces were decimated in the war with the Army of the Ten Billion Spiders and a great sadness fell upon the place. And now this!'

'The sword might still be here,' Mallory said. 'Let's go.'

No birds sang as they made their way through the gates to the great front door, which hung open, unattended; the only sound was the constant hammering of the rain on the buildings.

They tethered their horses and Mallory led the way into the atrium. It was cold and silent. Jerzy made intermittent whimpering noises until Mallory glared at him to stop.

They passed through room after room, all deserted. In some, they found an upturned table or chair, occasional shattered glass, enough to hint at trouble, but nothing that indicated an invasion by overwhelming force.

'I do not understand,' Jerzy whispered. 'Queen Rhiannon's warriors had renounced violence, but they still would have defended the court with their lives.'

'Maybe they were surprised.' Even as Mallory said it, it didn't ring true.

Eventually they came to the iron-studded oaken doors of the great hall. They had been sealed shut with chains, and warning sigils were scrawled all over them. The carcass of a gutted dog lay before it, now just fur and bone.

'Can you read those?' Mallory nodded towards the sigils.

Jerzy cowered. 'They are marks of great power, warning of destruction to anyone who crosses the barrier to this room.'

'Looks like this is where we need to go.'

Jerzy moaned, but Mallory was already in search of the armoury. In the dripping darkness of a stone sub-cellar, he located several barrels of gunpowder. He forced Jerzy to help him carry two barrels to the door of the great hall, leaving a trail of the black powder along the corridor.

'Master, are you not scared of bringing destruction upon your head?' Jerzy asked as Mallory prepared to strike a flint.

'Firstly, I'm not anybody's master and you really need to stop calling me that. Secondly, I don't think I'm coming out of this whole business in one piece so there's no point being timid.'

'You remind me of my good friend Church.'

'Insult me, why don't you. I'm a party guy. He's got the world on his shoulders, and we all know what all work and no play lead to.' Mallory struck the flint and the gunpowder fizzed into life.

They dashed around the corner before the deafening explosion sent a flare of heat that scorched the walls of the corridor. Smoke and stone dust clouded the air as they clambered over the rubble to where the doors had been. The rain now fell through a large hole in the roof, and part of the wall had been demolished.

The hall was dark and windowless. Mallory lit a torch and progressed cautiously into the gloom. Halfway across the hall, amidst the echoes of his footsteps, the torchlight illuminated something glowing at the far side.

Jerzy tugged at Mallory's sleeve. 'Master . . . good friend, let us be away now. I am scared.'

'What is that?' Mallory tried to pierce the enfolding dark. He continued to advance. The golden glow came and went as the torch flickered, and finally he realised it was one of the Tuatha Dé Danann.

'Who's there?' he called out.

The figure made limited movements and a high-pitched whine that set his teeth on edge.

The torch finally revealed Rhiannon, the queen of the court, encased to her neck in an iron sheath, her arms pulled into a crucifix position by chains suspended from the ceiling. Hooks on wires kept her eyes permanently open. Her mouth had been sewn shut.

'God, how long has she been like this?' Mallory rushed forward to free her, but her whining increased insistently. As he struggled to release the iron sheath he saw why: tiny needles on the underside of the sheath dug deeper into her flesh with every attempt to remove it.

Jerzy fell to his knees, tears streaming down his face at the queen's suffering. 'What evil could do such a thing?'

'We know what evil.' Mallory looked into Rhiannon's eyes briefly, but what he saw there was too much to bear. His gaze fell on a long iron box on a stone plinth nearby. A thin blue light leaked from it. As Mallory examined it, soothing whispers filled his head.

'The sword's in here,' he said. But as he went to open the box, Rhiannon's muffled cries rose up urgently. Mallory backed away. 'Makes sense they'd booby trap it.' He returned to Rhiannon. 'There's got to be a way to free her.'

'Only the Enemy would make release cause more pain than imprisonment,' Jerzy said.

Mallory forced himself to look into Rhiannon's eyes again to let her know he would help. But she repeatedly rolled her eyes down and to the left. Mallory followed the direction she was indicating.

All he could see was a silver clasp at the shoulder of her dirty, torn dress; tentatively, he reached for it.

The clasp became fluid, turning into a silver egg that sprouted eight legs. Mallory snatched his hand back.

'It is a Caraprix,' Jerzy said. 'All the gods have them. Companions, confidantes . . . they have a strange power all their own.'

'She wants me to take it.' Mallory hesitated, then held out his hand palm upwards. The silver spider scuttled onto it, throbbing with light and power, though cool to the touch. Mallory held it up to eye-level.

Before he could react, it leaped, the sharp, silvery legs clinging to his face as it forced his lips open, then his teeth. He gagged, tried to rip it out, but it was like mercury, sliding through his fingers into his mouth and down his throat. The bulk of it closing his airway brought panic. Clawing at his throat, he saw stars, and then felt a sharp stabbing pain. A second later he was unconscious.

But the darkness led instantly to light. Fractured images passed before him, a world seen through oil, with a silvery landscape and a silvery sky merging into one. Enormous creatures moved against the distant skyline and after a while Mallory realised they were Caraprix, but greater and more powerful than he would ever have believed. With the vision came the knowledge that he, and everyone, had misjudged them: not pets or parasites, companions or confidantes. They were greater than anything in the Fixed Lands or the Far Lands, greater perhaps than everything.

He heard a voice saying, 'The closer things are to the heart of Existence, the more fluid they become.'

But then the image shifted, and in that dreamy vision he saw warriors dressed all in black with hoods over their heads. Flashes of perception: the warriors running through the Court of Peaceful Days; Rhiannon's warriors falling beneath sword and axe; and then the warriors advancing towards him, and Mallory realising he was seeing the scene through Rhiannon's eyes. Another flash. Frightening yet incomprehensible images, and then a slow, subtle revelation . . .

Mallory came round with a concerned Jerzy leaning over him and the Caraprix scuttling away from his mouth and back to Rhiannon.

'We have to get at the sword. We can use that to free Rhiannon,' he said.

'How do you know these things?'

'It told me.' Mallory examined the box again. 'Touch this the wrong way and it'll release a blade that'll take your hands off at the wrist.'

'You could just blow it up with gunpowder,' Jerzy said archly.

'Sarcasm. Good. You'll be one of us in no time. Actually, that wouldn't be a bad idea except I know for a fact that there's only one way into it.'

Mallory steeled himself and went over to Rhiannon. Of all the Tuatha Dé Danann, she was one of the most compassionate and it was a tragedy that she suffered so. The hope in her wide eyes made it even worse.

'There's no easy way to say this,' he began. 'The only way to free you without killing you is with the sword. And the only way to open the box is with your hand. That's the trick of the trap. Here you both are, a few feet apart, yet it's a puzzle that's impossible to solve.' He took a deep breath to hide the tremor in his voice. 'Or nearly impossible.'

She was trying to read his face, but couldn't see the answer.

'I can open the box if I cut off one of your hands.'

Her eyes stretched wider than he would have thought possible. The whine in her throat grew high-pitched once again. He wanted it to stop.

'We don't have to worry about shock or blood loss killing you. Your kind are tougher than that. But the pain will be unbearable. No anaesthetic, nothing to dull it. It could scar your mind for ever.' He fought to calm his pounding heart so that he didn't make it worse for her. 'Do you want me to proceed?'

Her eyes continued to scan his face, searching for another way, hoping against hope. Finally she signalled her agreement. A single tear trickled from the corner of one eye to the edge of her mouth where it moistened the dry stitches.

'Left or right?'

She indicated her left.

Mallory nodded as dispassionately as he could and turned to talk quietly to Jerzy. 'Bring me a boning knife from the kitchens.'

'Good friend, are you sure you can do this?' Jerzy whispered.

'The sick thing is, I've done much worse than this in my life. I can't afford to be pathetic. I have to do it for her.'

'You spoke of the pain scarring her mind. But this act will scar your own mind.'

'Just fetch the knife, Jerzy.'

Jerzy returned with a leather-bound box. He tripped and the glittering contents skidded across the flags, cruel blades all, with barbs and serrations and razor edges.

'Cool move, Jerzy,' Mallory muttered.

Jerzy frantically gathered up the knives and Mallory took them out of Rhiannon's view. He selected the one he thought would be quickest and cleanest and hid it behind his back.

'Still a chance to back out,' he said.

Tears swam in her eyes, but she indicated for him to continue.

'I'd do the same in your position. You're very brave.'

Mallory rested the edge of the knife on her wrist. It was cool, her skin smooth and delicately shaded. He fought to stop his hand from shaking.

The next five minutes were lost to him. He vaguely remembered the sounds that came out of her, but they would return to haunt him during the nights to come.

Then he turned, holding it, and what brought it all home was Jerzy, the jester, usually filled with life and dance, on his knees, sobbing hysterically, yet still grinning through it: an image of the insanity to which they had all been brought.

From the corner of his eye, he saw Rhiannon, her head slumped on her chest, but he couldn't bring himself to look directly at her. At the box, he placed the stiffening hand on the spot the Caraprix had shown him. The lid sprang open with a flash of blue sparks, and there was the sword, calling to him. In his hand, it felt warm, easing his pain. With one sweep, he severed the clasp that held the iron sheath in place. The second sweep cut the chains and Rhiannon fell into his arms. She was barely conscious.

Mallory laid her on the flags and took another of the kitchen knives to cut the thread sealing her lips. But as the first stitch was severed, her eyes fluttered shut and her head lolled to one side.

Jerzy leaned forward to test the shallowness of her breath. 'A secondary enchantment. When you cut the thread, it put her into the Sleep Like Death.'

'So she couldn't tell us what happened,' Mallory said bitterly. 'Can we help her?'

'Perhaps. Back at the Court of the Soaring Spirit – Math the Sorcerer could help.'

As Mallory carried her through her desolate home, a cold desire for revenge filled him. Nothing would deter him from it.

10

In the warm womb of her room, Sophie lay back on the cushions before the fire and watched the cat move across the furniture, its shadow sometimes swelling to panther-size. Sophie had summoned it with her will alone, and while she had tried to pretend it was a normal animal, she only had to glance into the depths of its eyes to know the truth.

It was a simple trick, a testing of limits to see if she was still able to manipulate the Craft, and her skill had exceeded her hopes. It was a product of memory and emotion. Regaining the knowledge of who she really was – artist, romantic, wanderer – and bringing Mallory back into her heart had opened up the wondrous landscape of her abilities.

Pleased with herself, she left the room and made her way along the cramped, dark corridors, still flushed with love from her sudden and surprising reconnection with Mallory. As she reached the level of the main court rooms, she heard the sound of crying. Cautiously, she entered the stifling heat of one of the chambers and found Niamh curled up in a chair so large it made her look fragile and childlike, her head buried in her arms.

Sophie hesitated, then ventured in. 'Is everything all right?'

With red-rimmed eyes, Niamh forced a smile and quickly tried to regain her composure. 'For most of my long existence, I have never cried. Church taught me how to, along with many other things, and I will always remember him for that.'

'You were close?'

Niamh motioned for Sophie to join her. 'I loved him in a way I have not loved anyone before. But his heart always belonged to another.'

'Ruth.'

Niamh nodded. 'Brothers and Sisters of Dragons have their own special gravity. At least, that is what I tell myself.' She gave a wan smile. 'Now I have other matters to concern me.'

'The war?'

'It threatens all the Golden Ones have ever held dear. My people are in disarray. The Great Courts have never worked easily together. Now any failure to unite will lead to our complete destruction. Yet still they will not talk.'

'There's something else on your mind, I can tell.'

'Your Craft gives you great perception. My brother is missing again, and I fear he may have fallen into the hands of the Enemy. Others, too, are missing. The Morrigan, of course. Math has not been seen for . . .' She waved a hand wearily. 'I am afraid the Enemy has infiltrated the Court of the Soaring Spirit. That no one here is safe. What kind of a queen am I to allow that to happen? In my darker moments, I believe I do not have the ability to lead. I wonder if I should give up my title for the sake of my people. Let someone else take charge, someone better suited to lead in these trying times.'

'Church told us all about you. No one could do a better job.'

'You are kind, as befits a Sister of Dragons. But still, the weight of these days lies heavily on me.' She dried her eyes, but her face remained taut. 'I am troubled by too many mysteries. My own existence . . . I have dreams that I died. I cannot recall how I returned to the Far Lands from your world.' Unsettled, she leaned towards Sophie in confidence. 'And now I am all alone.'

'You're not alone. We'll stand by you, in the way that you've always stood by us.'

This appeared to soothe Niamh, for she smiled warmly. They were interrupted by the crash of the door as Caitlin marched in.

'You've got to see this,' she announced.

Sophie and Niamh followed Caitlin up onto the palace's ramparts. In the north, fire flickered in the sky near the horizon.

'What is it?' Sophie asked.

'A candle, calling someone home.' Caitlin handed Sophie a brass spyglass.

The distant flame sharpened into focus. It was the burning outline of a man. Sophie estimated it must have been hundreds of feet high.

Behind then, Niamh began to mutter, 'They are bringing him back. They are bringing him back.'

'Bringing who back?' Sophie asked.

But Niamh appeared to be in a trance where something was speaking through her.

The wind carried the bitter smell of ashes, and the air of disaster drawing closer.

11

Instinctively, the guards averted their gaze or squirmed involuntarily as the Libertarian strode through the Heathrow Security Annexe. He knew they registered him as a blur of static on the periphery of their vision, an anomaly that their brains couldn't quite comprehend – unless he decided otherwise, or they were spider-ridden, of course, and then they had no choice but to see him, in all his glory.

In his room, the senior officer who had been tasered by Hunter was already sweating heavily in anticipation. He glanced nervously at the Libertarian as he entered, swallowed hard, couldn't find any words.

'Get rid of them,' the Libertarian said.

The man jumped from his chair and dismissed the guards. 'There was another one . . .' he began hesitantly.

'Excuses are so tiresome.'

The senior officer flinched as the Libertarian raised his hand to brush back his own hair. He said thoughtfully, 'Don't worry, I'm not going to hurt you. Not yet, anyway. Too messy. All those questions, doubts – it's not conducive to the smooth running of reality. Maybe later, when you're away from here, and I'm bored.' He flopped into the officer's chair and swung his feet onto the desk. 'Two groups of Brothers and Sisters of Dragons infesting the place. That is rather an irritation.'

'They won't get far—'

'Oh, they will. They're clever and instinctive and, quite often, counterintuitive. Your breed is not built to deal with that approach.' The Libertarian removed his sunglasses to clean off a spackle of blood. 'If I could only remember what happens in the coming months, things would be so much easier. But there's too much static.' He rapped the side of his head. 'Still, it all turns out nice, so—' He started. 'Are you still here? Go on, run along, before I change my mind and dismantle you.'

Alone with his thoughts, the Libertarian felt unusually uneasy. Memories of the future, memories of the past, intertwined, conflicted. Why was he thinking about the person he had been? Those days were long gone, and their loss had never really concerned him until the last few hours.

He thought of a deep, passionate kiss at the point of waking, a caress, whispered words, and he shuddered. Long gone, and glad of it.

'Who. Am. I?' he said to the empty room. 'I. Am. Who?' A palindromic existence in time.

Choosing activity to still his thoughts, he jumped to his feet. 'I think I will tag along for a little while.' He hummed to himself. 'See what sparkling notions are dancing in the heads of those Brothers and Sisters of Dragons.' Any analysis would have told him it was not the wisest course, but he was pulled by his own currents. And as if to reassure himself, he added: 'One death at the appropriate moment is all that it will take to drive them to the point of collapse. And I know exactly which one.'

12

Stillness suffused the hotel. The snow of the high country had swept indoors, blanketing everything. Hunter was on his feet, the fuzzy torpor of the alcohol already gone.

'Chill out, killer. It's only a stopped clock.' Dreamy and drunk, Laura stretched like a cat.

'It's affecting you. Fight it.'

The sharpness of his words cut through her hazy state. 'Shit. That was weird . . . trippy.'

Hunter took in the details of the scene quickly. The crackling of the fire was barely audible and appeared to be coming from the end of a long tunnel. The light had an odd cast; shadows fell from no obvious source.

Laura tentatively touched the glistening wall. 'Frost,' she said, puzzled.

'Stay with me,' Hunter ordered.

'Now you're confusing me with someone who does what they're told.' She stepped closer to Hunter nonetheless.

At the bar, the barman was nowhere to be seen. Nor was the heavily bearded, red-faced drinker who only a few minutes earlier had lurched from the restaurant to start downing the hotel's strong lager.

'I thought I saw Shavi and Tom come in.' Laura turned slowly. 'I can sense that grumpy old git within fifty yards. They couldn't have slipped by us.'

'The frost on the walls is growing thicker,' Hunter noted, 'but the room isn't getting any colder.' He leaned over the bar. A bloody smear ran from where the barman had been standing into the back rooms. 'So. We could follow that into obvious danger or we could walk away,' he said.

'As self-preservation is my default setting, I don't think I need to answer that,' Laura said. 'But as being a thick-headed man is your thing, I can see which way this is going to go.'

Hunter stepped behind the bar.

'I just hope that as you lie dying you're tormented by guilt that you sacrificed a young and innocent woman,' she said.

'You can be quiet now.'

'And you can take that gun you've got tucked away and shove it up your—'

Hunter pushed open the door to the back rooms to reveal the barman lying butchered in one corner. It looked as if he'd been attacked with an axe.

Laura glanced away. 'Well, Shavi is going to be pissed off.'

'Nice show of compassion. Very endearing.'

Hunter noted there was only one door leading down to what he presumed was the cellar.

Laura followed his gaze. 'Why would you want to go down there?'

'The other one might still be alive.'

'I thought Church was the one who did the right thing.'

'You really don't know me. I'm a sensitive soul underneath this sexy and charismatic exterior.'

A flight of wooden steps led down into the dark cellar. The only sound was a distant creaking. Hunter flicked the light switch and a single bare bulb came on somewhere out of sight. It was barely enough to hold back the shadows. The creaking grew louder when they reached the foot of the stairs.

Rounding into the main area of the cellar, they saw the bearded drinker hanging by his neck from an oily rope attached to a hook in a beam. He was naked. His body was covered with runes cut into the skin with a sharp knife. Laura pressed a hand over her nose and mouth to keep out the salty butcher's shop smell. Hunter first made sure the rest of the cellar was empty, then examined the body.

'Ritual marks,' he said. 'Don't know how they could have been carved so quickly.'

'Because time doesn't mean anything here. It's like a bit of the Other-world has crossed over. Those runes – they look Viking.'

'You've seen them before?'

'I belong to an environmental group – Earth First. A couple of blokes in my chapter are Odinists. They've got those runes tattooed on their chests.'

Hunter tried to make sense of the markings. 'Patterns,' he mused.

'What?'

'Everywhere. Patterns. Numbers – five. Names. Symbols. Systems. All of them repeating.' He paused thoughtfully. 'Almost as if they were programmed in.'

'When you've got your head out of your arse, can we actually turn our attention to who did this?'

The eyes of the hanged man snapped open, the whites crimson with broken blood vessels. Laura leaped back with a curse.

'You woke them,' the corpse said in heavily accented English. 'You crossed into their Great Dominion. You woke them!' It thrashed its legs around in fury, the ligature biting into its neck, the eyes bulging.

Hunter unconsciously stepped in front of Laura to protect her. 'All right – slightly weird, but here we go. Who did this to you?'

A sickening laugh rattled in the hanging man's constricted throat. 'He will get you next. They all will!'

The eyes snapped shut and the animation left the body. The creaking rope gradually stilled.

'I hate this life,' Laura said.

Hunter grabbed her hand and hauled her towards the stairs. 'We have to find the others. ' "They all will",' he said. 'How many of them are here?'

As Shavi and Tom entered the lounge, they realised Hunter and Laura were no longer where they had been. The haunting atmosphere grated on senses attuned to the Otherworldly.

'What do you see?' Shavi asked.

'Nothing. I can't move beyond this moment. You?'

Shavi felt the alien eye squirming in his head with a life of its own, but no images flashed into his mind. 'This does not feel like the Army of the Ten Billion Spiders.'

Cautiously, they moved from the frosted lounge up the wide pine stairs to the first floor. Their rooms were on the second, but they were stopped in their tracks by thick greenery. Along the walls of the corridor stretched branches of fir and juniper, their resinous aroma heavy in the air. Ivy hung from the ceiling and dense moss obscured the floor.

'Laura?' Shavi said.

Tom snorted. 'She barely knows what she's capable of doing.'

'I think whatever did this expects us to venture in there. That would be a mistake.'

'For once one of you lot speaks some sense.' Tom moved towards the next flight of stairs.

Before Shavi could follow he was gripped by a honeyed feeling rising from his groin. A night with his boyfriend Lee, shortly before Lee's death, eased from his memory. Sensual, warm, gentle touches growing harder. Then a shiver of remembrance from a time before, an older woman kissing him deeply, embracing him between her thighs. And then he was enveloped in sex with Laura beneath the summery stars of a Glastonbury sky. He loved her. He loved them all.

His erection was hard, his heart pounding. Desire flooded through him, swamping all other thoughts. He walked into the corridor where alien, powerfully scented blooms were now sprouting. The moss was soft and soothing beneath his feet.

'Where are you going, you bloody idiot?' Tom called.

The distant voice was a distraction that Shavi ignored. Amongst the vegetation, his arousal became even more intense. He was vaguely aware of Tom grabbing his arm and trying to drag him back, until the grip was relinquished as Tom also fell under the spell. Side by side, they progressed along the corridor until they were deep in the scent of pine and flowers, and there was no sign of the hotel.

Rounding a corner, they came upon a cool grove in which a woman stood. Her features swam, but long before they settled into an image of ravishing beauty, both Shavi and Tom knew she was the most sexually attractive woman they had ever seen. Long, golden hair cascaded past her shoulders. Her lips were full and parted in a teasing smile. She wore a semi-transparent white dress, belted at the hips, that revealed and then hid the figure beneath.

'I see the blue light in you.' Her voice was low and warm. 'Strange trespassers, indeed.'

'Who are you?' Shavi asked.

'I live in the ice and the fire, in the roar of battle and the silence of the bedroom, in the pulse of the blood, in forests, in passion.' She looked from Shavi to Tom, pleased with her control over them. 'Those of your kind called me Freyja, once of the Vanir, now of the Aesir.'

'Freyja,' Tom repeated. Shavi felt his companion struggling. *Why fight?* Tom thought. *Why not give in to the sensual delight?*

'For so long we have slept in the Halls of the Dead,' she said. 'But now you have woken us. What made you think you could enter our Great Dominion unbidden?'

'They are Brothers and Sisters of Dragons.' Tom's voice was small, wavering. 'Champions of Existence. They go where they please.'

Shavi found her laughter even more arousing. But Tom's resistance had cast a shadow upon the golden world that now existed inside him. 'If . . . if we should have asked your permission to come here, then I apologise,' Shavi said hesitantly. 'But our safe passage is imperative. We are on a mission of the greatest importance.'

Freyja came closer, and closer still, moving her lips to within a fraction of an inch from Shavi's cheek, smelling his musk. It was all he could do to contain the heat rising in him.

'A Brother of Dragons,' she mused. 'So you fight for the World Serpent, which is curled around Midgard with its tail in its mouth?'

'Yes,' Shavi breathed.

'It is said that the World Serpent will burst forth at Ragnarok,' she whispered. 'Are these the End-Times? Is that why we have been woken?'

'It is.' The flint in Tom's voice shocked Shavi. 'Loki has already joined the Enemy.'

Freyja recoiled. 'That sly, malignant trickster? Are you lying, old man?'

'It is true,' Shavi said.

Freyja considered the information. 'This deserves our attention. But

101

that does not alter the severity of your transgression.' Her smile grew darker.

She motioned, and a figure detached itself from the vegetation. It had been there all along, but they had not seen it, for it appeared to be constructed from the greenery itself. A long green beard of moss trailed down its front, above which green eyes glowed.

'The Leshy,' she introduced. 'My dark brother of the woods. He does not abide trespassers, and his punishment is terrible. Look – he casts no shadow!'

The importance of this was lost on Shavi and Tom. Their attention was caught by the realisation that they could no longer move.

14

'You don't have to solve this on your own. Talk to me.' Church sat on the edge of the bed, one hand resting on the small of Ruth's back as she buried her face in the pillow.

'I want to. I want us to be just how we used to be.' She rolled over to look at him. Tears streaked her cheeks.

'If Veitch did something, we can find a way to put it right.'

'So we stop saving the world to save ourselves? You know that's not an option.'

'I'm not going to let us fall apart. You mean more to me than the world.'

'Maybe that's why he did it,' she said. 'A blow struck for the Army of the Ten Billion Spiders. You get me and the world is lost.'

Church didn't have to think. 'I want you.'

She laughed quietly, without humour. 'I knew you'd say that – that's why I love you. You're an idiot. Don't you get it? Veitch has made me a weapon to destroy everything we're trying to achieve.'

'It's a suicide mission, no hope of success. Everyone keeps telling me—'

'Shut up.' She swung her legs over the edge of the bed and wiped the tears from her face. 'Now that my memory's coming back, I know what my legacy is. I'm a conduit for the Craft, and all that represents. For life. All that responsibility, you know? I can't allow myself to be used to screw everything up. And I can't allow you to walk away from your own destiny. Not for me. Not for us.'

'What are you saying?'

'I'm saying goodbye, Church.' She brushed her fingers against his temple and Church pitched backwards onto the bed in a deep sleep.

For a moment, Ruth paced the room, kneading her hands in desperation. Then she grabbed her spear and kissed Church tenderly on the lips one final time. Before the tears started again, she marched quickly out of the room, descended in the lift, strode across the lounge – so driven she was oblivious to the frost – and outside. She wore no coat. Without hesitation, she continued through the thick snow towards the bleak horizon. The wind was bitter and well below zero.

It wasn't long before the warmth left her completely and she felt as if she was walking into a dream.

15

When Church came round, he rushed from the room. A vision of ice and a blast of north wind brought him up sharp. The corridor had been transformed into a frozen cavern. Icicles hung from the ceiling and hoarfrost covered everything, glimmering in the light from his room.

His breath clouding, he returned to fetch Caledfwlch from the holdall in the wardrobe. Blue flames fizzed and spattered in the cold, and with them came the first wash of bitterness. He wanted to be pursuing Ruth, bringing her back into his arms, not standing there, sword in hand, fighting again for something so immense he could barely comprehend its importance.

The frost crunched under his boots. At the top of the stairs, he paused and listened to a distant scraping of metal on stone. The noise made him feel unaccountably queasy.

Down one flight of stairs, then another, the scraping growing louder as he descended. In his hand, the sword hummed in protest.

As he neared the last few stairs, Church saw the shadow first. Enormous, it fell across the hallway revealing someone out of view sharpening an axe. Sparks flew. He came down another step and saw that the axe was double-headed, the edges nicked from long use, the handle black and rune-covered near the blade, and wrapped with black leather further down.

'Come, little fox.' The voice was a deep bass rumble.

'Who are you and what do you want?'

As Church continued down the stairs, the figure slowly came into view. At first, Church took it to be a wild animal, at least eight feet tall with a mane of black hair and a full beard, eyes the red of a summer sunset. The teeth visible through the thick beard were rows of needles, all blood-stained. The muscular body was nearly naked apart from an animal-hide tied roughly around the waist, but the exposed skin was nearly invisible beneath blue tattooed runes, hideous battle scars and body hair, thick and shiny.

He held up his right hand to reveal a cruel silver hook. 'That bastard wolf!' he growled. 'But I survived and I will slaughter it yet!'

'Who are you?' Church repeated.

'Your little fox-brothers called me Tyr. I am the thunder of the battle-field. Now I am returned, my power awakened by the sacrifice of the hanged man.'

Tyr saw Church sizing him up and smiled cruelly. 'You walk our Great Dominion. There are rules, blood and earth. You have taken a step too far. A prayer and a sacrifice may have bought your passage, but now there is no hope for you.'

Tyr swung his axe so fast Church barely saw it move. Only instinct saved him. It cleaved horizontally, shattering stair rails and reducing to dust a large part of a pillar.

Reactions and muscles honed by combat across two thousand years threw Church backwards onto the stairs, his sword coming up just in time to deflect another blow so powerful he was afraid his blade would shatter. The jarring impact almost plunged him into unconsciousness.

There was not even a second to recover. Tyr drove his silver hook towards Church's head. Church rolled and the hook smashed through the stairs a fraction of an inch from his skull.

The axe was already swinging again as Church jumped off the stairs over the arc. As he came down, Caledfwlch tore open Tyr's side.

Tyr's roar was deafening, but Church was surprised to hear it evolve into booming laughter. 'Not just a little fox after all!' he yelled insanely. 'I will enjoy carving you into food for the ravens!'

The axe whirling in a blur, Tyr launched himself with the strength and speed of a beast. He had no qualms about his own safety. Church sliced a chunk of the flesh from his bicep, but Tyr continued oblivious.

Church had already worked out a strategy to back Tyr into a space where he couldn't wield the axe when three shots rang out. Hunter stood on the stairs with Laura beside him. He waved the handgun towards Church. 'One of the perks of working for the Government.'

Tyr stopped, puzzled. He dug one meaty finger into the bullet hole in his chest and delved around for a few seconds before retrieving the bullet. He examined it curiously and then turned his attention to Hunter and Laura.

'You should not be in the shimmering. Why has my sister's *seior* failed?' He shrugged. 'No matter. More bones for the pot.'

Hunter examined the gun contemptuously. 'I tell you, what's the point? I should just throw this away and get a fish knife or a spoon or something.'

'All right, damsel in distress here,' Laura said insistently as Tyr began to advance. 'Aren't you tossers actually supposed to be doing something?'

'We're going to throw you to him as a diversion,' Hunter said.

Church tried to blindside Tyr as the god attacked Hunter and Laura, but a whirlwind of axe movements protected him. Chunks of masonry in clouds of dust flew wherever the axe hit.

Hunter propelled Laura through a gap in the shattered stairway, and they raced to Church before Tyr could turn.

'We need to find somewhere defensible until we can work out our options,' Hunter said.

'Agreed.' Church led the way into the dining area and then through to the kitchens. Hunter locked the steel door behind them.

'That's not going to keep the hairy bastard out.' Laura snatched up a meat-cleaver.

The thunder of the axe against the door made her leap back with a shriek. The door bowed, almost shattered.

'Here.' Hunter indicated a gas canister ready to be installed in one of the ranges. Church understood instantly.

When the door burst in, Church brought Caledfwlch down sharply, slicing neatly through the canister's nozzle. Hunter ignited the jet of gas, which roared directly into Tyr as he crashed into the kitchen. The conflagration engulfed him instantly. Flesh crackled and popped, fat sizzled, eyeballs burst.

They had to press their hands against their ears to cut out his ear-shattering bellows, but even then there was a hint of ecstasy in his cries. With flames leaping from him, he lashed out blindly until he could control himself no more and lurched back the way he had come.

'I wonder how long it'll take him to recover,' Church said.

'Time enough for us to get the hell out of Dodge,' Hunter replied. 'If you'll excuse me a cowboy moment.'

Laura hurled her cleaver across the kitchen. 'Aren't I the spare part,' she said angrily.

Burning fittings and the screech of the fire alarm marked Tyr's passing into the frozen outdoors where it had started snowing again.

But as they turned to the wrecked stairs, they were confronted by vegetation streaming down the remaining steps and railing.

'You ready?' Church gripped his sword with both hands.

'Fuck, no,' Hunter replied. 'I didn't pick up my spoon from the kitchen. I suppose I could use my teeth.'

Freyja rounded the turn in the stairs, her smile eliciting instant arousal in Church, Hunter and Laura. Behind her came the Leshy, twisted like an old hawthorn tree but his eyes blazing with a fierce light. He held two strands of ivy pulled taut over his shoulder. They stretched back to Tom and Shavi who were hovering a foot above the stairs, bound tightly with creeper. Both wore crowns of thorns that dug into their flesh with a life of their own, bringing streams of blood down their faces. They appeared unconscious, though their eyes were wide open, unblinking.

Hunter and Laura remained entranced, but the flickering power in Caledfwlch reached into Church and broke the spell. Instead of Freyja, he saw Ruth and that gave him all the strength he needed.

'Set them free.'

Freyja was intrigued by his resistance. 'That cannot be. They are to be crucified on the world-oak as small payment for your trespass. Be content that you do not join them.'

'That's not going to happen.'

'You would oppose the gods?' Her voice grew flinty.

'Anything that gets in my way. Set them free.'

A rustling, hissing sound escaped from the Leshy. He dropped the ivy bonds and advanced on Church in a jerky, creeping manner.

Church's resistance infected Laura and Hunter, who shook off their enchantment. 'These are the Scandinavian gods, right?' Laura shouted to Church.

'Germanic. Slavonic. I don't know how far their Great Dominion stretches. By the way, this really isn't the time for a theological discussion.'

'Odin's the big boss, right?' she pressed. 'Or Woden, or whatever?'

Church adopted a fighting stance. The Leshy did not appear the least bit scared by the sword or the power it represented.

Laura backed off, but Church could hear her muttering, 'Come on! I need you.'

The Leshy was only feet away when the main doors burst open and a blast of snowy wind rushed in. Behind it came a cloaked figure in a battered, shapeless hat, a gnarled staff in one hand. A raven sat on each shoulder.

'All-Father?' Freyja's confidence drained away, and she bowed her head. The Leshy stopped in its tracks and did the same.

The new arrival strode forward. He was a bearded man with an eye patch, but he exuded great power, and it was familiar. 'The Brothers and Sisters of Dragons have free passage through this Great Dominion,' the All-Father said. 'One of them wields Gungnir, my own spear. Did you not know?'

Freyja bowed sheepishly.

'Where is my daughter?' he asked Church gently. 'I cannot sense her.'

Church realised he meant Ruth. 'I don't know.' A chill ran through him. Why could the All-Father not sense her?

'Free them,' the All-Father commanded.

As the creepers fell away from Shavi and Tom, they dropped to the stairs. Hunter and Laura ran to reclaim them.

'We are all waking now, All-Father,' Freyja said. 'The Aesir . . . the Vanir . . . all the others. Is this it, then? Is this Ragnarok?'

'Yes,' the All-Father replied gravely. 'It is Ragnarok.'

Freyja blanched.

'In their cavern, the Norns are stirring their pot and whispering. Urd looks at what has been, Verdandi considers what is and Skuld counts down the moments to the End-Times.' The All-Father rested on his gnarled staff.

'Then the end is already foretold.'

'Only the Fates know.'

Freyja searched his face for a moment, then bowed her head and walked slowly out into the night, the Leshy trailing behind her. The All-Father turned to Laura.

'You called, daughter. I came, as I always said I would.'

Laura smiled uncomfortably.

'Brother of Dragons,' the All-Father said to Church, 'you face many dangers as you move through the Great Dominions, and I cannot help you with those. You must tread with caution, for the powers ranged against you are greater even than here.'

'I know you,' Church said.

'You know me, Brother of Dragons. I remain an anomaly amongst my kind. And I serve a higher agenda.'

He bowed slightly, and then moved away and out, changing into his familiar shape as he did, part-vegetation, part-bestial.

'I remembered,' Laura said when he had gone. 'All those names he spouted . . . the ones people knew him by. Cernunnos. The Green Man. And Odin. Somehow he filled that role, too.'

'You're not just a pretty face,' Hunter said.

'No. I have the ability to kill people in their sleep,' she replied, half-heartedly rising to the bait.

Shavi and Tom slowly came round. Laura remained with them while Hunter followed Church outside. Snow fell heavily. It didn't take them long to find Ruth's tracks.

They followed them for a quarter of a mile, but beyond that point the snow had covered them. With mounting desperation, Church turned slowly and searched the desolate landscape.

'There's no way she can survive out in the open.' Church couldn't keep his voice from breaking.

'She's got a lot of fire in her. If anyone can survive, she can,' Hunter said.

They searched for another fifteen minutes, but by then the cold was burrowing deeply into their own limbs and Hunter forced Church to turn back. At first, Church resisted, but in the end, devastated, he realised the hopelessness of the situation.

Ruth was gone.

16

From the line of pine trees two miles distant, a silver hand caught the moonlight as it traced patterns in the crisp snow. Veitch watched Church and Hunter make their way back to the hotel. He could almost feel their raw emotion.

'Life hurts, doesn't it, mate?' he said quietly.

Behind him, horses that were not horses stamped their hoofs and blasted steaming breath from their nostrils. Etain and the other Brothers and Sisters of Spiders stood silently. Frost rimed their hair and faces, but they were oblivious.

Ruth was nestled in the crook of Veitch's arm. He gently brushed the snow from her cheek. The blanket in which he had swaddled her would soon bring warmth back into her limbs.

'It's a funny old world. We see everything around us, and we know what it's like, but we always want something more. So we're never able to rest, never happy.' He kissed Ruth on the forehead. 'I love you, darlin'. Always have and I always will. We're setting off on a long road now. It's not going to be pretty, but it's the only way, right up to the bitter end. Ryan and Ruth, side by side against the world, like it was always meant to be.'

In Etain's dead eyes, there was a faint glimmer, like the twinkling of a star in the furthest, coldest reaches of space. And the cold wind blew, and the snow fell, and silence lay across the land.

chapter five

some kind of karmic-chi love thing

1

Black feathers gleamed across a vast arc around the hotel as if darkness was welling up out of the ground and across the pristine snow. Shavi watched the *Morvren* as he dabbed at the still-bleeding thorn marks on his temples.

'The birds are responding to Church's thoughts,' he mused. 'Almost an extension of his personality.'

'He's a bloody idiot.' Tom rapped on the glass to try to scare the ravens away. Beady black eyes stared back at him unflinchingly. 'He has a job to do and he's mooning over some woman.'

'We are all addicted to being in love. It is the human condition.'

'I wouldn't know about that, would I?' Tom said sarcastically. 'Ever since those so-called gods cut me up and put me back together, I've not been much of anything.'

Hunter came over, swigging from a bottle of Jack Daniel's. 'He'll be all right. He's a tough bloke.'

'Why did she do it? It is not like Ruth,' Shavi asked.

'Something between the two of them,' Hunter replied. 'Don't ask me – I don't do all that relationship shit. But you're right – it's not like her, given the little I know of her, which leaves me thinking she's still alive. Can you see anything?' he said to Tom.

Concern briefly softened Tom's harsh expression. 'Nothing of her.'

'But you are starting to see snatches of the future now?' Shavi asked.

'I've had a few flashes in the last half hour. As events happen, more and more falls into place. The future is becoming solid.'

'And not good, by the look on your face,' Hunter noted. 'What happened here to make a bad outcome more likely?' He brushed the question off instantly. 'No point thinking about what might be. We need to find our target. Are you ready to locate him?'

'I am ready to try,' Shavi replied.

'Not going to lose any more body parts, are you?'

Shavi smiled tightly. 'I have the upper hand now.'

2

Dawn was breaking when they left the hotel in a four-wheel-drive. They had found several other people sacrificed to Tyr, hanging in their rooms. Hunter had been keen to burn the hotel to the ground to cover their tracks in what would be seen as another terrorist outrage, but Church was adamant that the bodies needed to be left intact for their relatives to claim.

'You recovered now?' Laura lounged in Shavi's lap in the back. 'You looked like shit when you came out of your little ritual room.'

'It is becoming easier, but never easy. At least we now know where we are going.'

Church brooded in the front. His eyes flicked continually across the landscape, always searching. 'Interpol's going to be looking for us,' he said. 'This isn't going to be easy.'

'I know a few tricks,' Hunter said as he steered onto the deserted main road.

Church allowed himself one last look for Ruth. Even after everything that had happened, he still had hope.

Behind them, the *Morvren* blackened the sky.

3

In the Court of the Soaring Spirit, the night was white with lightning flashes. The storm whirled ferociously around the foothills, bringing with it rain as hard as bullets and thunder so loud it shook the glass in the windows.

Mallory sat beside the bed in the room at the top of the tallest tower, where he had sat for most of the day. Rhiannon barely stirred. Occasionally her eyes would flicker as if she was in the throes of dramatic dreams, but she showed no sign of waking from the Sleep Like Death.

Caitlin slipped in. 'Still nothing?'

'Maybe I'm wasting my time. I keep hoping she might come round long enough to give us a hint as to what's going on here.'

'Sophie's been in the ritual for hours. She looks exhausted.'

'She found nothing?'

'The Market of Wishful Spirit might as well have fallen off the edge of the world. That's what she said.'

Mallory cursed under his breath. 'Everyone's counting on us.'

'She's doing her best. We all are.'

Mallory gently mopped Rhiannon's forehead with a damp cloth; it appeared to soothe her. 'I keep thinking there's something staring me in the face and I can't see it. The Brothers and Sisters of Dragons that Church rescued are missing. Lugh and Math and some of the other Tuatha Dé Danann are missing. The whole population's terrified. And the Market of Wishful Spirit has gone into hiding. We just need to find the pattern that links it all together and then we'll start getting somewhere.'

'You think the Enemy's already here in the court, undercover?'

'I'm certain of it.'

Caitlin thoughtfully fingered the axe she now carried at her waist. Mallory was impressed by the transformation that had come over her; she appeared more together than at any time since he had met her.

'I think we should start questioning people,' she said. 'They know something. We just have to find a way to make them talk.'

Mallory was acutely aware of her standing beside him. She had an odd but appealing musk, a hint of lime, which he guessed might be a by-product of her troubled mental state affecting her body chemistry.

'You holding it together okay?' he asked

'Yeah.' She smiled. 'Give me an axe and the chance to chop something into bloody chunks and I'm a picture of mental health. How dysfunctional is that?'

'I wouldn't say any of us are pictures of stability.'

'You seem okay.'

'Yeah, I thought I was, until . . .' He dried up. He could feel Caitlin's eyes on him but she was too polite to prompt. 'I did something really bad,' he continued. 'Killed somebody.'

'They deserved it?'

'No. The exact opposite. At the time I felt I didn't have a choice. I was forced into it by some nasty people. But I wonder . . . if I'd been stronger . . . smarter . . .'

She rested a sympathetic hand on his shoulder. 'We've all been through so much. Death is the catalyst that transforms normal people into what we are now.'

'Whoever thought up that idea was a real sadist. So I murdered an innocent, and you lost your husband and son.'

Her voice grew unbearably fragile. 'I'm glad my memory's back so I can think about them again, but it also means I have to remember them passing. Is that one of the lessons we're supposed to be learning: you can't have the good without the bad?'

Another flash of lightning filled the room with white.

'More like the value of things is defined by the loss of them. No potential loss, no value.'

'You're a bit of a philosopher, aren't you, Mallory?' she said wryly. Her hand was still on his shoulder.

'Not me. I'm a man's man. None of that thinking stuff.'

'Before the Void got to me, I'd started to come to terms with my loss. I'd even begun to see someone else. Thackeray, that was his name. I wonder where he is now. I wish I could see him again.'

'Maybe you will—'

The door burst open with a crash and Caitlin took a sharp and unconscious side-step away from Mallory. It was Jerzy.

'Good friends, come quickly!'

They followed him down the winding stairs and out into the driving rain where the storm was so loud it was impossible to hear what Jerzy was saying. At the main gates there was a group of guards in a circle of torches, their capes swirling as they surrounded a large man on horseback clutching a bundle to his chest. The guards brandished spears and swords threateningly.

Jerzy grabbed Mallory's arm tightly. 'You must help her!' he shouted.

Mallory thrust his way through the guards. They rounded on him, swords pointed at his chest, but backed off when he half-drew Llyrwyn.

Evgen, the captain of the guard, blocked Mallory's way. 'You are not required here. Leave now.'

'Who is that?'

'It is none of your business, Brother of Dragons—'

'Ho!' The rider threw back his hood to reveal a mane of black hair and glowering features. A ragged scar ran above and below his left eye. 'A Brother of Dragons, you say!'

Mallory pushed past Evgen. He could feel the captain's hateful eyes on his back.

The rider peered into Mallory's face. 'Yes, I can see it now. Soft features, but it is there.' He half-fell from the horse and caught himself at the last. 'I have ridden for five days and nights to escape the Enemy. I need a bed, ale and a woman, not necessarily in that order.'

'Who are you?' Mallory asked.

The rider grinned. 'My name is Decebalus, once of Dacia, then a bastard of Rome, now a Freeman of Existence.'

Mallory recalled Church's description of fighting alongside Decebalus centuries ago in the earliest days of the Brothers and Sisters of Dragons.

Decebalus raised the bundle cradled in his arms. 'I return with a great prize.' He pulled back the blanket to reveal a girl of about eight, blonde ringlets framing a dirty, tear-stained face and wide, frightened eyes. 'Give greeting to Virginia Dare, first child of the New World.'

4

Wary of returning to the Palace of Glorious Light, Mallory, Caitlin and Decebalus slipped off to the Hunter's Moon, the barbarian carrying Virginia tenderly beneath his heavy cloak. Evgen set a guard on their trail, but Decebalus knew the dark, winding lanes intimately and they lost him within five minutes.

In a tiny, low-ceilinged backroom before a fire, Decebalus steadied himself with three flagons of ale in quick succession.

'I have been away from the court for many, many moons, tracking the frontier of the Enemy's territory,' he said. 'I have seen some bastards in my time, but they are the worst. The devastation . . . the slaughter . . . But that is not the most awful thing. It is the feeling they leave in their wake. Hopelessness. The end of it all.' He wiped his mouth with the back of his hand, his eyes haunted and faraway.

'What happened to the other Brothers and Sisters of Dragons who were here?' Caitlin asked.

Decebalus looked at her, puzzled. 'They are gone?'

'Missing. No one knows where.'

'I left to spy on the Enemy's weaknesses. It was a long and dangerous mission, hiding and running, living off the land. Most of the others were soft, like you. I was best-suited.' He ground his teeth. 'I thought the risk was mine, not theirs.'

In his lap, Virginia stirred, lulled asleep by the warmth of the fire after the chill of the night.

'Where did you find her?' Mallory asked.

'In the blasted lands, not far from the Enemy's fortress. She had discovered a secret way out of their damnable captivity.' He paused. 'And she knows a secret way back in.'

Mallory instantly saw the tactical significance, but Caitlin was overcome with sympathy for the child. 'Poor girl. She's the one the spiders stole from Roanoke with all the other settlers.'

'Four hundred years ago.' Mallory couldn't forget Church's expression when he had recounted his failure to save Virginia and the others.

'She was a baby then,' Caitlin said. 'She's spent eight years of her life with those things. What she must have been through—'

'Children are hardy,' Decebalus said. 'She will recover, given time.'

'Evgen was keen to stop me getting to you,' Mallory mused. 'Perhaps he is the Enemy's spy. Or,' he added, 'perhaps Niamh didn't really have that spider removed after all.'

'She sounded honest,' Caitlin protested. 'And if she is working with the Enemy, why hasn't she sent us the way of the other Brothers and Sisters of Dragons? Or killed us in our sleep?'

Decebalus finished his ale. 'Because she wants something?'

'Could be the Extinction Shears,' Mallory said. 'The spiders can't find them. They might think we have more information.'

'We can be away from here within the hour,' Decebalus said.

'No. Everything we need is here,' said Mallory.

'We stay,' Caitlin agreed. 'You hide here with Virginia. We'll remain at the palace, try to pick up some information about what might have happened to the others.'

'A risky, some would say foolish strategy,' Decebalus noted. 'I like it.'

5

Sophie emerged from the ritual so weary she could barely stand. Using the Craft in the Far Lands was a rush, all her senses on fire, her mind experiencing things that would change her for ever. But even abilities that had been a wild dream a few days earlier could not uncover any sign of the Market of Wishful Spirit. It was as if it had never existed.

Niamh waited in the anteroom, hands clasped behind her back as she stared into a mirror with a sunburst design. She gave a troubled smile.

'Have you had good fortune in your search?'

'Not yet, but I'm not going to give up.' Sophie flopped onto a sumptuous couch, feeling as if she could fall asleep in seconds. 'Can I help you with something?' she asked wearily.

'Counsel.' Niamh sat beside her. She curled her legs under her and stretched, cat-like. The movement revealed a striking vulnerability that Sophie had not seen before. 'I cannot discuss my doubts and fears with my own people. It would be seen as a sign of weakness. If Church were here, I know he would help, but he . . . abandoned me.' The final words were barely audible, but Sophie could hear the longing in them.

'He's got a big responsibility.'

'I know. We all have. There is no room for the personal in our lives.'

'But we have to have that. It's what keeps us going through all the hard times. Everyone who knows me says I'm strong, able to cope with anything. And I am strong. But if I didn't have Mallory, I'd be . . . lost. I love him so much.'

'And he loves you?'

'He says so. I . . . I believe him. Our relationship is weird. We never really tell each other our feelings. We just sort of know. Although . . . I don't think he knows exactly how much I need him.'

'Then you should tell him.'

'It's not that easy. I don't want to appear weak – or desperate. And when you love somebody that much it makes you weak on some level. It makes you scared, because you have something to lose.' Long-suppressed memories of the heartache that Mallory had healed threatened to rise. She fought to hold them back, knowing they would tear her apart again. She closed her eyes, and gradually calmed herself. Sleepiness crept up on her.

'I understand what you say. We all fear abandonment. We need that love. For me, there are times of great loneliness . . . at night . . . during the stillness after dawn. I have grown fond of your people. I miss your companionship.'

Sophie was aware of Niamh's closeness, the arm trailing behind her, gently touching her hair. An atmosphere of honeyed warmth enveloped her. It appeared to be exuding from Niamh, and it brought a fluttering deep in Sophie's belly. 'How can we help you?' she asked lazily.

'Advise me in my negotiations with the other courts, and in my preparation for the coming battle.'

'Of course we'll do what we can.'

'Fragile Creatures . . . so beautiful,' Niamh said gently.

Sophie smiled. 'Oh, that's good, coming from you.'

'The Golden Ones do not see the surface. We look deep inside. And that is where the beauty lies in all you Fragile Creatures.'

Sophie felt Niamh's fingers gently play with her hair. She almost jumped when the fingertips brushed her scalp.

'Church opened my eyes to the beauty of your people,' Niamh continued. 'Each of you shines like a star. So far beyond us . . . rising so fast.'

Sophie lost herself in Niamh's ethereal eyes.

'It takes my breath away,' Niamh whispered. 'All of you. You.'

Niamh's fingers exerted a slight pressure on the back of Sophie's head, easing her forward. Niamh's eyes pulled her in with the depth of her yearning.

'I am so lonely,' Niamh whispered.

Sophie felt the bloom of Niamh's breath on her cheek, then on her lips. The shimmer of golden light blinded her. A touch on her lips, an electric jolt, pressing harder. Heat rose inside her. Slowly her mouth responded, warm and soft.

6

Dombas was a small town almost lost in the folding snow of the majestic Norwegian highlands, about an hour's drive from the hotel. At five a.m. it was deserted, but the tiny railway station was open for business, though equally devoid of life. In the warm waiting room, Hunter continued to swig Jack Daniel's while keeping watch. The others huddled by the fire.

'We could call the Last Train,' Shavi mused. 'Perhaps it would help us reach our destination quicker.'

'What?' Tom said with angry disbelief. 'You have ridden the Last Train?'

'It wasn't exactly the Orient Express.' Laura's face was lost in the hood of her parka. 'More like a cattle carriage for freaks. And it smelled just as bad.'

'Stay away from it!' Tom shouted. 'Do you know where it has come from? Do you know where it is going?'

'No,' Laura said in a couldn't-care-less tone.

'Be thankful you don't.' Tom delved into his pocket for the tin that contained his roll-up materials. 'Bloody know-nothing idiots,' he muttered.

'Oslo's going to be a problem,' Hunter said. 'Big city like that, we'll have to be careful wandering around.'

The sound of the approaching train rumbled through the walls. Church stirred himself from his brooding and went to the door for one final look out. 'She's not dead,' he said. 'She can't be dead.'

7

Veitch made his way down Karl Johans Gate, dodging the artists lining Oslo's main street. It was late morning and the bars, cafés and restaurants along the route were already beginning to fill.

There was a bright optimism to the city that dovetailed with his own mood. It was a strange feeling. The only other time in his life when he'd felt even vaguely hopeful was when he had discovered his heritage as a Brother of Dragons alongside Church, Ruth, Shavi and Laura. Good people striving to be better. It had given him a sense of purpose that had always been missing.

But then he had been manipulated by higher powers, forced to betray the only people in the world he cared about, and his reason for living was exposed as the sham it truly was. He blamed the gods, he blamed Church. But in his darker moments he knew the truth: he was a loser who had brought it all on himself. When the Void had originally brought him back into the world, he had considered suicide; there was no way to fill the emptiness inside him.

But now things were different.

On the edge of Vigeland Park, he paused and took a deep breath of the cold, crystal air. He thought he could smell juniper berries and a hint of the fjord beyond. So many experiences since he had returned, so many new sights and thoughts that it was difficult to process it all. He remembered Church telling him once that every new experience turned you into a new person. So who was he now? That was the question.

The park was a vast, green sprawl of trees, lawns and duck ponds interspersed with life-size statues by the sculptor Gustav Vigeland. Veitch found his target in the dead centre, near the most impressive piece, a forty-six-foot-high sculpture of a mass of writhing bodies called *The Monolith*.

Standing next to the sculpture was a man in his mid-twenties with a sickly appearance, pale skin and lank brown hair. Every now and then someone would come up to him – an elderly person with frailty etched in their features, or a mother with a child swaddled tightly. With a kind expression, the man would exchange a few words with them, then take the person's hand lightly. After a moment the visitor would try to press money upon him, and he would politely refuse.

Having seen enough, Veitch strode up to him. The man greeted Veitch cheerily in Norwegian.

'Sorry, mate. Don't speak the lingo.'

The man's face brightened. 'You're British.'

'London born and bred.'

'Every time I hear the accent, I always get homesick.' He took Veitch's hand tentatively. 'Jez Miller. From Swindon.'

'Somebody has to be. Ryan Veitch.'

'Are you here for help?'

'What kind of help?'

Miller shifted uncomfortably. 'People come to me . . . y'know, when they get sick.'

'And you heal them?'

'It's a gift,' Miller said bashfully. 'I have to use it to help.'

'Yeah, you're the one I'm looking for all right. Come on, walk with me.'

Miller was taken aback, but did exactly what Veitch said. 'You've been looking for me? But no one knows I'm here. I've lost touch with my family, and . . .' His brow furrowed.

'You can't even remember why you're here, right?'

'Things have been a bit fuzzy for a while. I've been going to the doctor, but the medication isn't working.'

'You are so off the radar, mate, you don't know it. Not even the big evil bastard running the universe could find you. But I did.'

'I don't understand.' Miller looked troubled, as though he was half-remembering something long-forgotten. 'How did you find me?'

Veitch held up an amber stone that glowed with a dull, warm light. 'Picked this up in the Temple of the Dead in the Grim Lands. They've got all sorts of weird stuff stashed away there. It's called a Trace-Stone. Locates missing objects. Or people.'

Miller tried to evaluate how sane Veitch was. 'Why did you want to find me?'

'Because you're one of the two Keys.'

'To what?'

'To a whole load of trouble. Success or failure. My future.' Veitch smiled tightly. 'You got anyone here? Wife, girlfriend, kids? Boyfriend?'

Miller shook his head.

'All right, here's the deal. You come with me and I'll show you everything you need to know. Why your memory's so screwed up. The whole reason you're here. Who wouldn't want to know that?'

The hope in Miller's face was evident. 'You're lying. How could you know something like that? Who are you?'

'If you don't come with me, you'll never know.'

Miller dropped onto a bench and thrust his head into his hands. 'I'd be crazy to go with a complete stranger. You might be someone who kills people.'

'Yeah. I might.'

Miller looked deep into Veitch's eyes. 'Whatever I've got inside me, it makes me a good judge of character. I can see, deep inside you, there's something good.'

'Now you're talking bollocks,' Veitch snapped. He caught himself. 'And just to prove you wrong, I'll give you a choice. Come with me of your own free will, 'cause I reckon you're a nice bloke and I'd really like you to think good things about me. Or I'll make you come with me.'

Once again Miller tried to read Veitch. 'Well . . . okay,' he said hesitantly. 'But I'll yell if you try something.'

'Like a girl, I bet. All right, shut the fuck up and follow me.'

Veitch marched along the network of paths with Miller constantly asking hesitant questions that got no answers. In the car park, Veitch motioned for Miller to get in the front of a four-by-four, while he went to the rear and checked all around before opening the boot.

Ruth lay inside, hands and feet tied together, tape across her mouth. She glared at Veitch hatefully.

'How you doin', darlin'?' he said chirpily. 'I hate treating you like this, but I needed to get our man in the bag before we sat down and had our little heart-to-heart. Won't be much longer now.'

Just as the boot swung shut, Veitch had the vague impression that Ruth was mouthing something behind the insulating tape. He shrugged. She had a lot of fire in her, and he expected a broadside when they finally did sit down and talk.

As he climbed into the driver's seat and pulled away, he didn't notice a couple of stones in the car park begin to roll slowly of their own accord. They came together, then another, and another.

8

Cabs from Oslo's railway station took Church, Hunter, Shavi, Laura and Tom into the centre of town. Burying themselves in their seats, they watched the flash of police cars passing regularly.

'How many spiders?' Laura said from the depths of her parka hood.

'Impossible to tell.' Church's attention never left the street scene. 'It only takes one or two at the top. People are good at obeying orders without question.'

Arriving at Vigeland Park in the early afternoon, they separated to lose themselves amongst the trees and duck ponds, eventually coming together again at *The Monolith*.

Shavi paced around for a few minutes, then said uneasily, 'I do not understand. He should be here.'

'Maybe he's gone to feed the ducks,' Laura said.

Shavi unconsciously rubbed the skin around his alien eye. 'No. He *should* be here. But he is not.'

Tom had been scanning the park while they spoke. 'Something is happening,' he said.

What they had taken to be one of Vigeland's sculptures was moving. It resembled a brutish man with a low brow and long, muscular arms, built from rocks and stones. A dull amber light leaked from its eyes. With each step, tremors ran through the ground.

Laura and Tom edged away.

'Hang on,' Church said.

'Crazy leader,' Laura muttered under her breath.

As the rock-thing approached, the park underwent a rapid change. Ponds and lawns faded away to be replaced by a wilder landscape of rock, gnarled trees and drifting mist. Bonfires were just visible in the distance.

The craggy Neanderthal lumbered up to them and levelled its burning gaze on each in turn. 'Heroes all,' it said in a voice like cracking granite. It nodded slowly as if this fulfilled a requirement. Gesturing with one heavy arm, it added, 'This is the land as it was in time past when the warriors ground bone and blood into the soil. And this is how the land is now beyond Bifrost: timeless and wild where the true powers live in every rock and tree.'

'What do you want with us?' Church asked.

'I bring a message from one of your kind. She summoned me from the dark place beneath the earth where I live with my people.'

'Ruth?'

'A Sister of Dragons who knows the practice of *seior* as only the great and wise Freyja knows it. She has been taken by another of your kind, he who carries the blade of black fire.'

Church grew cold. 'Veitch? He's alive?'

'He lives. The Sister of Dragons wants you to know that he has the Creator Key and now he hunts the Destroyer.'

Hunter clapped a reassuring hand on Church's shoulder. 'We'll find him before he hurts Ruth.'

'How? We have no idea where he's going or where this Destroyer is.'

'The Shavster could ask his spooky friends again,' Laura suggested.

'I have already exhausted any advantage I might have over the Invisible World,' Shavi replied. 'I must wait a while before I contact it again.'

Tom pushed past the others to face the rock-creature. 'Freyja brought the practice of *seior* to the Vanir and Aesir, did she not?'

'She did.'

'And Ruth is the greatest practitioner of *seior* in the Fixed Lands. The two are bound by the principles of the Craft. Freyja *must* help us.'

'It is unwise to be so forward,' the creature rumbled. 'But should you

121

wish to petition the goddess, travel to yonder hill and the grove where the golden apples grow.' And with that, the creature shambled away, losing form as it went, disintegrating into rocks and stones.

'Is that a wise course?' Shavi asked. 'You saw how Freyja was at the hotel.'

'We can't trust any of the blasted lot of them!' Tom snapped. 'But we do what we have to.' He strode out for the hill without looking to see whether any of the others were following him.

The air was chill at the top of the hill and autumnal mists floated amongst the trees where the apples glittered in the wan light.

'I'm going to have me one of those,' Laura said. Tom called out for her to stop, but she had already plucked the golden fruit. In her eyes, Tom could see the gleam of a strange attraction overcoming rational thought.

'Chill out, Grandpa,' she said, until she saw Tom's horrified expression. A second later blood began to speckle the apple's shimmering surface. Laura threw it away in disgust. 'Jesus. It's bleeding.'

'The blood of the gods,' Tom whispered.

As Laura tried to wipe the gore from her hand, it began to spread, sticky and wet. Soon her entire arm was dripping. Blood continued to run from the apple, across the floor towards the others; the faster they moved away, the faster it ran.

Tom sprinted into the trees, which now formed a dark, dense forest. He allowed himself one backward glance and wished he hadn't. Laura, Shavi, Church and Hunter were covered in blood from head to foot, fighting for their lives as it flooded into their mouths.

9

Tom felt the full weight of his age as he ran. His knees protested, his chest burned, his heart pounded so hard he thought it would burst. He felt as if he had lived with fear from the moment the queen of the Court of the Yearning Heart had taken him from the world. Always running, always scared of the past, the present, the future. He hated himself, but he couldn't stop running.

The blood continued to drip from the fruit overhead. He had avoided every splash so far, but it was only a matter of time before he was tainted. Behind him, his friends were dying, like the others he had left behind to their fate at the Court of the Final Word.

The irony made him sick. Across his homeland he was known as a great hero: Thomas the Rhymer, who would return to save the land in its time of greatest need. In truth, he was selfish and weak and scared. Worthless.

Tears stung his eyes. He tried not to think of Church, who had befriended him and shown him so many valuable lessons, and of the others who each in their own small way had made his dark life a little brighter.

He drove himself on, but after nearly eight hundred years of sickness and self-loathing he had finally reached his limits. He crashed onto the soft loam and cried out, 'Take me, damn you! Take me and let them go!'

For a long moment he lay face-down, his head reeling with the insane rush of emotions. When his mind finally began to clear and he realised it was not all over, he slowly looked up to see Freyja standing next to a tree, her smile teasingly sexual, but her eyes dark and unfathomable.

'Mortals can never resist the golden apples,' she said.

'Save them,' Tom pleaded.

Freyja plucked one of the apples and held it before her so that the glow illuminated her beautiful face. 'You are offering your life in exchange for theirs? Of what value is that to me?'

'The All-Father ordered you to give us safe passage,' Tom gasped.

'And so I did. But this is a new matter. A transgression greater still. The golden apples are the very power of the gods. To steal one is a crime that demands the highest penalty.'

'You set a trap. You knew once we were in the grove it was only a matter of time until one of the apples was taken.'

Her laughter was soft and gentle and contemptuous. 'Your little sister has a great mastery of *seior*, but she is far beneath me. After all, I brought *seior* to the gods. When she conjured here in our Great Dominion, she presented an . . . opening.'

'What do you want? Revenge?'

'Revenge implies some notion of equality. You are mortals, for all your great abilities, and consequently barely worthy of my attention.' Holding the apple delicately, Freyja sat on a fallen tree. As she examined the fruit's gleaming skin, Tom had the strangest feeling that it was not an apple at all, but something sentient.

'This is the axe-age, the sword-age,' she continued, 'that precedes the great catastrophe Ragnarok. The seeds of this destruction were sown in the beginning, when this flawed existence emerged from the fire and the ice.'

Tom was struck by how Freyja's mythic account echoed the Gnostic beliefs that Church had come to understand as the truth: of a flawed universe ruled by the Void.

'The one your people know as Loki has a part to play and now he has already joined the forces of dissolution. Will the World Serpent curled around Midgard with its tail in its mouth soon burst forth? Will Asgard fall? Will Bifrost burn? Can such wonder and beauty ever fail?'

Her haughty expression faltered. Tom instantly recognised the familiar emotion.

'You think you know what this means, but you do not,' she said. 'Fenrir will break free and roam the Fixed Lands with his savage brothers, spreading death everywhere. The wolves will swallow the sun and the moon, and Yggdrasil, the Life-Tree, will shake to its roots. Hel will rise from misty Niflheim with her armies of the dead and sweep across the Vigrid Plain. And all the worlds shall burn, and Earth shall fall into the boiling ocean.'

A silence followed her words that extended far into the forest. The images she had conjured reminded Tom of the biblical Revelations he had read as a youth. There was only one story, filtered through different cultures, different beliefs.

Freyja stood before him, and her face was almost too fierce to look upon. 'If you wish to live – if you wish to save your comrades at this moment – you must make a bargain with me. Even though it could mean the betrayal of your own and all they stand for.'

Tom steadied himself against a tree, fighting the deep chill of desolation rising through him. 'What do you want?' he said.

10

Church coughed and retched until his throat was raw. Finally he cleansed the last of the blood from his system. His gore-soaked clothes clung to him. Hunter and Shavi coughed up blood nearby, but Laura sat in a daze.

'Okay, I am not taking the blame for that one,' she said.

They were back in Vigeland Park. On the other side of the pond, a couple feeding the ducks watched them uneasily.

'Drenched in blood in a public place. Not the best look for a bunch of wanted terrorists.' Hunter helped Shavi to his feet. 'We need to get cleaned up and out of sight. Where's the Grateful Dead?'

On cue, Tom lurched out of a nearby copse. They were all transfixed by the intensity of his haunted expression.

Shavi took his arm. 'What happened?'

Tom took a second to steady himself. 'I persuaded Freyja to give us this.'

He showed them a gold ring in the shape of a dragon eating its tail. 'It's called *Andvarinaut*,' he said. 'When you wear it, you feel a pull in the direction of whatever you are searching for.'

'Ruth,' Church said, relieved.

Tom nodded non-committally.

'Better give it to Church—' Hunter began.

'No!' Tom's eyes blazed. 'Only I can wear this! Do you understand?'

'Take a stress pill,' Laura said. 'Bit of a Frodo moment there.'

'Only I can wear this,' Tom repeated. He held out his hand. It twitched with the pull of the ring. 'We head south.'

Church shifted his posture so he could feel the comforting weight of the sword on his back. 'Whatever else happens, Veitch has had his last chance. If he's hurt Ruth in any way, I'm going to kill him.'

The emotionless intensity of his words shocked them. Church went to the pond to wash some of the blood from him. No one followed.

chapter six

the bull, the serpent, the ivy and the wine

1

'This world is a beautiful place.' Shavi stood at the rail looking out over churning black waves towards a sunset of red and gold against which storm clouds roiled, occasionally throwing out bolts of lightning.

Laura thought how delicately handsome his features looked in the depths of the hood of his bulky parka. The winds across the Baltic were biting. 'You've just done too many drugs,' she said.

Shavi laughed. They had grown easy in each other's company as their memories of past times returned. 'There has been a lot of pain on our journey together, but I would not change any of it.'

'Not even the old git's rambling stories about the good old days of the sixties?'

'We come from such different backgrounds, but events have forged us into a unit. Underneath it all there are bonds of friendship that run so deep they are profound. Who would have thought such people could come together and like each other?'

Hunter lurched out of the door that led to their rough-and-ready quarters alongside the crew. 'Bloody hate ships,' he moaned. His words belied the effort to which he had gone to secure their passage after they had only just slipped through the fingers of a Security Service sting while crossing the border into Sweden. There had been roadblocks every mile of their eight-day journey south, forcing them to double-back, abandon vehicles, march miles through the cold and eventually stow away on a river barge before they eventually made their way to the port of Malmö.

'Where is Church?' Shavi asked.

'Sleeping, finally – he was determined to keep going until he dropped. Bit worried about the old guy, though. Something's eating away at him. But you know what he's like – he won't talk about it.'

Laura clutched at the rail as the ship crested a swell. 'On the bright side, at least when he's moping he's not being a pain in the arse.'

'What are our plans when we reach Germany?' Shavi asked.

'Steal a van. We can cut through the country pretty quickly on the autobahns, depending on which route Veitch takes. If we get past security, that is. I thought we'd have more trouble in Sweden.'

'*More* trouble?' Laura said. 'It was touch and go all the way.'

'Trust me, we've had it easy.'

Laura watched the sunset colours swimming on the ocean. 'Why didn't Veitch just kill the guy we were after? That would have stopped us dead in our tracks.'

'He is unpredictable,' Shavi said simply.

'He's smart and sly, too,' Hunter added. 'He's got some sort of plan.'

Urgent activity broke out amongst the Russian crew further along the deck. They were leaning over the other side, pointing into the water. Far below the surface a dim light was visible, powerful enough that it could pierce several fathoms.

'Is that one of those deep-sea fish, way off course?' Laura said. 'Or a submarine?'

Hunter questioned the sailors in Russian. 'They're calling it a USO – unidentified submarine object,' he said afterwards. 'They've seen one or two on this route.'

'Wait,' Shavi said. 'Is it rising?'

The light grew brighter as it emerged from the depths. The crew shouted anxiously, and one man ran to inform the captain.

'Let's get under cover,' Hunter urged.

In the shadows of a metal staircase, they watched the waters boil as light streamed from below. Something broke the surface, reflecting the sunset and the distant lightning. At first they thought it was a metallic craft, then some mythical sea-beast and finally realised it was a little of both.

Rising up from the swell was some kind of insectile construct, black carapace, extensions that could have been legs, and an overwhelming stink of spoiled meat. Water streamed from it as it lifted into the darkening sky to hang over the ship. They instinctively recognised it as something that had come from the Void, searching for them.

'Shit, if it attacks here, game over,' Laura whispered. 'Five minutes in this water and we're dead.'

Hunter held her back, but his touch was also calming. He weighed

127

things neither Laura nor Shavi saw. 'If it was ready to attack, we'd be gone already.'

Lights flared again, eyes levelling, a forensic stare. A beam fell upon the sailors and held them for a moment before moving off across the surface of the ship. Hunter, Shavi and Laura pressed back into the shadows.

When it completed a circuit, the eye winked out and the insect-ship sank slowly back beneath the waves. The crew ran about in relieved excitement, hugging each other.

'I thought the idea was that the Void didn't try to break the Mundane Spell,' Laura said.

'This'll just be one of those fish stories that gets told in bars and then forgotten,' Hunter said. 'But it's pushing at the limits of what it can get away with. These kinds of things must be patrolling everywhere, scuttling behind the scenes, trying to find us.'

'But whatever was in the craft was not wholly intelligent,' Shavi said. 'It sensed we were here, you could see, but it could not work out why it could not find us. That is one thing in our favour.'

At the rail, they watched the lights growing dimmer as the vessel sank into the depths.

2

Two days later, at Rostock, Hunter bribed a sailor to stow them in crates of machine tools, who in turn bribed the customs official to let the container lorry through without scrutiny. Ten miles inland they were freed to buy a van from an unscrupulous backstreet dealer unconcerned about paperwork. They picked up the autobahn east of Hamburg and headed south.

Tom sat silently in the front, feeling the gentle tug of his ring. At the wheel, Hunter watched faces, seeing the scars of a world without magic, feeling the slow, black suffocation of the Void pressing in on all sides. He was sure it would only be a matter of time before that desolation enveloped them all and they rejoined the non-people with their non-lives. He started to beat out a rhythm on the steering wheel, but it sounded like the ticking of a clock, counting out the seconds of hope that remained.

'There's still hope,' Tom said quietly, as if he could read Hunter's mind. 'There's always hope. That is what the secret Gnostic knowledge tells us.'

'Somehow that doesn't feel like enough,' Hunter said.

'Ah, but it is. To understand that is to win. This world is about the base and the material. It is about struggling for money and power, about fighting for *people like you* against *people like them*. You can see it engrained in every aspect of our culture, locked in so tightly that there is no room for the opposite point of view to gain a foothold. Innocence, love, hope – these things are derided and their power diminished. And yet there is a place where they can survive even the most tumultuous attack.'

Shavi leaned forward between the two of them. 'The human heart,' he said.

In the back, Laura yawned loudly and pointedly. 'Here come the hippies.'

'The Gnostic secrets tell us that fragments of the true power of Existence, the Blue Fire, are lodged in every human, waiting to be fanned from a spark into a flame,' Tom continued. 'Those fragments are the basis of the Pendragon Spirit. And if that knowledge tells us one thing, it is this: that every person can make a difference. That by looking within, the outside can be altered.'

'That's a nice little story,' Hunter said, 'but nobody's going to wake up of their own accord. They've got too much to keep them occupied – cash, drink, drugs, sex.' He paused. 'Not to be knocked, of course.'

'That is how the Void wins,' Shavi said. 'It has built a prison that we love.'

'Still doesn't get away from my point: who's going to start making people fan those sparks?'

'You,' Tom snapped. 'Do I have to spell it out? Why am I cursed to be surrounded by thick-heads?'

While Laura launched a caustic attack on Tom, Church sat silently in the back, turning over Tom's words, convinced they were directed at him. As always, Tom cut through to the heart of him, slicing past the encysted negativity that had grown around Ruth's disappearance.

'We wake them by shattering the Mundane Spell,' he said. 'We show them the magic that exists behind the scenes.'

As they passed Frankfurt a few hours later, they realised his words had more than metaphorical meaning. Cars veered wildly across the autobahn and came to a halt on the hard shoulder as people jumped out to stare into the sky. Overhead, a winged horse dipped and soared in the morning light. Hunter pulled the van to the side and wound down the window. The cries of the observers were filled with wonder that suggested they had been changed for ever.

'This Great Dominion is awake,' Tom said, 'and the magic it contains is now unfettered. You did that, simply by passing through.'

'So all we've got to do,' Laura said, watching the horse dreamily, 'is to wake each Great Dominion. Simple. We open the box, the weird stuff pours out and the Mundane Spell shatters.'

Tom sighed. 'First, you have to survive each Great Dominion.'

3

The Tower of the Four Winds stood amidst minarets and flat-roofed white stone buildings, an echo of Moorish architecture that was compounded by the aroma of spices on the hot wind. It was one of a pair, an exact duplicate of one that stood in the Court of Soul's Ease. Though all around the streets were as claustrophobically packed as any in the Court of the Soaring Spirit, Math's tower home stood in a spacious walled garden that felt like breathing again after a prolonged period of stress.

'So Math is some kind of sorcerer to the Tuatha Dé Danann?' Mallory whispered as he searched the shadowy garden, a lantern hidden beneath his cloak.

'Scary guy,' Sophie replied. 'He wears a mask with four different animal avatar faces that keeps rotating while he speaks.'

'Was he a threat to Niamh? Is that why he's missing?' Caitlin gripped her axe tightly.

'I'm not convinced Niamh is the threat,' Sophie said hesitantly. 'I don't get any sense of that.'

'The Tuatha Dé Danann are very good at hiding their motivations,' Caitlin responded. 'Did you have any trouble getting Rhiannon out of the palace?'

'Decebalus smuggled her out.' Mallory unsheathed Llyrwyn, which sang as the blue flames licked the warm night air. 'He's got rooms at the Hunter's Moon under an assumed name. He'll guard Virginia Dare and Rhiannon with his life.'

'They'll find them sooner or later,' Caitlin said.

'Then we'd better not waste any more time chatting.' Mallory led the way up the path to the tower's door.

Ivory, glass and gold combined in perfect balance, the overall aesthetic implying that it was a place dedicated to the study of higher things. But an underlying tone of menace was hidden in the architecture like a ghost of the truth.

The door hung open, the lock shattered. Cautiously they climbed a staircase running around the inside wall. Halfway up, Caitlin and Sophie shared a look of apprehension, but the only sound was the wind rushing through the space above them.

They emerged into a room at the very top of the tower with open windows at the cardinal points. In front of the windows, iron rings had been set in the wooden floorboards with a broken chain attached to each one. Purple drapes marked with magical symbols had been torn from the walls. An upturned brazier, books, charts and lanterns were scattered all around. Mallory examined deep scarring in the floorboards where it looked as if they had been hit repeatedly with an axe.

'If he's such a scary sorcerer, that means whoever took him down has to be even scarier,' Caitlin noted.

Sophie picked up some of the magickal items. They made her fingers tingle as if they were calling to her. 'Do you think he's dead?'

'That'd make sense if he was a threat,' Mallory said. 'But if he is, that means all the Brothers and Sisters of Dragons Church rescued are dead, too.'

Sophie righted the brazier and started to set the books and amulets and crystals back on the tables. The disorder was unsettling her. 'He is a powerful sorcerer,' she said thoughtfully. 'They couldn't have taken him by force alone. And they couldn't have taken him by surprise, not here, in his own tower.'

'Then why didn't he run?' Caitlin examined one of the broken chains, then looked out of the window across the jumbled rooftops of the dark city.

Mallory perched on the main altar table and slowly took in the details of the room. 'He knew there wasn't any point in running. They were more powerful. They saw him as a threat. They were going to get him sooner or later.'

'So he just sat here and waited for them?' Caitlin said.

Musing, Mallory watched intently as Sophie laid out the magickal items. 'What would you do if you knew an enemy was coming for you and there was no escape?'

Caitlin tapped her axe rhythmically against the stone lintel of the window, lost in thought.

'He was working on something just before they took him.' Sophie examined two crumbling leather-bound volumes, various pages marked by hide strips. She trailed her fingers across a gold chalice studded with gems, a half-burned green candle, a polished crystal, a human skull branded with runes. 'These . . . I can't read the words, but these diagrams . . . and these ritual items – Math was trying to contact the Grim Lands.'

'Why would he want to get in touch with the dead?' Mallory asked.

'Even the gods are banned from going there. But there's something here about souls . . . What was he doing?'

'There's a message here somewhere,' Caitlin interjected. 'If I was trapped with no way out, that's what I'd do – leave a clue for someone who might come looking for me.'

'We have to look for patterns,' Sophie said. 'That's what magic is – repeating patterns that influence the underlying patterns of the universe.'

'Patterns,' Mallory repeated thoughtfully. 'You know how I feel about magic – about the same as I do about gods, God and religion. But patterns I can understand.'

Mallory returned to the entrance to get a better view of the room. His gaze fell upon the fallen drapes, the position of the brazier, his recollection of where the magickal items had been before Sophie moved them. He sheathed his sword and extinguished the lantern.

The darkness smothered them until their eyes got used to the faint light falling through the windows. The moon was high and almost full, its rays a bright beam through one window. From another, illumination came from an eternal flame that burned atop another tower nearby. One light white, one ruddy. Mallory returned the brazier to its fallen position. In the moonlight, a handle carved in a serpent shape produced a finger of shadow across the floorboards.

'Where did the other stuff go?' he said.

Caitlin placed the chalice on the floor, hesitated. 'No, that's not right.'

Sophie adjusted the chalice by a few inches, realigning it with the moonbeam. Another finger of shadow extended to bisect the first.

'Doesn't make sense.' Mallory examined the point where the shadows crossed. 'The moon wouldn't be in the same position now as when Math laid all this out.' Frustrated, he paced the room. 'Maybe we're wrong—'

'No,' Sophie insisted. 'This feels right. We're just missing something.'

'Four winds . . . four windows,' Caitlin mused. 'The old philosophers had four elements. Wasn't that the basis of some magic?'

'Earth, air, fire and water,' Mallory added, nodding.

'Five,' Sophie corrected. 'Those are the four earthly elements. There was a fifth, quintessence, which was heavenly, incorruptible.'

'Okay.' Mallory knelt to examine what they had. 'The brazier stands for fire, obviously. I'm betting the chalice is water. What lines up with the earth window?'

Sophie held up the skull with a shrug.

'Mortal clay.' Caitlin's voice was hollow, her eyes downcast.

Sophie placed the skull where it had been when they entered. 'I think the fourth one is supposed to stay empty, for air.'

132

Mallory stepped back to survey the ritual pattern. 'And the fifth?'

Sophie picked up the polished crystal. 'A guess. Or instinct, if you prefer. This was still on the table when we came in. I think we have to place it in the right spot to complete the pattern.' She weighed the crystal in her hand, then went to select a position.

'Wait,' Caitlin cautioned. 'It might not be wise to put it in the wrong spot.'

Sophie hesitated.

'If it's supposed to be heavenly,' Caitlin began, 'shouldn't it be above the corruptible elements?'

Sophie looked to Mallory. He nodded. Tentatively, she held the crystal ahead of her and moved towards the middle of the room. When she was above the centre point, she felt a bodiless tug on her hand that made her shiver. Slowly, she opened her fingers and the crystal remained suspended in the air.

'Now what?' Caitlin said in hushed tones.

The crystal rotated slowly.

'Light the lantern,' Sophie whispered.

Mallory struck his flint, and the flickering lantern light made the shadows retreat. The moment it struck the crystal, the room came alive with shimmering patterns circling the walls as the crystal turned: words in an alien language, runes, diagrams.

Sophie, Caitlin and Mallory were mesmerised. Each pass reflected information on their retinas, burning it deep into their unconscious.

'It's a calendar,' Sophie said dreamily. 'What does it mean?'

The moment the words left her lips, the light winked out and the crystal fell, shattering on the floor.

'MAT,' Mallory mouthed as the images continued to play across his mind. 'ANM. Those letters keep coming up. I don't understand.'

'It's as plain as the nose on your face or the tower in the city,' Caitlin said in Brigid's throaty rumble. Mallory winced at the relapse: what had brought one of her buried personalities to the fore?

'What are you saying?' Sophie asked.

Caitlin/Brigid gave a chilling laugh. 'Go to a library if you want to understand. It's all up here!' She tapped her temple.

A noise on the edge of his perception snapped Mallory out of his reverie. He motioned for Sophie and Caitlin to remain silent. At first there was only the wind, but then came a faint sucking sound like gas escaping from a marsh. Behind it, high and reedy and drawing closer, were child-like voices, but whatever they were saying made no sense; an idiot's chant.

Mallory peered out of the south window. The foot of the tower was lost in the darkness, yet even so he thought he could see something moving, darker still than the shadows that concealed it.

'Stop that noise! It's scaring me!' Caitlin said in her little girl's voice. The axe slipped from her fingers and clattered on the floorboards.

Mallory ran from window to window. Waves of shadows lapped all around the tower.

'They're coming!' Caitlin whined.

The grind of the tower door being dragged open. Tiny feet clattering up the steps; empty, idiot voices growing louder.

Mallory slammed and bolted the trap-door that led to the stairs.

'What are we supposed to do now?' Sophie said.

'You can either let down your hair, Rapunzel, or find something we can use to get out of here.' Mallory began to ransack the chests and cupboards.

Caitlin sat against the wall, hugging her knees and rocking gently.

The clattering of feet came right up to the trap-door, the insane voices now shrill and giggling. The bolt rattled amidst a flurry of clawing with what sounded like birds' talons.

'How did they get up here so quickly?' Sophie breathed.

Head deep in an enormous chest, Mallory emerged with an extensive coil of silken cord.

'Will that hold us?' Sophie asked. The clawing and giggling almost drowned her out.

Mallory stamped his boot on one end and tested it. 'Yeah. Look, you need to do that thing you do. The other end has to be attached to the nearest building.' Sophie's face betrayed her lack of confidence. 'You can do it, combat honey,' he said softly.

While Mallory secured the cord to one of the iron rings set in the floorboards, Sophie leaned out of the window and silently attempted to summon one of the bats she'd seen circling the tower earlier.

The trap-door burst open with a crash. From the dark beneath erupted what looked like six-year-olds but with grey, mortuary skin, jagged, broken talons and pale eyes like saucers. Their sharp-toothed mouths snapped hungrily.

'Any time now would do,' Mallory shouted. With surprising tenderness, he pulled Caitlin next to him and stood between Sophie and the dead children with Llyrwyn drawn.

Sophie forced herself not to look back, but could hear the sizzle of the flames as the sword cut the air, and the sickening sound of bone and meat cleaved, and the hysterical screams and incongruous shrill laughing, so loud she wanted to scream herself.

Concentrate, she thought. *Don't be so pathetic!*

The bat was so large that at first she thought it was a bird of prey. Soon the cord was unravelling out of the window. When it was taut, she yelled to Mallory.

'You go first!' he replied. The unnatural children swarmed at him like rats. He hacked and thrust in a blur, piling up bloodless limbs and dismembered bodies.

'Caitlin—?' Sophie said.

'I'll carry her! Go!'

Sophie paused as she took in Mallory holding Caitlin about her waist, pressed hard against him, using his own body as a shield. Caitlin clung to him with a touching hope.

Sophie swung her legs up to grasp the cord and then shinned along it like a monkey, feeling the sucking gulf beneath her once she was out of the window, forcing herself not to look down.

Bats flapped around her head, and the cord burned her hands and feet as she gathered speed, but she clung on. Soon she was on a flat roof nearby, allowing herself to breathe as Mallory dropped from the cord next to her, bleeding from numerous wounds. Caitlin hung around his neck, her face pressed close to his.

'Thank you,' Caitlin said, with what sounded to Sophie like breathless adoration. Just the little girl inside her friend, Sophie told herself.

Mallory steadied himself. 'Okay, that's put me right off having kids.'

'Whoever's behind this isn't going to let us blithely carry on trying to find out what happened,' Sophie said.

'We knew it was just a matter of time before they caught up with us. Let's find that library.'

4

While Mallory bathed his wounds in one of Decebalus's network of secret rooms at the back of the Hunter's Moon, Sophie sat with Virginia Dare, brushing and braiding the little girl's hair. More resilient than Sophie could have hoped, she had recovered from the worst of her ordeal, but her eyes still held a haunted look that Sophie feared would never fade.

'When will you rescue my mother?' Virginia asked.

'Soon.' Sophie averted her eyes from a network of scars peeking above the neckline of the girl's shift.

'Do not talk to me about that place!' Virginia snapped, as if she could read Sophie's mind.

'Darling, you're with friends now. We're going to look after you.'

'Nobody can look after anybody. You are always on your own.'

'That's not true—'

'It is! My mother could not protect me!'

Sophie winced. 'I know what that's like. To feel you've been abandoned by people you count on. You're lost. You're scared. You're afraid you can't stand on your own. It hurts, doesn't it? And you never forget that hurt.'

Virginia watched Sophie intently for any sign that she was lying or patronising. 'You are not alone. You have the Knight.'

'Mallory? Yes, I do.' Sophie looked around to check that Decebalus was not in earshot and then whispered conspiratorially, 'I haven't even told Mallory this. It's a secret, between you and me, all right?'

Virginia's eyes grew wide. She nodded.

'Before Mallory came along, I felt exactly like you. I couldn't cope on my own, and I was ready to give up. I didn't show anybody – I'm not like that. I put on a big, brave smiling face, but inside I was clinging on by my fingernails.'

Sophie could see that Virginia understood.

'And then Mallory came along and he saved me,' she continued. 'Not in an "I've got a big sword to kill the monsters" way. Instead he made me realise there was somebody to watch my back when I wasn't up to the fight. He showed me the truth – that none of us are superheroes who can always cope on our own, and it's not a sign of weakness to accept that. All we need to do is find somebody we trust and put our faith in them to look after us when we stumble. And once you give up fighting on your own – once you share that burden of struggle – you're stronger.'

Through the open door to the next room, she watched Mallory move about, wincing when one of his wounds pulled.

'You are very lucky to have found him.'

'Yes,' she said. 'I am.' She let her own deeper fears subside and turned back to Virginia with a reassuring smile. 'And now I'm asking you to trust us. Can you do that?'

Virginia looked into Sophie's eyes for a moment and then nodded, before nuzzling her head into Sophie's neck and hugging her tightly.

5

To Ruth, the scenery had the look of a seventies summer holiday snapshot with colours that were too saturated to be real. A clear blue sky, verdant trees, sun-bleached grass and rolling, dusty, boulder-strewn hillsides. The white walls and pink-tiled roofs of the village glowed in the morning light.

It was warm and beads of sweat trickled down her brow, but her bonds prevented her from wiping them away. The tape across her mouth itched and she was sure she was developing an allergic reaction to the glue.

'Why don't you let her go? She won't try to get away. I can't believe you've kept her like that for a week.' Miller became upset every time he saw Ruth, his discomfort made worse by his awareness that he was too ineffectual to do anything about it.

'It's not the getting away that I'm worried about.' Veitch reached over and wiped Ruth's damp brow with a handkerchief, not unkindly.

'I know you say she's some kind of witch, but I can't believe that.'

'This from a bloke who can cure any illness with a touch.'

'That's not witchcraft!' Miller said, outraged. 'It's the power of God—'

'Yeah, yeah, whatever. Now shut up. Your whining voice really gets on my tits.'

Miller fell silent, plucking at the grass beneath his legs like a spurned schoolboy.

Pensive, Veitch leaned back against the wheel of the car and watched Ruth for a moment. 'You know I don't want to have you trussed up like a Tesco chicken.'

Ruth glared at him.

'Yeah, I know. Words are cheap. But I've seen what you're capable of. You're an A-bomb just waiting to detonate, only you don't know it. You're getting your memory back, I know, but you still haven't remembered how to tap into that whole witchy Craft business. Which is good for me. Not too keen on waking up a toad, or with my insides on the outside. But pretty soon even that gag and those ropes aren't going to stop you doing what you do. Then we'll have to make a choice—'

'Even you wouldn't kill her!' Miller interjected shrilly.

'I told you to shut up.'

'No!' His voice cracked with emotion. 'I've had enough of this. I don't know why you've got us both. I was stupid to come with you. But I trusted you! You don't feel like a bad man—'

'Yeah, well, you're an idiot.'

'Why are you so horrible? What do you want?'

Veitch gently tapped one silver finger on the well-used map as he surveyed the landscape.

'Why have we driven halfway across Europe?' Miller continued. 'What are we doing in Greece? Where are we?'

Veitch sighed. 'Village down there is Myloi. They reckon Pythagoras used to have a mansion here . . . walked around the streets doing his studies and everything.' He eyed Ruth slyly, but she showed absolutely no interest in his attempt at perspicacity.

'But why—' Miller whined until Veitch's cold look cut him short.

'Time's running out. I'm not really what you'd call patient, but that ticking clock is making me worse. So I'll say this once: don't piss me off, either of you. We're here because we're going to my favourite holiday resort.'

'Kalamata?' Miller ventured.

'The Land of the Dead.'

His mouth gaping, Miller tried to read Veitch's face, then returned to his sullen grass-plucking.

A lazy, heady peace lay over the still countryside. Ruth enjoyed the sun on her face after being bundled up in the suffocating boot all the way down into the Peloponnese, with only the occasional stop on isolated back roads where she was allowed to stretch her legs. She'd been plotting different ways to break free, but Veitch was clever and no opportunity ever arose. The longer the journey continued, the more she feared for her safety. She recalled Church describing all the Brothers and Sisters of Dragons that Veitch had brutally murdered over the years. Quite why he was taking his time over her she wasn't sure, but sooner or later her moment would come.

He had been right about one thing: her control of the Craft was growing stronger. Her attempt to use the Craft in Oslo had drained her completely, and the iniquities and exhaustion brought on by her captivity had made it difficult to focus and concentrate. But it felt as if it was built into the architecture of her mind, and as soon as she fully understood the pattern of it she would be able to utilise it to its fullest. All she needed was time.

'What's that?' Miller startled her out of her thoughts. He was on his feet, pointing into the trees down the slope towards the village.

Veitch was beside him in an instant, alert and threatening.

'I couldn't tell if it was a man, or an animal, or a bit of both. It was watching us. You think I'm mad, don't you?'

'You're not playing with a full deck, mate, that's for sure, but I've seen enough weird shit not to dismiss something like that.' He looked round at Ruth uneasily. 'I should stick you back in the boot while I check this out.'

'Let her stay out longer,' Miller pleaded. 'She must be going insane in there all that way.'

'I don't trust her or you. Frankly, I don't trust anyone.' He looked down the dusty road. 'When are Etain and the others coming back?' he muttered irritably to himself before appearing to make up his mind. He

138

grabbed another length of rope from the car and tied Ruth's wrist bonds to the bumper. 'That'll hold. All right, you're coming with me,' he said to Miller.

He set off down the slope. Miller hesitated for a second before scuttling over to Ruth. He slipped something into her hand before smiling weakly and hurrying after Veitch. It was a Swiss Army knife.

Ruth's muscles ached from too many hours tied up in the boot of the car, but she feverishly opened the knife and struggled to work the blade against the rope at her wrist. It was slow, and difficult, and within moments blood was flowing from numerous cuts. Anxiously, she watched Veitch and Miller clamber over rocks as they made their way down to the tree-line.

After the third time she dropped the knife, frustration set in. It always looked so easy when she saw it on film. She could tell from Veitch's body language that he could see nothing in the trees, and soon he would be making his way back. She'd never cut the rope in time. Tears of anger burned her eyes.

But just as Veitch turned to make his way back up the slope, there was a sensation like a shadow falling across the land. Ruth had the briefest notion of the sky turning black, and then of a sapphire snake moving sinuously towards her across the ground.

Why is the Blue Fire coming to me? she thought, confused.

And then a face filled her whole vision, so close she could only get an impression of it – part animal, part human, but with blazing eyes that were filled with a disturbing madness, and a smile that suggested uncontrolled sexuality. And then she knew no more.

6

Veitch returned to the car to find Ruth gone. The blood-spattered Swiss Army knife lay in the dust next to the coil of rope from her wrists. Furiously, Veitch grabbed Miller by the collar and dragged him over to see, before cuffing him around the ears.

'You left her that, didn't you, you traitorous little toe-rag?'

Miller whimpered and shrank back. He was surprised when Veitch only gave him a rough shove.

'Right. You help me find her. Up that way.' Veitch pointed along the road in the direction they had travelled earlier. He turned in the opposite direction.

'Wait.' Miller picked up the coil of rope. 'This hasn't been cut.'

'Stop lying. There's no way she could have got free from those knots.' Veitch examined the rope only to see that Miller was right. 'All right,' he said slowly, 'this is fucking weird.'

7

A scarlet sun hung hot and heavy in the black sky. Ruth walked along the main street of Myloi with a sound like the sea in her ears. Next to the low, white-walled village school stood a tomb, reeking of age, and on either side a labyrinth of alleys ran off into shadows. There was a coffee shop with the steam still rising from the gleaming machines behind the counter, and a bar with a bottle of ouzo on the table nearest the door, and shops selling olives and dried meats. But there were no people anywhere.

Somnambulantly, she took in every detail without contemplating the strangeness of it all. She was there, and there was no other place she should be.

In the middle of the road stood a large bull with eyes that mirrored the sun. It snorted a blast of hot air and dragged a lazy hoof in an unthreatening manner. Ruth came to a halt before it.

'Listen,' the bull said, 'can you hear the music?'

And then Ruth could, the lilting tones of a flute floating down from the hillside somewhere ahead of her.

'And look, there is ivy and wine,' the bull continued. The houses and shops on either side were now festooned with ivy, and nestling amongst the leaves were large stone jars of wine. Ruth could smell its heady, fruity scent.

'The season is turning once more. New shoots of growth break through the hard ground. And you, woman, tend to them with the serpents in your wake. The season is turning within you, too, but first what is hidden must be revealed.'

Ruth found herself swallowed up by the bull's red eyes and realised that it was not a bull at all.

8

The afternoon was already drawing on when Ruth found herself sitting in the shade of a grove of olive trees on a hillside overlooking the village. Her head rang and her throat was dry. The details of her escape from the car and encounter with the bull were already fading like a dream, but the

140

impressions remained at the back of her head, making her queasy with the sense of mysteries and secrets.

'Are you all right?'

The woman's voice was rich and deep and heavily accented. Ruth squinted against the sun until a figure emerged from the glare, black hair, olive skin, a shapely figure accentuated by a tight-fitting white dress. Ruth estimated she was in her early forties.

The woman helped Ruth to her feet, carefully inspecting the raw marks on Ruth's wrists. 'You have been attacked?'

'No . . . yes.' Still dazed, Ruth fought to order her thoughts. 'A man kidnapped me. I managed to get away, but he might still be around. He's dangerous!'

Ruth tried to place herself in the landscape and estimated that somehow she was on the other side of the village from where the car had been parked.

'We must call the police—' the woman began.

'No!' Ruth had visions of spider-controlled authority figures swarming from vans. 'Just . . . just take me somewhere till I can get back on my feet. Please.'

The woman nodded and took Ruth's arm. 'My name is Demetra. My grandmother built this place. It was the first of its kind in the Peloponnese.'

Ruth could now see a small but well-tended white farmhouse sur-rounded by more modern buildings. Beyond them were olive groves and fields that contained rows of what looked like cabbages. Ruth could see several women working diligently.

'What place?' she said.

Demetra looked puzzled. 'A refuge. For women like yourself. Who have suffered at the hands of men.'

'But . . . I didn't come here because of that . . .' Ruth caught herself. She couldn't begin to explain why she had come there.

It was cool inside the main farmhouse. The kitchen was clean and modern with a white stone floor and pine furniture. Instead of sitting at the table, Ruth ran from window to window, searching the rolling landscape.

'Do not worry. You are safe here,' Demetra said in a soothing voice. She placed a coffee pot on the stove.

'You don't understand. He's not like other men. He can do things . . .' Ruth realised how she must sound and quietened.

'We have very good security here. Fences and cameras. No one can get onto the site without us knowing. No men,' she stressed.

Anxiously chewing a nail, Ruth sat at the table as she considered her options. Veitch was relentless and brutal. She could only presume he hadn't killed her instantly because somehow she fitted into his plan, and if that was the case he would not allow her simply to walk away. But was it best to lie low there at the refuge, or to attempt to lose herself in Europe? And Veitch still had her spear. She wasn't wholly sure what powers lay within it, but she knew it shouldn't be in the hands of the Enemy. It was her responsibility to get it back.

'We have space. We can offer you a bed.' Demetra sat opposite her. 'Do not feel you have to talk about your experience. But I should warn you, this is a difficult time.' She paused. 'And a strange time, too.' Her smile faded to reveal a troubled, weary expression.

They were interrupted by a tearful woman in her thirties, slight and verging on anorexic. 'It's Roslyn,' she said in a desperate American accent.

Blanching, Demetra rushed from the kitchen after her. Ruth found them near the security fence that surrounded the farm. Five other women had gathered, of different ages and nationalities, but all their faces were shattered by grief. Demetra knelt over the body of another woman. She was probably in her twenties, Ruth guessed, but it was difficult to tell for her face had been beaten so badly it was a mass of bruises.

Demetra cried silently. 'Why did she leave the compound?'

'He told her he was going to hurt the kids if she didn't see him.' The American's voice cracked.

'I'm sorry,' Ruth said. 'The police—'

Demetra shook her head. 'Roslyn's husband is a powerful man. He pays to get what he wants, and he has already ensured that the police and the other authorities support him.'

'He's been trying to shut us down,' the American sobbed. 'Just because we took Roslyn in.'

With surprising strength, Demetra picked up Roslyn and carried her with dignity towards the farmhouse. 'We will not inform the authorities,' Demetra said in response to Ruth's querying expression. 'Roslyn requested to be buried here in accordance with our beliefs.'

'What are those?'

Demetra smiled, but gave nothing away.

'Look.' The American pointed behind them with astonishment. Along the path Demetra had taken with Roslyn's body, tiny golden beings with gossamer wings were appearing from nowhere, rising up like moths to catch the sun before flitting towards the trees. In their wake, they left a feeling of contentment.

The women watched in amazement. 'Magic,' one of them said quietly.

'But the land is supposed to be dead,' Ruth said quietly to herself.

'The season is turning.' Ruth felt a frisson at Demetra's echo of the bull's words. 'The land is waking.'

9

'Why don't you just let her go?' Miller said hopefully. He gripped the dashboard for dear life as Veitch sent the car hurtling down deserted dusty lanes barely wide enough for one vehicle.

'Will you shut up? Jesus Christ, I tell you, Miller, one more word and *you're* going in the boot.' In the grip of his rage, Veitch slammed a fist on the steering wheel. 'She can't have got far. Bollocks, Etain can find her in a bit.' He saw the sign he wanted and jammed a foot on the brake so hard that the car fishtailed wildly before it came to a halt.

'You're going to kill us!' Miller said.

'Tempting.' With a scream of tyres, Veitch sent the car down a side lane, past long, yellowing grass and scrubby bushes towards the blue Aegean Sea. He eventually brought the car to a halt on a rocky, rough piece of ground not far from a large modern structure. All around, insects buzzed, their too-rich colours shimmering in the sun.

'Where are we?' Miller asked.

'If there's one thing that bastard Church taught me, it's do your homework.' Veitch got out of the car and walked towards the large structure. Miller followed meekly. 'That roof covers American excavations of an old fort going back six thousand years. Most important Stone Age site in the area.'

'We're sightseeing?'

'Nah, we're not here for that. This used to be an area of springs, and there was a bloody big lake here before it dried up. Lerna, it was called. Famous. In those old stories, Hercules fought some big fuck-off monster round here.' Veitch strode towards the sea and Miller had to skip to keep up. 'Now if you were as smart as me, Miller, you'd know those old Stone Age geezers weren't like Fred Flintstone. They knew what they were doing when they built their settlements. The big ones, the special ones, were all thrown up where the power in the land was strong. So strong it could cut through between here and . . . other places.' He flashed Miller a grin. 'You're going to have to take my word for it, mate.'

Veitch stopped within earshot of the rolling waves and knelt down, holding his hand a few inches above the ground, feeling for something

Miller couldn't see. 'I thought it'd cut me off after I went against it,' he said to himself, 'but I can still feel it.' A note of awe rose in his voice.

'Why are we here, Ryan?' Miller said wearily. He glanced over his shoulder towards the deserted Tripoli road and the rising bulk of Mount Ponticos. 'I want to go home. And . . . it doesn't feel right here. I keep thinking something bad is going to happen.'

'You've got to stop being scared by life, Miller. It'll kick you in the arse all the time, but that doesn't mean you've got to stick your bum in the air.' He grinned. 'You want to see something really cool?'

He slammed his hand palm down on the ground. To Miller's surprise, blue sparks flew up and the air smelled of burned iron; even more surprising, it was oddly familiar to him. After a second, the ground began to rumble and soon a rift opened revealing a large, dark tunnel.

'Lake Lerna was supposed to be bottomless,' Veitch said. 'Instead, there was a tunnel to the Underworld, so everyone said. And you know what? They were right. You can cross over to the good old Otherworld all over the place, but this is one of the few spots that lead directly to the Grim Lands. The Land of the Dead. My place, now. My people.'

Miller was transfixed. From deep in the tunnel, he could hear the echo of hoof-beats drawing closer. Within seconds it became thunder and then Etain and her three comrades burst from the ground on their supernatural mounts. Sickened, Miller looked away from the dead, pale skin blooming here and there with lividity.

'The Brothers and Sisters of Spiders,' Veitch said by way of introduction. 'Might have to think about a new name for them.' He nodded to Etain. 'Hello, darlin'.'

She levelled her dead, emotionless eyes at him and Miller was convinced some unspoken communication passed between them, for Veitch's face darkened.

'Shit. What's going on?' He turned to Miller, but he was speaking to himself. 'The way's been blocked. They're on to us.'

'Oh, well done! How did you ever guess?' The theatrical voice was punctuated by slow, mocking clapping.

The Libertarian sat on a baked, muddy dune, dressed all in white like a colonial aristocrat, with a wide-brimmed hat adding a touch of flamboyance above the sunglasses that hid his lidless red eyes. Though he exuded an air of condescending wit, there was no humour in his face.

'Treachery comes so easily to you, doesn't it?' He sighed. 'We pick you up – from your grave, actually – dust you down, give you purpose and power, and how do you repay us?'

Veitch made a subtle motion for Miller to move closer to him. 'You made the big mistake of pissing me off.'

'As we're in Greece, it would be rather fitting to discuss the concept of hubris with you in relation to that arrogance, but I fear an intellectual debate really isn't a dish you like.' The Libertarian rose to his feet and effetely dusted down his pristine trousers. 'What is your plan now? I can't believe the other side has welcomed you with open arms, not after you slaughtered a small army of their kindly, decent-hearted sheep.'

'They're all bastards, same as your lot.'

'So it's the Veitch way, is it? A pox on both your houses. How wonderfully ambitious. You think a Fragile Creature can stand alone in the vast sweep of reality? Light-dark, good-bad, heaven-hell – there is no middle ground for you to occupy, Ryan. Where do you really think you're going to find a place where you can survive, let alone make a difference?'

'Nowhere.' Veitch shifted his body weight. Miller knew Veitch carried some kind of weapon in a harness on his back, but he'd never seen it. 'I'm going to bring the whole mess tumbling down. Back to the foundations. Then maybe we can start over again with something that actually works.'

'Ah. Feeling a little spurned by both sides? What are you going to do? Huff, and puff, and blow really hard?'

'Nah, I'll leave it to the Extinction Shears, mate. I've seen what they can do, you know that. Plus, this decent bloke here, and the other one – I know they can help screw you up.'

The Libertarian fell silent for a moment. Then: 'You know where the Extinction Shears are?'

Veitch grinned. 'Your big mistake is you always underestimate me.'

'You utilised our inability to register your presence very well, I'll give you that. And obviously anyone who travels with you falls into that self-same peculiar blind spot. But the minute they leave your side . . .' The Libertarian made a melodramatic gesture.

'Ruth.' Veitch grew grave.

'Yes, the Sister of Dragons. Clearly you've stopped murdering them now. Turned over a new leaf? Or is it just because this one makes your little heart go pitter-patter?'

'Shut up!'

'You love her?' Miller said. 'That's why you kidnapped her. I knew you were good deep down—'

The Libertarian roared with laughter.

Veitch slipped one hand into the covered harness on his back and withdrew a sword. Black fire danced along the blade and reflected darkly in Veitch's eyes. 'I still have this.'

'Oh, I bow to the power you wield. I'm no fool. Quite the opposite. You see, I know I could have brought a minor cadre of Lament-Brood here and overwhelmed you by sheer force of numbers. But where is the sport in that? A little emotional suffering always sweetens any mundane job, I say.'

Veitch was still wrestling with the Libertarian's twisted logic when Miller made the connection for him. 'He's going to kill Ruth.'

'No real need for her any longer. I let that little group of naive dragon-brood wander across this world with impunity to see if they could turn up the two Keys and/or the Extinction Shears. Oh, I threw an obstacle or two in their way, just so they didn't get suspicious. But here you are, and you've done the job for them!' The Libertarian squinted at Miller as if he couldn't quite see him. 'And I think once this one is chopped up into meaty chunks,' he added hesitantly, 'the other one will be superfluous. Two together or none at all.'

Terrified, Miller backed behind Veitch.

'Don't worry – I won't let him take you,' Veitch hissed.

'I wager you always hear the James Bond theme in your head when you say things like that.' The Libertarian bowed his head slightly and walked to the top of the dune. 'Think of your lady-love while you are sadly unable to help her.'

Realisation came a second too late for Veitch. As he raced forward to cut the Libertarian in half, black spiders burst from bubbles in the air to shower in vast numbers on the ground. They formed a crescent around Veitch, Miller and the Brothers and Sisters of Spiders.

'Where did they come from?' Miller gasped.

'They're always there. Crawling behind reality.' Veitch hesitated.

'We can run through them—'

'No! If they touch you, they'll wipe you out as if you never existed.'

The spiders advanced. Cursing under his breath, Veitch backed towards the tunnel leading to the Underworld until he stood on its lip, one arm across Miller's chest.

The Libertarian waved his hand theatrically. ' "There go the loves that wither, the old loves with wearier wings; And all dead years draw thither, and all disastrous things." '

'I'm going to get you, you bastard!'

'Shout all you want, no one will hear you. You're going where you belong, Ryan, down amongst the dead men.'

Something wrapped tightly around Veitch's ankles and then he was dragged backwards into the dark. As he fell, funereal cloth wrapped tightly around his head, and the last thing he heard was the sound of the ground closing above him.

chapter seven

cult of souls

1

It was a night for whispers and memories, dreams and magic. A full moon hung over the purple mountains at the heart of the Peloponnese and the warm air was filled with the scent of cooling vegetation and olives. Occasionally the wind would bring the salty aroma of the sea.

'You do not have to join us.' Demetra's face was still filled with the weight of her grief.

'I didn't know her,' Ruth replied, 'but I feel I want to be there.'

Demetra flopped onto the swing-seat on the farmhouse porch. 'So strong for so long, for everyone relying on me, and tonight I feel as if I cannot go on.'

'It'll pass. We all feel like that sometimes. And if we didn't, we wouldn't know what it was like to feel on top.' Ruth sat next to her.

'You are strong. I see a quality in you . . . it is hard to define . . . but it has the colour blue.' Demetra peered deeply into Ruth's eyes, then looked away with a smile. 'I am sorry. I have strange ways.'

'I think you're under a lot of pressure. It must be difficult, trying to manage this community, keep these women safe, while all those powerful people have been trying to close you down.'

'It has been a difficult road. The world has not been safe for women for a long time. Three years after my grandmother walked the many miles from Athens to find a safe place, she was raped and murdered by a gang of men building a road. It was not about sex. It was about control. They did not like what she was doing here, and wanted to punish her for it. Eventually, my mother took over the running of our community. She died when I was twenty, beaten to death on the hillside here. Her murderer was never caught.' The moonlight illuminated the defiance in her features. 'I fear my own end will be the same. But if we do not stand and fight for what we believe in, then nothing will ever change. And change always demands sacrifice.'

Ruth's owl flapped onto a perch on a tree in the courtyard. Demetra eyed it curiously, as if she could see its true nature.

'I try to understand the patterns of life, but it makes so little sense. The world would be a better place without the brutality, and the hatred and suspicion, the desire for money and power. Everyone knows that, yet we embrace this sour existence. We are condemned prisoners cheering as we walk to the gallows.' She smiled sadly. 'Why do we want to live in a world without magic?'

'The world can be changed. You're doing your piece—'

'How small and ineffectual it is. I could not save Roslyn. In the end, what have I achieved?'

As Demetra went to meet Lou, the American woman, who was approaching carrying a candle, she looked diminished somehow, worn down by grief and the demands of the life she had chosen. Ruth's heart went out to her.

'We're ready,' said Lou.

The women had gathered just beyond the courtyard, all dressed in white flowing dresses that glowed spectrally in the moonlight. There were twelve including Demetra, each carrying a candle. Hidden beneath a shroud, Roslyn lay on a wooden stretcher amongst them.

'We welcome Ruth into our celebrations,' Demetra said to them. 'And this *is* a celebration, for when we move from this harsh world into a better place, it should be recognised with ecstasy.'

A large wine flask hung from each woman's waist. In turn the women took a long draught and made a solemn speech.

'My name is Alicia. My arm was broken in three places, but I survive. I wish my sister Roslyn well, for she is now beyond our pain.'

'My name is Melantha. It took six months before I could look at myself in a mirror, but I survive. I wish my sister Roslyn well, for she is now beyond our pain.'

When the final woman had spoken, Demetra offered Ruth her own wine flask. 'Drink deep. Experience the joy of detachment from this world.'

Ruth swallowed a mouthful of wine and was surprised by its potency. It was not like any wine she had ever tasted before.

Six of the larger women shouldered the stretcher and a slow procession set off up the hillside towards the olive groves. The flapping of Ruth's owl disturbed her, but when she tried to see the cause of the commotion she noticed the lights of a vehicle making its way across the dark landscape in the direction of the compound. Though a commonplace sight, Ruth felt oddly uneasy.

The women began to sing a quiet, lilting song that contributed to the dreamlike atmosphere. As they walked, they took repeated draughts of wine, not for the flavour but to get drunk.

'The Cult of Souls has been a part of our culture in Greece for thousands of years,' Demetra began. 'They called us a mystery religion, and one of the mysteries we taught was the strength of the true, primal being that lies at the heart of all of us. The real person, the rider of the mare that is our body.'

'The soul,' Ruth said.

Demetra smiled. 'That word has too many connotations. It is a mystery at the heart of a mystery. Our beliefs underpinned, and preceded, the Orphic Mysteries, and Gnosticism, and even Christianity. Some trace it back to the Osiris Cult of ancient Egypt. They believed the spirit existed in three forms. The *akh* was the form the dead existed in when they travelled to the Underworld. The *ba* was a bird released at death that contained the individual's personality and character. And the *ka* was a double that could be released in dreams, but was finally released at death.'

'And you're all part of this cult?'

'No one is forced to join. There is no religious text, no rules and regulations. At its heart is one simple idea: that what is inside us is stronger than our bodies and can go on for ever. It is not about any religion, rather an idea, just an idea. And we believe that by freeing ourselves from the body, and the care and worry that come with it, we can access that deeper being and through it glimpse the true nature of Existence.'

Ruth smiled. 'So get drunk—'

'And dance, and sing, and leave the world behind.'

As they moved into the dense trees, Ruth had the strangest sensation that the women's song was now accompanied by the playing of a flute, but it faded into the background whenever she strained to hear it clearly. Golden lights moved high in the branches, like will-o'-the-wisps, and Ruth realised it was the winged figures they had puzzled and argued over earlier.

'There's magic here,' Ruth said firmly.

Demetra looked troubled. 'I would so like to believe . . . Everything is changing so quickly that I no longer know what is true any more. It began yesterday. We noticed the olives were bigger and more bountiful than ever

150

before. The wine was stronger. The water and soil tasted and smelled richer.' She shook her head. 'And now those . . . beings. Perhaps it is just a trick . . .'

As they progressed further into the trees, the scent of the vegetation on the warm night air became almost hallucinogenic; or perhaps it was simply the effect of the wine. Ruth felt a sense of well-being rise up from her belly; her fingers tingled; the hairs on her neck stood erect.

The sensation took the edge off her profound longing for Church. When she considered it, the sacrifice she had made had been almost physically painful, and the best she could do was to try to keep it out of her mind. That was the most difficult thing of all, for he was always there, on the edge of her thoughts.

The tiny flying figures swooped low, dipping in and out of the branches, following then leading the procession. Every now and then, Ruth thought she glimpsed movement away in the dark, neither beast nor man but something in-between, yet oddly unthreatening.

What is happening here? she asked herself.

Finally they came to a large clearing. Roslyn's shrouded body was placed in the centre and then the women stripped off their white dresses unselfconsciously. Ruth felt no pressure to join them. She sat back against an olive tree and watched as they played music on an old CD player, and danced and drank and sang. The heady, languorous atmosphere was punctuated by moments of grief when they would start to cry softly, before the dance and the music took them away again on an upward spiral of euphoria.

This is very strange, Ruth thought to herself. *I feel as if I'm here and not here at the same time.*

The wine went straight to her head, and at some point she fell asleep. When she came round, she felt as if she was still in the throes of a dream. The women were lost to ecstasy, dancing in such a frenzied manner that they no longer appeared to know where they were or who they were. Their whirl reminded Ruth of film she had seen of voodoo rituals, wild limbs, thrashing hair, rolling eyes. They left trails in the air behind them, and in her detached state, Ruth had to accept she was as drunk as the rest of them.

Strangely she found she was lying on a bed of ivy that had not been there before, and when she squinted she thought she could make out snakes of blue fire like the ones she had seen earlier sinuously weaving across the ground.

'*Come to me.*'

The voice was deep and resonant like the call of an animal and she

151

couldn't tell if it was real or in her head. She pulled herself to her feet and moved into the trees. A shape circled her, and another, and a third, but however much she looked she could only catch impressions, like the flash of a shadow on a summer wall.

Lost in her dream, Ruth hurried through the trees until she eventually stopped and turned, and was confronted by a face that made her black out for an instant. She saw red eyes and fur and horns, but the rest was lost to shadow.

'Do you know my name?' it said in the deep, throaty rumble she had heard before.

Ruth tried to see who was talking to her, but every time she focused her head swam. 'No,' she replied in a voice that appeared to be coming from somewhere else.

'I am a lover of peace and a lover of madness. On the boundary between the living and the dead, you will find me. I am of the trees, and of fertility, and of destruction. I was ancient even when the Greeks worshipped me in the grove of Simila, strange and alien to them. In Mycenae, they knew me as DI-WO-NI-SO-JO, and many other names were mine in the time before that time. I am not the oldest thing, but I am one of them.'

'What do you want with me?' The god terrified and entranced her at the same time.

'You are favoured by the oldest things – the mark of my kin is upon you.' Ruth realised he was talking about the brand of Cernunnos she carried. 'You have a part to play in the great, unfolding pattern. But first you must give in to the madness and the ecstasy to unleash your hidden self.'

Ruth tried to back away. It felt as if there was a field of electricity around the god that made her heart pound and her anxiety and excitement rise in equal measures.

'Drink.'

A wine sack was thrust into her hands. Though she fought it, she was unable to resist and when the warm, powerfully intoxicating liquid ran down her throat it felt more like a drug than wine. Her vision fractured; colours shifted, glowing with heat and life; sounds boomed and echoed in unnatural ways. Music swelled around her and she felt instantly aroused.

'What's happening to me?' Her hands went to her belly where a heat was rising.

'See my little brother? He brings the fear of wild places and the joy of congress.'

Ruth caught sight of a distorted image, goat legs, human torso, animal

152

horns, an erect phallus. 'The horned one,' she gasped, recalling her Craft. 'Pan . . .'

Another figure slipped by furtively, sleek, seal-skinned, with a dangerous grin and glowing eyes, gone before she could comprehend more.

'The oldest thing in the land,' the god growled. 'We three stand beside and behind you as the pattern unfolds. Know you this, and act accordingly.'

'What am I supposed to do?' Ruth asked desperately. 'I don't understand any of this!'

The god cocked his head, listening. 'Too late now!' he boomed. 'Great danger approaches. Run. Run!'

2

Darkness so intense, Veitch could see nothing. Thin air, cold and dusty-dry and filled with the stench of decay. With an effort he overcame the slowly fading paralysis that had infected him since he had been dragged down into the Underworld, and tore off the shroud that was clinging to the lower half of his face.

Tentatively, he felt around. Bones rattled next to him, along with some minor grave goods. Stone was hard against his back, on either side, just above his face. Breathing slowly to remain calm, he realised he was in a box, perhaps a tomb. The sword was still with him – he could feel its dark whispers in his head – but there was not enough room to use it.

'Miller!' he called out. Then: 'Etain?' There was no response. 'All right. You're on your own.'

An image of being buried far underground crashed into his mind and claustrophobia swelled in his chest. 'Stay calm, you wanker,' he snarled. He rammed the balls of his fists against the stone over him. The pain reduced the constriction growing in his throat, but there was no movement from the lid of the box. The dull thud told him that there was no space above him, and despair curled in his stomach.

Quickly, he hit out at the four sides. The wall to his left rang hollow. With relief, he felt along the edge and was convinced there was a join: a door of some kind.

Forty minutes later, the stone burst outwards and a thin, icy light leached in. His fists were torn and bloodied and the mess that had been his left elbow protruded from his tattered shirt. But the pain was already lost beneath his fierce determination to get to Ruth before the Libertarian did; the possibility that he might already be too late was instantly rejected.

Letting his eyes grow accustomed to the light, he swung his legs out of the shattered door before a rush of vertigo forced him to grip onto the edge. The ground was at least fifty feet below, at the foot of a wall of coffin-sized tombs that reached another hundred feet above his head. Stretching out before him in the vast cavern was a monumental necropolis of tombs and mausoleums constructed of dull, grey stone or set into the rocky walls, slumbering under an oppressive atmosphere of dust and age and uneasy stillness. Yet for all its enormity, Veitch knew it was only the suburbs of the Grim Lands. What lay beyond this crumbling fringe of the Underworld was a place as immeasurable and unknowable as death.

On the crepuscular limits of the cavern, he could just make out the tunnel that led to those Grey Lands, now sealed by iron gates that reached from floor to roof. No chance of hiding away amongst the vast ranks of the silent dead, who had accepted him in a way he had never wholly experienced in the living world.

'Miller!' he called out. 'Etain?' The way his words dropped like stones across those silent buildings unsettled him, and he recalled the dry, grasping hands that had pulled him into the Underworld; not the dead, but something stronger and more dangerous. He resolved to remain as quiet and silent as that place.

With an effort, he found handholds and deep cracks in the tomb-wall that would allow him to climb down. Pausing to check the tombs on either side, above and below for signs of movement, he began his descent without looking down.

The cracked, ancient flagstones of the street between the towering mausoleums were covered with a fine layer of dust. Most of it was undisturbed, but there was a trail where he had been brought to the tomb-wall. Following it, he came to a large area of tracks and scuffs on the edge of a frozen river that bisected the cavern. One trail led up a slope towards the tunnel where he had been brought in. Another went to the river's edge.

Cautiously, Veitch approached the ice, white with hoar-frost, and wondered why it was frozen when the air temperature was well above freezing. The query came and went as he put one tentative boot on the ice. It took his weight without cracking, and he strode out a few feet, noticing that he left footprints in the frost. There were no other prints, so Miller had not been taken across to the far bank.

As he scuffed the ice with his boot, he noticed something glimmering in the dark depths beneath. Dropping to his knees, he frantically scrubbed the frost away to reveal a surface like glass. And just beneath it lay Miller, floating, his body unmoving but his eyes wide and alive and pleading.

The ice flew up in diamond-hard shards as Veitch repeatedly rammed the sword down, the black flames hissing as they met the cold. After ten minutes he was slick with sweat, but he had broken through almost six inches and the water beneath had begun to seep through the ice. Miller continued to drift around mysteriously in one spot, not drowning, un-moving, alert and awake. An almost pathetic gratitude was etched in his features.

Gentler strokes shattered the final half-inch, and Veitch carved a big enough hole to drag Miller out. When Veitch immersed his hands in the water, a dreamy lethargy came over him. He fought its seduction and it faded when he had Miller lying on the ice.

Veitch shook him roughly. 'Come on, you fuck-wit. We haven't got time for this.'

Life gradually returned to Miller's limp body. A smile spread across his face. 'You saved me. Thank you.'

'Stop talking. Don't do anything but follow me. We're going to find Etain and the others and get to Ruth.'

'You love her.'

'I told you to shut the fuck up.' Veitch clipped Miller roughly around the ear.

As he ran back up the bank, he realised Miller wasn't behind him. He turned to see Miller poised on the edge of the frozen river, one foot hovering above dry land.

'What are you doing?' Veitch called.

Miller was disoriented. 'I don't remember who put me in there, but . . . there are words in my head. A warning. If I walk again on the land I—'

'Just do it!' Veitch snapped.

Startled into action, Miller put his foot down. In that instant, a sonor-ous tolling echoed across the still city of the dead. The bell's tones had a toxic effect on Veitch's emotions, poisoning him with the first wash of dread.

Miller was locked in place, terrified. Veitch ran back and grabbed him. 'Run!'

'What's that bell?'

'Run!' Veitch dragged Miller up the bank and thrust him so hard he almost fell. Within seconds, they were both sprinting up the steep street towards the tunnel leading out of that place.

At a crossroads they spied a collection of statues, apparently ancient from the thick layer of dust that blanketed them. From one of them stared a pair of unblinking eyes that Veitch recognised instantly.

Brushing away the dust revealed Etain's charred, damaged face, the beauty still evident to him in what remained. 'Thank God. I was worried I'd have to leave without you, darlin',' Veitch muttered.

Etain was in the same kind of trance that had gripped Miller, but as Veitch pulled her cold form into an embrace, she gradually came round. Her eyes made a mechanical movement towards Veitch when he planted a kiss on her cheek.

Miller watched queasily until distant echoes distracted him. 'Ryan, hurry! People are coming. Lots of people!'

'Give me a hand, then.'

Sickened, Miller helped Veitch scrub the dust from Branwen, Tannis and Owein, and from their otherworldly mounts. 'Can't we leave them?' he said anxiously. Further down the street, past the towering mausoleums, the sound of many feet could now clearly be heard.

'You don't leave your mates!' Veitch snapped.

Miller watched the dead Brothers and Sisters of Spiders clamber onto their horses and felt a twinge of concern for Veitch's sanity.

The swarm rounded onto their street at the foot of the slope near the frozen river, hundreds of grey bodies, more joining them every second. They were naked and hairless, their limbs lithe and powerful, but their skin sickly and purple-veined. Their yellow eyes were fierce. They looked like a tribe of relict humans, barely human at all, and they carried as weapons human thigh bones that had been picked clean.

Miller was rooted to the spot, one hand half-raised to his mouth. Veitch caught the back of his shirt and dragged him into action. They ran up the street, the dry air searing their throats. The tolling bell continued to chime, and the sound of feet became thunder, yet their pursers were eerily silent.

The tunnel was already in sight when Veitch accepted they were not going to make it. More grey figures were beginning to emerge from side streets ahead.

'There's no end to them,' Miller whined.

The Brothers and Sisters of Spiders were already at the tunnel mouth. Etain reined in her mount and drove it back down the slope, trampling the grey men under hoof; they died as silently as they lived.

But then the wave of pursuers closed off the street ahead, washing down towards Veitch and Miller as quickly as the ones approaching from behind.

'What are we going to do?' Miller sobbed.

'Two options: die or live.' Veitch gripped his sword in both hands, comforted by the flaring black flames.

Across the city came a loud voice, the words alien, with an unreal quality that jumbled Veitch's thoughts. Blood trickled from his ears.

On the top of a tower on the other side of the frozen river stood a figure radiating such power that Veitch knew it could only be a god. The figure swam as if in a heat haze until Veitch's mind settled on a form it could comprehend: sable robes and a pale, bald head. Even at that distance, Veitch could tell the flesh was covered with the black markings that signified control by the Army of the Ten Billion Spiders.

Contemptuous, he turned back to the fray, neither knowing nor caring what god might rule that twilit world bordering the land of the dead.

Black lightning crackled as Veitch tore into the rushing enemy with his sword. Heads were cleaved, limbs fell away and thin blood the colour of gruel splattered across the dust.

The tunnel to the upper world was tantalisingly close, but the grey swarm appeared endless and not even the ferocity of the Brothers and Sisters of Spiders could dent their numbers.

And over it all the god of the underworld continued to wail his song of despair and decay and the winding down into nothing.

3

Ruth staggered amongst the olive trees, trying to fight off the heady, mesmerising intoxication of the otherworldly wine. Every sense was heightened: the rough touch of the bark under her fingers, the aromas of the verdant grove, the crashing through the undergrowth that faded in and out and was impossible to pinpoint.

Fighting to control her thoughts had little effect for they moved like the tides under their own power, focusing on each new fascination before flashing to a distant memory or fleeting notion. The three mysterious beings that had come to her, neither human nor animal, but rather some hybrid representation of an ancient, eternal power – had that been real? Were they still around?

Further off amongst the trees, pale wraiths flitted. No, not ghosts, she realised, but the women who had accompanied her to that place. Dancing naked, filled with abandon and the joy of life. Ruth came to a halt, smiling, feeling an unusually affecting bond of sisterhood. Drifting dreamily.

A jolt, like a lightning flash.

Not dancing, running.

Ruth shook her head to clear the suffocating blanket. Sounds rose through the haze. In the distance, the CD was still playing its loop of trance beat; and surfacing through it, a scream, two, cries of fear and anger. Ruth ran towards the confusion.

The women tore through the undergrowth, searching for cover. They were not alone. Men, swarthy from labouring under the sun, bearded and heavy with muscle, pursued them, calling and barking and sneering. They carried shotguns and pickaxe handles. Some laughed at the exhilaration of the hunt.

The lights Ruth had seen making their way slowly up the road to the compound. The constant threat of violence from the men who had murdered Roslyn. Her death had been like a chunk of raw meat thrown to a voracious pack. They wanted more. They could no longer accept the terrible threat of twelve women who were determined to live the kind of life they wanted to live.

A thick-set man who smelled of beer caught Alicia by the arm and roughly threw her to the ground at his feet. She was completely defence-less, but he still decided to hit the softness of her face with the iron-hard, use-smooth handle of his axe. Horrified, Ruth heard bone break and saw a gout of blood spatter down Alicia's naked chest. The man smiled at this, as though he had found something small and amusing. He hit her again. Alicia no longer moved.

Ruth threw herself at the attacker, clawing and punching and tearing at his hair. He was surprised at first, but then with one flick of the wrist he brought the axe-handle up into Ruth's face. She saw stars, fell back.

The man barked something at her in Greek, but though the language was alien, his meaning would have been understood by any woman anywhere in the world. With a nicotine-stained grin, he raised the handle, ready to strike.

'No!' Demetra's cry was like thunder.

The man stopped mid-blow and glanced towards her. In the trees, Ruth saw other women and their pursuers also come to a halt.

'No!' Demetra cried again, and this time frantic wings flapped in the branches above them, though no birds flew there.

Demetra's face terrified Ruth. Little sign remained of the woman who had welcomed Ruth into the community. The wine had consumed her, but that was only part of the story. Within her features, or overlying them, or underneath them, was the essence of the god of the groves, madness and terror and sex and death all mingled into one.

She began to scream, then trill, the notes building and shaping into a hypnotic song, and as she sang she tore at her hair until it became a wild mane, and she threw her head this way and that, and writhed in an ecstatic dance.

Ruth's attacker was mesmerised, as were all the men poised with their weapons. The women began to mimic Demetra, subtle jerks becoming a dance they all shared; a hive-mind, lost to passion.

As the song became a howl of fury, Demetra launched herself at the stunned man standing over Ruth. Clinging onto him with her arms and legs like a wild animal, she sank her teeth into the meat of his cheek and tore it away.

As the man screamed, desperately trying to tear Demetra off, Ruth saw the white of cheekbone and the dark inside his mouth. Demetra would not be deterred. She was lost to a whirlwind of teeth and nails, the man unable to lift his axe-handle in the face of it. His last expression was of faint surprise that a frail woman could have brought him to this, and then his features disintegrated before Demetra's assault. Her nails rammed into his eye sockets, bursting the orbs. Her teeth ripped open his throat and she gulped back the crimson spray.

By the time Ruth attempted to restrain Demetra the man was dead. Even then Demetra did not stop. She tore off his shirt and ripped into his bulging belly, tearing out the pale intestines and whipping them into the air.

'Stop!' Ruth cried, but the wide, white eyes that peered out of the bloodstained face through a curtain of dripping hair were feral, barely human at all.

Her hallucinogenic intoxication made the scene and the sounds all the more horrific. Fighting to remain calm, Ruth lurched back into the depths of the grove, but there was no peace anywhere. The naked women hunted the men like a wolf pack, bringing them down as they ran, disembowelling them or ripping off limbs with ferocious strength.

Ruth slumped at the foot of a tree, covering her ears, but the hideous sounds continued as the pale figures flashed back and forth amongst the dark trunks like strobe images at a club.

After a while it was easy to believe that the sounds were not coming from humans at all, and that gave her some comfort, but the noises went on much longer than she would have expected. Finally, the pleading became faint whimpering, became silence.

When she was sure it was over, Ruth steeled herself and made her way past the piles of gore to where Demetra sat. Her breasts, belly and thighs were stained red, and in her lap was the head of the man who had murdered Alicia, torn off in the final moments of her frenzy. The madness had just started to fade from her eyes, but the presence of the god of the groves still hung over everything.

A flash of white and brown in the branches startled Ruth. It was her owl-familiar, but in the heightened atmosphere it appeared oddly changed. As it descended, it changed more, until a man with disturbing owl features stood before her.

For a moment, Ruth was struck mute, unable to tell if this was another hallucination. 'I saw you like this before,' she began hesitantly, 'in a dream.'

'No dream.'

'This is how you really look?'

'Nothing has a *real* look. Only what lies inside remains unchanged. All else is fluid.'

'What are you?'

'I come from the oldest things in the land, as does the Craft that gives you your strength. Of all the Brothers and Sisters of Dragons, you are closest to the true beginnings and the higher powers.'

His voice had a jarring edge that was always on the brink of becoming the screech of an owl. Ruth was unnerved by him, but comforted, too.

'I have always served your line,' he continued, 'bringing power, and knowledge, and communication from the forces that shape you.' He turned to Demetra. 'Once, long ago, I aided one of her ancestors, another Sister of Dragons, cut down in the snow too soon, and then reborn, as all things are.'

'What happened here tonight?'

'You do not know?' He stared at her with those wide owl eyes. 'You are an anomaly in the world the Void has created, as are your Brothers and Sisters. Wherever you travel you break the Mundane Spell. You wake the magic. You bring back old forces, and wild ways, and exhilaration, and wonder, and terror, and all the things that cannot abide the way of the Void. And this day you have awakened the Liberator, one of the oldest things, but not the oldest, who was known by many names, amongst them—'

'Dionysus,' Ruth interjected.

'He loves peace, and will not accept anything that prevents it. And he will not tolerate the injustices of men, for he loves women, as all the oldest things do, for they are givers of life, the source of all power in this world.'

'I brought him back?'

'And his brother Pan. Magic lives, here, now, in the groves and on the mountaintops and by the lakes. The Void's power is weakening. It still seeks to maintain control, but it can only do so through the Mundane Spell.'

'But the spell is shattering—'

'And soon the illusion can no longer be maintained. And then it will be forced to confront you. I come now with a warning. Your days of being tolerated are long gone. Threats lie everywhere. You must be on your guard at all times.'

'But you'll be here to help me, won't you?'

'Of course. The oldest things in the land watch over you, Sister of Dragons. For these are the End-Times—'

Ruth was taken aback. 'The End?'

'All that has happened has been leading to this moment.'

'You talk as if the "oldest things in the land" want the end to happen?'

The owl-man did not answer.

'Tell me!'

'Listen to the message of the Cult of Souls. Understand the *Gnosis*. In the rites carried out in the name of Dionysus, the truth lies.'

Demetra rose to her feet, holding the head by its hair. Comprehension slowly returned to her face. 'Something is wrong,' she said, puzzled. 'I can hear him whispering to me . . . the god of the groves . . . and his brother . . . Pan-ic . . . Panic! Something is coming!' Her words ended on a shrill note of anxiety.

In the pale, eerie eyes of the owl-man, a moment of puzzlement rose briefly. 'I sense . . . an empty space,' he said with troubled curiosity. 'Where something should be, there is nothing.'

The blade burst from his chest with a liquid sucking sound. Trying to make sense of this further strange occurrence, he examined it even as life drained from him. The blade was twisted and then yanked brutally upwards through his sternum to break free from his collar bone. The owl-man's eyes rose up, the pupils froze and he slid to the ground to reveal his murderer.

'You know he ate mice?' The Libertarian wiped the blade on the owl-man's back. 'Nasty habit.'

Ruth turned and ran. Careering down the slope towards the farmstead, she bounced off trees, skidded, tripped and fought to keep her balance. To her left, there was a sudden bright fluttering as scores of the small golden figures soared in frantic flight, up high and then away over the sun-baked landscape.

There was no sound of pursuit, and that unnerved her even more. If she could get to the kitchen she could pick up a knife, and she was sure she had seen an old shotgun somewhere. Perhaps Demetra had left the keys in the jeep and she could just drive hard and fast out of there.

She skidded out of the grove and sprinted towards the lights of the farmstead. Passing the well-tended herb garden, she had a clear view of the grounds. No surprises. She glanced back to find the Libertarian right

161

behind her. His fist smashed into the back of her head and she hit the ground hard.

Dust filled her mouth. Blood splattered from her temple and her head rang. She kicked out at the Libertarian, but he caught her ankle and flipped her over, sitting astride her and pinning her arms back.

Ruth glared at him.

'No clichés? No "do your worst"? Or are you hoping I won't realise you're working on one of your conjure-thoughts?' The Libertarian punched Ruth in the face. Blood ran into her mouth. 'Pain makes it very difficult to concentrate, doesn't it? Best not to try.'

Ruth looked into his eyes and saw that she was going to die. A surprising calmness and clarity suffused her. There was no hatred or anger, no regret, just an acceptance that felt like a burden being lifted from her shoulders. She thought of Church and wished him well, of Shavi and Laura; even, surprisingly, of Veitch.

Surprised by her reaction, puzzlement crossed the Libertarian's face, but only fleetingly. 'Knowing you as I do, I should have guessed you wouldn't give me any pleasure at the end,' he muttered. He shrugged. 'For so long it was impossible to harm you or your dragon-brethren, but here at the source we are equals.'

He moved his hands to Ruth's throat and began to squeeze. 'You can fight,' he continued with irritation. 'You can cry. You can scream.'

Ruth smiled. 'We'll win. You know that.'

The Libertarian's face darkened. The grip on her throat tightened. Her breath faded and the pressure on her chest became unbearable. Stars flashed, trails of Blue Fire exploded, and then she was flooded by a dreamy warmth that signalled the end.

4

On the side of a deserted road on the Albanian-Greek border, Church was stung by a lone tear and a devastating sense of loss that he couldn't begin to explain. Tom leaned against a tree next to him, smoking and watching the flames dance in the campfire. Hunter slept – he had an ability to doze off anywhere – and Shavi meditated on the edge of the gloom. Laura had wandered away into the trees, complaining of boredom.

'If I decided to walk away tonight, what would you do?' Church asked.

'I'm not your keeper.'

'You act like it.'

'And you act like a hopeless, besotted, soft-headed fool, as you have from the moment I first met you.'

'I can't carry on doing this without Ruth. I spent so long looking for some kind of meaning in my life and she's it. I always thought that was a stupid, romantic idea – that in the end it all came down to one person. But it's true.'

There was a long silence during which Tom exhaled blue smoke, his eyes closed. Eventually he said, 'The Fool finds wisdom on the road of life, and in your thick way you seem to have stumbled across it. Everything comes down to love. When we're young, it's all we want. When we're comfortably married and the routine has set in, we yearn for its exhilarating rush. When we're not getting it, we seek out money, sex or power to try to fill the gap.' He eyed Church askance. 'Love drives everyone insane. It makes the best of us do wonderful things and terrible things. Yes, you're right – it's the root of everything. It's the magic and the curse of Existence.'

'You seem to have survived pretty well without it.'

'That shows how much you know.' His spectacles caught the light of the campfire so his eyes could not be seen. 'I left my love behind near eight hundred years ago. There won't be another. Now don't go asking me any more stupid questions about that.'

Church looked towards the south. Would it really be so bad if he left the world to the Void? People would continue to live their lives, find love, have children, the sop that made the rest of it bearable. He could reach Ruth faster on his own. They had been forced to take detour after detour to avoid the net of the security services, hiding out for days in damp, stinking warehouses, going nights without sleep, constantly changing vehicles.

As he weighed his decision, Shavi staggered up to the campfire, ashen-faced. 'I fear . . .' he began, choking back the words. 'I fear something has happened to Ruth.'

5

Ruth's hair was stirred occasionally by the light night breeze so that it gave the illusion of life. Beside her, the Libertarian sat in the dust, studying her face, pondering on what he saw there. He scooped up a handful of the dry earth and slowly let it dribble out of the bottom of his fist.

'There is nothing left for me here,' he said eventually. 'Without you, the Brothers and Sisters of Dragons cannot achieve anything meaningful.

Indeed, this is the beginning of their end.' Throwing the remainder of the earth away with an incipient anger that puzzled him, he added, 'Back to the Otherworld it is, then. There are cities to raze, and genocide to complete. My days will be pleasingly full. No more of this sickening rat-hole. Good riddance to it.'

He made to get up, and then paused to study Ruth's face again. After a few seconds, he kissed her quickly on the lips, and then marched away without once looking back.

6

From the rumbling, soil-and-pebble-raining entrance to the Underworld spewed Veitch, filled with all the fury of a devil let loose from hell. His sword blazed with the blackest flames, and he was covered with the grey gore of two hundred brutal deaths. Miller was dragged along in his wake, struck dumb by terror and the horrors he had witnessed. Flanking them were the Brothers and Sisters of Spiders, weapons and hoofs still drip-ping.

'Get me to her,' Veitch barked.

There was only a momentary pause before Etain swept him up onto her horse, and then they were off on a wild ride across the Greek countryside, beneath implacable stars and a cold moon, along still-hot roads, through trees that tore at their hair and skin, across dusty, rock-strewn slopes, until they finally arrived at the still puddle of light that was the compound.

Veitch instantly recognised the motionless form, carefully laid out in a cruciform, and threw himself from the horse before it had come to a halt. Sprinting to Ruth's side, he kneeled and checked her vitals. She looked as if she was sleeping.

The reality of her death took a moment to break through the barrier of his hopes. As he ran his fingers through her curls, and stroked the pale curve of her cheek, he recalled the first time he had seen her, when they were still naive about their own potential and the future course of their lives, and he remembered how stupid he had felt, like some animal rising up out of the mud to look at a higher form of life. Ruth was always *better*, not just cleverer or wiser, or more experienced than a South London thug like him, but she was more moral, with a profound emotional awareness and a heart as big as the world. Sometimes he had been shocked that the others hadn't seen it. It was his secret, their bond.

Over the intense, dangerous, uplifting months they had spent together during that Age of Misrule when the gods first made their move, he had come to realise there was an emptiness at the heart of his life that only she could fill. For her, he could strive for better things. Without her he was back at the gates of hell.

Too *grandiose*? That was a Church word, but Church understood those things as much as he understood Ruth. No, not too grandiose. A pure and simple truth.

Veitch took her hand and made his fifth futile fumble for a pulse. And then he cried for the first time in two thousand years and more, silently at first, and then with juddering sobs, as all his pathetic dreams leaked out and he was left with nothing but self-loathing and the harsh realisation that he was damned.

Miller's hand fell on his shoulder. 'Let me help.' The words were so gentle they were almost an exhalation.

'She's dead, you fucking idiot.'

'I might be able to do something. I don't normally. Once they're gone it's best to leave them that way. But . . . it doesn't look like it's been long. Let me help.'

Wiping away his tears and snot, Veitch allowed Miller to pull him gently away. He stood next to Etain, still in the saddle, and rested one hand on her cold thigh.

Miller squatted next to Ruth and pressed both hands on her breast above her heart. Bowing his head, he grew still. For long moments, Veitch watched, transfixed by grief. Just as he was about to start raging at Miller for his stupidity, he became aware of a faint blue light that cast flickering shadows with no obvious source. As Miller continued to meditate, blue sparks fizzed from his fingertips and the air became suffused with the odour of burned iron. Veitch realised that the light was coming from within Miller. A blue glow appeared at Miller's midriff, increasing in intensity until his stomach and lower back became transparent, though Veitch realised he was not looking at muscle and bone but through them to another plane entirely. And there Veitch saw a serpentine movement like a blue shadow against a brighter glow, coiling gently as Miller increased the force that flowed into Ruth. It looked for all the world like a tiny Fabulous Beast nestling deep in the heart of Miller's being.

Veitch barely dared draw a single breath. Finally the light went out as if a switch had been thrown, and there was only silence.

Veitch didn't move. Miller rocked back onto his heels, covering his face, exhausted. It had failed, like everything else in Veitch's life had failed; why did he ever dare hope for anything when there was only disappointment?

A tremor ran through Ruth. It could have been the night breeze stirring

165

her clothes, but there was another, and then another, and then finally she pushed herself up on her elbows, blinking.

Veitch's jaw sagged, and then a barely believing smile leaped to his lips. He whispered to himself, 'And the crowd went wild.'

'I dreamed I was in such a misty place,' Ruth said. 'Why do I feel like I've got a hangover?'

A rush of exhilaration filled Veitch and for a moment he thought he would cry again, for joy this time. It would have been the easiest thing in the world to rush over and sweep her into his arms, but it would not amount to anything, he knew that. He allowed himself one secret grin in the dark and said, 'Looks like you've got some uses after all, Miller.'

Ashen-faced and shaking, Miller came over. He was smiling. 'You don't fool me with your act, Ryan. I can see how much you love her,' he said quietly.

'Bollocks. What do you know?'

'I know that somebody who shows so much care for another person that he would risk everything to save her can't be as bad as he pretends.'

'If you go on thinking that, you're making the kind of mistake that could get you killed. I've hurt a lot of people to get here. I'm the bad guy, Miller. I know it and I don't care.'

Miller continued to smile knowingly. It unnerved Veitch, so he went over to Ruth who was sifting through her woolly thoughts.

'Did the Libertarian do this?' Veitch asked.

'I think so . . . yes. I remember him strangling me.'

'You died, darlin'.'

Ruth's eyes widened.

'Whatever part of you matters went over to the Grey Lands. I've been there – it's not Club Med. You hang around for a bit before you move on to wherever you go after that.' He jerked a thumb towards Miller. 'He got to you in time.' Veitch's hands were trembling; he hid them behind his back.

Ruth's eyes narrowed. Something in his words or manner puzzled her. 'I remember what you used to be like, Veitch. It's coming back to me.'

Uncomfortably, he looked away to the east. 'Sun'll be up soon. We need to move. Those bastard spiders are going to be all over us now. Need to think . . . where to next? Fuck. I planned this really well.'

The landscape appeared to revolve around him, a vertigo-inducing moment that almost made his knees give way. When it came to a halt, the shadows had altered and were no longer fixed to the light sources, and there was an intense quality to the silence as though the landscape was listening. The Brothers and Sisters of Spiders, Miller, the compound buildings, all were gone.

'What the fuck—?' Veitch drew his sword, but the black flames were so subdued they were barely visible.

'Where are we?' Ruth looked round, disoriented. 'I don't recognise this place.'

'Knavery abounds. Why, you arc pouk-ledden.' The voice was filled with a sly humour. A second later the Puck appeared.

'What are you?' Veitch growled.

'My names are many, in many lands,' the Puck said with a sweeping bow. 'Call me Robin Goodfellow, but do not call me blackguard if you wish good fortune.'

'Watch him,' Ruth said to Veitch. 'He can't be trusted.'

'Night wanderers, you are,' Robin said slyly. 'And so, by my right, I mislead you. Or not. And therein lies the mischief, for you to divine.'

'You're not making any sense.' Veitch lowered his sword. 'Like all your bleedin' kind. Never saw you with the spiders, though.'

'Robin plays his own game. A long one.' From behind his back, he pulled a black box etched with gold-filigreed hieroglyphics. He offered it to Veitch.

'Is that . . . the Anubis Box?' Ruth asked with mounting anxiety. 'You can't give that to him! It's too powerful. It controls gods!'

Ruth lunged for the box, but her hands closed on thin air. The Puck was now curling round behind Veitch, the box held aloft. Veitch took it curiously.

'No!' Ruth said. 'I thought you were helping us!'

'Mischief does not follow a straight path.'

Veitch examined the box. It hummed in his hands as if it was alive, one of the objects, like his sword, that was nothing like it appeared to be. A thought struck him, and he looked to Ruth, who was thoroughly destabilised. 'Not happy for this to be in my hands? I could just open the box—'

'Don't!'

'Maybe you'd better come along and keep an eye on me, then. In the car, not tied up in the boot. But one wrong move and the lid comes off.'

Ruth's features grew flinty. 'I always thought there might still be a little spark of goodness buried in you somewhere. But there isn't. You're worthless. And if I ever get the chance to stop you, I will.'

'You'll fall for my charm sooner or later.' He turned back to the Puck, who was circling them like a hunting wolf. 'What am I supposed to do with this?'

'It will buy you passage in the most dangerous domain. Now go. More mischief awaits and . . . Robin is gone.'

Between blinks, Veitch and Ruth found themselves back in the compound where Miller shifted uncomfortably near the Brothers and Sisters of Spiders, unaware they had been anywhere.

Ruth eyed Veitch hatefully, but there was nothing he could do about that. She was still alive and that was all that mattered.

7

The sun rose red and raw behind the olive grove. Ruth watched the trees become stark black silhouettes against the scarlet, and tried to find a path through all that had happened that night.

The death of her familiar left a deep ache in her heart, compounded by fears for what it meant for the future. He had been a companion and an aide for so long she felt as bereft as if she had lost a friend, though there had been times when he had truly scared her.

Her encounter with Dionysus, Pan and the Puck frightened her, too. They were not like any of the other gods she had met – the 'oldest things', they called themselves. What did that mean and what did they want? There were so many questions, and so many threats at every turn, that she no longer had any idea what the real agenda was, or what her role in it should be.

Veitch was communicating in his creepy way with the Brothers and Sisters of Spiders, sending them on ahead. Now that he had the Anubis Box he was an even bigger threat; she had to stay with him. She hoped when it came to a head she could count on Miller, but he was almost childlike in his simplistic view of the world.

Movement alerted her to the women trudging down from the grove, naked, blood-stained and dazed. Ruth took Demetra's arm.

'Alicia is dead,' she said in a strained voice.

'I know.'

'We avenged her.' Demetra's face showed a dawning acceptance of power. She looked at her brown, blood-caked hands. 'It was horrible. But it was . . . strength. And defiance. What we discovered tonight . . . We will not be beaten again.' She closed her eyes and breathed deeply of the fresh dawn air. 'There was madness and death, and freedom and life. And we were at the heart of it. This night we awakened . . . to something else.'

'The whole world is awakening,' Ruth said. 'It can't stay the way it has been any longer.'

'You had something to do with what happened tonight.' Demetra searched Ruth's face. 'I do not know what. I do not know who you are, really.' She hugged Ruth warmly. 'But I thank you. And I thank you for all that I know you *will* do. But you must take care. I feel in my heart there is great danger ahead for you, and sacrifice.'

They held each other for a moment until Ruth sensed Veitch watching them. 'Time to move on,' he said.

'Where does your journey take you?' Demetra asked.

Ruth looked to Veitch, but his dark eyes gave nothing away.

chapter eight

the victorious city

1

The blue waters of the Mediterranean sparkled in the afternoon sun. At the rail of the cruiser, Veitch peered past the flecks of foam on the churning wake into the cool depths. Once, in a different life, he had seen mermaids swimming alongside his boat. That single glimpse had been a moment of transformation that opened him up to the infinite wonders of the universe, but sometimes he wished it had never happened; nothing had ever lived up to it since.

They were half an hour out of Paphos, heading south, and trying to make up for the time they had lost stealing a boat in a Greek harbour because the authorities had banned all charters to Cyprus. Another hour and a half to land, and then he could divest himself of the Anubis Box, which throbbed dully beneath his arm.

'Thinking of jumping?' Ruth had come up silently behind him.

'You wish.'

'I could make you, you know. My command of the Craft is getting stronger by the day. A powerful wind, a gentle nudge . . . over you go.'

'Do it,' he said flatly. He could feel her gaze heavy on him. She was struggling to comprehend his mood; he didn't really understand it himself.

She hesitated, then said, 'Miller told me how hard you tried to save my life.'

Veitch glared at Miller, who was sauntering in the sun next to the passenger lounge. He saw the murderous look in Veitch's eyes and darted inside. 'I might hate you lot, but I hate that Libertarian bastard even more. If he wants you dead, I want you alive.'

He could see in her eyes that she suspected the truth. Feeling raw and exposed, he turned back to the sea. 'Anyway, I was just paying you back. You could have killed me in London at your flat.'

'I try to be better than that.'

'You should have killed me. Tying me up . . . that was just stupid. Did you think I wouldn't get free and come after you again?'

'I thought it would buy us enough time to sort things out.' She paused thoughtfully. 'When you caught up with us in Cornwall and tried to kill yourself, and that power jumped from you to Church and me . . . what did it do? And why did you do it?'

'Because I wanted to see if the mermaids were still swimming.'

Fire lit her face at the thought that he was contemptuously dismissing her question, but she controlled herself. 'You're right, I should have killed you. All those people you've slaughtered, all the harm you've done . . . But the fact is, Ryan, despite all that, I still think of you the way you were when we first met. Someone who was selflessly trying to do their best. Someone who cared.' She weighed whether to continue, and then threw her caution aside. 'I remember a time we shared—'

'Stop it.'

She came up sharp at the emotion in his voice, and that stung him even more. He expected her to press harder, but instead she said, 'Just because you've given me my freedom, don't think I won't look for a way to trip you up.' The expression she presented was supposed to be challenging, but there was an odd note of uncertainty in her eyes.

'I expect it.'

She returned to Miller. Veitch stared back into the depths, but his mind was racing. He sensed deep currents moving in Ruth, and a strange new life within them, but he was afraid to examine them too closely for fear of disappointment.

2

The wind blasted down from the mountains with the cold threat of rain. Behind them, the lights of the Court of the Soaring Spirit had long been lost to the inky night. There were only the bleak, rising foothills of scrubby grassland, outcropping rocks and stunted, wiry trees.

Mallory led the way on horseback, with a lantern hanging from a staff attached to his saddle to guide them over the treacherous land. Sophie and Caitlin followed, heads bowed against the gale, and Jerzy took the rear on a small pony, frightened and jumpy.

Mallory kept one hand on his sword. The countryside all around the court was dangerous, and from the walls they had seen many of the Enemy's outriders and small, marauding groups. Tension ran high within the alleyways and inns, fuelled by the expectation that it was only a matter of time before the Enemy was at the gates. And what was the queen doing to protect them?

It was a question Mallory had asked himself – and Niamh. But as much as he had questioned her, and spied on her whenever he had the opportunity, she appeared honestly concerned about her subjects and the court's security. She made no attempt to stop them when they set out in search of the great library of Ogma, which Jerzy had heard about in the Hunter's Moon; indeed, she barely paid any heed to them.

'How much further?' he shouted above the wind.

Jerzy spurred his pony to Mallory's side. His frightened eyes were fixed on the dark. 'Something tracks us,' he whimpered. 'Oh, master, please deliver us safely. Oh, why come under cover of night? Why not in the beautiful light of day?'

'Because we're an easier target then.' Mallory followed Jerzy's gaze. Behind them, several dark shapes moved close to the ground, keeping pace with them. 'So, how far?'

'A mile, perhaps.'

Mallory beckoned Sophie to his side. 'Give us some cover. Just something to keep them occupied. Can you do that?'

'If you have to ask that, you really don't know what I'm capable of.' She flashed a grin.

'That's what I'm worried about.' Surprising her, he grabbed her cowl and pulled her in for a deep kiss. 'For luck,' he said.

'Not that I need it.'

'Not that you need it.'

She bowed her head for a second, and when she raised it her eyes had rolled back so that only the whites were visible. Her lips moved silently. An orgasmic shudder led to a moment of grace and then she gave a spent smile. 'I wouldn't hang around if I were you.'

Mallory beckoned to Caitlin, who had carried an air of sadness with her since they had left the Tower of the Four Winds. She smiled wanly and spurred her horse on.

Jerzy whimpered again as he indicated an undulating shadow moving up the hillside behind them. As it neared, they could see it was made up of a multitude of bodies: rats, fat and sinuous. A desperate hunger informed their rabid motion. Jerzy cried out and drove his pony as fast as it would carry him. The others followed, heads down into the wind. The rats surged towards whatever was tracking them, now the nearest source of food.

After about a mile, when the hillside was becoming increasingly rugged, Mallory reined in his horse. The way they had come was clear of any movement. That didn't mean the threat had gone, but Mallory recognised the opportunity for a breathing space.

'You enjoyed that,' he said to Sophie.

'It was invigorating.' She threw her cowl off and shook her hair so the wind caught it. 'The Craft works so well here. It's such a buzz.'

'A slight chance we could have ended up as the first meal break for your furry little helpers.'

'What's life without a little danger?'

'Safe?'

'You need to live a bit, Mallory. All my early years were safe. Middle-class home, middle of the road. But no meaning, in anything. The only time I started discovering what really mattered was when I threw all that in and left home. Travelling all over the country with a group of people all searching for the same thing.' She stretched and shivered with pleasure. 'You only discover the truth – about yourself, about the world – when you take risks.'

'The trouble with risks is it can go either way.' Mallory watched Jerzy gallop up to them from reconnaissance along the increasingly treacherous path.

'We are here,' he said with excited relief. 'Finally, sanctuary.'

Without Jerzy's explicit directions, they could easily have missed the entrance. Overgrown with dry, brown bramble and long yellow grass, almost obscured by fallen rock, there was only a dark passage disappearing into the hillside; it looked as if the library was retreating from the world.

Mallory's horse grew skittish as he led it down the tunnel of dense vegetation until they came to the front porch of a large stone building set into the hillside. Above the porch was a tower topped by a weather-vane in the shape of a dragon. Caitlin tethered the horses while Mallory hammered on the door.

A moment later it swung open to reveal a tall man in robes so white they appeared to gleam with their own light. There was the familiar moment of disconnection while his features swam, but they eventually settled into a high, artistic brow, piercing grey eyes and long black hair and a bushy beard, both streaked with silver.

'You don't know us—' Mallory began.

173

'I know who you are, Brother of Dragons. I know your Sisters.' He eyed Jerzy. 'I know you, and who you represent. And I know why you are here.'

'How could you?' Caitlin asked.

'I am Ogma, and my library contains records of all that has happened, and all that will happen, if one but knows where to look.'

'That must really ruin birthdays and Christmas.' Mallory had kept his hand on his sword, but there was no sense of threat coming off Ogma, just a calm wisdom that made him feel more secure than he had done in a long time.

'We hoped you would let us use your library,' Sophie said. 'And we would be grateful for any guidance you could give us.'

Ogma motioned for them to enter. 'Everything I have is given freely and without obligation.' He picked up a candelabrum from a table beside the door and led them into the gloomy interior.

The library stretched into the hillside, a warren of dusty rooms and corridors, niches and vast halls, festooned with strands of silky cobwebs and filled with shelf after shelf of books, parchments, maps and mysterious objects of glass and silver that moved their position between blinks.

The portentous atmosphere gave Sophie a fit of the giggles that she made a poor job of stifling. Jerzy, though, was at peace, gambolling beside them, his fixed grin for once matched by the joyful expression in his eyes.

As they moved amongst the stacks, Caitlin grabbed Mallory's arm and pointed. Shavi was examining a book, which, when opened, was only filled with light.

'Shavi!' Mallory called out. Uneasily, Shavi returned the book to the shelf and walked away.

'He cannot hear you,' Ogma said. 'What you see has already happened – or will happen, in your terms – and the same is true of many of the events you will witness in this place.'

'Then how do we know what *is* happening?' Caitlin asked.

'*You* do not.'

They entered a large reading room with several small tables set discreetly amongst the books, each with a small crystal lamp. Mallory had been thinking hard since they had entered the library, and said to Ogma, 'We were told the library contained all the knowledge there is. Is that correct?'

'It is.'

'And you know where that knowledge is and how it all fits together?'

'I do.'

'Then you can tell us where Math is, and the others. Where the Market of Wishful Spirit is. The location of the Extinction Shears.'

'That and more.'

'We need that information. Everything depends on it.'

Ogma smiled and Mallory thought instantly of his father. 'You are confusing knowledge, or wisdom, with the journey to achieve that wisdom. Both are separate, both equally important. For the journey is transformational, and is necessary to impart the power to use the wisdom once it is achieved. One without the other is worthless.'

'So find it yourself – that's what you're saying.'

'The key to your search is here and within your ability to locate.'

'But people could be dying while we waste time looking! All I'm asking is to cut a few corners—'

Sophie restrained Mallory with a hand on his arm. 'Everything valuable has to be earned. That's the lesson of the Craft. We can do this.'

'All right. But you'll give us some help if we ask the right questions?'

'Of course.' Ogma gestured expansively around his library. 'Open yourselves to Existence. It will help you.'

'Yeah, yeah,' Mallory muttered. 'No such thing as coincidence. I know the drill.'

While Jerzy sat next to the blazing fire, the others drifted off amongst the stacks in search of inspiration. Superficially it appeared a hopeless task – there were more volumes than they could examine in several lifetimes – but their instincts told them otherwise. What they had witnessed during the ritual in Math's tower still flickered across their deep unconscious with two words rising repeatedly – MAT and ANM.

Some of the books were in unknown languages that gradually became comprehensible the more Mallory scanned them. Others left him with inexplicable emotions, euphoria or dread, and he was forced to close them quickly.

Occasionally he would glimpse figures flitting amongst the stacks, ghosts of the past or future, some like wisps of smoke in a shaft of light, others unnervingly substantial, their feet dragging on the flags.

One, a chilling figure with a body constructed from twisted blackthorn and a face that appeared to be made from crushed and folded paper, paused then turned slowly to stare at him. Mallory sensed a threatening aura emanating from the creature. The paper shifted gradually into an expression that appeared to say, 'Perhaps we'll meet again, soon.'

Mallory hurried on.

After a while his attention was caught by a full-length mirror trimmed with ebony on a silver stand. It caught the torchlight in an unsettling way.

A legend was inscribed in gold on the top: *We are all books, our experiences writ large for everyone to read.*

Don't look in it, a voice in Mallory's head warned. He looked.

A sensation of falling came a second after he saw the reflection of a Mallory he did not recognise. Memories swam before his eyes. The cocky young man who thought the world couldn't touch him. Nights in the club, the music vibrating through his bones. The rushing joy that only came before you realised troubles might wait just over the horizon. And then the hard men who had taught him a hard lesson. The realisation that some choices are impossible, but you have to make them anyway, and the price is etched on your soul. He saw the blood on his hands and relived the feeling that nothing would ever be right again. He'd come to terms with what the sickening criminal thugs had forced him to do – worse, what he'd chosen to do – but he knew he would always be trying to make amends for it.

Death was always the catalyst, the philosopher's stone whose alchemical touch transformed the base to the sublime, sadder, more frightened but wiser. That terrible night had given him new eyes. He recalled the next day, walking down the street and being able to tell at a glance those who had had their first experience of death, and those who were still innocent; you always remember the first time.

And then Sophie had come along and shown him that there was still life after death, a new life, more vibrant than the one before. Sophie who had saved him.

Blue flames flickered in the depths of the glass and Hal appeared briefly, superimposed over Mallory's own reflection. A sad smile appeared on the flaming face and it mouthed the words, 'Hold on to moments of joy – they slip through your fingers like sand.'

3

Caitlin's three constant companions bickered incessantly deep inside her head. The old crone Brigid cackled and mocked, much to the irritation of the neurotic Briony, while Amy pleaded and whimpered for them to stop. Caitlin had learned to fade them out so that she had some respite to hear her own thoughts, but every now and then they would break back through. No peace, ever.

'You can't have him. He belongs to someone else,' Briony was saying in her snide tones.

'I don't want him. That doesn't mean I can't like him,' Caitlin said, then looked around in case any of the others were near enough to hear her talking to herself.

'She's already forgotten Grant.' Brigid cackled. 'Out of sight, deep in the ground, out of mind.'

'I haven't!' Tears sprang to Caitlin's eyes. Was there some truth in what Brigid said? Was she forgetting her husband? It couldn't be – the grief was still sharp.

'And what about Thackeray? Isn't he your boyfriend?' Amy's innocent voice made her questions even more poignant.

'I don't know where he is. Leave me alone!' Caitlin clutched at her head. Silence, that was all she wanted, and there were times when she thought she would only find that in death. Never alone, she felt so alone.

She caught sight of Mallory across the aisle and three stacks down. He didn't see her. A tingle ran down her back and into her groin, followed by a pang of guilt. The feelings were mysterious in origin, and she did her best to suppress them, but they were growing stronger. As long as she could keep them locked away there wouldn't be a problem.

4

Sophie watched Caitlin watching Mallory and instantly saw every thought inside her head. It felt like a betrayal. Her feelings were already a stew of guilt and doubt and confusion; now she could add mistrust to the mix.

Was Caitlin attempting to steal Mallory away behind her back? Or was she just going to be barefaced about it? And if she couldn't trust these two, who could she trust? It only confirmed her feelings that they were wrong about Niamh. She'd only ever showed Sophie kindness, and love, and what had happened between them was wrong, a betrayal of her relationship with Mallory, but it had only been once, an accident arising out of closeness, and there had been a lot of good in it, and it wouldn't happen again, so that was all right.

Anger bubbled up in her. She hated losing control, and that made her angry at Caitlin even more. Why couldn't she control her stupid crushes? Didn't she realise how much was at stake?

Unable to look at Caitlin any more, she turned and let out a cry when she found Ogma standing behind her. His gaze delved into the deepest part of her. She shifted uneasily, but could not escape its focus.

'You remind me of the other Sister of Dragons,' he said. 'The other mistress of Craft.'

'Ruth?'

'Both of you so fragile behind the face you show the world, both searching, inside and out.'

'I've found what I'm looking for. And now I'm going to make sure I hang on to it.'

Ogma grew puzzled. A silver pin at his shoulder grew and changed shape. The Caraprix crawled down his body, unable to settle on a new form.

'Here!' Distracted by Mallory's cry, Sophie found him examining a large, leather-bound tome. Caitlin was close at his side, scrutinising the pages. Sophie flinched.

'Serendipity.' Mallory grinned. 'I looked round and saw Caitlin looking at me. This book just caught my eye behind her head.'

'Let me look,' Sophie said sharply.

Inscribed at the top of facing pages were the words MAT and ANM. Beneath were two large circles surrounded by markings that resembled astrological symbols, drawings of the sun and the moon and writing in a language that none of them recognised.

'Definitely looks like a calendar of some kind,' Mallory said.

'What is this?' Sophie said to Ogma, who was watching them with a hint of a smile.

'Your kind know it as the Coligny Calendar. It was a gift, from me to the tribes, to a group known as the Culture. Ancient knowledge that would help them on the long road to ascension.'

Caitlin closed her eyes to focus on Math's images in her head. 'I can see it. The sun and the moon turning . . . all these different symbols. Why did Math leave us with a vision of a calendar?'

'What do these words mean?' Mallory pointed to MAT and ANM.

Ogma indicated MAT. 'In the tongue of one tribe, *Maith*, in another, *Mad*, meaning "good".' He circled ANM with his index finger. '*An Maith*, or *Anfad* – "not good".'

Mallory pondered on this as he studied the drawings. 'The year is marked into two halves. This one's black—'

'Winter?' Sophie suggested.

'And this one's light. Summer. But what's this word between the two halves? *Atenvix?*'

'Renewal.' Ogma pronounced the word with gravity.

'I don't get it. What was Math thinking?' Sophie asked.

As they debated the significance of the calendar, a loud grating rang through the halls of the library. It was the sound of a long-closed door opening.

Ogma looked around sharply, hearing other noises beyond their range.

His placid face grew grave. 'You must leave this place,' he said. 'Great danger has arrived.'

Mallory drew Llyrwyn. The surge of blue flames took their breath away.

'This library is the greatest source of knowledge in all Existence,' Ogma said. 'Its power is a threat to the Great Authority. It remained untouched for as long as it maintained its neutrality, for the Devourer of All Things does not act as long as the constant state stays in balance.'

'But you've helped us. And now you need to be taken out,' Mallory said.

'You didn't have to help us,' Sophie said. 'Why did you risk it if you knew this was going to happen?'

'We all have a part to play. Tiny actions may have large repercussions. Everything – every apparently insignificant thread – makes up a vital part of the great tapestry.'

'Come with us,' Mallory urged.

Ogma shook his head. 'I must do what I can to protect my library.' He nodded to them with a troubling finality and then moved quickly away.

Mallory put the book into his backpack. 'I don't think he'll mind us taking this under the circumstances. Anybody remember the way out of here? This place is a maze.'

'I can help. Just give me a moment.' Sophie leaned her head against the stacks, eyes closed.

Distant, but drawing closer, came the measured, heavy tramp of feet. The sound was accompanied by a faint whispering that dampened their spirits, and a gradual change in the atmosphere like the building charge before an electrical storm.

Sophie jerked as if in the throes of an orgasm. At her feet, tiny azure flames crackled briefly before a single thin line of blue moved out across the floor, indicating the way to the entrance.

'One slight problem,' Mallory said: the light disappeared into the shadows in the direction of the approaching threat.

Mallory led the way through room after room with the noise of the intruders growing ever louder. Whatever was coming disrupted the peculiar atmosphere of the library, and the time-lost spectres jumped and broke up as if there was interference on a signal. Those that were more solid somehow sensed what was coming; in one aisle, a naked, green woman sat sobbing, tearing at her hair, her eyes wide with fear.

Signalling for the others to move off the main aisle, they hid at the far end of a stack as a deafening metallic dragging entered the chamber. With it came a sound that was not a sound, like an enormous heart beating or the steady rhythm of a war drum.

The torches cast a huge shadow down the central aisle. Sophie's own heart began to thunder, and she thought she was going to be sick. Whatever it was carried its own noxious psychic atmosphere that assailed her emotions.

Finally she saw it. The intruder rose up above the stacks, nearly eight feet tall. Rusty iron plates hung down its front and back from chains, and its body reminded Sophie of an abattoir worker, muscular, arms smeared with blood. The chains that held the iron plates were fastened to its flesh. It wore a helmet of smaller rusty iron plates, roughly bolted together, and behind it the creature dragged a bloodstained sword as big as itself.

Mallory gripped Llyrwyn with both hands, but Sophie urged him not to attack. They both knew he wouldn't stand a chance.

Slipping around the rear of the stacks, they passed the Iron Slaughterman. Beyond the huge figure, the library swarmed with other things just as terrifying: some had the heads of rats or wolves and stopped periodically to sniff the air until Sophie was filled with dread that they would be found; others leaked purple mist, weapons rammed into their decomposing bodies.

The companions ducked behind stacks or scurried quickly into the shadows, diverting into rooms away from the blue line to avoid being discovered. Eventually they huddled in a corner of a large chamber, unable to move forward or back.

'There's only four of me,' Caitlin whimpered in her little-girl's voice. 'I'm missing a part. I need to be whole.'

'Stop whining,' Sophie hissed, and then hated herself for it.

The grating sound of the Iron Slaughterman's sword drew near again, this time approaching along the rear of the stacks. Mallory moved them towards the central aisle, but there was also movement there.

In the brightly lit central area of the chamber near two rows of reading desks, the sound of another door opening heralded the air peeling back to reveal a rectangle of darkness like deepest space. From the reaches of the void, a white cloud roiled towards the door, revealing a figure at its heart. Emerging into the library, it hovered several feet above the flags, black robes sparkling with starlight. In one hand it held a large golden key and in the other an ironwood stick. Waves of power rolled off it, worse than the Iron Slaughterman's aura, and it took a long moment for Sophie's see-sawing mind to settle on features it could accept.

Finally she saw bone-white skin framed by black hair, a sharp nose and slanted eyes. After a few seconds, it flipped to negative – black skin, white hair – and then back again, continuously.

'Janus,' Mallory whispered.

Divom Deus, the god's God. Sophie recalled Church's account of how he had been tortured by the dual-faced god of doorways and new beginnings in ancient Rome.

The creatures prowling the library emerged from the stacks and gathered before the god. 'Destroy everything.' Janus's voice rolled out like a tolling bell.

Sophie, Mallory and Caitlin were so mesmerised by the scene that they failed to realise that the Iron Slaughterman had rounded the stacks behind them. They were only saved by Brigid shrieking through Caitlin, 'Ware! Run! Run!'

Sophie and Caitlin were thrown to one side by Mallory as the great sword cleaved in an arc, smashing a stack and tearing through the priceless volumes. Where the tattered books fell, light radiated from them, and some jumped and shook like living things.

Mallory attacked furiously, but Llyrwyn clanged with little effect against the Slaughterman's breast-plate. Mallory only escaped the edge of its sword by a hair's breadth.

Sophie cursed her inability to marshal her Craft under pressure. There was movement all around her. Something with snapping jaws gnashed an inch from her face. It took her a second to realise she had only survived because Caitlin had dragged her clear.

Confusion erupted as the creatures swarmed. But from nowhere came a pure sound, like the ringing of crystal, and sudden flashing light that brought all the things to a halt. Along the central aisle surged Ogma, the light coming off him. His face was too terrible to examine, and the creatures fell away from his path as he rushed towards Janus.

A soundless explosion washed through the chamber as the two gods met. Half-blinded, Sophie grabbed Caitlin and Mallory and hauled them past the dazzled creatures. She kept her attention fixed on the blue line barely visible on the flags, driving the other two before her until they reached the entrance hall.

Caitlin was crying as they tumbled out into the night, where their horses stamped and snorted fearfully. Flecks of snow blew in the chill air. Jerzy emerged from behind a bush where he had been hiding.

'I sensed danger. I couldn't find you. I ran . . .' He hugged Mallory pathetically. 'I'm sorry, I'm sorry, I'm a coward.'

'Why did Ogma do that?' Caitlin said through her tears. 'He didn't know us, didn't have any connection with us or what we wanted.'

Mallory comforted her with an arm around her shoulders, a gesture Sophie did not miss. 'I'm guessing he thought we were worth the sacrifice.'

They clambered quickly onto their horses and set off for the Court of the Soaring Spirit. But as they thundered down the hillside, Sophie's thoughts were not turned to the mysteries of the calendar or the threat that lay ahead, but to Mallory and Caitlin and issues of trust and betrayal.

5

Cairo was crushed beneath layers of oven-heat that baked the dusty streets and made even the slightest movement an effort. The languid drift of the Nile divided the city along clear architectural lines. To the west were the public gardens, wide boulevards and open spaces that allowed the great, gleaming skyscrapers and modern Government buildings to breathe easily. To the east, the winding lanes and crowded tenements jostled for space against the hundreds of age-old mosques, seething amidst a cacophony of voices, music and traffic noise, stewing in the smells of spices and cooking meat and discarded rubbish. Beneath the surface, ancient fault-lines divided it on a deeper level, between the mythological and the real, where ancient histories and barely forgotten beliefs whispered threateningly down the ages.

Church was clearly aware of those conflicts as he attempted, without much luck, to shelter from the stifling heat on the edge of the great souk, Khan el-Khalili, under the awning at a pavement table of the El-Fishawi café, which also went by the name of the Café of Mirrors. An elegant echo of more peaceful days, quietly resting down a side street off Sikkit al-Badistan, it was an oasis of reflection within the teeming market, where artists and writers talked quietly over coffee, scribbled on pads or tapped on laptops, lost to their thoughts. After the constant motion of the latest four-day leg of their journey, Church welcomed the opportunity to sit still in one place for a while.

Amidst the noise rising from the souk, Church found an odd sort of peace, and the strong, treacly coffee gave him the kick he needed to make a decision.

'I was here five years ago.' Hunter now occupied the formerly empty seat next to Church. 'Bunch of extremists threatening to blow up British tourists. Sorted it out. Not pretty, but effective.'

'How do you do that?' Church said, exasperated.

'Secret stealth powers.'

'Are we safe?'

'Got my mate Omari Maisal to check the GDSSI system. It flagged us up as suspected terrorists, so Omari did a bit of jiggery-pokery and shuffled us into a non-alert file. So if the Egyptian Secret Service are no longer looking for us, that's about as close as we'll get to a clean bill of health around these parts.'

'Until somebody in high office with a spider embedded in them decides otherwise.'

'Nothing we can do about that. Still, got a bit of satisfaction from dumping that spider-guy overboard on the cruiser from Limassol.'

'They're just innocent people the spiders choose to control, Hunter.'

'Nobody's innocent.' He paused to watch a beautiful Egyptian woman walk by. She flashed her eyes at him. 'Casualties of war. It's us or them, and there's no getting away from that.'

'I know, but I don't like it. We're supposed to be protecting people.'

A waiter brought Hunter a coffee. 'You remind me of me, before I turned into the lovable, cynical, twisted bastard I am today.'

'How long ago was that?'

'A long time ago.' Hunter sipped his coffee, the cloying sweetness masking the bitter flavour that laced his words. 'Been doing this since I left school. When I signed up, they noticed I had an . . . aptitude.'

'Glad to be out of it?'

'You're never out of it. Yeah, it never scored high on the job satisfaction stakes. All this, it's like a holiday after a hard year.' He laughed silently at Church's disbelieving expression. 'Doing something good – clearly, definably good, something that matters – makes me feel like I'm not a total monster.'

'You wouldn't have been chosen to be a Brother of Dragons if you were.'

'Maybe Existence just needed someone with my particular skills.' He stretched lazily, soaking up the atmosphere. 'And it's been good hanging with you and the others. Learning a lot, about things I never really got the chance to think about. That'll make it all worthwhile when I go out in a blaze of glory.'

'That's fatalistic.'

'Pragmatic. Somebody like me, the things I've done, no way it's going to end nicely. I've known that for a long time. You accept it. Learn to live with it. To be honest, it's probably all for the best.'

'You're a difficult person to understand, Hunter.'

'Yeah, my mate Hal used to say that.'

Through the crowd, Shavi appeared, grinning broadly. 'There is no doubt about it. Ruth is alive.'

'You're sure?' Church thought his heart was going to stop.

'The visions I have been experiencing since Greece were confused. But I have just done a ritual in the room, and there is no doubt.'

'What's going on? One minute she's dead, the next she's alive.' Church's relief turned quickly to anger. He had been tearing himself apart ever since Shavi had had his first vision on the Albanian border, and only Laura had stopped him from leaving. She'd told him that if he went he was sacrificing them all to the spiders – typical Laura emotional manipulation, but it had worked.

Shavi unconsciously rubbed his alien eye. 'I do not know the context, but let us just celebrate the fact that she is alive.'

'The old guy's magic ring says Veitch and your girl are somewhere here,' Hunter said. 'Except he's suddenly gone off the radar. What's that all about?'

'I do not know, but I am nervous,' Shavi replied. 'We have entered another of the Great Dominions, and I am apprehensive about the forces that are awakening here.'

'More gods.' Hunter sniffed. 'We got past the ones in Norway. Why should Egypt be any different?'

6

'If you can't keep up I can get you a Zimmer frame.' Laura pushed her way through the crowds on Mar Girgis Street. In the heat, Old Cairo breathed steadily under eight thousand years of history.

'I'm actually choosing to walk several paces behind so people don't think we're together.' Tom was red-faced and sweating, and yearning for the moderate climate of his Scottish home.

Laura's white-blonde hair stood out amongst the veiled women who were in the majority on the streets of Masr al-Qadima as it stretched down to Coptic Cairo, but she had chosen to cover her shoulders and legs in deference to the local custom. 'I'd have thought you'd finally want to boost your reputation now you've got a few hundred years under your belt.' She glanced back at him. Her eyes were hidden by the expensive sunglasses she'd stolen from a tourist shop on the edge of the souk, but her smile gave an edge to her mockery. 'Hot?'

'Of course I'm bloody hot! It's one hundred and four in the shade!'

'One of the advantages of being not quite human. I don't feel the heat.'

'Yes, it's easy to forget you're a plant. In my experience, one of their finer attributes is that they're always silent.'

Laura came to a halt before the ancient rounded towers of the western gate into Coptic Cairo. She checked the guidebook. 'Looks like this is it. Built by Emperor Trajan in AD ninety-eight to enter the Roman fortress of Babylon. Like anyone cares.' She shoved the guidebook into her pocket and marched through the gate into the cooler and less popular religious compound.

South-west of the gate was El Muallaqa, the Hanging Church, the oldest Christian church in Egypt built into the walls of the Water Gate of the old Roman fortress. Its twin white towers looked down on a peaceful avenue.

'How will we recognise them? How are they going to know we're who we say we are?' Laura asked.

'Did you hear that thing I said about silence?'

In the cool confines of the white-walled Hanging Church, Tom waited beside the central haikal screen, the dark ebony a stark contrast to the white marble pillars nearby. 'Amongst his many attributes, Jack Churchill is a very clever man,' Tom whispered. 'Long ago he saw the benefit of establishing a vast network of spies and helpers linked to the places where the Blue Fire is strongest, in every religion, every path. Over the centuries, the Watchmen grew like a vine, spreading across the globe. In the earliest days, Church gave them their secrets and mythologies, descriptions of the Brothers and Sisters of Dragons who would exist at this time, ways to contact you, ways for you to contact them—'

Laura cut him short with a loud theatrical yawn. Tom fumed quietly and continued to watch.

After ten minutes they were hesitantly approached by a balding cleric with a clipped white beard. Tom subtly extended the first and fourth fingers of his left hand and touched the other two fingers to his palm to make a surreptitious 'W'. The cleric repeated the gesture.

'It is you. Here. Now. Of course,' he whispered. He could barely restrain his excitement.

Behind her sunglasses, Laura rolled her eyes. 'Don't have a kitten. You'll get used to our God-like brilliance.'

'Ignore her,' Tom snapped. 'She likes to torment small animals. You expected us?'

'Then you do not know? This is beyond coincidence. Proof, then, of God's work. Come with me.'

As he hurried out into the heat, Laura whispered, 'We just need him and his religious nutters to keep an eye out for Veitch, right? Don't waste time letting him show you his action-figure collection.'

Tom ignored her and followed the cleric out.

'It's all right for you, you boring old git,' Laura called after him. 'This road trip keeps you out of the care home. Meanwhile, I'm missing out on sex, drugs and alcohol. You know, a life.'

In the forecourt before the Coptic Museum, the cleric consulted with an imam, who glanced towards Tom and Laura and then handed over a key.

The cleric returned to Tom, fishing a second key out of some hidden pocket. 'I apologise for the secrecy, but we cannot talk of these things in the open. I fear what is happening.' He steadied himself and marched towards the monastery and the Church of St George, its twentieth-century architecture incongruous amongst the ancient religious buildings. He took them through a side door and down several flights of steps. Moving quickly through the cool depths of the monastery, they arrived at an unassuming door that led through much older stonework into catacombs beneath. He paused in a derelict area beside a door with two locks.

'I am so glad you have come,' he said with relief. 'We have debated what to do during the two days since he appeared. We felt the only option was to constrain him here because of the potential danger, but his power is growing daily. He was like a newborn when we found him, wandering in a daze on Mohandiseen, but soon he will choose to leave here and we will be unable to stop him.'

'Who've you got in there?' Laura asked.

'We know who he says he is,' the cleric replied. 'And we hope and pray this is not true. For it cannot be true!'

'Just give us the keys.' Laura sighed. 'One simple answer. How hard is that?'

As an added security measure, the locks had to be turned at the same time. The cleric backed away as the door swung open to release a blast of humid air heavy with the scent of vegetation.

Laura caught Tom's shoulder. 'Let me go alone.'

'This is no time for your usual stupidity.'

'No, I feel something.' The Cernunnos brand on her hand was burning. Whispers came and went in her head.

What had once been a chamber cut into the natural bedrock on which Cairo rested was now filled with the lush vegetation that sprang up in the Nile Valley after the great river's annual life-giving flood. Laura pushed her way through it until the door was lost to view and her only link to the modern world was the sound of Tom urging her to take care. On some level she knew this was one of *her* places, where her own peculiar abilities flourished, and that gave her confidence.

The room appeared to go on for ever. Laura knew she was in one of those places that lay on the border between her world and the other, where different rules applied. Yet the chamber itself had once been perfectly normal so she guessed the cause of the dissonance had to be the occupant.

She pushed her way past the final frond and found herself on the edge of a cool oasis beneath a starry night sky. The pool was ablaze with Blue Fire, though it was silent and without heat. Beneath the surface, Laura could make out a serpentine form swimming: a Fabulous Beast.

'Great Apep, the serpent of chaos and destruction, who dwells in the Duat and accompanies the dead on their journey to the Underworld.'

Laura started at the voice. From out of the dense vegetation emerged a figure wrapped in the bandages of mummification. The features swam as he neared, eventually settling into a face that combined characteristics of human, animal and vegetation.

'Okay, Tutankhamen. Back off.' Laura forced herself in tune with the vegetation. It moved slowly at her will to bring a barrier between the two of them. The approaching figure waved one arm and the growth fell away; Laura felt a kindred power, but one much greater than her own.

She realised she had backed calf-deep into the burning pool, though there was no sensation from the flames beyond a subtle well-being. The bandaged figure stopped on the edge.

'Who are you?'

The figure held its head as if it was having difficulty recalling. 'I am the Good One,' he said after a moment. 'Onnophris.'

'Doesn't ring any bells, dude.'

'I have another name . . .' He struggled. 'Osiris.' An unsettling smile crept across his face.

'You're some kind of nature god. Like Cernunnos.' She held up her hand to show the brand of interlocking leaves. 'So that makes you my uncle, right? Same family, another branch?'

'That is one aspect. Only one. You are in a different place now. Things are not the same here.'

'All right, you're feeling a bit out of it. You've been away for a long time so I'll give you the catch-up: there's a war going on. Spiders versus snakes. No sitting on the fence allowed. And because you're the "Good One" you're with us.'

'Good is a matter of perspective. It is the quality of one who obeys the main directive of the ruling power.' Osiris was changing; Laura watched with a queasy fascination as the vegetation and animal characteristics fell from his face to reveal yellowing bone.

'You're obviously going to be busy now you're back in the world. Mummies to wrap and all that. I'll leave you—'

'This is my greater aspect.' A pair of bloodshot eyes now watched Laura out of a cracked skull. 'I am the King of the Dead.'

'You're missing a few clues. Here's one: I'm not dead.'

'You are dead. All you mortals. You simply do not realise it.'

His words touched something deep in Laura that she couldn't and wouldn't recognise, and it made her shudder.

'Come with me.'

'If you think I'm taking one step out of this lake, you've got your bandages wound too tight.'

'Laura.'

It chilled her to hear her name coming from the skull. 'All right, you know my name. Big whoop.'

'A lost child. Unloved. Beaten and scarred by her mother. Unprotected by her father. A sense of worthlessness. Self-hatred. What value could you have, then?'

Laura felt sick to hear the deeply protected secrets of her life unfolding. 'Stop it.'

Osiris appeared to be reading something just above her head. 'Driven, as all mortals are, by circumstances beyond your control. Choosing a path of self-destruction and succeeding – until you were saved. By four others, Brothers and Sisters of Dragons. For the first time you were accepted, with all your flaws and your burden of troubles and your desperation. For the first time you had a home, and friends, and love.'

'You know I'm going to keep standing here? Even when you get down to what shoes I wore on my first day at school?'

A moment of silent calculation and then Osiris said, 'You have a choice, as all the dead do. Come with me or I will take another, and what will happen to them will be worse than anything you can imagine.'

'I can imagine a lot.'

'Every culture established by mortals in this world has shared one belief – that life continues in some way after death. It is known by peoples that have no contact with any beyond themselves, from the dawn of your ages, from the darkening west to the gleaming east. Because it is the One Truth embedded in the deepest recesses of your construct. The gift you were given when you were made.'

'Yeah, I always knew I was going to live forever.'

'The greatest threat to any being is that the endless cycle of death and rebirth could be ended. Complete termination. Never to exist again. More – never to have existed at all. Wiped from Existence.'

'Except you're making one big mistake. I'm a coward. In a world of cowards, I'm queen. Saving my own skin is my number-one priority in

188

any situation. So whoever you choose, I'm going to be sick and sad, and hate myself, but I'm still not coming out of this fire.'

'And still you lie to yourself.'

An image of Hunter flashed before her eyes. Laura felt a corresponding twist in her gut that shocked her. 'You really picked the wrong one there.'

'A lost child. Unloved. Ignored by his parents. Dragged into a friendless world of deceit and cold hearts. A man who loves, and loves love, but can never be allowed, and can never speak of it. Who must hide his loneliness and his sadness and his suffering. Who is honourable, and trustworthy, and who would give up his own life for others, but who is punished every second of his life by being forced to bring death, and to know all of the deaths he has brought. A man who loves you more than any man has loved you, and who cannot himself believe that he has found this depth of feeling.'

In the silence that followed his words, Osiris's bloodshot eyes stared at Laura with uncompromising harshness. She hesitated, and then said, 'You're wasting your time. Run along now.'

'I will take him.' Osiris began to retreat into the dense vegetation.

'Wait.' Laura thought she was going to be sick. Every fibre of her demanded self-preservation, yet still she was torn. She had no control over the deep, oceanic swell of her response. 'I won't be wiped from Existence?'

'No.'

'But it's not going to be nice, right?'

Osiris did not answer.

She barely knew Hunter. Of all the people Osiris could have chosen, he was the least likely to be important to her. Yes, they had made a connection, but it was nothing, not really. Everything for them lay in the future, unborn. She could resist.

She took a step towards the edge, hesitated. Osiris waited.

7

The sun hung fat and red over the West Bank where the dead had been taken for centuries. The great pyramid of Khufu rose in silhouette as the lights of the Sharia al-Haram began to flicker on, and the air was filled with the ethereal, soaring sound of the muezzin calling the faithful to prayer.

Not long ago, Church would have drifted into the mystical atmosphere that had transformed Cairo into a city of wonders for millennia, but his fears for Ruth and his hatred for Veitch isolated him. He sat on the terrace of the rooftop apartment they had rented in an old boarding house, with the shadows growing long around him, waiting for some sign.

As the stink of the day's traffic fumes gradually gave way to charcoal smoke and the aroma of barbecuing lamb from the street sellers, Shavi entered with an armful of books and pamphlets.

'Research,' he said brightly. 'I thought it wise to know what magic might have awakened in Cairo before it descends on our doorstep.'

When Church didn't respond, he pulled up a chair next to him and opened a bottle of mineral water. 'Napoleon Bonaparte said that from the top of the pyramids, forty centuries look down on you. How many thousands of people, if not millions, have looked back at them during that time?'

'You're trying to make me feel insignificant?'

Shavi smiled. 'Oh, that would be far too simplistic for me. On the one hand, I could be suggesting that all our lives, and our problems, are like the sand out there – tiny grains lost to the great, sweeping grandeur of the desert. Or I could be implying that as Brothers and Sisters of Dragons we are not insignificant. Of all the generations that have looked up at the pyramids, we are the first to be tasked with a destiny that could change everything.'

'Or both.'

'Or both.'

'Insignificant in the ups and downs of our lives, the loves, and betrayals, and suffering. And uniquely important in the job we forgettable, pitiful people have been given to do.'

'Exactly.'

'Nobody likes a smart-arse, Shavi.'

They both smiled and watched in silence as the sun finally set and night fell across the Victorious City.

'What have you found?' Church asked.

'Plenty. This is a place where myth and legend are carved into the very fabric of the city. But so far there appears to be no sign of anything out of the ordinary.'

'That doesn't give me much comfort.'

'The city is quiet for now. Let us enjoy this moment.'

Church examined the milky river of stars overhead. 'I'm starting to wonder what I'd do without you, Shavi. Sometimes I'm afraid all my brooding is going to drive me insane. I worry about everything – about Hunter, there's so much going on inside him, and Laura, the same. About poor Tom—'

'And they are concerned about you. That is what friends do. Now . . .' Shavi opened one of the books to change the mood. 'So much about the Kingdom of the Serpent – and the war with the spiders – and the myths and legends of the world! All there, in the old stories. That secret history again, just waiting to be read with the right eyes.'

'Gnosticism taught us a lot.'

'But the symbolism in the myths is so much more potent!' He began to read, summarizing as he scanned the pages. 'So much, even in the Middle East alone. As with all myths, another story playing behind the words. In Hittite mythology, Illuyankas was the monstrous snake, or dragon, who waged war against the gods and was eventually slain. This tale was assimilated into Canaanite mythology as the struggle of the gods against Leviathan. Illuyankas's death was believed to signal the start of a new era.'

'So the dragon is the bad guy?'

Shavi smiled, but did not answer. 'In Iranian mythology, the monstrous dragon Azhi Dahaka was supposed to embody falsehood, and was the servant of Angra Mainyu, the god of darkness. It is told that at the end of the world, Azhi Dahaka will break free of his chains and ravage the Earth. Even here in Egypt, the great serpent Apep is a force of destruction and chaos, who attacks the life-giving sun every day. Even in the mythology of the Bible, the snake in the Garden of Eden was demonised. For giving knowledge! How can that be a bad thing? The message of that story was that humankind was supposed to stay in ignorance—'

'Not rise up, not reach its potential. You know, you might have a few Christian scholars querying that reading.' Church grinned, but was briefly distracted by small fires springing up here and there across the city. A celebration of some kind?

'Propaganda!' Shavi continued. 'Politics is everywhere. When a ruling power wants to maintain control, it creates stories that demonise the other side, to win over the hearts and minds of the population. As you well know, the Christian Church did this effectively when it first arrived in Britain and attempted to supplant the Old Religion. Witches were damned! The Horned God, representing the great power of nature, was cast as the Devil.'

Church's attention was drawn back to the fires. They appeared to be burning on rooftops across the city.

'In fact, the demonisation of women went hand-in-hand with the serpent—'

'Yeah, I've read *The Da Vinci Code*,' Church said distractedly.

'—because women controlled the Craft, which is fuelled by the Blue Fire, the serpent power. You have only to look to Hebrew legend. Lilith was the first woman to be created – part woman, part snake. In the Old Testament she is a demon whose name means "storm goddess" or "She of the Night", and her talismanic creature is the owl. And why did she become a symbol of evil? Because according to Talmudic legend she refused to lie beneath Adam and believed herself to be equal! The message again is clear: women, know your place! Do not use your power. And these stories have changed the thinking of generations. Just stories, people say. But stories create belief, and the imagination has the power to change ideas into reality.'

Church moved to the edge of the roof terrace. The fires concerned him; there was something unnatural in the way they danced. 'What you're telling me is that in this particular Great Dominion, the serpent was cast as the enemy.'

'Yes, perhaps because there is a source of its power here. Maybe even the main source of the Blue Fire in the world. The original node of energy where the great serpent originated.'

'The Garden of Eden.'

'And that makes this a very dangerous place for us. The gods of Egyptian mythology may well be allied against the serpent—'

'Working for the Void.' Church gripped the parapet. More fires were mysteriously lighting, drawing closer. 'And we've awakened them.'

8

With Coptic Cairo at his back, Hunter looked over what appeared to be a vast rubbish dump, but which he knew was one of the most important Islamic archaeological sites in the world: Fustat, the first Islamic city in Cairo, razed to the ground when the Fatimids took the area. Piles of rubble, isolated fires, trenches and apparently random holes were interspersed with occasional heaps of plastic and cans left by locals with less of a sense of history.

He'd wandered the length of Old Cairo, but there was no sign of Laura anywhere. He'd sensed she was in trouble while he was enjoying a late-afternoon coffee in the Café of Mirrors. He hadn't discussed such an amorphous feeling with the others, and he certainly wouldn't raise it with his former Government comrades, who would have mocked such a feeling as a by-product of a woolly mind. But he had acted on such blind instincts for much of his life, and he was convinced it was what made him good at the terrible things he did. With his current knowledge, he wondered if it had always been the Pendragon Spirit at play in him, in the same way it had clearly influenced Shavi's spirituality, or Church's leadership abilities.

Another fire erupted in the dark depths of Fustat. Kids, he thought, gathering for sex or drugs away from the eyes of their elders.

As he headed in the direction of the Mosque of Amr Ibn al-As, he was almost knocked over by a man in his twenties fleeing in blind panic.

Hunter grabbed him by the collar. 'What's wrong?'

The man had an intellectual look about him, stylish glasses slightly askew beneath long, curly black hair. He glanced over his shoulder fearfully. 'The fires—'

'Calm down. Who are you and what are you doing here?'

'Fayed Osman. I'm an archaeologist. Let me go!' He struggled, but couldn't break Hunter's grip.

'I don't want to give you a slap.'

'It's the fires, don't you see?' Fayed gestured to the small blazes springing up across Fustat. They were burning across the city, too. 'They're smokeless!'

A fire burst into life not far from the road, on a piece of rough ground amidst a network of trenches. No one could have ignited it. The intense yellow flames gave way to scarlet edged with green, and within them a dark shape appeared and began to grow, like an insect metamorphosing through all the stages of maturity in seconds.

What emerged was a blur as Hunter's perception skated all over it without finding any traction, yet he got a sense of insectile limbs attached to an animal's body and head, perhaps a wolf.

Fayed began to rave. Hunter's own mind convulsed as the fire-being stirred madness in him. Still holding on to Fayed, Hunter ran back to the mazy streets of Old Cairo and only came to rest when he was sure the thing was no longer following. The unnatural insanity passed.

Hunter hauled Fayed into a dark alley filled with boxes of discarded vegetables and a scavenging dog. 'You know what that thing was?'

Fayed shoved Hunter's hand aside and gave a deep sigh as his panic passed, too. 'I work for the Council of Antiquities. I was despatched to investigate reports of a disturbance in Fustat. The illicit trade in antiquities is extensive – looters descend when night falls. But it was the fires and the djinn—'

'They're like devils, right?'

'Before Islamic times it was believed they were nature spirits capable of driving people mad. They roamed all the lonely, wild desert areas, invisible most of the time, but they could also take on any shape, human or animal. Islamic belief said they were intermediaries between humans and the higher powers. They are said to live with other supernatural forces in the Kaf, a range of mountains that circle the earth. A metaphor for the Invisible World. Iblis, or Satan, is their chief.' He took a deep breath to steady himself. 'They are born of smokeless fire.'

'All right, you're coming with me.'

'I have to report back—'

'Not a request.'

Fayed read Hunter's face and complied. Hunter led the way back through winding streets, the main thoroughfares clogged with honking traffic. Occasionally, they came across people staring anxiously at the rooftops, or street cafés that had been abandoned.

In the centre of one such street, a policeman tore bloody streaks across his face with his nails as he raved against his invisible tormentors. Further along, the streetlights cast quickly moving shadows on a wall from no obvious source.

'Looks to me like they've come out of hiding to take back what's theirs,' Hunter said.

9

Caledfwlch glowed brightly in the gloom of the guest-house stairs as Church and Shavi cautiously made their way down.

'We need to find the others, regroup somewhere till we find out what's happening,' Church said.

'Those fires may not signify any threat,' Shavi cautioned. 'They may simply be random events, signs of this Great Dominion awakening.'

'After two thousand years of doing this shit, I'm not inclined to agree. The Pendragon Spirit attracts bad like nothing else on Earth.'

The stairs opened onto a cool living area with a tiled floor. Large potted ferns and screens surrounded a few items of furniture. There was no sign of the owner.

'If we seal the perimeter, we could hold out here until the others get back,' Church suggested.

They both started as they rounded a screen. Tom sat on a long, black sofa, smoking.

'Jesus Christ, you sacred the living daylights out of me,' Church said. He put a finger to his lips before Tom could respond. Church and Shavi continued towards the front door, which hung open. The smoky, dusty aroma of a Cairo night drifted in on the breeze.

'Just Laura and Hunter now,' Church whispered. 'Lock the door and we can try to reach them on their mobiles.'

'This counts as an emergency?'

'My call. Yeah, I know Hunter said only use them once and discard them in case the GDSSI are monitoring calls and track our location. But I'd rather we were together now.'

When Shavi had locked and bolted the front door, they instantly felt more secure. Church dialled Laura first, but the call went straight to voicemail. Only instead of the abusive message Laura had left earlier, there was now an insane shrieking.

Hunter answered immediately. 'I was just going to call you,' he said. 'I'm on my way back. Lock the doors until I get there.'

'Already done. You saw the fires?'

'Yeah, and I've seen what comes out of them.' The signal kept breaking up so Hunter sounded miles out at sea. '. . . threat.'

'I didn't get that,' Church shouted. 'What comes out of the fires?'

'Djinn.' The word was loud enough for Shavi to hear. His eyes widened. 'Some sort of shape-shifting demons,' Hunter continued. 'They can become anything to get under your guard. Major threat level. Don't approach them until I'm there. Even with your big sword.'

'They can become anything?' Church repeated.

He didn't hear the reply. His attention was caught by Shavi's expression. A shadow had fallen across his tranquil features, his eyes fixed somewhere over Church's shoulder.

'Tom,' Church said.

He had a fleeting glimpse of Tom sitting on the couch, smoking. Something was wrong with the scene that he would have noticed earlier if he'd paid attention. Tom was hollow-eyed, his irises red-rimmed, and there was a quality to his expression that was mean-spirited, his shoulders hunched like an animal waiting in its lair.

As soon as Church registered this, Tom was gone, the couch empty, a ghost of smoke drifting in the air.

Church dropped the phone. He could hear Hunter barking questions on the other end. He knew the djinn was still in the room, but he couldn't see it.

'Over there,' Shavi called.

Some peculiar aspect of the djinn's nature was fracturing Church's vision; his mind's eye held an image, and then a good second passed before a new image replaced it in his head. A jagged flash: an indiscernible shape halfway across the room near the right-hand wall.

Another flash: the shape, like a hunched man seen through dense fog, on the opposite wall.

Church began to swing Caledfwlch. Too late.

With the third flash, the sword slipped from his hand and clattered on the tiles. He was forced to bend backwards at the waist by something he hadn't yet seen. Fog closed across his vision and in it two red eyes glowed hatefully. Dimly, he heard shouting, but the words were lost to him.

In those eyes was his world, and in them he was younger, and living in London with Marianne, the woman with whom he had thought he would spend the rest of his days. His life spooled before his eyes at rapid speed, heading relentlessly towards the terrible inevitable: boxes appearing in the empty flat, contents spewing out to fill shelves and cupboards and to stack up around the now lived-in rooms; Marianne's birthday, the surprise party he had arranged with all her friends; the expensive bottle of red wine he had spilled on the lounge carpet, desperately trying to scrub it out before she got home.

And then, with his new eyes, he saw something that threw him off-kilter. The spreading stain formed the shape of a man on fire. No randomness, no mistake; it was as clear as if he had drawn it himself.

How long had the dark force been wrapping around his life, prodding him, pushing him towards mishap? How close was it to everyone, the Invisible Hand that shapes us and the things we do?

And then everything in his vision span out of control: coming home, finding Marianne dead, her blood spreading into the shape of the Burning Man, too, a detail he'd never noticed before, now chillingly clear.

Back then he'd thought it was suicide, and cursed himself to the point of dissolution for not seeing the signs and helping her. He later learned it was murder but still cursed himself for not preventing her death. What kind of hero was he if he couldn't save those who loved and relied on him?

The vision wouldn't break. It was going places that pulled madness from the depths of his mind. Marianne sat up, soaked in her own blood, and pointed one red, accusing finger at him. 'You did this,' she said, and her love turned to hate. Lurching awkwardly, she came towards him, red teeth bared. 'You didn't love me enough.' It was the blade that he always feared. Her arms clamped around him, and he could feel the sticky soddenness of her clothes, smell the iron of her blood. She was red, all over, for red was the colour of the Burning Man.

Marianne would never let him go. He would be looking into those eyes for evermore, whether his own eyes were open or closed. His sanity became a brittle thing.

Ruth will save you.

The words came from nowhere. It was Shavi's voice, distant but clear.

The desolate sense of horror shifted on unsteady ground. Church lost sight of Marianne, and once again saw the dense fog within which the red eyes burned.

Before the djinn could reassert its control, he was grabbed and thrown backwards. Hunter was there with an Egyptian man. Still locked into the fading remnants of his vision, he needed Shavi's help to get to his feet.

'You all right?' Hunter barked.

Church nodded.

'The djinn can drive you mad. And they're all over the city.'

Church cleared the last vestiges of haze from his head and reclaimed Caledfwlch. As the Blue Fire rushed into him, he instantly felt stronger. On the periphery of his vision, the djinn left trails of movement, already gone by the time his gaze settled on them.

They backed to the door and slipped through it just as Church sensed the djinn launching another attack. What sounded like a frenzied jungle beast thundered against the just-closed door, shrieking cries, making their blood turn cold.

Church caught Shavi's arm. 'Thanks.'

Shavi smiled shyly. 'Instinct. I am glad it worked.'

Searching the street, Hunter cursed loudly. 'What's the point in looking for something you can't see?'

A familiar figure weaved towards them, keeping close to the buildings. Tom came to a halt and doubled up, wheezing from his exertion.

'How do we know if he's the real thing?' Church said.

'Stick your sword in him. See if he squeals.' Hunter had already made his mind up.

'Very funny,' Tom snapped. 'While you're having your fun and games, one of your own has been taken.'

He proceeded to tell them about Laura. 'I waited, but she never came out. And when I went in after her, the room was empty. No prisoner . . . no Laura. Only this.'

He held up a key with a handle in the shape of a jackal's head.

'A mortuary key!' Fayed took it in awe. 'I have not seen one of these outside the museum. They are ritual objects used to unlock the Night Door, when the dead are taken to the mortuary complex for the final judgment.'

'Where's the mortuary complex?' Hunter asked.

'*Imentet,* my ancestors called it – west, the traditional direction in which the dead travel, towards the dying sun.' He indicated down the street

197

where they could see the searchlights shimmering on the Great Pyramid of Khufu. 'Also known as *kher neter*, the Necropolis. The Land of the Dead.'

chapter nine

the lone and level sands

1

Hunter kept the pedal to the floor as he steered the stolen truck along Sharia al-Haram towards the Giza plateau. The road was lined with night-clubs and casinos, a tacky neon strip permanently in conflict with the majesty that lay beyond. At that time of evening, the pavements should have been thronging with tourists with too much money, posses of Egyptian businessmen and the street trade that preyed on both groups. But the road was eerily deserted. No traffic moved, which made it easier for Hunter to ignore the red lights.

Occasionally, impossibly beautiful women would attempt to flag them down, or injured, desperate children. Hunter never slowed. Sometimes they would step into the path of the truck, but there would never be an impact.

'Are you sure we're doing the right thing?' Hunter said without any sign of emotion.

'Why are you asking me?' Church said.

'We're going right into the heart of where these gods exist. The chances of getting Laura out are almost non-existent.'

'She is one of us,' Shavi said quietly.

'I know,' Hunter said, 'but this is in direct opposition to our primary mission. We make a hopeless attempt to go in there, we stand to lose everything. Smart strategy suggests we abandon this futile gesture and focus on what we're meant to be doing. Or lose everything.'

'You are suggesting we abandon Laura?' Shavi said incredulously.

Hunter didn't reply.

The truck sped past the Maryutia Canal, the pyramids huge against the night sky. Behind them the stars formed a milky river across the heavens, as though the Nile was reflected above.

'We save Laura,' Church said. 'No argument.'

Fayed leaned between Hunter and Church. 'We are nearly there.'

'You can take the truck straight back,' Hunter said to him. 'It'll be too dangerous to wait for us.'

'No. I have spent all my life studying the great culture of Ancient Egypt. If what you say is true and the gods really do walk the Earth, then this is too great an opportunity to miss.'

'You idiot,' Tom said quietly.

The road passed the security perimeter of the Giza complex where armed guards would normally have been patrolling, but it was as deserted as the city's suburbs. Hunter brought the truck to a halt before the ancient monuments. Not far away, three jackals tore at bloody remains that did not appear animal. As two of them fought over a long bone, another loped up, but although jackal-headed, this one had the body of a man. It attacked the remains with relish.

Filled with awe, Fayed scrambled to get a better look. 'Anubis,' he whispered.

The jackal-headed creature looked up as if it had heard him, and then loped away across the moonlit sand.

'I'll stay here,' Tom said.

'It's not safe,' Church responded.

'Oh, it's *much* safer going in with you,' Tom replied sarcastically. 'I think I'll take my chances.'

The night was warm. The aromas of the city had been replaced by the dry scent of the desert and the cooling stone of the pyramids. Disturbed, the remaining jackals ran. Church decided not to check what they had been eating. There was an air of foreboding that put them all on edge.

'Where's the mortuary complex?' Hunter asked.

Fayed made an expansive gesture. 'The entire site has been a necropolis almost since the beginning of pharaonic Egypt. In fact, there are two distinct areas separated by the wadi. Here are the more familiar monuments. There—' he indicated a ridge to the south-east '—are the private tombs of citizens of various classes.'

'Such monuments to the dead,' Shavi said in awe.

'They believed that death was not the end,' Fayed replied, 'just a point of transition from this world to the next.'

'Like the Celts,' Church noted and glanced at Shavi, 'and just about every other culture.'

Shavi smiled. 'Do you think they were on to something?'

200

Nearest was the smallest pyramid of Menkaure, with a causeway leading to the mortuary temple before its entrance. The pyramid of Khafre had the same layout, with the Sphinx lying next to its causeway. And beyond was the Great Pyramid of Khufu, still breathtaking even without its sheath of gleaming white stone that had been stolen many generations before.

A figure separated from the shadows near the causeway and came towards them. Church drew his sword when he recognised Etain, her dead face as white as the moon.

Fayed fell to his knees. 'What is this? The dead come for us?'

'No sign of Veitch or the others,' Hunter said. 'Why's she not riding that freakish horse you talked about?'

Curiously, Church sensed no threat. Despite her appearance, he saw the Etain he had first met in the Iron Age, beautiful and strong, the woman who had fallen in love with him and paid the price.

'No visible weapons,' Hunter said. 'Take her down?'

'Wait.'

Etain came to a halt in front of them. Church tried to read her intentions, but there was nothing in her eyes beyond the suffocating blankness of death. She waited for a moment, fixated on Church's face, and then turned and walked north.

'Well, I've followed worse,' Hunter said. 'Shall we?'

Sand swirled around their ankles as they made their way past the two smaller pyramids. After fifteen minutes they were standing before the Great Pyramid, and only at its foot did its scale become truly apparent. A mountain of steps rose up high overhead, a single star peeking out behind the summit.

'Each block weighs around two and a half tons and there are more than two million of them covering thirteen acres,' Fayed said, recovering from his shock and clearly finding comfort in graspable facts and figures. It was as if he was seeing the monument for the first time. 'The mystery of mysteries. A true wonder.'

'Yep, it's a building,' Hunter said. 'Now, a woman, *there's* a mystery of mysteries. And one worth spending your life uncovering.'

'I spent two thousand years getting back to my own time,' Church said, 'and this was ancient when I started the journey.'

Fayed clapped a hand on Hunter's shoulder. 'You are a military man, I can tell. Where you stand now, Alexander the Great once stood, ruminating on the great mysteries.'

'I'll do my ruminating when I'm a few hundred miles from here.' Hunter scrambled after Etain as she made her way to the entrance.

The transition from the heat of the evening to the dank cave-chill of the tunnel made them all shiver. Hunter took out his pencil-torch, but Etain appeared to need no light.

'Is it true that no body of Khufu was found, nor any tomb goods?' Shavi whispered. His words echoed much further than he had anticipated. 'Indeed, is it not said that this pyramid was not a tomb at all, but served some other mysterious purpose?'

'The Supreme Council of Antiquities does not accept that theory,' Fayed replied with some hesitancy, which suggested he was not wholly convinced. 'I do not know what you expect to find in here. For the vast size of the pyramid, there is very little space inside. A few passages, a shaft, the tiny Queen's Chamber and the slightly larger King's Chamber. Nowhere for the gods to gather.'

'The space you see is not always the only space there is,' Church replied.

'Don't get him started,' Hunter said to the baffled Fayed. 'Next he'll be drawing you diagrams.'

They hauled themselves up the steep, treacherous Ascending Passage, breathing heavily from the exertion in the claustrophobic tunnel. But when they entered the Grand Gallery and the quality of the echoes changed with the high ceiling lost to the shadows above them, Etain came to a halt.

'What's she doing?' Hunter whispered.

'Listening, I think,' Church replied.

'It's too dark in here,' Hunter said. 'Why couldn't they set up their camp out in the desert?'

'Hush,' Shavi said. 'Can you hear it?'

A whisper of movement, a scratch and a scurry, growing louder.

'It's coming from the other side of the wall.' Church pressed his ear to the stone.

'This can't be good.' Hunter shook the torch. The beam was growing noticeably dimmer.

'The batteries?' Fayed suggested.

'They're new.'

In the growing gloom, Etain's face glowed spectrally. She moved further along the Gallery and waited. The scurrying and scratching behind the wall was now clearly audible, and magnified by the odd acoustics of the passage.

Church pulled away from the stone. 'Spiders. They're moving behind the walls.'

Hunter glanced at Etain. 'She led us into a trap.'

'I don't think so,' Church said.

Fayed picked up on the others' anxiety. 'Then we must retreat,' he said, skidding down the steep slope to where the Grand Gallery met the Ascending Passage. He came to a sudden halt. Peering into the dark of the tunnel, he caught sight of tiny fronds waving from the almost imperceptible gaps between the monolithic blocks. The impossible logic of the sight meant it was a moment before Fayed realised he was seeing the legs of the spiders Church had mentioned as they pulled their bodies out through a space that could not possibly admit them. The first emerged with a plop, black and shinily metallic. And then they were falling in streams from the ceiling and bursting from the walls, a seething wave rising up the passage.

His eyes wide with fear, Fayed scrambled back up the Grand Gallery. 'Yes, spiders. Thousands of them.'

'What if,' Shavi said, 'the entire pyramid is filled with them. A repository, a base, perhaps even the place that allows them passage into our world.'

'Now you're just trying to upset me.' Hunter bounded up the slope behind Etain.

'Stating-the-obvious time: we can't go back,' Church said, watching the spiders spilling into the Grand Gallery. 'We have to stick with her.'

They followed Etain into the stark King's Chamber, which contained only an empty granite sarcophagus.

'No exit.' Church cursed under his breath. The Grand Gallery was now alive with spiders rushing across every available surface towards the entrance to the King's Chamber.

'Might as well draw your sword,' Hunter said. 'We could probably squash a couple of dozen before they take us apart.'

As the torrent washed towards the entrance, Etain stepped past them and placed one hand on a barely visible indentation in the stone. Instantly, a block fell from above and crashed into the door space. Once the dust had settled, they saw they were sealed in.

As they breathed with relief, Shavi held up a hand to his ear; from every side of the small chamber came the sound of spiders.

'Let's review our situation,' Hunter said. 'We're trapped in a tiny room, at the heart of a mountain of stone, surrounded by what could very well be ten billion lethal spiders.' He looked to Church. 'Now's the time to tell us your plan.'

Etain gently edged Church towards the sarcophagus and made it clear that she wanted him to lie in it. Unsure, he complied. When he was lying flat in the cold stone box, Etain pressed something out of his line of vision.

The bottom of the sarcophagus fell away, and Church plummeted into the dark.

2

Miller wrung his hands together. 'Where are we? Inside the pyramid? Or not?'

'You'll get used to it.' Ruth watched the door for any sign of Veitch returning. He'd been gone for at least two hours with the Anubis Box. Ruth had tried to accompany him, but the gods had barred her way.

She waited with Miller in an opulent state-room covered in hiero-glyphics and decorated with gold and lapis lazuli. Water splashed from a graven lion's head into a large rectangular pool that reflected the torch-light. Everywhere appeared cool and peaceful, but there was an under-lying air of tension.

Way out of his depth, Miller hugged his knees. 'Are they really gods?'

'They like to think they are. Higher powers, say. None of them can be trusted – they've all got their own agendas.'

'I wish Ryan would tell me why he needs me.'

'Why do you keep giving him the time of day?' Ruth replied with frustration. 'You should brain him with a rock the first chance you get.'

'Ruth!' Miller tried to see if she was joking. 'He's a good man. He just doesn't know it.'

'He's murdered hundreds of decent people, if not thousands. That's not any definition of "good" that I know.'

Miller shook his head defiantly, but Ruth noted he didn't press her with any more questions.

'I'm sorry you got dragged into this,' she said. 'You seem all right.'

'I just don't understand what part I have to play.'

'A big part.' Ruth put a maternal arm around his shoulders. 'You're not alone, Miller. We're all pawns that those higher powers shuffle around the board, and most of the time we've got no idea what part we're playing in this big, incomprehensible game.'

'I wish I was like you. Confident.'

Ruth was surprised; she didn't feel confident. Most of the time she was acting on instinct, trying to hold it together. Was that really how others saw her?

'And that spear you've got. Sometimes when I look at it out of the corner of my eye, it doesn't seem like a spear at all. It's like a . . .' He thought for a moment, then shook his head.

'I'm surprised Veitch lets me keep it.'

Miller laughed. 'You don't know how he feels about you!'

'What?'

'He thinks you're special. He trusts you. And he . . . oh, it's not for me to say.' He looked away shyly, but his meaning was clear.

'You're joking. He really thinks he's got a right to fall for me?'

'If you knew how strongly he feels—'

'Shut up. I don't want to hear it.'

The great gold doors at the far end of the room swung open soundlessly. Four guards in headdresses and silver kilts flanked Veitch, who held the Anubis Box tightly against his chest. The guards had a plastic quality to their faces that Ruth had seen on the younger members of the Tuatha Dé Danann, as if they had been newly constructed.

'Sold the human race down the river yet?' Ruth asked.

'You've got it all wrong,' Veitch replied. 'The gods are as scared of this as you are. They don't want to use it, just keep it safe somewhere.'

'That doesn't make sense. They created it.'

'Who cares? All I know is that it's going to buy us safe passage across all the Great Dominions. No more of these bastards preying on us. Then I'll be able to find the Second Key without any hassle and get down to business.'

Miller eyed the box warily. They could all feel some kind of force coming off it in waves. 'Why haven't they taken it away from you?'

'They said they need to prepare for it.'

'You trust them?' Ruth asked.

'No. But they know – like you – that if anyone tries to screw with me, I'm taking the lid off this thing. Then we'll see what happens.'

3

Ethereal string music echoed distantly and the sweet aroma of incense filled the air. Laura opened her eyes. She was lying on a cold slab, unable to move her arms or legs. The last thing she remembered was stepping out of the oasis of Blue Fire and following in the footsteps of Osiris. Craning her neck, she saw that she was bound from feet to waist with linen mummification strips; further wrappings pinned her hands to her sides and continued up her arms to her shoulders. She only perceived these details peripherally, however, for her attention was almost immediately transfixed by a horror so great it took a second to comprehend. Her chest had been cracked open. She could see her organs glistening from her breastbone to her navel, yet she felt no pain. As the shock subsided, she screamed long and hard and blacked out briefly.

When she came round again, it was with the reassuring thought that she wasn't human. She could survive this, had already survived things that would have killed anyone she knew. Unable to bear the view, she closed her eyes, calming herself. And when she opened them next, she was not alone.

His skull-head yellow in the flickering torchlight, Osiris sat on a stone throne at the end of the chamber beyond her feet. Beside him stood many other beings, a number of them with animal heads, which Laura guessed were his fellow gods.

'You have been brought into the Court of the Two Ma'ats to declare innocence of wrongs before the great god, and before the full tribunal of forty-two divine assessors,' Osiris intoned. 'You must defend yourself successfully or be destroyed for ever.'

'You told me I wouldn't be wiped from Existence,' she said angrily. Laura was shocked to hear her voice, a rustle of autumn leaves, barely holding on.

'And you will not. If you defend yourself successfully.'

Laura released a foul-mouthed tirade that at least made her feel a little better.

'The Brothers and Sisters of Dragons are an anomaly in this world,' Osiris continued. 'You were created for a world that does not exist, by a power that does not rule, which is an echo of the one true god that made this place.'

'I get it. You're just a bunch of arse-kissing collaborators. You see who's in the driving seat and you get right behind them. "Yes, boss, no, boss." I've seen your kind in every awful job I've tried to do in my miserable life.' She was proud that she sounded so defiant.

'What is the point in offering the promise of magic to a people dwelling in a place where there can *be* no magic?' Osiris continued. 'In offering hope where there can be none? It only makes the people restless and bitter and sorrowful. It disrupts the tranquillity of their lives and ruins what little joy they might find in their short existence. What you do is cruelty. What you bring to this stable world is terror. The Brothers and Sisters of Dragons are not a force for good, but for harm.'

'So you're saying we should give up and accept the world's a mess? Just because people are stumbling along blindly—'

'They are content.'

'Because they don't know what they *could* have.'

'They never will. Not in this world.'

'Then we'll blow the damn thing up and start again.'

'You must recognise the absurdity of your words: that a handful of mortals could unseat the great architect of the universe.'

'You're not recognising something, bonehead,' she spat. 'We've got the Pendragon Spirit, and it's alive. And every human being has a shard of that power in them, just waiting to be awakened. That's why you want to destroy us, and the big bad Void wants to keep us contained and living in ignorance – because you're scared of what we might achieve if the human race ever opens its eyes.'

There was silence for a long moment, and then Osiris raised a hand. 'The judgment will commence. And if you are found wanting, the Pendragon Spirit will be removed and destroyed. And one by one the lights will be extinguished, and the Blue Fire will die, and there will only be the comforting, endless dark.'

'You don't get to judge me,' Laura said. 'No one does.'

'I call forth the Lord of the Sacred Words.'

The ranks separated and a god with the hunched body and features of a baboon stepped forward. He unfurled a papyrus scroll, which he set on a lectern, and then took up a reed pen, poised to write.

'Thoth, god of wisdom, will record the judgment.'

Then came Anubis, jackal eyes glittering coldly. He held a pair of golden scales with a feather resting on one dish.

'The god of embalming will weigh your heart against the feather to see if you are worthy of joining the ancient gods in the Fields of Reeds.'

'Why do I get the feeling you've already made up your mind?'

Laura was overcome by a deep sense of dread. A shadow fell across her, and it was the coldest thing she had ever experienced. Webs of frost bloomed on her skin. Something loomed over her just beyond her field of vision; she had the feeling she would go mad if her eyes were to fall on it.

'If you are judged unworthy, if you are found false and wicked, the daemon Ammut is here. She is the Devourer of the Damned. She will eat your heart, and then she will eat you, and you will die the ultimate death – wiped from Existence, never to have been.'

Laura closed her eyes and tried not to tremble but failed. She wanted to say something brave and clever, but no words would come.

'Let the judgment begin,' Osiris announced.

Church found himself in a stone tunnel lit by torches. Along one wall there was a beautiful relief of brightly coloured images that appeared to tell a story. The hieroglyphics made no sense to him, but amongst the scarabs and stylised men and animal-headed gods, there was a scene of a row of gods bowing down to what was unmistakably a Caraprix.

His thoughts were interrupted by the sudden arrival of a cursing Hunter, then Shavi, Fayed and finally Etain.

Church took Etain's cold, dead hand. 'I don't know if you can understand me, but thank you for bringing us this far. I'm sorry for what happened to you. I didn't mean for you to die, and if there's any way I can make up for it, I will.' He let the words hang in the air. Etain continued to stare at him with wide, unblinking eyes.

After a moment, she marched along the passage. As they followed her, the atmosphere in the tunnel became increasingly heady, and an unreal quality permeated everything.

'Someone is coming,' Shavi said. Church had noticed that Shavi's perception was now so sharp he was aware of things long before anyone else.

Church drew his sword. They waited.

Running footsteps echoed off the stone. A figure hurtled around a bend in the tunnel, and Church was shocked to see a duplicate of himself. The new-Church, however, did not appear to be shocked at coming into contact with his doppelgänger.

He ran up to Church and the others. 'Is this it? Is this the right time?' he gasped. 'You have to listen to me. This is a warning.' He looked around, confused. '*Is* this the right place? Am I too late?'

A chill ran through Church. 'This doesn't make sense.'

'When you're in Otherworld and they call, heed it right away. They're going to bring him back. They're—'

Church turned to Hunter. 'I've experienced this before. It was an echo, or something like that, some breakdown in time and space, between when I was in the other place . . . after the casket of spiders . . . between there and when I was in Edinburgh . . .' He dried up, unable to explain the bizarre sequence of events clearly.

'Okay, the medication is clearly not working,' Hunter said.

Church turned back to his other self. 'That was a closed loop, an echo. It shouldn't be happening here.'

The new-Church became gripped with fear. In panic, he yelled, 'Too late!' and then he was running back along the tunnel. The footsteps quickly faded to nothing.

Church was filled with a deep anxiety. 'What is going on?'

Shavi rested a hand on his shoulder. 'Some say moments of great trauma can resonate through all time, through reality itself, imprinted on the very essence of what is. A fingerprint on a window, a trace memory of what was.'

'When I was in that cavern, before I met the Caretaker and I made that warning, it felt unreal,' Church said, 'as if I was mouthing someone else's words.' He sheathed his sword. 'So what was I really trying to warn myself about? What's waiting for us?'

'It is best not to try to second-guess the future. That is a guarantee for living in fear,' Shavi said. 'Follow the Buddhist code: live in the moment. It is the only way to find peace.'

Unsettled, they continued through enormous, ringing chambers, some filled with reflecting pools, others with shafts piercing upwards through the stone to frame stars or the moon. There were palms and strange, alien flowers, statues of cats and crocodiles and hawks, and an overwhelming air of grandeur.

'I don't like this,' Church said. 'Where is everybody?'

'Do you hear that? Ritual music?' Shavi cocked his head. 'And I smell incense.' He broke off to the left, following the sound and smell. It brought him to a row of lattice windows, each barely bigger than a hand. Peering through, Church and Shavi saw Laura lying on the slab.

Church blocked Hunter from seeing. 'We need to get into that room,' Church said.

'Let me see.'

'No. It's Laura. They've cut her open.'

Hunter thrust Church to one side. When he turned back from the window, his face was like iron. 'She's still alive. She's a tough kid. Let's get her out.'

'The chamber is filled with gods,' Shavi said. 'We could not survive.'

5

'Will you shut the hell up? You're driving me crazy!' Veitch ranged around the chamber, followed closely by Ruth.

'I'm just trying to get you to see sense. We were a team once. Come back and work with us—'

209

'I preferred you when you were ready to stab me in the back. At least you were quiet.'

'I'm not saying I've forgiven you for what you did. Jesus, who could—'

'You think that's a good way to win me over?'

Ruth glanced at Miller, who urged her to continue. She chose her words carefully. 'I know you've had some hard times. And it's made you bitter. And you've done some . . . questionable things. But Miller is right. Existence wouldn't have chosen you to be a Brother of Dragons if you weren't inherently good. Screwed up, massively flawed – clearly, but good nevertheless.'

'There you go with those compliments again.' Veitch glared at Miller. 'Should have realised this had your fingerprints all over it.'

'No, this is me talking to you, Veitch. Ryan. From the heart. For old times' sake. Don't hand over the Anubis Box. Come back to us. Do the right thing.'

'You really think I can wash all that blood off my hands just like that?'

Ruth remained silent.

'Yeah, didn't think so. Fact is, I'm the wounded party here. I'm the one who was led on – yeah, by you, right? Remember that? I'm the one who was abandoned by my mates and then screwed by Existence, left to rot until the Army of the Ten Billion Spiders gave me a leg-up.'

'It wasn't like that, and you know it! They used you, as much as those gods who manipulated you.'

'And I've had enough of it. I'm bringing the whole fucking building down, and fuck the lot of you.' He gripped the Anubis Box so hard, Ruth was afraid it would shatter.

'It's a childish gesture,' she said. 'Wreck everything just so you can stamp your foot and get back at everyone who's hurt your feelings. And I so mean wreck *everything* – the whole universe! How insane is that?'

'Yeah, well, I don't do anything by half-measures.' Veitch stared into the waters of the reflecting pool, deep in thought. 'Okay,' he said after a moment. 'I'll do it. I'll come back and help you lot out.'

Ruth could barely believe her ploy had worked. 'All right—'

'All you've got to do is tell me you love me.'

Ruth's mouth fell open. She could see in Veitch's face that he was serious.

'And mean it. I'll know if you're lying.'

'I can't do that.'

Veitch nodded slowly. 'I know. Whatever you say, I'm not an idiot.'

The door swung open and Owein, Tannis and Branwen entered. Veitch was briefly puzzled by Etain's absence, but then turned back to Ruth. The sadness in his face shocked her.

'See, there's no point in me doing the right thing.'

'Of course there is. Do it for yourself.'

He shook his head. 'I'm a lost cause, darlin'. You're the only thing that matters, the only thing worth fighting for in this fucked-up world. For you, I'd do anything.'

Ruth was speechless.

As Veitch went over to the Brothers and Sisters of Spiders, Ruth sat down with Miller, touched and confused. 'Why does he feel that strongly about me?' Anger followed the confusion, but she didn't know why.

The electric sound of Veitch drawing his sword demanded their attention. The black fire that leaped across the room was mirrored in his face. 'Traitorous bitch,' he snarled. Then, to Ruth: 'Betrayed again, see? That's what life is for me.'

'I don't understand. How did they communicate with you?'

Ignoring her question, Veitch replied, 'Etain has brought that bastard Church here to get me when my guard is down. Only I'm going to get him first, and this time I'm not making any mistakes. He dies.'

6

Laura sat on the top of a dune and stared into the heat haze hanging on the horizon. The desert stretched out as far as the eye could see in all directions, as desolate as her heart. She smelled the odour of carrion long before the jackal appeared around the foot of the dune and sat on its haunches on the slope just below her. Its glittering, intelligent eyes fixed on her and it said in a low voice, 'Laura, with the chosen name DuSantiago.'

This made perfect sense to Laura. 'Got it in one.'

'You are lost. You have been lost all your life. Is that correct?'

Laura didn't answer.

The jackal looked to its left where a six-year-old blonde girl was being hit with a Bible by a woman. The girl was crying, but trying to smile through the tears.

'Were you a dutiful child? Did you follow the path of right?'

'You're joking, aren't you? First chance, I was out of there with one mission: take whatever life had to offer.'

A thirteen-year-old Laura swallowing an E before lying down to have sex with a long-haired man with a back covered with tattoos.

She watched herself in coitus. 'I never did get his name,' she said dispassionately. 'You always remember your first time. I wish I could scrub it out of my mind with a wire brush.'

Another jackal wandered around the foot of the dune and settled to gnaw on a thigh bone.

'Did you give back for the life that had been given to you?' Anubis asked.

'The life given to me?' Laura snapped. 'A mum who beat me into next week from when I was old enough to walk, and a dad who sat back and watched, making sympathetic noises and doing nothing. Yeah, it was one big celebration.'

'Did you have any friends?'

'I had myself.'

'Did you honour your parents, who brought you into the world and nurtured you?'

Tears sprang to her eyes. 'Let's see that, shall we.'

To her right, she lay on the sand while her mother carved *Jesus loves you* into her back with a kitchen knife. 'No, I don't think I honoured them.' She wiped her tears away with the back of her hand, leaving a gritty trail of sand on her cheek.

'What value did your life have?'

Laura watched numerous scenes play out of her drinking, taking drugs, having sex, committing petty crime. 'None,' she said. The weight on her heart was growing heavier by the minute.

More scenes unfolded, desperate and pathetic.

'You agree that your existence was worthless?'

'Yes.' She stifled a sob. She had always known it, deep in her heart.

'You have squandered that vital resource given to all living things?'

'Yes, yes, yes! I always knew life was pointless. I learned my lesson well.'

Behind her, the sound of heavy movement. Fear bloomed inside her, taking root in the despair. She didn't dare look around as the cold shadow fell on her back.

'Does anyone stand with you?'

'No,' Laura sobbed. 'Who'd stand with me?'

'We would.'

Laura saw Church standing next to her, Caledfwlch in his hand, the blue flames licking gently in the desert breeze.

'Lives are filled with disappointments and failures. It's easy to focus on them, and once they've happened, they're always there, tugging at your memory. It feels as if you can't escape them.' Church gently brushed the hair from Laura's forehead.

'You have no authority here,' Anubis said.

'It doesn't matter what happened in Laura's old life,' Church continued regardless. 'It doesn't matter what flaws she still carries around with her – the kind of flaws we all carry. Because she's aspiring to be something better, and that's what really matters. She pretends she doesn't care about anything, but we can all see the truth. She's chosen to walk this path. She's put her life on the line for others. She's risked everything when there appeared to be no hope of ever winning. But do you know what the real proof of her value is?'

'You have no authority here.' Anubis's words turned to an animal growl.

'She's found friends, the kind of friends you rarely make, who would lay down their lives for her.'

Laura thought she would cry.

'*You* have no authority here,' Church said. 'We're Brothers and Sisters of Dragons. We stand for Life. And I'm taking Laura away from here now.'

'The judgment is not complete!' Anubis bared his teeth and howled. As the furious sound rolled out, the desert melted away and the desolation faded with it until Laura was lying back on the slab.

'Hello, darlin'. That's going to leave a nasty scar.' Hunter stood on the other side, pretending to be aloof.

'You love this, don't you? Playing the big hero saving the girl,' she croaked.

'Yeah. It's my job.'

'I think we should save the witty repartee until we are actually out of here,' Shavi said as he lifted Laura off the slab. 'I'm going to bind your chest with mummy wrappings,' he said to her gently.

'Good old Shavi,' Laura replied dreamily. She felt as if she was slipping away.

Osiris rose from his throne. 'I expected more of the Brothers and Sisters of Dragons. You stand here in the Court of the Two Ma'ats before the lords of the greatest of the Great Dominions. No stealth, no cleverness, just futile bravado. Now you will all be judged, and afterwards the Pendragon Spirit will be torn from you, and you will be devoured by the daemon Ammut.'

A shiver in the dark at the back of the chamber.

'Your legend gone for ever. Everything you did, everything you stood for, forgotten. And this will eternally be the world of the Devourer of All Things. Without magic. Without hope.'

'He's got a point,' Hunter said. 'How were you planning to get out of here?'

'I was planning on them recognising our superior ability and just letting us leave,' Church said.

'Can you two cut the comedy routine and get us out of here,' Laura croaked. 'I'm starting to feel in desperate need of a serious drink.'

Church and Hunter shared a brief look. Beyond them, Laura saw the gods not in the shapes they had given themselves, but in the essence of their power, their animal-totem wildness, so uncontrollable and destructive that any one of them could crush Church or Hunter in an instant.

'Thanks for trying, guys,' she said weakly.

She wondered why Church was looking towards the door. When it swung open, she realised he had arranged some kind of diversion to help them escape.

'Always the man with the plan,' she whispered. Now that she was off the slab, pain was creeping into her limbs.

Church's expression grew dark.

The door crashed against the stone wall and a young Egyptian man came sprawling in. Behind him walked Etain, her dead eyes fixed on Church, and behind her came Veitch, his blade of black fire pressed against the nape of Etain's neck. His anger was barely contained.

'Jack Churchill, you bastard,' he snarled. 'You're not going to rest until you destroy everything that matters to me, are you?'

'Etain came to us, Ryan. You'd better ask her why she did that.'

Confused, Veitch glanced at Etain, but didn't ask the question. He removed his sword from her neck and brandished it at Church. 'You and me. Now.'

'Slightly busy just at the moment.' Hunter gestured to the gods, but Veitch could only see Church.

'I beat you the last time we fought, Ryan. I killed you.'

Veitch grinned. 'You were meant to. It got me just what I wanted.' He advanced, taking in Laura, and Shavi, kneeling next to her and binding her wounds. 'Come on. Now.'

'I'm not going to fight you, Ryan.'

'You don't have a choice.'

Now grave, Hunter said, 'If we don't get Laura out of here, she's going to die, no matter how special she is.'

Laura heard the concern in his voice and smiled.

'You're saying that like I care,' Veitch spat.

'I think you do,' Church said. Laura could tell he was fighting not to reveal his true feelings about Veitch. 'You used to care a lot, for all of us,' he continued. 'Those kinds of feelings don't go away. They just get buried beneath all the crap.'

'Is that what you call what happened to me?' Laura met Veitch's eyes, but he looked away. 'No chance,' he continued. 'It's too late.'

A scuffle outside the door ended with Ruth bursting in, the other Brothers and Sister of Spiders scrabbling to hold on to her.

'Ryan, don't be an idiot!' She grabbed Veitch's shoulder to hold him back.

'Ruth, get over here!' Church called, elation and concern fighting in his voice.

At Osiris's command, Anubis and a hawk-headed god approached. Laura tried to warn Church, but her voice was now too feeble to carry.

'Don't let Laura die,' Ruth said to Veitch. 'You have the power to save her. You can do something right.'

'Why should I?'

'Do it for me.'

Veitch wavered. 'Will that change your mind?'

'I don't know. It might.' Ruth's voice had grown quiet, almost disappearing beneath the growl that issued from the back of the room.

'You are unreliable, Brother of Spiders,' Osiris boomed.

'That's not my name.' Veitch hesitated, then turned to face the gods. 'I'm not standing with you,' he said to Church. 'As soon as we're out of here, I'm going to end this.'

'Sounds good to me,' Church said.

'As unlikely as it is that I'm the voice of reason,' Hunter interjected, 'but do you want me to do a quick headcount and tell you how seriously we're outnumbered?'

'I always keep a little something in reserve,' Veitch said.

Hunter grinned. 'You're a man after my own heart, Veitch.' He removed something from his shirt that he kept hidden in his palm.

'You and that utility belt, Hunter,' Laura whispered. 'Always full of surprises.'

'That's me, baby. And when we're out of here, I'll show you another one.'

'I'll hold you to that.' Laura's vision dimmed. She couldn't tell if Hunter's bravado was just for her sake.

God, I'm dying, she thought. Shavi dragged her towards the door, pausing to finish binding her wounds with unsettling urgency. She tried to offer him words of comfort, but she began to slip in and out of consciousness.

Distantly, she heard Osiris issue an order and there was wild, terrifying movement from the back of the chamber. She heard Ruth scream. A freezing shadow fell across her as Ammut rushed from the shadows.

Everything began to come in flashes, like snapshots dropped before her eyes. Disconnected sounds came and went like the surf. There was a small explosion and the room was filled with acrid smoke. Hunter said something about thanking Omari and the Egyptian Secret Service. The Egyptian man was beside her saying, 'Will she live?' and Shavi hushed him.

And then she had the most amazing vision of Blue Fire and black lightning flashing across the room. Church and Veitch were involved in a graceful, athletic fight with the daemon, ducking, leaping, their blades slashing in shimmering arcs.

When her gaze fell on their target, she dry-retched and her brain would accept no clear images of it, but she had residual flashes of fangs and red, hateful eyes.

And then Hunter loomed over her, and he was grinning as she always remembered, but there was an intense, incongruous sadness in his eyes.

'Don't worry,' she said. 'I can't feel it any more.' But he didn't appear to hear.

'Get her out of here,' he said urgently to Shavi. 'She's going.' He kissed her gently on the lips with a surprising tenderness that she hadn't seen in him before. She remembered what Osiris had said in the oasis about both of them being lost, and she wondered oddly if they were now found.

He put his lips to her ear. 'I—'

She never heard the rest.

7

In the confusion, Hunter, Shavi and Fayed carried Laura out into the corridor. Church, Ruth and Veitch fought for their lives as the Devourer of the Damned drove them back. Numerous blows had been struck, but its true form was too slippery for their perception to tell how badly it had been wounded.

Through the curling smoke, Church could see the gods becoming more animal than human with each step. Anubis loped on all fours, preparing to attack. Sobek slithered in his crocodile form, jaws gaping wide.

'Get over there and hold them back,' Veitch snarled. Etain instantly led the Brothers and Sisters of Spiders to protect Veitch's right flank.

'They're going to be slaughtered,' Church shouted.

'Serves her right.'

'She brought me here to take Ruth away. God knows how or why, but I think she cares for you.'

'Can't believe someone likes me?' Veitch lashed out furiously. There was a roar of pain from Ammut as the black lightning struck.

'She's dead, Ryan.'

Veitch didn't respond.

Wielding her spear expertly, Ruth came between the two of them. 'Stop it. In about three minutes we're all going to be dead.'

Anubis's snapping jaws tore a chunk out of Owein's arm. He continued to hack at the god regardless.

'For God's sake, can't one of you useless males do something?' Ruth snapped. She fell back with a yell as the Devourer raised blood on her cheek.

Veitch cursed loudly. 'Can you hold it off for a few seconds?'

'What are you going to do? Run?'

'What I'd like to do is ram this sword up your arse. Instead, I'm going to give up my "Get Out of Jail Free" card.'

Ruth retaliated with a ferocious spear strike. 'Don't be an idiot. You can't control it.'

'They're scared of it – that's a good enough reason to use it. Are you seriously telling me it's going to be worse than this?'

'Would one of you tell me what the hell's going on?' Church yelled.

'The Anubis Box,' Ruth replied breathlessly. 'Ryan was going to trade it for free passage through the Great Dominions.'

'It's too dangerous!'

'Sometimes you've got to take a leap in the dark.' Veitch stepped back and removed the Anubis Box from inside his shirt. In one swift move-ment, he tore off the lid.

Church and Ruth yelled as one, but their voices, and all sound in the chamber, were sucked into the darkness in the box. For one moment everything hung, silent, motionless.

A barely audible susurration. Then tendrils as black and shiny as oil erupted from the box, lashing out with intelligence, accompanied by a deafening roaring. Veitch could barely hold on to the box, so great was the force of the evacuation. The gods ran in terror, but the tendrils sought them out, latching on to their faces, their limbs, pouring into their mouths, noses and ears.

217

When Church had last witnessed the contents of the box in action, it had been controlled by the crystal skull, but here it was untrammelled. The gods began to disintegrate at its touch.

Other tendrils splattered against the walls and ceiling, seeking out the minute cracks between the cyclopean blocks of stone. Soon after there came an ear-piercing squealing that drowned out even the deafening roar emerging from the box.

'It's attacking the spiders!' Church yelled.

When they had all reached the door, Veitch hurled the box into the chamber, his arms shaking from the strain of holding on to it. The sound that followed would haunt them for ever: the shrieks of dying gods.

With the fabric of the building shaking as the contents of the box sought out every hidden part of the structure, they ran through clouds of dust and falling masonry until they reached the place where they had entered the pyramid-space, where the others waited. As each crossed the mark of a scarab inscribed in the flags, they were flung upwards, blacking out briefly before finding themselves in the sarcophagus in the King's Chamber.

The pyramid continued to shake, though not as devastatingly as its counterpart in the Otherworld, and there was no sign of the spiders, but still they ran, and didn't stop until they were in the chill night air beside the Sphinx.

His face drawn, Hunter carried Laura's unmoving form to one side. Miller ran to help, but though he hung over her for long minutes he could do nothing to revive her. 'I can't find the spark,' he said tearfully.

Veitch was oblivious to the distress that drew Shavi, Fayed and Ruth to Laura. He turned to Church, eyes blazing. 'Let's do it.'

The anger that had been eating away at Church had been fired by Ruth's troubling responses in the pyramid. It left questions that he wasn't sure he wanted answered. 'I've had enough of you screwing things up,' he said, drawing his sword.

'I've barely started.' Veitch drew his own blade.

A shadow crossed the moon. In a thunderous cloud of feathers, the *Morvren* swept in from the direction of the city, emitting their cry of dismay and suffering. Within seconds of their descent over the pyramids and Sphinx, flakes of snow began to fall. A bitter wind whisked them into a blizzard that soon coated sand and rock. Church and Veitch backed away from each other, shivering. With the unnatural localised storm came an abiding sense of presence.

Out of the swirling snow, a figure appeared. The cries of the *Morvren* took on a desperate, frightened edge. It was a god, ten feet tall and wearing the traditional Egyptian clothes of the ruling class. Despite its aristocratic manner, its features were brutish, part pig, part ass. It carried a staff mounted with a single golden eye.

Fayed pressed himself against the stone of the Sphinx. 'Seth,' he said in a voice almost lost to the icy gale. 'God of evil and the desert.'

Seth loomed over them. 'Sheathe your swords, Fragile Creatures. There is nothing to be gained by confronting you at this time.' His voice sounded like a boulder being dragged over gravel. 'The destruction you have wrought here will reverberate across all Existence. You have slain gods, the source of wonder that your own ancestors worshipped.'

'You shouldn't have sided with the Enemy,' Church said.

'Are these, then, your morals? The near-eradication of an entire race to achieve your aims?'

Church was bowed by his words. 'It was them or us,' he responded feebly.

'My people took the decision to walk with the Devourer of All Things a long time ago. But I was the first. When the spiders came to me in the long dark of the desert night, I recognised our place in the vast sweep of everything. To rule—'

'To serve!'

'To be part of something greater.' Seth's piggy eyes lay heavily on Church. 'And for a long time we were. Now only I remain.'

'So why all the bleedin' chat?' The black flames of Veitch's sword cast odd shadows across his snow-flecked face. 'If you want to get your revenge, give it your best shot.'

'I have observed you from the moment you crossed into this Great Dominion, and I have learned a great deal,' Seth continued. 'Existence has found powerful champions, but the seeds of your own destruction lie within you. That information is valuable and will be returned to the source.'

Near the foot of the Sphinx, Hunter and Shavi were hunched over Laura, oblivious to Seth. Church couldn't tell if she was alive or dead.

'Run back to your safe-zone with all your ugly bastard pals, then,' Veitch said. 'You're done here.'

A glimmer of contemptuous humour crossed Seth's face. 'And you run on your way, Fragile Creatures, like the frightened vermin you are at heart. You may have slain the most wondrous of wonders today, but you are not gods. You will never be gods. You think if the Mundane Spell fails, if you find the two Keys, that you will have a chance to build your shining city. You will not. This is a world without hope, yet you appear blind to that fact. How wilfully stupid, how very typical of Fragile

Creatures. So go now. Run. I see there is nothing in you to truly fear. Go to the Forbidden City and ask the location of the Second Key. It will do you no good.'

Church tried to pretend that nothing vitally important had been said, but he could see Veitch had registered it, too.

Seth stepped back into the gusting snow. 'Ask the King of Foxes. He has learned many things to which even the greatest power is blind.' The words were delivered flatly, but there was an inherent note of threat: Seth clearly did not believe they would survive any meeting with the King of Foxes. More snow swirled, and when it cleared Seth was gone.

Church and Veitch studied each other's faces for a moment. Then they turned and ran, Church for the truck, Veitch for a battered taxi cab abandoned near the edge of the necropolis.

Tom was asleep in the passenger seat of the truck and jerked awake when Church fired the ignition and sent the vehicle lurching towards the Sphinx.

'Is the Devil after us?' Tom spluttered, still half in a dream.

'No, we're racing him for the prize.'

Veitch in his taxi reached the Sphinx a few seconds ahead of Church. He leaped out and threw Miller into the back seat.

Church was out and running as Veitch grabbed Ruth's arm. 'Fight him till I get there!' Church yelled.

In Ruth's face, Church saw the same inexplicable uncertainty he had witnessed in the pyramid. Her eyes met his for a fleeting instant, which only confirmed his doubts, and then she was being bundled into the cab with no resistance.

He watched the cab roar away in a cloud of dust towards the lights of Cairo until Fayed gripped his elbow. 'The others need you. Your friend has little time left.'

Throwing off his troubled thoughts, Church ran to where Shavi and Hunter crouched over Laura. The desperation in Hunter's eyes made him look more acutely human than Church had thought possible.

'I don't know what to do,' he said to Church.

'No pulse,' Shavi said.

'I don't know if she ever had a pulse after Cernunnos changed her,' Church replied.

'Still, the life is leaking out of her. Nearly gone now.' Shavi rubbed the skin around his alien eye, seeing something invisible to the rest of them.

'What are you saying?' Hunter asked bitterly. 'We give up? I thought we were supposed to be some kind of heroes.'

'We can't do anything for her here,' Church said. 'But in the Other-world, anything is possible.'

Hunter's face came alive. 'Some spell . . . magic . . . the Blue Fire. Or one of those golden-skinned gods.'

'But you have never visited Tir n'a n'Og,' Shavi said. 'How will you cope?'

'I'll go anywhere,' Hunter said. 'To hell's door and beyond.' He looked down at Laura's face. 'Nothing's going to stop me.'

'Then we need to find a place to cross over,' Shavi said.

His words gave Hunter pause. 'I can't hold you back. You need to catch up with Veitch.' He paused, shook his head. 'What am I saying? You need me here. I can't go running off . . .' He tore his gaze away from Laura. '. . . just for personal reasons. None of us matter. Only the mission's important.'

Church looked from Hunter to Laura, and saw Ruth instead. 'Take her. This isn't just about saving the whole universe. Some things are more important than that.'

Hunter's haunted eyes thanked Church silently, and as he carried Laura to the truck, Shavi said to Fayed, 'Are you coming with us? This is your chance to see wonders of which you have only ever dreamed.'

'I am returning to my home, and I will never speak of these events again,' Fayed replied.

'But you wished to see the gods.'

'I have a wife and a child and another on the way. I have a job that is slow and laborious and dusty. I am human, only human. These things I have seen – these wonders and horrors – will haunt my thoughts for the rest of my days. I can never go back to being the man I was. You were meant to experience these things. I was not.'

'We're only human, too,' Church said.

'Perhaps you were once. But your experiences have changed you. You stand against the gods with impunity. You wield weapons that were not meant for men. You are as far beyond me now as the gods are beyond you.'

He turned without another word and trudged towards Cairo. Church watched him go, desperately afraid that what he had said was true, for if it was, the lives they knew, and to which they hoped to return, were over.

8

The cauldron of the southern Sahara was beginning to heat up. The first curve of the sun wavered in the haze on the horizon, but the moon and a scattering of stars still glowed ghostly in the lightening sky.

'Hard drive.' Church was swathed in a scarf wrapped tightly around his head to keep the biting sand at bay.

'I do not know how Laura continues to hang on, neither alive nor dead,' Shavi said.

'I hope you're both satisfied,' Tom said harshly. 'Three days we've wasted on this wild-goose chase. Veitch must be halfway to China by now.'

'You really think we could just let her die?' Church replied.

Before them lay a complex of standing stones that stretched for miles: a circle of flat stones surrounded by four pairs of tall stones, and further afield megaliths that rose up ten feet above the desolate landscape.

Shavi indicated some of the stones. 'You can still see the solstice and cardinal alignments. Here in Nabta, this circle was used six thousand years ago, and probably earlier. At least a millennium before Stonehenge. Is that not amazing?'

'Wonderful,' Tom said tartly.

'Religion, science and human society, all coming together at one point. The Egyptian civilization started here.'

'Is there enough Blue Fire left in the sand?' Church asked.

Shavi scanned the ground. 'Thin currents, but I believe it will do.' He shielded his eyes from the sun. 'The Blue Fire is starting to dry up now that it has been cut off from the source. Soon we will not be able to travel between here and Tir n'a n'Og. We will be trapped on Earth.'

'That's what the Enemy wants,' Church said. 'To cut us off from the universe.'

Hunter emerged from the truck with Laura in his arms. 'Are we ready to do this?'

'Are you?'

'Why haven't I got a sword like yours? That would make things so much easier.'

'You think?'

'A warrior without a weapon? Not good.'

'Stop moaning and find something,' Tom snapped. 'You've been complaining about that ever since I met you. Anyone would think you didn't want a weapon.'

Hunter laughed quietly, and then made his way into the centre of the circle. 'All right, throw the switch. Press the button. Say the magic word. A whole new world in which to indulge myself. I like the sound of that. And nobody knows my reputation.'

'Good luck,' Church called.

Tom and Shavi moved to the tall menhirs on either side of the circle. When the rising sun clipped the top of the stones, they placed their right hands firmly on the rock. The earth energy pulsed beneath their fingertips, increasing in force with each beat of their hearts until it rushed upwards to form a blazing azure structure high over the circle. Discharges crackled amongst the stones.

Church had one last sight of Hunter, cocky and grinning, with Laura in his arms, and then there was a flash of blue light and they were gone.

9

Even in the first light the interior of the truck baked as they drove north along the empty desert road. Shavi had remained silent ever since they had set off, staring through the open passenger window across the bleak expanse of sand. Without any warning his head pitched forward and then back, and he gave a low moan.

'You all right?' Church asked.

After a moment, Shavi replied weakly, 'I saw . . . I saw . . .' One hand made a claw over his alien eye, as if he was about to pluck it out. 'I saw death.'

'No surprise there.' Tom sniffed. He turned the ring on his finger with repressed anxiety.

'For the Brothers and Sisters of Dragons. It follows us closely, like your ravens, Church, and not all of us will survive what is to come.' He sighed. 'One of us will die soon.'

'Laura?' Shavi was only confirming what Church had felt instinctively since the ravens had started to follow him.

'I do not know. It is not clear. But I fear for her, Church, and for Hunter.' Tears rimmed his eyes. He looked back out through the window, and no one spoke for the next hour.

chapter ten

the way

1

What is the Burning Man? The question was whispered throughout the claustrophobic, labyrinthine streets and alleys of the Court of the Soaring Spirit, and in the back rooms of the Hunter's Moon, and in the coffee houses and grocery stores and anywhere people passed, quickly, for no one gathered long in a place. It was as if every resident instinctively felt they were being pursued by forces unknown. There was no rest in the court, and little hope, for the distant sound of the Enemy's war drums never ceased, and there were ashes in the wind, and whenever they raised their eyes from the gutter, the Burning Man was there, in the sky on the horizon, hanging over them, a mystery and a threat.

In the secret network of rooms tucked away at the back of the Hunter's Moon, the goddess Rhiannon still lay in the Sleep Like Death. Decebalus cared for her around the clock, with assistance from the young Virginia Dare, but it was not work for a barbarian and he was growing irritable with the constraints of his small existence.

'She's not improving?' Mallory paced by the fire. He had barely rested since they had returned from Ogma's library.

'She muttered one word in the throes of a fever dream, but it made no sense to me.' Decebalus slurped noisily on mutton broth. 'How much longer must I wait here? She will not awaken.'

'We don't know that.'

'She has been like this for days. What will change?'

'Stay positive. She's all we've got. She knows who did this to her, and probably why.'

Grunting, Decebalus pushed back the empty bowl, eyeing Virginia who was curled up asleep in one corner. 'So your trip to the library was a waste of time.'

'You need to kick back, Decebalus. Those veins on your neck are starting to pulse.' Mallory ignored Decebalus's glare. 'For some reason, Math implanted in our minds the image of a calendar split between the good months and the bad. MAT and ANM. Summer and winter.'

'So it was a waste of time.'

'Only till we crack the code. Math probably expected one of his own kind to find it, and that they'd know what he was getting at. We're in the dark.'

'Until you find the light. You are not going to ask one of those golden-skinned bastards?'

'We don't know who we can trust.'

'You cannot trust any of them, ever.'

Mallory looked to Rhiannon. 'I could trust her. She was good to me once.'

'Then you find yourself in a difficult situation. Where next?'

They both started at a knock at the door; Decebalus went for his axe, Mallory for his sword. Another coded knock followed. It was Caitlin, her features delicate against the coarse hood and cloak that swathed her.

'You made sure you weren't followed?' Decebalus said.

'Of course.' She marched in and flopped onto a large wooden chair before the fire. 'I looked all over for Sophie.'

'She said she was going to use her Craft to try to find something,' Mallory said.

'She wasn't in her room, so where's she doing it?' She kicked off her boots and curled her legs under her. 'She seems to have a real downer on me at the moment. What's wrong with her?'

Decebalus sighed loudly. 'I need a drink. Find me in the bar when you are done prattling.'

After he had gone, Mallory said, 'I think we make him uncomfortable.'

'Why would that be?' Caitlin didn't look at him when she spoke.

Mallory steeled himself and drew up a chair. 'We've been stuck with this Pendragon Spirit and none of us knows what it really means.'

'You like your non sequiturs.'

'We do know it creates a bond between us,' Mallory forced himself to continue. 'The kind of bond you rarely find in life.'

Caitlin grew serious. 'That's true. I feel as though I know you . . . all of you . . . better than anyone. Like the friends you always wished for as a kid, but never found.'

'That's it exactly. It's a spiritual thing, if that doesn't sound all hippie and girly.' He let the words hang for a moment, aware that Caitlin was watching him intently. 'That connection is on a spectrum. Friendship merges into—'

'Love?'

He nodded. 'Church and Ruth. Me and Sophie. Patterns repeating. Always patterns.'

'I know what you're trying to say.'

Her words brought him up sharp. 'There's that connection again.'

'Or maybe I'm just really smart.' She smiled, but it didn't ring true. 'I loved my husband more than anything. Yes, we had our problems, mainly down to me, but that love never went away. I miss him every day. I met someone else a while after Grant died, Thackeray was his name, and I started to grow fond of him. Until the Void turned the world upside down and now I've got no idea where he is. And then there's you.'

Her words still hit Mallory hard despite long knowing the unspoken emotions that lay between them.

'You're telling me the Pendragon Spirit may be causing the feelings between us, or it may be magnifying what would already be there,' she continued. 'The why doesn't matter, just that those feelings are there. But recognising doesn't mean acting on them. I know what I feel, and I know you feel something, too, and it's beating you up because you love Sophie. And I know you do because I see it so clearly whenever the two of you are together.'

He nodded, now entranced even more by the depths of her empathy.

'And I recognise what you two have, and I'm not going to go against that. Do you really think I would? The friendship that's the basis of my feelings means I don't want to see you or Sophie hurt, whatever that means for me.' She took a breath. 'I love you, Mallory. That's the first and last time I'll ever say it.'

Her words brought both relief and regret. 'You're a good person.'

'I know. And life would be so much easier if I wasn't.'

'And life would be a little less confusing if good things couldn't be bad, and vice versa. It's all MAT and ANM and ANM and MAT.'

'MAT . . . ANM.'

The words were so quiet they were almost an exhalation. It took Mallory a second to realise they had come from Rhiannon. He raced Caitlin to her side.

Rhiannon was still in a coma, but now her lips moved soundlessly. Mallory put his ear close to her mouth. 'What about MAT and ANM?' he asked quietly.

After a moment he withdrew, lifting one of Rhiannon's eyelids to check her pupil. 'Still gone.'

'Did she make any sense?'

'She said, "Turn the seasons to find the Gateway to Winter." '

2

Sophie and Niamh sprawled on the queen's sumptuous bed in her private chamber. It was hot from the roaring fire and the air was filled with a heavy perfume. Sophie stretched dreamily while Niamh combed her hair with long, soothing strokes.

'You seem troubled,' Niamh said.

'It's that witch. And my boyfriend. I saw her stalking around the palace checking I wasn't around before she crept off to be with him.'

'I fail to understand such betrayal. I had come to believe that Brothers and Sisters of Dragons were noble, honourable beings. To find they are like other Fragile Creatures is dispiriting.'

'Maybe I'm jumping to conclusions—'

'But you saw the way she looked at him?'

'Yes.'

'And your instinct reveals the truth. We discussed that, did we not?'

'I know—'

'Perhaps you should observe them. Now. Then you will be sure of the truth.'

'Spy on them? I couldn't.'

Niamh slipped an arm around Sophie and pulled her head down onto her breast. 'In these dangerous times, would it not be wise to know whom you can trust? Is that not of the utmost importance to the Brothers and Sisters of Dragons? Is that not what Church would want?'

'I suppose. But how should I—'

'You have your Craft.'

Sophie paused. 'I shouldn't really use it for personal gain.'

Niamh stroked Sophie's hair, caressing her ear, her cheek. 'But this is for the Brothers and Sisters of Dragons, not for you.'

Sophie wavered.

'I have the herbs to make the balm. In fact, I shall help you in the preparation. Sisters together!'

Niamh slid from the bed and unlocked an ornate cabinet containing an array of jars and phials. Sophie browsed them for a moment before removing the necessary ones, and a cream to provide a base. As she ground them with a mortar and pestle, the leaves released the bittersweet aroma she recalled so clearly from her studies. 'Thank you,' she said. 'If not for you, I'd feel so alone.'

Niamh traced her fingers down the nape of Sophie's neck, releasing a shiver of pleasure. 'I told you,' Niamh breathed into her ear, 'I am here for you, always.'

Once the balm was complete, they returned to the bed. There was a moment of shyness as Sophie eyed Niamh, but the goddess simply leaned forward and kissed Sophie gently on the lips. Slowly, she undid Sophie's dress and eased it over her head. When Sophie was naked, Niamh pressed her to the bed, easing a pillow under the small of her back.

'People talk of witches riding broomsticks.' Sophie's breaths were short, her eyes closed. 'They don't realise it's just a misunderstanding of the word "riding".' She giggled, embarrassment and anticipation stirring her feelings. 'The wise women used their broomsticks to apply the balm to the vaginal walls so it was absorbed into the bloodstream quickly. But the flight part, that wasn't a metaphor. It was true.'

Niamh traced circles on Sophie's belly, bringing shivers of satisfaction. From the bedside cabinet, Sophie removed a spindle used to wrap parchment. Niamh whispered, 'Let me.'

Sophie acquiesced without a second thought. Niamh applied the balm to the spindle and then with her free hand stroked Sophie's pubic hair. Barely touching at all, she continued down between Sophie's legs, along her lips and back.

'Are you ready?' she breathed.

'Yes,' Sophie moaned.

Niamh kissed Sophie's pubic mound before easing one finger in to open her up. Sophie moaned louder and arched her back. Once she was lubricated, Niamh gently inserted the tip of the spindle and applied the balm.

Sophie was overcome with the most intense sexual desires. She had always found the ritual stimulating, but there was something in the atmosphere in the room, or in Niamh's company, or in the oddly heady wine that Niamh had encouraged Sophie to drink, that drove her instantly to the brink of orgasm.

As the balm entered her blood, the erotic charge retreated. Sophie felt her consciousness falling back into her head, into the soothing dark where the trapdoor of reality lay.

There was a rush like the most exciting fairground ride, and then she was out of her body and soaring up to the ornate ceiling. Looking down, she saw herself writhing in pleasure as Niamh ran a finger around her clitoris, still barely touching. In her pure state, a pang of guilt ran through her. It was ritual, but from her new perspective it appeared to be so much more.

Without a backward glance, she rose through the ceiling and the rooms above until she emerged from the blue-tiled roof into the smell of ashes and the night breeze, and to the sight of the Burning Man high on the horizon.

Exhilarated, she took a deep breath. She was a ghost. Nothing could touch her, but she could see, smell and hear as clearly as if she had substance.

Arching her back, she flew down the side of the palace and across the jumbled rooftops, faster and faster still. And then she dived down into the streets and alleys, flying inches above the cobbles at breakneck speed, shrieking with wild laughter before rising up sharply across a roof and down again. The court passed in a blur. Through windows, she fleetingly saw the occupants going about their private business. She flew with the owls and the bats, and drifted with the smoke rising from the chimneys, and then floated on her back to watch the stars. And then, finally, she was at the Hunter's Moon.

Her exhilaration faded rapidly. Slow-burning anger rose up from the fire that Niamh had stoked, and she knew that she couldn't rest until she had discovered if her suspicions were true. She eased through the tiles into an attic room where a man with scales and a forked tongue and a woman covered with fur were engaged in rough sex; down winding stairs, along twisting, claustrophobic corridors to the room that lay behind a door that resembled a painting of a door.

The instant she saw Caitlin and Mallory a jolt struck her heart, for everything she feared was laid bare in the subtlest of details: the arch of the neck, a look held a fraction of a second too long, the brushing of bodies standing slightly too close. They stood over Rhiannon with their arms almost touching, at an angle so they could look into each other's faces, occasionally glancing down at Rhiannon when she moaned and writhed feverishly.

Sophie ignored the possibility that the goddess might finally be waking. Her attention was held by Mallory and Caitlin; they may as well have been making love before her. Her anger flared as Caitlin touched Mallory's arm to point out some detail of Rhiannon's state. Her anger roared as Mallory whispered a response in Caitlin's ear, his cheek brushing her hair. Her anger became a conflagration as words broke through the dense fury surrounding her brain: 'We . . .', '. . . together . . .', '. . . nobody must know . . .' The rest of it didn't matter; the truth was plain: she had been betrayed by the two people closest to her. She was alone. Except for Niamh, who had been right all along but had never come out and said it for fear of hurting Sophie's feelings.

As the blaze consumed her, she rushed up through the building and into the night sky, driving higher and higher, a burning woman, as isolated as a star.

Gradually, her rage was dampened by a rising sadness, and that was when she looked down at the court far below and saw something that brought her to a sudden halt.

At ground level, the Court of the Soaring Spirit was such a sprawling, jumbled, incoherent city that it was impossible to guess its layout. But high overhead, all was clear.

The court was a perfect circle divided into clearly delineated and equal sectors. She had seen it before. From the air, the Court of the Soaring Spirit was a representation of the Coligny Calendar down to the smallest detail.

'MAT,' she mouthed, transfixed. 'ANM.'

3

The rains started soon after, sheeting from the heavens to cascade off the roofs and gutters, gushing from the mouths of gargoyles and spewing from rusty pipes until the winding, cobbled streets became streams rushing down towards the main gates.

Mallory and Caitlin emerged from the comforting light and warmth of the Hunter's Moon to find Sophie waiting beneath a leaking porch over the dark doorway across the street. She was wrapped in a sodden cloak with scant regard for the downpour.

Happy to see her, Mallory ran across the street and took her in his arms, and if there was a moment of stiffness, he didn't notice it. 'Why didn't you come in?' he asked, giving her a discreet kiss on the forehead.

Sophie eyed Caitlin waiting uncomfortably beneath the Hunter's Moon's front porch. 'I thought I was followed. I didn't want to lead anyone to you.'

'Smart move. From now on, we've got to be even more cautious.' He told her what Rhiannon had said. 'I reckon we're getting close to something.'

Sophie responded with her own observation of the court from on high. 'I don't know if the court is based on the calendar or vice versa, but it can't be a coincidence. It has to be what Math was leading us towards.'

'It fits. Switching the seasons. The Gateway to Winter has got to lead somewhere.' Mallory peered into Sophie's face. 'Is something wrong? You seem—'

'Just cold.' She pulled her cloak tighter as Caitlin crossed the road.

'Brigid says someone's coming.' She glanced up the slope where the street wound away into the dark. 'We need to hide.'

The sound of marching feet rose up above the driving rain. Mallory herded Sophie and Caitlin into an alley where they pressed themselves against a wall in the dark.

With torches sizzling in the rain, Evgen led an armed guard of twenty men, and in their midst was Jerzy, badly beaten and bound with chains that made him repeatedly fall into the gushing rainwater. Jerzy shrieked loudly, tears running down his cheeks.

As Mallory went for his sword, Caitlin grabbed his arm and pressed her body against him to stop him moving. Behind them, there was a cold, hard sound that could have been the wind.

Once the guards had passed, Mallory said, 'Niamh's given up pretending. Jerzy was the easy target. She'll be coming for us next.'

'Niamh didn't order this,' Sophie said.

'Come on, be real. You know it's her.'

'How can you defend her?' Caitlin added.

'Ganging up on me now, are you?' Sophie snapped.

'This isn't the time to argue,' Mallory said. 'I'm going to see where they're taking Jerzy. If I can get him out without facing the whole damn army, I will. You go and wait with Decebalus. We need to find the Gateway to Winter quickly.' Mallory slipped out into the street, keeping close to the buildings.

Caitlin peered out after him. 'Come on,' she beckoned.

'Wait.' Sophie put a hand on her shoulder. 'I have a better idea.'

4

The transition from the arid heat of the southern Sahara dawn to the chilly, gusting night rain on the grassy downs of Tir n'a n'Og left Hunter reeling. He found himself in the ruins of a watchtower on a ridge above the sweeping grassland, masonry crumbling with age and covered with ivy and lichen. His senses instantly came alive; every scent, every sound, every colour was heightened, more real than real.

Yet he found his footing rapidly and assessed his situation in a matter of seconds. He smelled ashes on the wind and behind the rhythm of the rain he could hear the clattering of metal, the steady tread of many feet and the beat of hoofs. Quickly, he carried Laura into the lee of one of the walls, afraid the cold rain would only worsen her condition. His attention was briefly drawn to the flaming outline of a man on the far horizon, but once he assessed it was not a threat, he quickly forgot it.

Laura was a poor sight. Bound to her armpits in mummy wrappings, her arms now free and lolling, she appeared to be dead. Her skin, which had always had a faint greenish hue, was bone-white, and her pupils were unresponsive. Yet Hunter had seen many dead bodies in his short, violent life and he was not convinced she was dead. Though she had no heartbeat that he could discern, no movement of her chest to indicate respiration, neither were there any of the changes that affected the body in the minutes and hours after death: no settling of the blood, no escaping of gases, no hint of the onset of rigor mortis.

'That,' he said to himself, 'is enough to give me hope, and while I've got that I'm not going to give up on you.' After a thoughtful pause, he added, 'And probably not ever.' Then: 'God, I hope you can't hear any of this sentimental bollocks or I'll never live it down when you wake up.'

He carried Laura beneath a sprawling elder in a corner of the ruins to shelter her from the rain and to hide her if they were discovered. 'Right,' he said, 'let's see what this world has to offer a plucky fellow with lots of ambition, an excess of charisma and the wherewithal to overcome any odds.'

Keeping low, he ran to the edge of the ruins and looked out across the downs. Through the rain, he could just make out hundreds of torches moving slowly, a river of flame in the dark. Occasionally, more intense bursts of fire flared up as if great furnaces were belching. It was a massive army on the move.

Crawling back to Laura, he sheltered beneath the elder. 'Now what?' he said aloud. 'Strange land, no idea of the terrain. Absolutely no idea which way help lies. Some might say I didn't think this through.'

'Are you . . . a Brother of Dragons?'

Hunter jolted. He had no idea anyone was in the vicinity, and he always knew; that was how he stayed alive. 'Come any closer and I'll kill you.'

'Are you here to free the Far Lands from the yoke of the Enemy?' the scared voice continued, unperturbed.

'Who are you?'

A pair of yellow eyes big enough to be human peered from the dark of a crevice amongst fallen masonry; yet the space looked barely big enough to hide a rat.

'I am but a simple denizen of the Far Lands, minding my own business, foraging for food. Until they came.' The voice grew tremulous. 'They killed my ma and my pa and my poor sissy. They killed them dead!' It began to sob loudly. 'And they're killing everything they come across, wiping the Far Lands free of us poor things. You know what they're really doing?' it babbled. 'Burning away everything. Starting again. The Far Lands have served their purpose. No need for a source of dreams and wonder any more. It's the end. And next they're going to do the same to the Fixed Lands, mark my words. Burn it all away and start again. Oh, the age of gods and Fragile Creatures is passed. The season is turned. Oh, woe is me. Oh, woe is us.'

Hunter began to feel sorry for the frightened creature. 'Come out. You're safe here for a moment.'

'No. If I come out now, I'll be forced to eat your hands and I don't want to do that. You won't help us then.' A pause. 'I've eaten the hands of lots of Fragile Creatures. Yum!' A faint smacking of lips.

Realising he had a lot to learn about Tir n'a n'Og, Hunter quickly withdrew the hand he had extended to help the creature out of the hole. 'My friend here is injured—' he began.

'Yes, she hangs between here and there. I can smell her. Nearly gone.'

'She needs help. Cernunnos—'

'Oooh, no. Long missing from the Far Lands. The Golden Ones are mostly gone. I think they know it's the Twilight Time.'

'Who can help her, then?'

After a moment's silence, the creature said hesitantly, 'Only the Court of the Final Word. They're still here. They'll be the last to go. They're enjoying themselves in these dark days, finding lots of what they need. Their river of blood is deeper and faster than ever. But you don't want to go there.'

'If they can help Laura, yes, I do.'

'To them, "help" means something different from what it does to you and me. They'll help you into a finer mess than you're in now.'

'I don't care. Where is this place?'

A long, grey hand with broken, bloody nails extended from the hole, stretching like toffee as it pointed towards the distant army. 'A long way. Through the Enemy's lines. You'll never be able to get there alive, not carrying your poor friend.'

Hunter watched the torches moving, remembering a similar scene in the Bosnian countryside.

'Take my advice: don't go! Even the Enemy haven't gone near the Court of the Final Word!'

Hunter scooped up Laura and eased out into the downpour. 'Thanks for the tip.'

'Wait! Are you going to help? Everyone knows the reputation of the Brothers and Sisters of Dragons. The old stories say you great heroes will free the land and lead us in our greatest hour. We need you, Brother of Dragons. We need you!'

'Don't worry. It's next on my list.'

With Laura in his arms, he clambered over the fallen masonry and began his journey across the downs towards Enemy lines. After six miles he could smell the greasy smoke from the torches and feel the ground shake from the relentless tread of thousands of marching feet. The downs had given way to a lush valley filled with copses and streams and boulders. Slabs of granite lay along the bottom of what appeared to be a dried-up river-bed. On the other side, the unbroken line of torches moved in the dark.

Hunter could wait until the army had passed, but there looked to be no end to it and he was afraid of wasting a single minute.

'Right now, I bet you're wishing someone with brains had fallen in love with you, who could think their way out of this mess.'

He laid Laura in the middle of a thick copse, half-afraid to leave her in case there were predators around, and then set off on reconnaissance, keeping low, moving from copse to copse, years of training making his actions as natural as breathing. As he slipped through the shadows, every regulated breath reminded him of another time, of Bosnia again, and Iraq, Belize, the Ukraine, Afghanistan, Lebanon, Tibet; and with the memory of each place came the images of the deaths, by knife, by gun, by bare hands. He remembered every face. It was his penance: keeping those features embedded in his mind would ensure that all the people he had slain would live on as long as he did; and he would never know peace.

For the final few yards, he crawled on his belly until he reached a broad bed of dry, dead reeds. The vast army was only yards away. The ground shook so much it made him feel sick, and he could smell the stink of sweat and blood and decomposition, of metal and leather. Purple mist drifted in the breeze from the Lament-Brood who marched at the heart of a terrifying rank of misshapen warriors, beasts and creatures, some of which had skin that gleamed like oil and changed shape regularly, sprouting carapaces and mandibles, multiple limbs, spikes and horns.

'I've seen worse,' he muttered.

He crawled to the edge of the reed bed, anxious that each rustle of movement would draw attention to him. He didn't know how long he had left till dawn, but he guessed it couldn't be more than a couple of hours and then he'd have no chance of getting through the ranks.

Frustrated, he scoured the valley until his eyes fell on fissures that ran through the rocky river-bed. It was tricky to discern details in the dark, but it looked as if they were wide enough to crawl through, and they appeared to run right under the army. It was a gamble – the fissures could end right at the feet of the Lament-Brood – but he had no other choice.

Returning to the copse, he stripped off his sodden shirt and belt, and did his best to fasten Laura to his back. The knots were good, but the wet cloth had a lot of give and she could easily slip off.

It took more than an hour to crawl on his belly down the slope, and by the time he reached the reed bed, all his muscles burned. At least the downpour had given way to a slight drizzle.

But as he dragged his way through the reeds, he realised he had miscalculated. The darkness was already thinning, the detail of the army emerging from the gloom. He was only a couple of feet away from the fissure he had selected, yet in a few minutes it might as well be a mile. He hauled himself out of the reed bed, his elbows and knees cracking painfully on the hard rock. Too-rapid movements would draw attention to him in the half-light; however fast his heart might be beating, he had to take it slow and steady, inching forward and hoping the shadows blanketed his bulk.

With his internal clock slowed to the beat of each precise movement, the sun appeared to be rising phenomenally fast. Grey spread out across the river-bed and the first hint of colour materialised in the soaking vegetation. The bizarre figures that made up the army became more terrifying as they emerged from the gloom: decaying features, blood-spattered, rusted armour raising sparks as they dragged their weapons on the rock.

I'm not going to make it, he thought.

The realisation cut through the numbness of damp, chill and exertion that had settled into his bones. Then a glimmer of a way out came to him. In the first pale rays of the sun, a mist was forming on the valley bed, thickening fast but not yet opaque enough to provide cover. He lay still and waited.

Light came up fast all around him. One curious glance in his direction would be the end. After fifteen minutes, he looked up and saw that the pearly mist now swathed the army. Crawling hastily across the river-bed, he wriggled into the fissure, relief flooding through him. But the gap ahead narrowed until it was barely shoulder-wide. Undoing the straps, he eased Laura off his back, fighting the random despairing thoughts that she was already dead and that everything he was doing was pointless.

With great effort, he manhandled her limp form through the tiny crevice. In the close confines, the heavy tramp of thousands of feet was deafening. Pebbles cascaded as the rock shook, and he feared it would all come crashing down on him at any moment.

When he was midway through the fissure, he looked up to see the bodies moving overhead, stepping over the gap one after the other.

Fifteen minutes later, he had passed beneath the army and was attempting to scale a steep incline of slick boulders where a white stream splashed. With Laura strapped to his back again, every sinew and joint ached.

'Okay, I was just spinning a bit of false modesty before,' he said. 'You got stuck with the right person after all. What can I say – I'm a hero.'

The climb took the best part of an hour. When the fissure opened out to reveal brilliant blue sky, with shaking arms he hauled himself onto a grassy slope with a breathtaking view along the valley to sweeping grassland and purple, snow-capped mountains beyond. Far below, the pearly mist glowed in the morning sun, hiding the black scar of the army and damping the martial tramp of feet.

Releasing Laura, he rested her head on his shoulder. 'A view like this deserves a bottle of good wine, music and someone to share it with.' He looked into Laura's pale face and tried to ignore what he saw there. 'Anyone listening would think I'm crazy, talking to myself. But whatever anyone says, I reckon you can hear me, somewhere, because that's the kind of woman you are. And if all the medical experts in the world lined up to tell me differently, I'd still believe it.' The view forgotten, there was only her face. Then he gathered her up in his arms and walked to the top of the ridge.

Beyond, the land rolled out to the horizon, mile upon mile of greenery that eventually thinned out to a rough, blackened zone in the distance. No sign of the Court of the Final Word.

'Looks like you're stuck with me for a while longer. No point hanging around . . . let's go.' He held Laura's cold form tightly and set out on weary legs for the horizon.

5

The truck smelled of hot oil and burning as it stood at the side of the dusty road beneath the baking Saharan sun. Shavi emerged from under the bonnet, a smudge of grease across his cheek. He shook his head. Church cursed loudly.

'Regretting being the Good Samaritan now?' Tom said superciliously as he sealed a roll-up in the only bit of shade at the back of the truck.

'It was the right thing to do,' Church snapped.

'Keep telling yourself that.'

Shavi looked along the road. 'We passed very little traffic all day. The map indicates no settlements for very many miles and it would not be wise to walk in this heat.'

Church retrieved the map from the cab and spread it on the flat-bed.

'I'll be interested to hear your options,' Tom said.

After Church had mulled over the map, he said, 'We're getting the Last Train.'

'What?' Tom scrambled to his feet. 'Have you taken a blow to your head?'

Church indicated a spot on the map less than a mile away. 'There's a track. Looks like it's some sort of goods line for the mineral works we passed. We can pick it up there.'

'No! I told you how dangerous that is!'

'You're always telling me things!' Church couldn't contain his anger. 'None of it any good. Useless snippets interspersed with dig, dig, dig about how useless I am, all of us are.'

'Stop whining. Sometimes you *are* useless. Sometimes you're not. You had a lucky escape last time, but if you take that train again it'll be the worst mistake you've ever made.'

'I've made so many I should be used to it by now.' Shavi stepped in to separate the two. 'We're taking the train,' Church insisted. 'We don't have a choice.'

Tom glared at him.

Church picked up the map and marked the direction. 'Coming?'

'Of course I'm coming,' Tom said sharply. 'I'm one of you.'

'Lucky us.'

'But if you get me killed I'm never going to let you forget it.'

The mile felt more like ten in the afternoon heat, but eventually they were standing beside a small-gauge track almost lost beneath drifting sand.

'Hardly used,' Shavi mused, 'if at all. Can the Last Train—'

'It can go anywhere,' Tom interrupted. 'And does.'

'How do you know so much about it?' Church asked.

'Because I keep my eyes and ears open, unlike you.'

With his knife, Church slit his thumb and dropped a spot of blood onto the rails. Within a moment they began to sing, and soon after the Last Train emerged out of the heat-haze, a mirage gradually taking substance.

It stopped next to them in a cloud of steam and smoke. The door in front of them opened silently.

Church hesitated before he stepped aboard. In the dry desert heat, the damp, vegetative aroma of the interior was much stronger than before and slightly unsettling.

'If you're going to do it, do it,' Tom barked.

Hands clasped, as if with excitement, Ahken waited just beyond the bright square of sunlight projected onto the floor, as if it troubled him. His eyes were hard and brittle and there was no humour in his smile. He appeared subtly changed from the last time Church had seen him, perhaps a note crueller, a degree more satisfied.

'Welcome once again,' he said.

'We need to go east. China. The Forbidden City. Can you take us?'

'Of course. The Last Train stops everywhere.'

Shavi and Tom boarded behind Church. 'Ah, True Thomas. So good to have you back. I thought of all our passengers you would be the last to return.'

Tom didn't meet Ahken's gaze. 'Just pay him and be done with it,' he said to Church.

'He didn't ask for payment before. It's free.'

'That was the first time. There's always a price, you idiot.'

'We can negotiate that later,' Ahken said with a bow. 'For now, enjoy all that the Last Train has to offer.'

He moved silently out of the carriage. Once he was gone, the doors closed with a hiss and the train moved steadily off.

Church rounded on Tom. 'Why didn't you tell us you'd travelled on here?'

'It wasn't relevant.'

'What else are you keeping from us?'

Tom stormed up the carriage and disappeared behind one of the brown leather seats.

'Leave him,' Shavi said. 'I sense he is troubled. He will tell us when he is ready.'

Through the windows, it looked as if they were sailing on a sea of yellow as the sands rolled out to the horizon. Soon the desert gave way to the flat-roofed buildings of eastern Egypt and then the scenery passed so fast it made Church queasy watching it.

They dozed intermittently, making the most of the opportunity to rest. Every now and then Shavi would rub his alien eye ferociously.

'Does it hurt?'

'I cannot feel it. But sometimes I see things, flashes, shapes passing by, colours, landscapes.' Shavi's face became drawn. 'Sometimes I see things from other worlds, sometimes from the past, sometimes the future. They are the worst. And once I saw my old boyfriend Lee, as bright as when he was alive.'

'That's good, isn't it?'

Shavi watched the scenery. 'He said the dead are waiting for me. For all of us. And that we would see them soon.'

'They lie, you know, all those things we deal with. They lie and they twist and they manipulate. If the eye's causing you trouble, take it out.'

Shavi shook his head. 'We need what it offers me. The hints, the information I can call forth—'

'But look at the price you're having to pay.'

Shavi laughed, and his face regained its bright hopefulness. 'You sound so surprised! We have all paid a great price to do what we do, Church. You shoulder your burden, Laura hers, Ruth hers. Why should I be any different? This is what we do! We were chosen to achieve great things. Our lives and our hopes and our dreams were all lost the moment we accepted the Pendragon Spirit.'

'We should get T-shirts printed: *No Happy Endings.*'

'As long as I can have mine in pink with blue letters.'

'You're a fashion wasteland, Shavi.'

'We do not need happy endings. Of all the people on the planet, we have been allowed to see the most wonderful things. We have been allowed into the greatest secrets, that there is meaning in even the tiniest thing, the erratic path of a butterfly, or the numbers of passing cars. We have learned that every single small thing we do is important. No gesture, no hand of friendship, no word of support is meaningless, for even the smallest thing can change the world. Is that not the greatest gift of all?'

'I wish I had your optimism, Shavi.'

'Ah, but that is why I am here, see.' He clapped Church warmly on the arm. 'The five of us each bring something important that is lacking in the rest of the group. Together we make all of us better.' He laughed. 'What we do here affects everyone and everything for all time. Who needs happy endings? Who needs the future and the past when the now is so potent?'

'You should write that down. You might get a self-help book out of it.' Church sat back and closed his eyes. 'Okay, you convinced me. No happy endings.'

6

Miller slept, curled up like a dog on the seat of the carriage. It had been a long, hard journey from Egypt, through India to their current location high up on Tibet's snow-covered plateau. Ruth observed Veitch, gripped by the view through the window of the hostile yet beautiful frozen land-scape and the majestic sweep of the Himalayas.

'You're a long way from South London,' she said, reading his thoughts.

'Never thought I'd see anything like this,' he replied dreamily.

She followed his gaze. Lhasa was long behind them, Qinghai Province ahead. 'They call this the "roof of the world". We must be near the highest point now – more than sixteen and a half thousand feet above sea level.'

Veitch rapped the window. 'That why this train is all sealed up like a plane?'

'We'd get altitude sickness if it wasn't.'

He poured her a coffee from the flask in his haversack. 'Least I showed you the world, right?'

'Shame I'm a prisoner,' she replied tartly.

'Are you?'

She didn't know how to answer, and changed the subject quickly. 'Do you think Church is behind or ahead of us at this point?'

'Don't talk about that tosser – you'll ruin my mood.'

'He's not going to give up, you know.'

'I know. That's what he does – carries right on to the bitter end. And I'm looking forward to him turning up again. Really. I owe him some payback, of the painful kind, and this time I'm finally going to get some satisfaction.'

'Don't hurt him.'

Veitch looked sullenly out of the window. 'When we were belting round the UK in that old van of Shavi's, he used to tell me about some ancient black and white movies he liked. Two old funny men on the road.'

'Bob Hope and Bing Crosby?'

'Yeah, that's it. *Road to Morocco* and all that shit. You know how he used to love banging on about that sort of stuff.'

The memories played out on Veitch's face, other aspects of his nature emerging from the hateful surface persona. Ruth was surprised to see a powerful hurt there.

'So here we are, then,' he continued. 'This business is one big fucking joke, isn't it? Road to Hell. Which one do you want to be? The one with the peanut head or the one who sang?'

'Can you sing?'

He shook his head.

'Then you get to be the joker.'

He could have taken offence at her comment, but instead he cracked a broad grin. It stripped away all the hardness and revealed the old Veitch who had once been one of them. She was surprised to realise how much she missed him.

'Ryan,' she began, 'I know you think Church, and all of us, let you down . . . that you were betrayed by everything we stand for. But it's not like that. You were manipulated. We all were – still are. Pushed around by higher powers. And we pay the price in our own lives.'

He watched her intently, trying to see where she was going.

'You can still do a lot of good. Help us—'

'It's too late for that.'

'You can make amends—'

'No, I can't. Don't treat me like an idiot. The things I've done – there's no going back. It's hell all the way.' He shrugged. 'Anyway, I've had enough of doing the right thing and paying the price. I'm looking after number one.'

'We need you, Ryan.'

He wouldn't meet her eyes for a long moment. Then, holding her gaze: 'There's one thing that would make me. In a flash.'

'Tell me. If I can help you get it, I will.'

'You. And me. Together.'

Her mouth hung open. Though she had known it for a long time, to hear it still shocked her.

'See – you can't even bring yourself to lie and say you'll do it to save the world.'

'It's not that.'

'I'd know anyway if you were lying. Now get some sleep, or you'll be knackered when we get to Golmud.'

He used his haversack for a pillow and curled up like Miller. But however tired she was, Ruth couldn't even close her eyes. She watched the frozen landscape pass, her heart beating in time with the rumble of the wheels.

Shavi woke to the sound of faint music, so sad it made his emotions swell. Church and Tom were still asleep. Outside the landscape had become lush with the kind of vegetation Shavi expected to see in the vicinity of the subcontinent.

Unsettled, he stretched and made his way down the carriage towards the source of the music. Two carriages back, he found the Seelie Court silently listening to a fiddle player calling the plaintive sounds from his instrument. He was accompanied by a fair-haired woman with no eyes, whose voice was filled with loss and grief and devastation. Shavi brushed away a stray tear.

When they had finished their song, the king summoned Shavi. 'Brother of Dragons,' he said in subdued greeting. 'You are the great seer. Do you perceive any hope in the times to come?'

'I see a great struggle.'

'You choose your words carefully.' He smiled. 'To shield us from the harsh blow of truth. It is a quality that has always endeared Fragile Creatures to the Seelie Court. But we are not children. We know we are approaching the time our cousins called Ragnarok. The twilight of the gods. Our time is passing, and yours, too, I fear. Will Fragile Creatures never achieve their destiny to rise to the rank of the Golden Ones?'

'Some of your people would be happy if that were the case.'

'But not us. We are proud to call Fragile Creatures friends.'

The queen stepped forward, hesitant and concerned. 'Your king—?'

'Church? He is here on the train.'

Her relief was palpable. She glanced at the king. 'We feared it was already the time—'

The king silenced her with a stern glance.

Shavi's attention was caught by a figure skulking at the end of the carriage. He shivered, refusing to believe, but it looked very much like his dead boyfriend Lee.

'Excuse me,' he said to the king.

He pushed his way through the Seelie Court until he reached the end of the carriage. The door to the next carriage hung open, and the figure that now looked even more like Lee was hurrying towards the back.

Shavi tentatively called out his name, then gave pursuit. Carriage after carriage passed without Shavi drawing any closer. Then he entered one carriage that was completely dark, with all the shutters drawn, and the door slammed behind him.

He rattled the handle, but it wouldn't open. Unease crept over him. There was no longer any sound of running feet, and he couldn't even hear the noise of the wheels on the track. Gradually, his eyes grew accustomed to the dark. The carriage appeared to be empty. With the door at his back locked, the only way was forward.

On the next door was a brass plate with the legend *The Hanging Garden*. He hesitated, then stepped through it. Once again the door slammed and locked behind him.

The first thing that assailed him was the stench of decomposition. The shutters were not completely drawn here and shafts of sunlight lanced through the gloom at irregular intervals. In the play of light and shadow, Shavi realised the grimly ironic meaning of the nameplate. At least thirty bodies hung by their necks from the carriage roof, the ropes creaking with the rocking of the train. The bodies were green and leaking noxious fluids, but their eyes were open and ranging back and forth, and their mouths moved silently. A mazy path wound amongst them.

A voice rose up. 'Pass the guardians if you wish to access the great secret.' Dark humour underpinned the words. 'But beware! Only those who are pixie-led will find the path.'

As Shavi took a step forward, the shutters slammed down and he was left in the dark and the stink.

'This secret must be great indeed,' he said. 'And is it of use to the Brothers and Sisters of Dragons?'

'Oh yes!' the voice hissed wryly.

'Then I am beholden to investigate. But you should know I am not scared of the dark.'

Shavi tried to recall the path he had briefly glimpsed through the hanging bodies. He moved a little way easily, but as he bumped into one of the corpses, a sigh escaped its lips and foul-smelling liquid splattered on him. Fingers caught briefly in his hair. He put a hand to his mouth against the overwhelming odour and edged forward. A third of the way down the carriage, he lost the path.

Steeling himself, Shavi took a guess and bumped directly into a corpse. It swung wildly, slamming back into him. Shavi recoiled and hit another, and then another. Each time he came into contact the corpse let out a low moan. Forcing his way through their midst, he soon realised the more he disturbed the bodies, the more animated they became. Almost bowling him over with their weight as they swung wildly, they tore at his hair and ripped at his face, drawing blood. The wounds stung as if they had been poisoned.

Shavi pressed on. In a frenzy, one of the animated corpses wrapped a seeping arm around his throat. Chunks of flesh came away under Shavi's fingers, but the pressure increased and he began to choke. Another attempted to claw at his human eye.

After a furious fight, Shavi tore his head free. He dropped to the floor to catch his breath, but the corpses continued to kick at him savagely.

Only those who are pixie-led will find the path, the voice had said.

And how did one see pixies? Shavi focused through his alien eye, and instantly saw a figure that appeared like an infra-red image in the dark. It was low to the floor, lithe and had characteristics that were both human and animal.

'Puck?'

The sound of laughter rang out. As the shimmering figure twisted and turned like an otter, Shavi followed in its wake. Over his head, the angry corpses desperately lashed out.

Finally, Shavi arrived at the far carriage door only to realise Puck was gone. Behind him, the moans subsided, the ropes stilled. The shutters slid up to admit the lances of sunlight.

The door before him had no name-plate, but it was covered in what resembled hide. He eased it open and stepped inside.

The carriage was bright, the shutters open and all the torches lit. Another door at the far end led to what Shavi guessed was the final carriage. A cauldron swung from a chain near the door, steam rising from it even though there was no fire beneath.

Shavi had thought the carriage was empty, but as he took a few steps towards the cauldron, three women appeared as if they had walked out of the walls. Like Greek peasants, they were dressed all in black, with deep cowls that cloaked their features in shadow. They approached in a jerky manner as if movement was not natural to them, and the closer they came the more queasy Shavi felt. They brought with them a palpable air of dread. When they halted ten feet away from him, Shavi's heart was pounding madly.

After a moment of rising anticipation, they spoke; or rather, one voice emanated from all of them.

'We are the Daughters of the Night.'

Shavi recalled hearing the name before somewhere.

'I spin.'

'I measure.'

'I cut the thread.'

The image troubled him; they were not talking about weaving. 'What is the great secret?' he asked hesitantly.

'What do you use to cut the thread?'

Shavi pondered. 'Scissors? A knife?'

The Daughters of the Night hovered in silence. At the back of the carriage, the door had opened slightly, as if someone was listening or waiting to leap out. He couldn't take his eyes off the gap. 'What is in the last carriage?' he asked, regretting the question the moment he had spoken.

'What waits there waits for all mortals at the end of their journey.'

Shavi could feel its presence, watching him through the crack in the door.

His throat dry, he forced his attention back to the Daughters of the Night. 'Show me what you use to cut the thread.'

'I cannot.'

Puzzled, Shavi thought hard until a notion came to him. 'The Extinction Shears. That is what you use to cut the thread.'

The Daughters of the Night did not reply, but Shavi could sense he had got it right.

'Where are they?' he asked.

'They are with us always, except when they are not.'

'They exist in all-times and all-places, but find their way to the moment around which the Axis of Existence turns.'

'You talk as if they are alive,' Shavi said.

'They return when we need them.'

'But this time they have not returned.'

'Some threads we can break . . . the threads of mortals. But we cannot cut the threads of events. We cannot sever that which is bound into the warp and weft of Existence.'

'We are searching for the Shears,' Shavi said. 'We believe they are somewhere in the Far Lands.'

'You are wrong.'

'They are in the place that lies beyond our task. The place we can never see.'

What lies beyond their task? Shavi thought. And then he had it. 'What the gods call the Grim Lands, or the Grey Lands. The Land of the Dead.' The Daughters of the Night remained silent, but once again Shavi could tell he was correct. 'Then we are looking in the wrong place!' he said. 'We must go to the Grim Lands to find the Extinction Shears.'

The Daughters of the Night began to retreat back into the walls. Soon the carriage was empty once more, but the atmosphere of dread did not leave with them. Shavi saw that the door at the rear of the carriage had opened a little more, and as he watched it opened further still.

He moved quickly into the previous carriage, where the hanging bodies

245

had now been replaced by rows of seats. As he hurried back to Church, he saw through the windows a new landscape of uniform factories with chimneys trailing smoke. Beyond lay modern skyscrapers. The signs were all in Chinese script. Shavi also noticed that it now appeared to be late summer. They had gained no advantage; the journey had taken almost as long as it would have taken Veitch to reach the same destination.

The Last Train finally came to a halt in a railway station that mixed traditional Chinese architecture with fifties design. As the clouds of steam finally cleared, the first thing that Shavi noted was that the entire station – one of the busiest in East Asia – was completely deserted.

ƒORBIDDEN

1

Tiananmen Square was deserted. The only movement came from the *Morvren* now nestling on every building, their unforgiving eyes turned on Church, Shavi and Tom who stood alone in the vast public space. Beyond, Beijing was still and silent beneath a brooding silver sky.

'Where is everybody?' Church asked.

'I don't think we need to be hanging around to find out, do you?' Tom said. He tugged at the ring uncomfortably.

'Veitch?' Shavi asked.

'He's here somewhere.' Tom shoved his ring hand into a pocket.

'If he'd already got the location of the Second Key he wouldn't be hanging around,' Church said. 'We need to persuade the King of Foxes to tell us. Then with the information Shavi got from the Daughters of the Night, we'll have the upper hand.'

'Don't sound so self-satisfied,' Tom cautioned. 'That is usually the most dangerous time. Or do you think all your feathered friends up there are mistaken?'

Church removed Caledfwlch from its scabbard across his back. It flared brighter than he had seen in a long time. 'The Blue Fire's much stronger here,' he said, puzzled.

The roosting formation of the silent *Morvren* appeared to be guiding them past the modern government and military buildings to the historic architecture of the Forbidden City beyond. It lay behind twenty-four-foot-high walls that gave the impression of a prison from which they would never escape.

Uneasily, they approached along the stone-flagged Imperial Way towards the imposing Meridian Gate set in the southern wall. Two grand protruding wings funnelled visitors towards five entrances, and from the top of each wing two deserted watchtowers looked down.

A shimmer like a heat haze revealed a man at least seven feet tall, his hair and beard a flowing white, his robes the green of a spring field. He held a staff topped with a hexagonal golden symbol, and around his neck hung a large clock, the hands whirling continuously. His eyes were purple.

'The King of Foxes bids me welcome you, honoured guests.' His tongue flashed out, thin, black and forked. He bowed. 'My name is Tai Sui, President of the Celestial Ministry of Time.'

'We are—'

'I know who you are, Brother of Dragons. And you, Brother of Dragons. And you, True Thomas.' His tone was hard, but he smiled broadly.

'And we're welcome here?' Church asked suspiciously.

Tai Sui bowed again. 'Of course. Good fortune follows you. Your deeds are well known to us here in Zilin Cheng. Enter our home and partake of all we have to offer, given freely and without obligation.'

Tai Sui led them through the Meridian Gate into a large square that at first appeared empty, but as the gate shut behind them, Church saw they were not alone. A shaft of sunlight illuminated scores of people moving somnolently across the square, their heads bowed. It was only after a moment that he noticed they cast no shadows. As they came to obstacles, they passed right through them.

'Ghosts?' Tom said.

'The Guei,' Tai Sui corrected. 'Spirits formed from yin, the negative essence of souls.'

'These are the people of Beijing?' Church asked.

'Some of them.' Tai Sui gestured to the grand square. 'This is Taihemen Square,' he said proudly, 'and you will see passing through it the Inner Golden Water River, which runs from this world to the next. It is said that even Fragile Creatures may sail along it between the worlds.'

They crossed one of five bridges and passed under another great gate before coming to another square. Rising from it was an elaborate three-tiered white marble terrace, and on top of it were three halls that were the focus of the palace complex.

Tai Sui indicated the largest, which towered almost ninety feet above the square. Along the roof ridge, ten gargoyles looked down. Church thought he saw them move, but put it down to a trick of the light.

'The Hall of Supreme Harmony,' Tai Sui said. 'It is from here that all power emanates in this Great Dominion. And its fortuitous construction and siting make it a power beyond all others. Numbers are power,' he added with a sly smile, 'but you would know that, Brother of Dragons. You will note that the hall is nine bays wide and five deep. This is the voice of Existence speaking. Nine and five are the numbers of power and majesty of the Emperor.'

'Five,' Shavi mused.

'Five,' Tai Sui repeated. 'Yet I see only two Brothers of Dragons. And one . . . other.'

'Not all numbers are equal,' Church said. 'Two Brothers of Dragons beat a thousand others.'

Tai Sui bowed. 'Your wisdom is recognised, honoured one. Please, enter the hall.'

The great imperial space was decorated everywhere with dragon motifs. At the far end of the hall, flanked by six golden pillars, was a large throne with five dragons coiled around the arms and back. Behind it was a screen with a further nine gloriously intricate dragons.

Church noted the numbers of the Fabulous Beasts and recognised a hint of some greater meaning not yet revealed to him. He could see that Shavi, too, sensed something.

'This place . . . it fees like home,' Shavi said. 'I cannot express it more clearly than that. It calls to me.'

'Why is it deserted?' Church asked.

'Deserted? Look again.' Tai Sui indicated the ceiling above the throne where there was a caisson decorated with a final coiled dragon. From its mouth cascaded a series of metal balls, like a chandelier. 'It is known as the Mirror of Xuanyuan, the Yellow Emperor.'

It showed a reflection of the room, now full of figures, all so hideous in appearance that Church reeled backwards in shock. When he raised his gaze, the hall was now as full as the reflection, but those present resembled men and women of the imperial court half a millennia gone. Church knew, though, that he had glimpsed their true form.

On the throne sat a man in purple robes, wearing a tall hat marked with Chinese characters. Green eyes stared from vulpine features; tufts of auburn hair protruded from the back of his head, running into mutton-chop sideburns and a short beard. His smile revealed yellow teeth.

'My advisors tell me you are blown by the winds of destiny, Brother of Dragons, but I sense destiny in your stride.' A smile flickered around the edge of the King of Foxes' mouth.

'We were told you had information that could help us,' Church said.

'Told? By whom?'

'Seth, one of your Egyptian relatives. I think he hoped that sending us here would lead to our destruction.'

'Ah.' The King of Foxes tapped his fingertips together regally. 'There are no other gods beyond the ones in this Great Dominion. We are exalted.'

'Yes, we've heard that before.'

'Tell me,' Shavi said, 'there are some beings of higher power who align themselves with Existence, others who ally themselves with the Devourer of All Things. Where do your people stand?'

The King of Foxes held up a medallion with a circle divided by a curving line into dark and light halves.

'The yin and yang symbol,' Shavi said.

'Everything that exists is determined by a natural order based on balance and harmony,' the King of Foxes said. 'The universe is held in balance by two interacting forces. Yin, the female, encompasses cold, dark, softness, the earth. Yang, the male, is associated with light, warmth, hardness, the heavens. Opposites, mutually dependent, but if they are in equilibrium, there will be harmony.'

'Is that supposed to answer the question?' Church said.

The King of Foxes gave a slight bow. 'The yin and the yang are present in every aspect of the world. You will see them in life and death, and in good and evil. You will see them in gods and Fragile Creatures, in the land, in animals. At the beginning of all things, the yin and the yang were there in the cosmic egg, and their struggle cracked the shell and begat the universe. And they will be there at the end.'

'The Gnostic secret again,' Shavi whispered to Church before stating loudly, 'You are saying that you are attempting to balance the two sides? That you are neutral?'

'One cannot be neutral in the currents of the universe. Sometimes the gods drift in one direction, sometimes in another.'

Tom stepped forward. 'Why would a king sit on an emperor's throne?'

The King of Foxes did not answer.

'Further, I do not recall the Chinese people ever worshipping a King of Foxes.'

'This is my throne now, Fragile Creature.' His tone was much harsher when he spoke to Tom.

'So you usurped it from the true owners,' Tom pressed. 'Where are the real rulers of this Great Dominion?'

The King of Foxes' eyes glittered. 'This Great Dominion is not like any other you may have encountered. It is the most powerful, and therefore the most dangerous. We did not need your clumsy, tramping feet to wake us from our slumber. We woke at the first stirrings in the chi, which is at its most potent in this glorious empire of heaven. Those who woke quickest moved fastest. And the fox is the fastest one of all.'

'You support the Void because it helps you maintain control here,' Church said. 'You're not going to help us.'

'The Brothers and Sisters of Dragons are a threat to the eternal balance. The Hu Hsien have already attempted to deal with your kind. Good fortune was not with them that day. But now the time is more auspicious!' The King of Foxes clapped his hands. 'Here in my great court there is nowhere to hide, little mice.'

Church turned to Shavi. 'Looks like it's time.'

'You are sure? You will be on your own.'

'Oh, stop it,' Tom interjected. 'He's been dying for his big moment ever since he got that sword.'

Shavi and Tom backed towards the door as the eight remaining members of the Hu Hsien emerged from the crowd. They flanked the throne, their human masks betraying hints of the foxes that lay beneath. One by one, they each adopted a fighting stance.

The clang of the door signalled Shavi and Tom slipping away as planned. Church drew Caledfwlch. Amidst a roar like a furnace, the blue flames rushed along the edge of the blade, so intense that even Church gasped. The brilliance of the blaze cast shadows dancing across the Hall of Supreme Harmony, and lit the King of Foxes' face with a sapphire glow.

'The chi,' the king said grimly. 'The spirit-fire fills you. I expected less . . . some pathetic Fragile Creature . . . but now I see—' He wafted his final words away with an imperious hand.

'We came here in good faith to find the location of the Second Key,' Church said.

'Not even the Devourer of All Things would be allowed that information. It plays a vital role in maintaining balance.'

'A bargaining chip to keep you on the throne.'

'If you will.'

'And you would dishonour yourself by attacking someone who came in peace?' Church chose his words carefully.

'There is no dishonour in facing such a powerful enemy.' He waved his hand almost imperceptibly and the Hu Hsien attacked.

Church was momentarily stunned by the ferocity of the assault. They came at him from all directions with a ritual cry, spinning and leaping twelve feet or more into the air, and as they moved they changed, their faces becoming vulpine, slavering jaws snapping savagely, claws breaking through the tips of their fingers.

'You've got to be kidding me,' Church said under his breath. 'Kung fu foxes?'

2

The sounds of battle echoed as Shavi and Tom moved quickly away from the Hall of Supreme Harmony.

'I do not like leaving Church behind,' Shavi said.

'We're not fighting men. Our job is to find something we can use to convince them to tell us what we need to know.'

Shavi scanned the expansive precincts of the Forbidden City, now bathed in shafts of sunlight breaking through the silvery clouds. 'What are we to look for?'

'If you had half a brain, you'd already know.' Tom polished the lenses of his spectacles superciliously. 'You saw the reflection over the throne. Those things are demons . . . usurpers. The true rulers of this Great Dominion are too powerful to have been eradicated by such as them.'

'So they will be imprisoned somewhere.'

'I'm sure they will be very grateful if we can free them. Now enough of your stupid mutterings and put that monstrous eye to good use.'

A moment later Shavi and Tom were running north, past the smaller Hall of Preserving Harmony, leaving the ceremonial Outer Court behind, with its discreet symbolism designed to represent heaven. Ahead lay the Inner Court with its more complex arrangement of halls and avenues, designed in the shape of the Kun trigram to represent Earth.

The Guei were everywhere, heads down in their grey spirit-existence, tramping their meaningless paths. But as Tom and Shavi approached the entrance to the Inner Court, a change came over the shadowless ghosts. Across the sweep of the Forbidden City, as one the Guei turned their pointing hands towards Shavi and Tom.

Tom cursed under his breath. 'I could have put money on that happening.'

The Guei nearest said in a high-pitched screech, 'I see shadows!'

'Why aren't you speaking Chinese?' Tom shouted back.

'I think you would be better off putting your energy into running.' Before Shavi could move, the Guei lunged. It reached him in the blink of an eye, talons tearing through his shirt and drawing blood.

'I thought ghosts were supposed to be insubstantial,' Tom snarled.

The Guei ran silently towards them from all corners of the city. As each one saw Tom and Shavi, it shouted, 'I see shadows!'

Shavi threw off the Guei thrashing viciously for his throat and ran with Tom towards the Palace of Heavenly Purity. The Guei swarmed, not even a single footstep echoing in the eerie silence.

'Bloody stupid idea,' Tom gasped. 'He's gone and got us all killed.'

Shavi and Tom ducked and leaped through the attacking ghosts, feeling fingers tear through their hair and scrape their cheeks, each blow coming a fraction closer. Ahead, the Guei swept to close off their path.

'See?' Tom shouted. 'I'm right. I'm always bloody right! Dead as a doornail in a foreign city, and I can't even pay my debts!'

Burning blue energy flared across the court.

Tom and Shavi were thrown to the flags and the Guei were driven back, hands in front of their dead eyes, shrieking silently. From the shelter of the Palace of Heavenly Purity darted Ruth, wielding the Spear of Lugh from which bolts of sapphire energy still discharged. She helped a beaming Shavi to his feet.

'You escaped Veitch!' he said.

'No time for talk. I'm tapping into some huge reservoir of power here, but I don't know how long it's going to last.' Her features were defiant, her eyes constantly watching the circling Guei. Shavi thought how much she had grown in stature since she had thrown off the Void's fake persona.

'You don't *have* to leave it to the last moment to rescue me,' Tom said. 'Earlier will do.'

With the Guei close at their backs, Ruth led them at a run into the shade of the Palace of Heavenly Virtue.

'They aren't going to give us the time to do what we need to do,' Tom said.

Yet barely had the words left his mouth when the Guei came to a halt and turned as one to look back towards the Hall of Supreme Harmony, their heads bowed deferentially.

'Are they worshipping?' Shavi said.

In the distance, a figure moved quickly through the ghosts.

3

The Hu Hsien attacked Church from all sides, a blur of whirling bodies and limbs. As they shapeshifted, snapping jaws and flashing feet and hands appeared from nowhere, lunging for his throat, then disappearing just as quickly.

Church was forced to draw on all his fighting skills. Blue Fire crackled through the air as Caledfwlch swung in constant motion, creating a defensive wall of flame and steel. He couldn't drop his concentration for even a fraction of a second.

But the relentless attack was taking its toll, and more and more blows were getting through his defences. Teeth raked across his forearm. A rib cracked from a high kick that sent him sprawling, and though he was on his feet in an instant, claws tore open the back of his neck. It was only a matter of time before one blow laid him low, and then they would be on him in a frenzy of tearing jaws.

Satisfied he had given Tom and Shavi enough of a head start, he checked the path to the door. His opening came when one of the Hu Hsien telegraphed an attack. Church brought the sword up and put all his weight behind it. With the sizzle of cooking meat, his attacker was bisected mid-change. The two halves fell apart, internal organs flipping and twisting as they continued to morph between man and beast.

A rush of shock ran around the crowd. The King of Foxes half-lifted himself from his throne in disbelief.

In the brief lull, Church sprinted for the door. As he laid his fingers on the handle, Tai Sui appeared. He bowed quickly and lifted the clock that hung around his neck. With one slim finger, he spun the hands forward.

The world spun with them. The Hall of Supreme Harmony blurred into complete darkness and after a moment of queasy disorientation Church realised he was somewhere else.

It was dark and cold and there was the damp smell of deep under-ground. Echoes rang distantly in a great space, and here and there lonely torches flickered in the gulf. Church was on his knees, his body wracked with pain. Blood spattered onto stone. Beside him, Caledfwlch lay shattered, its outlines blurred and continually changing, the Blue Fire extinguished.

Rough hands grabbed his jacket and hauled him up. His head spun with the blood loss.

'Three minutes till you're dead, Brother of Dragons.' It was the Libertarian. His scarlet, lidless eyes glowed in the gloom, and his broad smile was triumphant.

'Everything has been leading up to this point, when you wave goodbye to what has gone before.' The Libertarian's voice rang with irony. 'All your sacrifice, all your pain and suffering, all your minor victories and your great losses. And know, as your life fades into the black, that you threw it all away – you and only you – because of your pathetic, doomed love for a woman.'

The Libertarian shoved Church viciously and blood flew everywhere. He shook his head with weary theatricality. 'Ah, the things people do for love. It makes us strive for greatness, drives us on when all hope is gone. It makes us do terrible things, like the mindless slaughter of generations of Brothers and Sisters of Dragons. And ultimately it turns us into the things we hate.'

The Libertarian glanced over his shoulder, and behind him Church saw for the first time a burning wicker man, its feet lost somewhere in the abyss. Inside it, figures squirmed as they were consumed.

'At the moment of your death, I will toss you into the fire,' he continued, 'and you will come out of those flames reborn, transformed. The final, absolute victory of the Devourer of All Things. The end of all hope for Existence. That is what you have thrown away with your stupid love.'

Church tried to speak, but his lips were dry and the words would not come. The Libertarian pressed his ear close to Church's mouth and proclaimed, as if performing in a pantomime, 'What's that you say? "What will I become, Mr Libertarian?"'

He drew his red eyes level with Church's so that they filled his vision. 'Can't you see the resemblance?'

The darkness spun wildly and with a shock that felt like a hammer blow, Church was back in the Hall of Supreme Harmony, almost driven to his knees by the disorientation of the devastating revelation.

Tai Sui had reset the hands of the clock to their previous time. Church lurched, heard the running footsteps of the Hu Hsien and realised that only a second or two had passed. Recovering, he knocked Tai Sui to one side and snatched at the door handle.

Before his fingers closed on it, the door flew open. Framed in the doorway against the silvery sky was Veitch, his sword drawn. Behind him the Guei watched with a mixture of adoration and fear.

'Bleedin' hell, you get everywhere,' Veitch said.

As Church raised his sword, the Blue Fire roared into a sheet of flame that leaped the gap to Veitch's sword. The black fire limning the blade surged – Church could feel the intense cold increase. The flames from his own sword gradually winked out.

'You see what I did there?' Veitch said. 'These days you just make me stronger.'

The strength ebbed from Church's limbs. Veitch stepped forward and rammed his blade right through Church's side, the tip emerging from his back. Cold mixed with hot pain rushed through Church's body and he fell backwards, black stars flashing before his eyes.

The Hu Hsien halted in surprise. Their uncertainty turned to unease as the Guei tramped in, bowing to Veitch. He moved past the first of the Hu

Hsien, taking off its head with a slice so fast Church barely saw it. A second Hu Hsien fell just as quickly, disembowelled.

The rest of the Hu Hsien adopted fighting stances. Veitch gave a weary sigh. 'All right, let's do it.' He made a summoning gesture.

The Guei fell on the occupants of the Hall of Supreme Harmony.

Badly injured, Church lay in the growing pool of his own blood as the first cries of, 'I see shadows!' rose up. The Hu Hsien were the first to fall, their fighting prowess useless against the weight of numbers. Next, the members of the court were rapidly dismembered as they attempted to flee for the doors. Even when they returned to their true hideous forms they were shown no mercy.

As the frenzied slaughter died down, Church saw Veitch on the throne, his sword at the throat of the King of Foxes.

'See, mate, your watchdogs have a new master.'

Only when Church saw the terror in eyes of the King of Foxes did he realise the extent of the power Veitch wielded.

'Now,' Veitch said calmly, 'you need to tell me the location of the Second Key.'

'The great city,' the King of Foxes shrieked. 'New York!'

'Where in New York?'

'On the great island at the heart of the great city in the shadow of the towers. The Key is a boy who walks with a girl who has killed and will kill again. They are guarded by a man who stands on the brink of ending his days, for he is cursed to remember all the stories. And the word that binds them to their spot is "empire".'

'Give me something solid.'

'That is all I know!'

'Yeah? Okay.'

Veitch sliced his blade across the King of Foxes' neck, only the slightest cut, but the black fire roared into it. The King of Foxes went rigid as the cold flames consumed him from within. A moment later he was just a sheath of skin that slid slowly down to the floor.

Veitch put away his sword and splashed through the gory soup that now covered the floor. He stood over Church, who was fighting to stay conscious.

'I should chop you into chunks, finally get it over and done with here and now. But . . . I'm not going to do that. I gave my word and I'm an honourable man.' Subterranean emotions flickered across his face.

'Don't do this, Ryan.' Church tried to ignore the pain. 'There's nothing to be gained by destroying everything.'

'That shows how much you know. The whole thing is a mess. There's

256

no point to it. No meaning to all the pain. Better to wipe it away and give someone else a chance.'

He stepped over Church and walked towards the door.

A lake of blood surrounded Church. He could feel every laboured beat of his heart.

'You're not going to die,' Veitch said. 'Not here. It won't let you. But at least you'll get a taste of it, just so you know what I've been through.'

He gave Church one last, curious look, and then he was gone.

4

As the Guei trooped off in their grim procession, Shavi grabbed Ruth and hugged her joyfully.

'I am so glad you are well,' he said. 'We were all worried Veitch would hurt you.'

'He hasn't hurt me.' Ruth wallowed in Shavi's hug. 'In fact, he helped save my life.'

'Church will be so pleased to see you. He has been broken-hearted, though he has striven to hide it from the rest of us—'

'I'm not coming back with you, Shavi.'

Shavi slowly released himself from the hug.

'I'm going with Veitch.'

After the embrace, the flicker of betrayal across Shavi's face was doubly stinging.

'I made him swear that he wouldn't kill Church, or any of you,' she said hurriedly. 'The price I had to pay for that was that I'd stay with him.'

She was aware of Tom watching her intensely.

'He's done some terrible things, but the good Ryan we all remember – he's still inside. I know he is. And if I can reach that part of him . . . save him . . . then I'll have done some good.' She looked from face to face. 'Won't I?'

'Oh, you want to *save* him,' Tom said sardonically. 'No other reason at all.'

'What are you saying?' Ruth snapped.

Tom only smiled.

'Come,' Shavi urged. 'The ghosts may have gone, but they could be back at any moment.'

As he led the way through the Gate of Heavenly Purity, Ruth sensed a barrier between them and that hurt her more than she could have believed.

The palace had double eaves and was set on a white marble platform. A raised walkway led from the gate to the door.

'Nine bays wide,' Shavi counted. 'Five bays deep. Did the Chinese understand the underlying pattern of Existence before anyone else?'

'Just open the door,' Tom said. 'Are you sure this is the place?'

'Yes. I sense restrained power.'

As Ruth crossed the threshold, a familiar energy coursed down her spine. An atmosphere of cathedral-like sanctity and the burned-iron odour of the Blue Fire lay within. The tip of her spear flickered with ghostly sapphire flames. Even Tom allowed himself a brief smile.

Their footsteps rang off the marble floor. A sumptuous design of red, gold and black covered the walls. In the centre of the palace, on an elaborately carved platform, stood a throne and a desk. Set into the roof was another caisson featuring a coiled dragon, and above the throne hung a tablet marked with Chinese characters.

'I wonder what it means,' Ruth said.

'It says "Justice and Honour".' The familiar voice rang out across the room.

'Someone's let the genie out of the bottle again.' Tom sniffed.

Ruth approached the throne. When she stood directly before it, blue flames leaped from her spear, soaring up ten feet into the air. Lines of fire rushed out from the throne, criss-crossing the floor before rising up to form a pyramidal structure of lines of force, centred on the grand chair. The breath caught in Ruth's throat as a figure faded in and out of the flames crackling over the throne.

'Hal?' she said.

'More pithy comments,' Tom said sourly. 'I am all ears.'

Laughter rippled out from the fire. 'Hello, Tom, Shavi, Ruth. I'm here because you've reached a really important juncture in the proceedings. Frankly, from this point on it could go either way. It's all down to you – and the others, of course.'

'So it's a pep talk, is it?' Tom muttered.

'Why is this moment so important?' Shavi asked.

'You'll see shortly. Suffice it to say, the balance of power is about to shift dramatically. You've done well to get here—'

'Well?' Ruth said. 'I died—'

'But you're alive now.'

'We were forced to split up. Church and Veitch are on the brink of killing each other . . .'

Hal was silent for a moment, and Ruth had the oddest feeling he was smiling at her words.

'And now you're here,' he said, 'in the Forbidden City, above one of the most important nodes of the Blue Fire, part of a network of subterranean energy that flows across south-east Asia. Now why do you think events led you here? Happenstance? Coincidence?'

Shavi smiled. 'There are no coincidences.'

'A prize for the mystic with the dodgy eye. Let's review a few things, shall we? Here, the dragon has always been paramount. Of all the three hundred and sixty scaly creatures in the hierarchy of Chinese myth, the dragon was at the top of the list. And it was always linked with chi – the spiritual energy that runs through the body, as seen in the meridians of acupuncture – and through the land. Man and world, both linked by the Fabulous Beast. How important was the dragon? It was one of the four animals chosen to symbolise the cardinal points. The dragon got the east. It stood for sunrise, spring and life. The white tiger got the west – death. We all know the Land of the Dead lies where the sun sets.

'In fact, in the folk religion, the Long Wang – yes, great name – were dragon kings who ruled over life and death. They were gods of the oceans, lakes and rivers – the liminal zones where you could cross over to other worlds – and they represented wisdom, strength and goodness.'

'Is there a point to this?' Tom said.

'It is a part of the secret history,' Shavi said. 'The true history of Existence, encoded in myth and legend. The Chinese put it at the centre of their beliefs.'

'Why?' Hal asked.

Nobody answered.

'Because from here you can access the well-spring of the Blue Fire – it's located right in this region of the world—'

'Wait,' Ruth interrupted. 'Church said the source of the Blue Fire was sealed off, back in the sixties.'

'Don't you think it might be possible to unseal it?'

'Why, if we could do that it would provide a battery for the Pendragon Spirit,' Shavi said. 'A tremendous battery!'

'More importantly, it wouldn't be the Void's world any more,' Ruth said. 'Can we do that?'

'You can't. But with help . . . In fact, a big step to achieving that help has already been taken by Ryan Veitch. The King of Foxes is dead. The throne is empty.'

'Then where are the true rulers imprisoned?' Tom said.

'I can't tell you that.'

'Oh, for heaven's sake!' Tom threw his arms into the air.

Shavi smiled. 'You are only annoyed because he sounds just like you. A hint here and there, but do it yourself or you will never learn.'

Hal's image fell into sharper relief in the flames above the throne. 'The Void already knows what you're planning to do. Beyond the walls of the city, the spiders are moving. The army will lay you under siege.'

'But they can't enter the city because of the Blue Fire,' Ruth realised.

'Then how are we supposed to leave?' Shavi asked.

'You'll find a way. Ask Tom.' The Blue Fire began to retreat along the lines of force towards the throne. 'You were all chosen for a reason – even you, Tom. Don't lose hope. Never lose that. Just look for the patterns that lie beneath the surface of reality and you'll always find your way.'

With a *swoosh*, the flames rushed back into the throne and Hal was gone.

'Useless waste of space,' Tom grumbled.

Shavi looked around. 'There is something hidden in this place, but what . . . ?'

Animated, Ruth organised Tom and Shavi to search the palace, but after fifteen minutes they had found nothing.

The door to the ornate entrance chamber clanged open and slow footsteps made their way in. Sallow-faced and leaking blood, Church staggered in.

'Oh my God!' Ruth ran to take his weight; Shavi joined her.

'You're here,' he croaked, his joy breaking through the pain.

'Hush.' Ruth gave him a kiss on the cheek as Shavi examined his wound.

'Veitch,' Church said weakly. 'Bastard took me by surprise then left me to bleed out.'

Ruth blanched. In the brief exchange of glances between Tom and Shavi she saw a transitory accusation.

'Lie down, save your energy. Don't talk,' she said, helping Church to the floor where Shavi attempted to staunch the bloodflow.

Church squeezed Ruth's hand. 'I'm glad you're here.' His smile, too, felt like a mark of betrayal. 'I don't get it – I should have died by now.' He coughed weakly.

'The Pendragon Spirit is keeping you going,' Shavi said.

Ruth became aware that Tom was not helping. He stood a little to one side, stroking his chin thoughtfully, apparently unmoved by the scene. 'He's your friend! Do something!' Ruth knew she was turning her guilt outwards, but couldn't help herself.

Tom eyed her coldly. 'I am doing something. The little snip in the fire said we should be looking out for patterns.'

'Now?' Ruth raged.

'It would seem like the most important time of all, don't you think?' Tom suddenly grew rigid, his gaze fixed on Church.

'What do you see?' Shavi asked.

'I see further proof that there are no coincidences. Everything has meaning if only you adopt the right perspective.' He knelt next to Church and gestured towards Church's blood flowing across the marble floor. 'I see a pattern,' Tom said, quietly triumphant. 'Indeed, I see a picture.'

Tiny grooves in the marble invisible to the eye were gradually filling with blood. Each pump of Church's heart added more blood to a growing picture of a coiled Chinese dragon, mirroring the one in the caisson above their heads.

'Quick, now,' Tom said.

As the head was completed, the eye winked at them with a flicker of blue. Ruth rammed the tip of the spear in the eye. A crackle of sapphire energy brought a rumble as the marble tore open in regular lines, section by section dropping to form spiral steps leading down into the dark.

'I'd have missed that,' Ruth said.

'You weren't looking for patterns,' Tom replied. 'You can applaud now.'

'Would you settle for me not strangling you?'

Shavi quickly gathered Church into his arms and together they descended.

5

At the foot of the stairs there was a long stone tunnel that eventually led to a great hall so bright they had to shield their eyes. A reservoir of Blue Fire stretched into the distance. The walls were illuminated with astonishing designs of Fabulous Beasts in jade and gold that appeared to be telling a story. Small silver creatures scurried amongst the coils of their tails.

Church, Ruth, Shavi and Tom's attention was drawn by a series of terracotta statues lining the burning pool, all different, all incredibly lifelike.

'Dump him in the flames,' Tom ordered.

As Shavi lowered Church into the Blue Fire, the pain began to drain from his features. Ruth had to look away, for the relief that flooded her almost brought her to tears. Instead, she examined the scores of terracotta figures. Some resembled men and women, others had the look of hybrid animals and lizards.

261

'These are the gods, aren't they?' she said.

'Imprisoned, with just a hint of torture – as you would expect from the King of Foxes,' Tom replied. 'Close enough to see the Blue Fire, but not close enough to use it. Pitch them in, too.'

Shavi and Ruth moved along the edges of the pool, pushing the statues into the flames. Within seconds they began to move, the terracotta cracking then falling away to reveal the living beings beneath.

Ruth shied back as one imposing figure rose from the Blue Fire. His black beard trailed down to his ankles, and his robes and tall hat were embroidered with Fabulous Beasts. Blue sparks fizzed from his eyes as he looked at each of them in turn.

'My name is Yu Huang.' His voice echoed into the dim distance. 'I am the August Personage of Jade. Whatever happens on Earth and in heaven is mine to determine.' His attention fell on Church and he nodded. 'The Brothers and Sisters of Dragons. It was only a matter of time until you found your way to the heavenly palace. You have my gratitude, and that of my Transcendental Administration.'

Other gods rising from the flames gave a clipped bow.

The Jade Emperor raised his head slightly as if sniffing the air. 'The King of Foxes and his demon-court are no more. Balance has been restored.'

Hesitantly, Ruth stepped forward. 'Sir . . .' She bit off the word, cursing her awkwardness. 'The Blue Fire has been closed off from its source.'

'Even in our deep and dreamless sleep, we heard of this tragedy.'

'The flow was cut by the Extinction Shears. Is there any way to restore it?'

Yu Huang's expression grew dark at the mention of the Shears. Raising one hand, he summoned a hugely overweight figure with a bald head and glaring eyes. In his left hand he held a chain that led a strange, squat animal resembling a one-horned goat.

'The question has been asked, Gao Yao,' the Jade Emperor said to the new arrival, 'and if our Empire of the Sun and Moon is to prosper still, it is one that must be answered in our favour. What is your judgment on this issue?'

Gao Lao lowered his huge frame to communicate silently with the goat. When he looked up, his eyes were wet with tears.

'August Personage, my judgment in this matter is clear. Even this transgression can be breached—'

'Even though the weft and the weave were cut by the Extinction Shears?'

'August Personage, yes.' Gao Yao bowed several times until Ruth became concerned he would not stop. 'However, a sacrifice is needed. The spirit of a heavenly presence burns brightly and only that will break the dam.'

Dark thoughts played across Yu Huang's face.

From the ranks of the gods, a muscular figure stepped forward. Bald, with a long, black ponytail, he carried a large silver axe marked in red with Chinese characters. A jagged scar ran across his face, and his left eye was covered with a patch. 'August Personage, I will do this task for you. It is a small thing, and my battle-cry will echo through all eternity.'

'No, Lei-Gong. The sun is setting on Existence, and I fear we will have need of your thunder before too long.'

One by one the gods stepped forward to offer their service, and one by one Yu Huang rejected them.

Finally he turned to the gods and said, 'Return to the Palace of Heavenly Purity and make plans. The Transcendental Administration will be needed in the days to come. Let this be your legend: Honour. Fortune. Wisdom. Justice.'

When the gods had trooped by him into the stone tunnel, the Jade Emperor turned to Ruth. 'Your spirit burns brightly. Believe in yourself, flower of the west, and all will be well.'

And then he turned to Church, Shavi and Tom. Church had recovered enough to stand unaided, but he was still pale and weak. 'One of you must accompany me to the source of the Blue Fire.'

It took a second for them to realise what Yu Huang was saying. 'One of us has to be the sacrifice?' Shavi asked.

'Why?' There was force in Church's question despite his physical weakness. 'Because we're not gods? Because we're lesser?'

'You would set yourself alongside the gods?' Yu Huang's tone and expression gave no hint of his thoughts.

'We're not lesser. Everything we've done shows that we deserve recognition.'

The Jade Emperor nodded thoughtfully. 'Perhaps, then, it is time.' He turned to Ruth. 'You will accompany me?'

'No,' Church said. 'I'll go.'

'You don't have to keep protecting me,' Ruth said sharply. 'The Brothers and Sisters of Dragons are equals. I have as much right as you to be sacrificed.'

'Typical,' Tom said. 'Fighting over who should be the first to die.'

'You're the leader,' Ruth said to Church. 'You're the one who's most needed. Not me.' Ruth tried to stop her voice from breaking.

Out of the corner of her eye, she saw Church pitch forward. As she turned to see what had happened, a hard blow struck the back of her head. The last thing she heard was Shavi's voice: 'I will do it.'

6

Shavi felt as if he was flying through a brilliant blue sky. Hanging on to the Jade Emperor's sleeve, they hurtled through hall and tunnel and cavern in immeasurable number, all of them lit by the brilliant glow of the Blue Fire.

Eventually they came to a halt in a cavern that Shavi guessed was the one Church had accessed in Vietnam in the sixties. He centred himself, trying not to consider what lay ahead.

'Where does the Blue Fire come from?' he said.

'The source of everything under Existence.'

Something in the face his mind had chosen for the Jade Emperor reminded him of his grandfather. 'And you and your kind stand with Existence?'

'We stand for balance. The yin and the yang in eternal harmony. One cannot exist without the other: day needs night; love needs hate; peace needs war. Each defines the other.'

'But the Void has been in control of the world for so long—'

'In your terms.'

'For the sake of balance, Existence should get its turn.'

A ghost of a smile. 'Yes.'

Shavi imagined for a moment. 'A golden age. Mankind in harmony with nature, not driven by the urge for money and power.'

'A golden age indeed,' Yu Huang repeated.

'Then I am ready,' Shavi said. 'If my sacrifice could help bring that about, it is worth it.'

'Why did you choose to put yourself before the one I had chosen, and the one who sought to take her place?'

'They are my friends.' It didn't feel like enough of an explanation, so he added, 'They love each other. They deserve a chance to be together.'

'More than you?'

'Yes.'

'Do you fear death?'

Shavi smiled. 'I do not welcome it. There is much more I feel I need to do before I leave this life. But no, I do not fear it. I believe it is not an ending in itself, rather that it leads on to something great and mysterious.'

Yu Huang nodded. 'A wise answer. Your Brother spoke of his desire

264

for Fragile Creatures to be considered equal to gods. He gives voice to a timeless prophecy of an age when the chi of Fragile Creatures will rise and advance. And in that time the age of gods will pass. This may well be that time.'

He approached a place in the cavern wall that was seared black, and for a second he appeared to be made of nothing more than blue light. 'Tell me, little Brother of Dragons, if you could keep only five memories, which would you choose?'

The question felt like a request for a valediction. Shavi closed his eyes and thought. 'My father and mother, hugging me on my tenth birthday. Before my father realised I was not going to walk his road and his heart hardened towards me.'

Shavi opened his eyes and was surprised to see that the thin pool of Blue Fire had licked up into a column three feet above the ground. Yu Huang watched it intently.

Closing his eyes again, Shavi searched his memories. If he was going to die, it would be good to do so with his best thoughts in his head. Was it an act of compassion from Yu Huang?

'A kiss in the dark on Clapham Common.' He saw Lee's face, sweet and mysterious, and accepted how much he had loved him. 'Lying on the Downs, looking over Stonehenge as the sun came up, listening to music on my iPod and feeling a part of something wonderful.' His emotions surged and he thought he might cry. 'Holding my grandmother's hand while she died, and seeing her smile one last time, hearing her tell me everything would be all right.'

He took a deep breath, lost in the vast Otherworld inside his head, Yu Huang, the cavern, his impending death all forgotten.

'The final one . . . sitting around a campfire at night, with Church, Laura, Ruth, Ryan, all of us laughing, and realising in such a powerful way that it shook me to the core that these were the best friends I could ever want. That they had enriched my existence just by being there, that they had changed my life, like the philosopher's stone changed lead into gold.' He let the image settle into his thoughts. 'I will miss them.'

When he opened his eyes he was shocked to see that the column of Blue Fire now soared to the very roof of the cavern. Yu Huang studied it carefully before turning to Shavi with an almost reverential expression. 'You have built a monument of wonder. A beacon in the deep dark of the Void.'

With a gesture, he raised another column from the Blue Fire, half the height of the one Shavi had created. 'I bestride the heavens. I have seen all, done all, yet that is the height of my own monument.' He looked from one column to the other and smiled. 'These are strange times, great times.'

'I am ready,' Shavi said.

After a long moment of silence, the Jade Emperor said, 'The season has turned, Brother of Dragons. It is your time now.' He reached out to the scar on the cavern wall and there was an explosion of Blue Fire that knocked Shavi from his feet.

When he regained his equilibrium, Yu Huang was gone. Blue Fire gushed through an opening, filling the reservoir in the cavern, and rushing out across Vietnam, across China and the Far East, across the world.

Shavi was stunned. As he struggled to comprehend why he was still alive, Hal's voice rang out warmly. 'Looks like the king has returned to the land, just as he did in the Age of Misrule. Congratulations, Shavi. The Fiery Network is back. And commiserations – you've just ushered in the most difficult time of all. It's going to be war, hard and brutal.'

Through the gap leading to the source of the Blue Fire, Shavi could make out movement. They came through with the flow, writhing sinuously as they struggled to adapt their nascent bodies to the new environment. The newborn Fabulous Beasts slipped into the stream one by one and made their way into the world. Shavi was overwhelmed by euphoria as their essence touched him in passing.

'Come on,' Hal said. 'Let's get you back to the others.'

7

Church came round to find Tom shaking him roughly.

'Bloody hell, Tom. I was dying a few minutes ago.'

'Shut up. You're alive now, aren't you? Stop being a little girl.'

Tom hauled Church into a sitting position. Rubbing the back of his head, Church recalled what had happened. 'Shavi?'

'Gone. He reached his potential – I always knew he would. The man's as quiet as a mouse, but he's got the heart of a lion. You probably didn't realise, bickering with your girly like a lovesick teen.'

Ruth came over, choking back sobs. 'He went in my place—'

'Your sword,' Tom interjected. 'Look at your sword.'

The blade had been cold since Church had left Veitch, but now tiny blue flames flickered around the edge. They grew stronger until, with a whoosh, they roared out like a torch. Tom pointed across the cavernous hall to where a tidal wave of Blue Fire rushed towards them.

'Dammit, he did it,' Tom said in awe.

The flames crashed against the stone lip of the pool, but didn't wash over the companions. A second later, Shavi stepped out of the cold inferno, grinning broadly. Ruth threw her arms around him, no longer holding back her tears.

'Yu Huang sacrificed himself in my place,' Shavi said.

Tom reeled. 'The Jade Emperor sacrificed himself in your place?'

'Yes.'

'The ruler of the Chinese pantheon – the highest of the high in this Great Dominion?'

'He said "yes", you old fool,' Ruth said sharply.

The flaming outline of Hal appeared in the Blue Fire, this time sharp and clear. Church had an impression of a shy young man overcome with the optimism that was spreading through them all.

'All right, team, you're on the last leg,' he said. 'Get the two Keys together, and then it's backs to the wall for the fight to end them all.'

'But we are still trapped in the Forbidden City with the spiders outside the walls,' Shavi said.

'I told you, for people like . . . people like us – there's always an exit. Right, Tom?'

'Your magic disappearing act,' Church said. 'That's right. You know how to jump along the lines of earth energy, move between the nodes—'

'No,' Shavi cautioned, 'it is too dangerous. I have heard tell that once you immerse yourself in the Blue it is so wondrous, so magical, you could lose yourself in there for ever.'

'That's right,' Hal said. 'The Blue is very seductive. It's the place we all want to go home to after a hard day's work, where we can finally rest. But you have to know there will be time enough for that later. You can free yourself from the pull of the Blue if you stay focused on your mission.'

'It can take us straight to New York?' Church said.

'It can take you anywhere.'

'Then let's do it.' Church turned to Tom. 'You know how to get this thing going?'

Tom nodded, crouching next to the pool, his head bowed.

'Church . . .' Ruth began hesitantly.

'Don't worry. We're going to be all right.'

'We need to talk.'

'When we get to New York.'

There was a whoosh as the Blue Fire swirled in a vortex. 'Come on,' Tom said. 'It's not going to stay open for ever.'

'Good luck,' Hal said. 'I'll be with you all the way. And beyond. The real journey starts here.'

Hal faded into the flames as Tom stepped into the vortex and was gone. Shavi followed.

'Church,' Ruth said forcefully, 'I'm not going with you.'

In her face, he saw a glimpse of the earlier betrayal and knew the truth. 'You're staying with Veitch.'

'I have to. I can't explain now.'

'You don't need to.'

'You're right there.' Veitch stepped from the shadows in the tunnel. Behind him, Miller cowered. 'Bad pennies and all that.' The black flames sucked hungrily at the Blue Fire in Caledfwlch.

'You're not going to take her,' Church said.

'She's making the choice, mate. That's always how I wanted it. I never wanted to force her to do anything.'

Ruth wouldn't meet Church's eyes.

'See, you're all better, just like I said.'

'So you can try to kill me again?'

'Nah, I just wanted to teach you a lesson. Make you feel some of the pain I felt. You see, now I've won. You've lost. Game over.'

'It's not over,' Church said coldly.

'Ooh, scary talk.'

'Church, leave it,' Ruth pleaded.

Veitch entered the hall and stood next to Ruth. When she didn't move away from him, Church felt as if Veitch had stabbed him all over again.

'I just needed you to do the dirty work, open up the path into the Blue,' Veitch said. 'It's the smart way to travel.'

Church raised his sword, ready to fight until one of them died. And then Ruth did come over to him, but just as he convinced himself that she had changed her mind, she whispered, 'Go,' and thrust him into the vortex.

As he was whisked away into a soothing sapphire world, he saw Veitch take Ruth's hand and prepare to follow. Still reeling from the revelation that he and the Libertarian were one and the same, this was the final blow. He wondered if disappearing into the peace of that blue world for ever might be the only way to soothe the pain.

chapter twelve

the burning man

1

The prison stood in the shadow of the great watchtowers that flanked the entrance gate to the Court of the Soaring Spirit. In a grim city, it was the grimmest building of all, built of gargantuan blocks of stone with only a smattering of windows, each barely bigger than a hand. Even in the dark, no light escaped from it, and no sound, but a reek of damp, blood and excrement hung over all.

In an alleyway that offered some respite from the driving rain, Mallory watched. There was only one way in and out, and it was blocked by iron gates with armed guards beyond. But Jerzy was in there somewhere, and if what Mallory had heard about the Hall of Bright Beyond was true, the Mocker needed to be rescued sooner rather than later.

Nearby, an old mare whinnied and stumbled slowly through the thick mud of a roughly built pen next to a smoky shack. Picking up a coil of rope, Mallory also took a thick woollen cloak that hung in an adjoining shed and wrapped it around himself before leading the mare out of the pen. He rode the animal towards the prison, hunched low over its neck with the hood of the cloak pulled forwards to obscure his features. Anyone seeing him would have thought him wounded or dead.

The mare came to a halt at the gates. Keeping still, Mallory could hear movement beyond. Lantern light splashed across the puddles that surrounded him.

'Move away,' a voice barked. 'No one is allowed to approach the Hall of Bright Beyond.' Mallory didn't move. The voice came again. 'Move away or I will loose an arrow into you.'

Mallory tensed, but no attack was launched. The lock clanked and the gate creaked open. Rumbling thunder added to the deafening sound of the downpour.

The guard lifted the lantern to peer into Mallory's hood. Reacting quickly, Mallory brought the pommel of his sword up sharply against the guard's temple. By the time the guard hit the ground, Mallory was off the horse and had reclaimed the lantern. Dragging the guard out of sight of the gate, Mallory bound him tightly with the rope, then slipped inside the prison, pulling the gate shut behind him.

There was no sign of the other guards. A maze of foul-smelling corridors led off the keep. He was grateful for the lantern for there were no torches, and occasionally, when its light fell on the doors that lined his route, he heard pitiful cries from within.

He searched through the labyrinth for more than an hour until he caught sight of a dim red glow eking into the corridor through an open door. Faint voices rumbled through the stillness, and as he neared he heard muffled cries that were unmistakably Jerzy.

Mallory crept to the edge of the door. Beyond was a large, low-ceilinged room lit by the glow from a brazier. Straw covered the floor to soak up the blood, excrement and urine. In a rack on one wall were rows of stained, rusted tools of indeterminate use. Arms outstretched, Jerzy hung like a monkey, naked, chained by his wrists to two wooden posts. A dirty rag had been forced into his grinning mouth, and his eyes were fixed wide with horror. Numerous gouges and burns scarred his chalky body.

Two of the queen's guards stood watch while a thin man in dirty robes and a pointed hood went about his work.

'He will not talk,' one of the guards said.

'He must,' the other replied. 'The queen shall know the secret plan that drives him or we shall be here alongside him.'

'What if there is no secret plan?'

'There is. He rides the Brothers and Sisters of Dragons like mares to achieve his ends. The queen has evidence, though I know not from where.'

'Shall I remove the rag to ask him again?'

'No, I cannot bear to hear his sounds. Two more turns and then we shall try again.'

The one in the hood had spent some time contemplating the rack of tools and finally made his choice, what looked like a wire brush fitted with three parallel razor blades. Humming to himself, he examined the tool distractedly as he approached Jerzy. The look in Jerzy's eyes made Mallory queasy, and then the glimmer of unbelievable gratitude in those same eyes when Mallory stepped into the doorway affected him just as powerfully.

'Let him go.' The blue flames licking around Llyrwyn made a stark contrast in the red room.

Swords drawn, the guards advanced cautiously. 'Walk away, Brother of Dragons. The queen is not of a mind to play games with you any longer.'

'Shame. I was hoping to challenge her at Twister.' He advanced. 'Once more, in case you didn't hear me the first time: let him go.'

The guards rushed him together.

The moves he had learned as a Knight Templar in the compound in Salisbury came instinctively. As the guards attacked from two sides, he stood holding the sword horizontally above his head, eyes closed.

When he opened his eyes, the sword moved so quickly that no one in the room saw it; three planes and then back in the scabbard. Both guards fell dead. The torturer in the hood retreated to the gloom at the rear of the room.

Mallory hacked through the chains supporting Jerzy, then caught him as he fell. The minute the rag was plucked from his mouth, the Mocker let forth a flow of desperate thanks.

'I think talking can wait, don't you?' Mallory said.

Jerzy nodded uncomfortably.

2

At the Hunter's Moon, Mallory found Decebalus pacing his quarters like a cornered beast.

'Where's Sophie and Caitlin?' Mallory asked.

'Not here. I have not seen them. But, look here.' Decebalus led Mallory to Rhiannon who rested more peacefully than she had since they had brought her there. Virginia hugged her knees in a chair beside the bed. The barbarian brushed matted hair from Rhiannon's forehead and her eyes flickered open. 'He is here,' Decebalus said softly, 'as I said he would be.'

Rhiannon gave Mallory a weak but warm smile. 'Mallory.' Her voice was low and soft. 'Again we meet. I knew we would. So good.'

'I'm sorry about your hand,' he said.

'You did what you had to do, as a Brother of Dragons always does. Do you remember when we first met, when Llyrwyn chose you?'

'For a long time I'd forgotten. The Void wouldn't let me have that memory. But now it's back. Those hours in your court were the last time I felt at peace.'

'I fear none of us will know peace again for a very long time.'

'It was Niamh, wasn't it?'

She nodded, her expression haunted. 'She has turned on her own kind. I would never have thought to see it. She came to my court with a large force and took us by surprise. All who remained were slaughtered, save me. And I . . . I was tortured, and was left as a warning to any of my kind who found me. Have you noticed there have been no visitors here from any other court? Because they fear her. All things in the Far Lands fear her. She has even taken her own brother captive. Not in your darkest thoughts would you imagine what she is capable of, Mallory. Not in your darkest thoughts.'

'Why didn't she kill me and the others the minute we got here?'

'There are currents moving deeply and secretly throughout all Existence . . . alignments and patterns that have been shifting since the first days. She will not act rashly. She sits in her web, gathering information, sifting motivation and rumour, manipulating and scheming. And when she is sure, and the power that she serves is sure, then she will strike.'

'Have you heard of the Gateway to Winter?'

'It moves through this city as the ages change, hidden from all eyes. Unless you have the map that plots its course.'

'I have the map.'

Rhiannon peered at him curiously. 'It is rumoured only Math has that.'

Mallory tapped his head. 'He left it here for me. A map that's also a calendar. Two aspects designed to hide its true meaning, I suppose. Do you feel strong enough to draw me a map of the city?'

Decebalus brought her paper, quill and ink, and Mallory went back to the fire in the other room where Jerzy huddled, weak and shaking, wrapped in a blanket.

'Are you all right?'

'They had only just started. And I come from hardy stock. As a boy I was beaten night and day to work the fields.'

Mallory pulled up a chair. 'The guards said the queen has evidence that you're acting on some secret plan. That you've been manipulating us.'

Jerzy stared into the fire uncomfortably.

'Are you working against us, Jerzy?'

'No!' The passion in his voice shocked Mallory. 'My good friend Church saved me and set me on the path to redemption. I owe him everything. And by association I owe all the Brothers and Sisters of Dragons everything.'

'Then what's going on?'

'I serve higher powers. They want the same as you, good friend. They do!'

'Church told us you were captured by the Puck, and spent a lot of time in his company. Afterwards you were changed somehow.'

Jerzy remained silent.

'Is the Puck the higher power?'

'The Puck serves a greater plan, as do all the oldest things in the lands. And the things that came before them.'

Mallory ignored the nonsensical comment and asked, 'If these powers want the same as us, why didn't you tell us? Why don't they reveal themselves and work with us?'

'Because they see a greater pattern. And you, with your limited perspective, may not accept the value of the choices they make. For in the greater plan, there are hardships that seen in isolation are shattering.'

'So we can't be trusted, is that it?'

Jerzy would say no more.

Bitterly, Mallory returned to Rhiannon. But the moment he glanced at the map she had drawn, his mind was assailed with colours and symbols and all the information Math had implanted there. It was too much, and he crashed across the bed, unconscious.

3

Some time later, in the thin hour before dawn, Mallory, Decebalus, Jerzy and a rapidly recovering Rhiannon made their way across the city in a storm that, if anything, had grown more intense. They had left Virginia tucked up asleep in her bed in the Hunter's Moon. Wind hurled protesting shop signs furiously and thrashed untethered shutters. Rain sluiced from the rooftops in sheets.

Mallory had the sense that the tiny, winding streets shifted their position in reality continually, confounding expectations, bringing confusion and doubt, and eventually despair. But Rhiannon's map continued to guide them. Every now and then they would shelter in a porch or the lee of a building, and study it beneath a cloak by guttering lantern light.

And that was how they found themselves in a small cobbled square with four roads leading off it. In the centre was a circular shallow pool enclosed by a low stone wall. Bloated by the rain, its black waters now lapped over the edge. And in the centre of that circle was a stone arch, simple in design, so rough-hewn it did not attract the attention and so slipped easily into the bleak background. The only detail was on the keystone, where a leafless tree had been etched.

'The Gateway to Winter,' Rhiannon said.

'Oh, what do we do now?' Jerzy scampered round and round the pool, raising large splashes.

'If it's a gate, the logical approach would be to find some way to open it.' Mallory stepped into the pool and stood before the arch. Up close, the impression that there was a clear view through the arch was an illusion. It was as if a fine gauze covered the gap, but he could pass his hand through it without meeting any resistance. Yet as he felt around the area where a handle would have been on a normal gate, his fingers closed around something hard. He pulled, and the gate opened.

The view through the arch showed the same buildings, but now the cobbles were covered with a thick blanket of snow, and flakes fell heavily from a night sky. Backing off, Jerzy gave a high-pitched whine, and even Decebalus shied away.

'Where is that?' Mallory asked. 'The past? The future?'

'Winter-side,' Rhiannon said in awe, as if that was enough.

Steeling himself, Mallory stepped through the gate; Rhiannon followed close behind, and after a moment's hesitation Decebalus and Jerzy came, too. Mallory shivered in the icy breeze, his sopping clothes leaching the heat from him.

'We need to move or we're going to freeze,' he said.

Sword drawn, Decebalus looked around at the snow-capped buildings. Everywhere was eerily still, as if the city was empty. 'But where do we go?' he said.

It was Rhiannon who pointed the way, so obvious the others had missed it. Along an alley between two faceless granite buildings the snow had been hard-packed by numerous feet.

The buildings rose so high on either side it felt as if they were moving beneath the earth. The snow continued to fall. The silence was unnerving. The alley twisted this way and that, picking an irrational path amongst the cramped buildings, each as blank as the last.

After a while, Jerzy began to tug annoyingly at Mallory's sleeve. 'Let us go back, good friend,' he pleaded. 'I do not like it here. We should come in the daytime. Perhaps even in the summer!'

Mallory realised that Jerzy was sensing something untoward, and after a few more paces he could sense it himself; they all could. It felt like someone standing just behind them, about to touch the napes of their necks. None of them could resist looking back from time to time as they hurried on.

The alley passed an area where a building had been demolished, the site sealed off with seven-foot-high wooden boards. After the claustrophobia of the route, the sudden open space was just as unnerving. A dim red glow emanated from somewhere on the other side of the fence – a fire, perhaps.

A low growl emerged from the sealed-off area. Then another, and another.

Jerzy whimpered louder.

Rhiannon caught Mallory's arm. 'Steady. I believe sentries have been posted to guard the way.'

Ahead, the alley formed a T-junction, and at the corner the boards had collapsed. As they approached, the growling grew louder. Mallory drew Llyrwyn just in time.

From out of the gap bounded a large dog, smeared a bloody red for it had no skin, and all its muscles and organs were in clear view. Blood spattered on the snow as it skidded around to face Mallory. On the other side of the fence, more dogs could be heard bounding towards the gap.

When the dog snarled, its red-stained teeth showed clear up to the hinge of its jaw. It leaped at Mallory with a force and fury that shocked him. It took all his skill with the sword to fend off its snapping jaws, but its momentum knocked him onto his back. Snarling, it went straight for his throat, spittle flying, uncontained eyes rolling insanely. There was no time or room to bring his sword up.

Just as its teeth brushed his skin, Decebalus brought his sword down, severing the dog's head from its neck and showering Mallory with a gush of steaming blood. The head rolled into a snowdrift where it continued to snap and snarl and roll its eyes.

'Foul hell-beast!' Decebalus spat.

Mallory just had time to scramble to his feet before three more ferocious dogs attacked. With Decebalus at his side, they hacked and slashed until there were only twitching, bloody chunks in the snow.

'That's the most disgusting thing I've seen,' Mallory said as he cleaned his blade.

'There may be worse things ahead,' Rhiannon warned.

As dawn began to turn the sky a fiery red, they followed the branching alley with the most frozen footprints and eventually came to another cobbled square. A large rock stood in the centre, in the middle of another low-walled pool, looking like the tip of a mountain bursting from the earth. In the side of it was a wooden door.

Mallory noticed Rhiannon's curious expression. 'You know where it leads?' he said.

'There is another one in Summer-side, but Niamh closed it off so none could pass through.' Awareness lit her face. 'It leads to the Watchtower between the worlds.'

Across rolling green downs and rushing white-foamed rivers, up steep boulder-strewn hills and over sweeping barren moors, Hunter carried Laura, fighting exhaustion, focusing on the horizon, driving one foot relentlessly in front of the other. Slow, laborious, wearing progress. Many times he felt he would fall to his knees and never get up again, but still he kept going. Even though there was not the slightest sign of life; nor was there any hint of a real, abiding death; and so he had hope.

'Nearly there,' he whispered. It had become his mantra, repeated too many times to count, although for all he knew they were a thousand miles away from their destination.

Finally the landscape gave way to a barren region where it appeared there had been a great fire. Charcoal trees sprouted from scorched earth peppered with blackened rocks. The air smelled like the industrial zone of a great city.

Tying his handkerchief across his mouth, he descended a slope that ended on the banks of a river of blood. To weary to be shocked, he followed it upstream to a sprawling white marble building: the Court of the Final Word.

Filled with relief, he found the energy to run the last few yards to the imposing doors, where he hammered furiously.

The doors were flung open by a startled, golden-skinned youth in red robes and a red skullcap. A red surgical mask hung from his neck. Behind him, more of the red-robed Tuatha Dé Danann moved with frantic purpose, carrying trays of strange implements, disappearing through doors into the bowels of the court.

'Begone, Fragile Creature,' the youth said angrily, before catching himself. He peered into Hunter's face. Whatever he saw there prompted him to turn and hurry into the depths of the building.

Hunter staggered in and yelled, 'I need help here! And if I don't get it I'm going to start breaking things.'

The youth returned at a clip accompanied by an elderly man with an aquiline nose and an aristocratic face. He gave a curt bow. 'Brother of Dragons, forgive any disrespect. I am Dian Cecht. This is my court. In our defence, these are difficult times. How may I be of service?'

Hunter held Laura out. 'She's hurt . . . could be dying. I was told you might be able to help.'

Dian Cecht eyed Laura. 'She has the mark of one of my brothers upon her.'

'You've got to help,' Hunter urged. 'Whatever it takes.'

Dian Cecht smiled but gave nothing away. He conducted a cursory examination of Laura. 'I cannot say for certain that there is anything I can do. And if there is, there may well be a severe price to pay.'

'Whatever. Just help her.'

This appeared to please Dian Cecht. He nodded to the youth, who took Laura and carried her carefully into the court.

'You are weary, Brother of Dragons. You need rest, food.'

'I'm fine.'

'It will not help the Sister of Dragons if you fall sick yourself. I will arrange for you to be taken to the rest quarters where you will be given sustenance. To such an esteemed guest, all is offered freely and without obligation.'

'Tell me the minute you know something.'

Dian Cecht clapped his hands and the nearest Tuatha Dé Danann put down the tray he was carrying and guided Hunter into a white marble room with crystal-clear water running in a channel from a spout in one wall. There was a low couch with sumptuous cushions. The god went away to fetch food and drink, but by the time he returned Hunter was fast asleep.

Dreams came in force, and he hadn't dreamed for a long time. They were hallucinatory, as if every image stored up since his first kill had been released as one, shouting and stamping their feet for attention, desperate to be set free. Though there was no clear narrative, he could pick meaning from the fires and the bones, the ravens and the single beacon glowing away in the dark that he could never reach.

He awoke slowly, fighting for freedom, to discover Dian Cecht sitting on a stool, studying him dispassionately.

'What have you found?' Hunter asked blearily.

'She is gone,' Dian Cecht replied.

Those three words took all the hope out of Hunter's life.

5

High up on the playa of the Black Rock Desert in Nevada, ninety miles north-north-east of Reno, a blasting wind flayed the skin and brought furious dust storms out of nowhere, and the sun seared the bleak land-scape to a hundred degrees. Yet in this inhospitable location, a ramshackle city had grown: tents and makeshift shacks, geodesic domes, soaring statues and art installations that doubled as living quarters, arranged into streets and esplanades with all the order of a fixed city's town planning.

The citizens wandered around in bizarre costumes – a Statue of Liberty, Wonder Woman, a tinfoil clown – or naked, body-painted, pierced, tattooed, dreadlocked, shaven-headed, surfer shorts, army fatigues, top hats, motorcycle jackets. They wore goggles and scarves across their mouths to protect against the seventy-mile-per-hour sand. Some drove vehicles that had been transformed into works of art, too, metal blossoming into staggering new mechanical creations. It was the day after the apocalypse, the end of the world, a nomadic tribe in the hinterland, and the party was only just beginning.

This was what Veitch saw when he tumbled from nowhere onto the prehistoric salt-pan. 'This isn't bleedin' New York,' he said as a man in a gimp suit wandered past.

Ruth dusted herself down as Miller, Etain and the others crashed out of the Blue behind them. 'I can't see Church,' she said. 'Why did we get spat out here?'

Beyond the tent city, a massive wicker man rose up against the silver sky.

A bare-chested, sandalled man with dyed blonde hair, carrying a surfboard, wandered up. His rolling gait suggested the influence of some narcotic. He went straight to Miller who was chewing on a fingernail, disoriented and frightened.

'Dude, you've got a blue dragon inside you!' the surfer said. His skittering fascination turned to the otherworldly mounts of the Brothers and Sisters of Spiders. 'Cool ponies!' He took a step back and began to sing 'My Little Pony' before breaking into a cackling laugh.

Etain took a step forward. Veitch made a subtle sign for her to stop.

'Where are we?' Ruth asked the surfer.

'Chica! So, what, you're a yahoo or a virgin?' He looked from her to Veitch. 'Nice sword, dude. And that silver hand . . . cool! If this is your first time, you fit right in.'

'Tell you what, mate,' Veitch said. 'How about you start speaking some sense or I give you a look at my sword close up?'

The surfer was oblivious to Veitch's threat. His attention was drawn to the horizon where the wind had whipped up a dust storm. 'Uh-oh, there's a white-out blowin' in. Gotta take shelter. Later.' Clutching his board, he ran awkwardly towards the nearest tents.

Ruth shielded her eyes from the sun; the moisture was rapidly being sucked from her body. 'He's right. Without the right clothes or provisions, we're in danger.'

With mounting annoyance, Veitch drew Etain to one side. 'You take the others out of sight till I can work out what we're doing. Don't want to freak anyone out.' He paused, read her face. 'Stop looking at me like that. I know you're feeling bad . . .' He glanced back at Ruth. 'We'll talk about it, all right? Soon.'

Etain took the reins of her mount and walked away into the desert. Branwen, Tannis and Owein followed.

'Do you really think she understands you?' Miller asked. 'Or do you just pretend you know what she's thinking?'

'I'm not mad, all right?' he replied angrily before marching towards the tents.

The dust storm swept in quickly. The surfer's name for it was fitting, for within seconds it was impossible to see more than a few feet. Veitch, Ruth and Miller were offered shelter in a large communal tent that resembled a Bedouin hall. Twenty or so others sat around on cushions talking quietly amongst themselves, or listening to trance music on an MP3 player fitted with speakers.

They all showed deference to a man in his sixties with snow-white hair tied in a ponytail and a long droopy moustache. He had brilliant blue eyes and an open, genial nature. He took the three of them over to where he'd been lounging on cushions and offered them home-made honey-cakes.

'I'm guessing you're virgins,' he said with a Southern drawl. 'Your clothes . . . not suitable, man, nah. My name's Rick.' He gestured expansively. 'Welcome to my domain. Enjoy yourselves. Everything is given freely and without obligation.' He chuckled throatily.

'Where are we?' Ruth asked.

Rick laughed, realised she wasn't joking. 'You don't know?'

'Just answer the bleedin' question,' Veitch said.

'You've got a lot of anger in you, I can see that. You don't need to let it eat you up here, man. You're with friends.'

'You're not my friends.'

'Yeah, we are. You just don't know it yet. We're a community, one of the last real ones left in this grasping, mean old world. We look after our own. You don't need to watch your back here. We'll do it for you. You can check all your anger and guilt and hatred at the door. We've all been there. We all know that pain. Here we can live the life we've always wanted to live and know we're safe.'

Veitch opened his mouth to speak, closed it again, shrugged, shifted uneasily.

Rick smiled. 'Good. We've got us an understanding. Okay, I'll take your question at face value. This is Burning Man Festival.' He looked from Veitch to Ruth to Miller, saw only blankness, sighed. 'You fell out of the sky?'

'Something like that.' Ruth said.

'Okay, Burning Man one-oh-one. An eight-day festival held up here in Black Rock every year ending on Labor Day. We come from all over, thousands of us, more every year, and set up this temporary city. You must know this if you're here, right?'

'We're pretty sure we're here for a reason. We just don't know why yet,' Ruth replied.

'Yeah, a lot of us Burners are like that. We're all searching for something here. Some even find it.'

'So what's the point?' Veitch asked.

Rick laughed. 'The point is the world has no point! Art, spirituality, friendship, community, love – all the things that matter are forgotten out there. Sacrificed on the altar of commercialism.' He spread his arms wide. 'This whole deal is an experiment. In community. In self-expression – you see the art out there? It's everywhere, a part of everyday life as it should be. And it's an experiment in self-reliance. This place is the antithesis of the real world. There are no cash transactions. No stores. You can't buy what you haven't brought with you. If you don't come well prepared you're in real danger out here. Or you can rely on the support of your neighbours. Offer to do something for them, they'll look after you. That's how a community binds together. What's your community?' He directed the question at Veitch.

Veitch shifted uneasily. 'I'm on my own.'

'How's that working out for you?'

Veitch didn't respond.

'We have ten principles here at Burning Man. Radical inclusion, gifting, decommodification, radical self-reliance, radical self-expression, communal effort, civic responsibility, leaving no trace, participation and immediacy. Now, to me that's a pretty good constitution for this new age we're moving into.'

Miller nodded. 'I like that. I like that a lot.'

Ruth struggled to see anything relevant in Rick's words. 'Maybe it was just an accident we dropped out here. Totally random.'

'There aren't any coincidences,' Veitch muttered. 'All right, I'm going to have a look around once that dust-storm's dropped.'

'Black Rock City is built in an arc with concentric streets. You'll find the Burning Man at the centre,' Rick said. 'Good luck with your quest. You look like you need to find some answers pretty quick.'

As they made their way out of the tent, a shaven-headed man offered them a comic book he had been reading. 'You want to take a look at this,' he said with a lazy smile.

Veitch examined it. '*Seven Soldiers*?'

'Grant Morrison. Celtic mythology. Seven heroes saving the world. Has all the best antecedents, if you know what I mean.'

Veitch handed the comic back. 'Seven is good. Five is better.'

'Rick's a nice guy,' Ruth said as they stood at the door waiting for the wind to drop.

'Reminded me of Tom. Only without the misery injection.' Veitch stared into the whipping dust, lost to his thoughts.

'I think we should split up, meet in the centre.'

Veitch eyed her suspiciously.

'I'll be there. You can trust me.'

'I've heard that before.' He turned to Miller. 'You come with me.'

'You can trust me, too!' Miller protested.

''Cept I can't trust you not to do something stupid, like getting run over or accidentally wandering into the desert. I need you where I can give you a clip round the ear when your brain packs in.'

Miller looked affronted.

Ruth surprised Veitch with a kiss on the cheek. 'Thank you for trusting me.'

'Don't let me down.' Veitch grabbed Miller by the collar and dragged him into the baking heat.

6

As Ruth made her way amongst the drifting crowds of bohemians, stopping every now and then to examine the spectacular art displays, she tried to make some sense of her own see-sawing emotions.

She knew she loved Church, but she was increasingly aware of a growing affection for Veitch, which both Tom and Shavi had clearly recognised in Beijing before she had even allowed herself to be aware of it. But how much of that was due to her own feelings, and how much had been caused by Veitch's power-sucking spell in Cornwall? Would she ever know the truth?

Veitch had done some terrible things, yet she could see that he was still at heart the hero who had been chosen by Existence. His great flaw was his emotional weakness. At times he was like a spurned child, lashing out at the things he believed had hurt his hopes and feelings. Could he be saved? It was her flaw to believe she could help him, and she was afraid it would all end in tears.

But love him? No, surely not.

From out of nowhere, the wind whipped up the dust into a choking smog in the avenue between the tents and shacks. A mutant vehicle, a three-wheeled motorbike with spider legs, roared by. The rider, a black woman wearing snow-goggles, yelled, 'You want to get under cover. There's another white-out coming on the back of the last.' She disappeared into the dust.

The storm grew stronger in seconds. It was already too late to attempt to make her way back to Rick's tent; her best option was to try one of the nearby homes.

Before she could move, the sound of hoof-beats began to draw near. From out of the swirling clouds came Etain, sword drawn. It took Ruth a second to realise she was the target and by then the Sister of Spiders was almost upon her.

At the last moment, Ruth threw herself out of the way. Disoriented by the dust blasting her eyes and face, crushed by the intense heat, she couldn't run.

Etain brought her mount round again. Her scarred and blackened face gave no hint of the emotions that drove her.

Ruth barely avoided the thundering hooves. 'Why are you doing this?' she yelled as she rolled out of the way.

As the words left her lips, she knew. 'You're jealous,' she said, stunned.

She was left reeling by the revelation that there was still some echo of life's richness deep beneath the surface of what she had considered a mechanical shell. And she knew that Etain would not stop until she was dead.

Etain was lost in the now-raging dust storm. Choking, Ruth could barely breathe, barely stand. She covered her face and turned her thoughts inward.

I can do this, she pressed. *Not so long ago I could have torn this world inside out. I can do it again.*

As Etain roared out of the dust, Blue Fire exploded in Ruth's head. The chaotic force of the dust storm bent to her will and smashed against Etain like a hammer, knocking her from the saddle. The impact probably broke several bones, but she was up in a second, sword in hand, marching towards Ruth.

Exhilarated, but unsure how long she could sustain it, Ruth said, 'I'm going to thank you. If not for this, I'd probably never have been pushed hard enough to realise what I'm still capable of.'

Etain lunged with the sword. Ruth concentrated. It was becoming more difficult to focus, but she increased the power of the storm, forcing Etain back. She hacked and slashed, her fury an eerie counterpoint to her frozen features.

'Okay, you love him, I get it,' Ruth said. 'You let Church into the pyramid because you hoped he might take me away and leave Ryan all to yourself. Now you've decided the only chance you have is to take me out of the picture completely. Is that right?'

Etain paused mid-strike and let her sword-arm fall to her side.

'I feel sorry for you,' Ruth continued. 'I know how much you've suffered over the centuries. I'm not even going to comment on a dead woman falling in love with a living guy. Frankly, I've seen weirder things in recent times. But if you come for me again, I will take you apart. Literally.'

Etain stood in the raging dust for a moment until Ruth saw a single glint on her cheek, the last drop of moisture leaving her arid body.

Ruth wanted to say something that would comfort Etain, but the gulf was too great to bridge; and it troubled her to think that even on the other side of death there was no escape from the pain love often bought.

As the storm blew stronger, Ruth took shelter amongst the nearest tents, and when she looked back, Etain was gone.

7

For half an hour, Miller had been chattering earnestly about how he'd adjusted to his role in events and was now prepared to do 'big things', and how Veitch was such a hero, though he hid it well, and such an inspiration, and how his eyes had been opened to all the magic in the world. During their months on the road, Veitch had learned to zone him out until he became a dim background buzz.

Instead he focused on the people moving around the tent where they had been offered shelter from the returning dust storm. He saw a man delve into his personal medical supplies to help a complete stranger who had gashed his arm. He saw a couple, desperate after their tent had been torn away by the storm and all their possessions lost, now given free use of their neighbour's home and supplies. He saw numerous acts of kindness played out without a second thought.

'Maybe we should stay here for a while,' he said, talking to himself, really. 'Maybe that's why we ended up here.'

He realised Miller had fallen silent. 'What?'

'You don't really mean that.'

'I do.'

'You've got a mission. You need to find the other Key or the Void wins.'

'I think we need to get a few things straight here. Firstly, I'm not after the Second Key to do some good deed. I want you two in my hands for revenge, pure and simple.'

'I know you've said that, but . . . you don't really mean it.'

'That shows how much you know. A – if it screws up that bastard Church's plan to be a big hero, then that's a win. Why should he get all the cheers? And b – with the two of you, I get the power to decide how everything should be. And if I decide it's going to be a wasteland, then that's how it's going to be.'

Miller looked hurt for a moment, but slowly he smiled.

'I mean it.'

'You don't fool me. I can see what you're really like.'

'Will you stop that!'

'You're a good man, Ryan—'

'You're a bleedin' simpleton. You wouldn't see the truth if it smacked you in the face. And when the time comes, don't think I won't throw you to the lions, 'cause I will. You don't mean anything to me, Miller. All the hours we've "shared" on the road . . . nothing. This is my time, finally. And I'm not going to screw it up.'

He gave Miller a sharp crack round the ear and then went to the tent-flap. The storm had moved on. 'Get your arse out here. And if I hear another sound out of you, you're going to be wearing your bollocks for a necklace.'

Veitch walked down one of the radial streets to the focal point of Black Rock City, with a troubled Miller hurrying to keep up. They weren't alone. The citizens were coming out of their homes in increasing numbers, following the same route.

'What's happening?' Miller asked, then skipped back when Veitch glared at him.

The sun was setting and the temperature was falling rapidly. As darkness spread across the playa, fires sprang up in the many neighbourhoods that formed the sprawling city. Music rose up everywhere, parties and dancing.

'Wow,' Miller said. 'I feel like I've gone back a thousand years.'

Veitch was too engrossed by his surroundings to retain his anger. By the time they reached the communal area at the heart of the city, night had fallen and it was already close to freezing.

'What kind of place is this to hold a festival?' Veitch said. 'An oven during the day, a freezer at night.' He stamped his feet to keep warm.

'It's about survival, man,' somebody said in passing. 'It's about proving that we're stronger than what the world throws at us. That working together we're stronger than anything.'

'Did you hear that?'

Veitch turned to find Ruth standing behind him. 'You look different,' he said. 'More confident or something. What's up?'

She smiled, then said, 'Look at that.'

Miller couldn't see anything, but Veitch did. Above the various communities, the Blue Fire came and went, shimmering like the aurora borealis. Veitch shivered, but not from the cold.

'It's here,' Ruth said, 'in this place. And they're bringing it to life, like our ancestors did thousands of years ago in the stone circles. You know what that means?'

'I'm not stupid.' Veitch refused to look at the lights, however much he wanted to, and continued to walk to the middle of the huge crowd that was gathering. The sense of community was palpable. In spite of himself, Veitch couldn't help but smile.

'I like it here,' Miller said.

'Shut up,' Veitch snapped.

Anticipation added a buzz to the feeling of well-being. Ahead, illuminated by the orange light of torches, was the wicker man, forty feet high.

'Wow,' Ruth said. 'I think we pretty much know what's going to happen now.' She added thoughtfully, 'The Celts used to build their own wicker men, as part of the harvest festival of renewal. Isn't that weird, seeing it here, after what we've been through?'

'Yeah, I've seen the movie,' Veitch said. 'Pity we can't stick a few coppers in there to stoke the flames.'

Over the next hour, the party atmosphere intensified. People sang and danced, hugged each other, gave performances that ranged from the touching to the bizarre. Finally, as if at some hidden signal, a low chant began. It grew louder, spreading through the crowd, until there was one voice, one heart. Veitch shivered.

Burn him. Burn him.

Suddenly silence fell for a minute or two. And then the flames rushed through the towering figure and a tremendous cheer rose up.

The Burning Man came alive in gold and scarlet and amber, the flames leaping higher and higher, reaching towards the stars, consuming the doubts and fears, the guilt and the hatreds of the old ways, and preparing the path for a fresh start. Veitch was mesmerised.

They watched the spectacle in silence, and then Veitch was overcome with a powerful need. He reached out in the dark and found Ruth's hand, barely hoping. A second of desperate anticipation and then she closed her fingers around his. They stood like that as the Burning Man blazed, not speaking, not looking at each other. The simplest thing. Veitch felt happier than at any other point in his entire life. He was afire, consumed, transformed.

After several minutes, Miller spoke and broke the spell, but Veitch didn't mind. 'I still can't see why we were sent here,' he said.

'Perhaps there was more than one reason,' Ruth said.

Reluctantly, they made their way back through the crowd towards Rick's tent. But when they reached the perimeter, a change came over everything, like one discordant note in a symphony.

Troubled, Veitch turned and looked back. Ruth sensed his unease and followed his gaze.

The Burning Man had altered. Around the licking flames, there appeared to be a visual distortion that suggested numerous other Burning Men stretching out to infinity. They merged, became one – not in this world, but looking over it, and in this Burning Man figures writhed: gods, their features tainted by corrupting lines of inky blackness.

'They're being consumed.' Miller's voice had an unnatural trance-like tone. 'Apollo . . . Ra . . . all the sun gods. Feeding the fire . . . the black fire . . .'

Veitch shook him roughly. 'What's wrong with you?'

Dazed, Miller rubbed his eyes. 'Can't you feel it? It's reaching out – across the world . . . across the worlds . . .'

The crowd was changing subtly, too. The exuberant mood had dissipated to leave a bleak anxiety that echoed the bitter cold of the night. It was in all the faces around them: smiles fading to reveal deep questions that had no answers; worries; a burden of troubles; an infecting emptiness. The Void.

Veitch looked back over Black Rock City. The shimmering patches of Blue Fire were winking out. The dark became darker still.

'No,' Veitch said. 'Leave them alone. They're not hurting anyone.'

'Hal said this was the most dangerous time.' Ruth looked around the unsettled crowd.

'Fighting back,' Miller muttered, dazed. 'Fighting back.'

Veitch cuffed him round the ear for good measure.

And then, in the non-silent silence of shuffling feet, a chant started, quietly at first, growing louder, like the one that had preceded the burning, except this one was grim and despairing. Veitch struggled to make out the words.

Croatoan, Croatoan, they appeared to be saying. Soon there was no doubt. The words echoed loudly to the heavens, one voice, one heart.

'What does it mean?' Ruth asked.

'What does it mean? What does it mean?' Miller whined.

Veitch grabbed Miller and Ruth and dragged them out of the crowd. 'We're going to nab one of those screwed-up cars and get to the nearest city. And then to New York.'

8

Hunter sat alone with his thoughts in the white marble room. He refused to give in to grief, though every time he thought about Laura and what she meant to him it became the hardest fight of his life. For a while there, he'd thought he might have had a chance of a normal life, but now he could see it was just an illusion. But as he battled with unfamiliar emotions, his analytical military mind began to reach other conclusions, and so he was not surprised when Dian Cecht came to him again.

'Here in the Court of the Final Word, death is not always the end,' the god said. 'We have examined the Sister of Dragons again, and we have plumbed the depths of our knowledge, and we have come to the conclusion that there may be some hope – though very slim – that we may be able to bring your Sister back from the Grim Lands.'

Hunter mustered a faint smile.

'You are not enthusiastic about this prospect?'

'I'm an optimistic man. Clichéd motto: where there's life, there's hope.'

'Before we continue, I must ask you: what are you prepared to do to ensure that the Sister of Dragons lives?'

'Anything.'

'Even give up your own life?'

'Yes,' Hunter said honestly.

Dian Cecht nodded thoughtfully. 'Then that will be the price. You submit to the Court of the Final Word for exploration and I will return the Sister of Dragons to life.'

'Exploration.' Hunter weighed the word. 'Why do you want me dead?'

'I do not want you dead as an end in itself. But to excavate the deeply buried secrets of a Brother of Dragons – that would be the greatest thing. Finally to have access to the mysteries of the Pendragon Spirit. What wonders might that open up for my people?'

'Why don't you just get what you want from Laura?'

'She has already been changed by one of my brothers.'

'Oh, yeah – the plant thing.'

'We need to divine the secrets of the Pendragon Spirit in its purest form.'

'Why?'

Dian Cecht hesitated. 'The Golden Ones, known to your people as the Tuatha Dé Danann, face a period of coming crisis. The Devourer of All Things leads destruction to our door, and though we are at the centre of Existence and can never be eradicated, what lies beyond is even worse. Stagnation. Decay.' The words were almost too difficult for him to say. 'Some say we will even be supplanted by Fragile Creatures.' He gave Hunter a piercing stare, trying to see how much he knew. 'The small victories of the Brother of Dragons Jack Churchill have allowed your people to take the first steps towards the next level of Existence. As wondrous as my people are, we lack the Pendragon Spirit.'

'And you want it.'

'The sole reason for the existence of the Court of the Final Word is to break down the very stuff of reality, to tear apart the fabric of all living things to find the constant mystery at its core.'

'You haven't found it yet.'

'No.'

'Perhaps you aren't meant to find it.'

Dian Cecht's face was like stone.

'So let me get this straight. I have to give myself up to you so you can cut me into pieces, break me down into my smallest constituent parts and then rip out my Pendragon Spirit. And I'm guessing that is going to be beyond painful. And in return, Laura gets to live.'

'That is correct.'

'I don't even have to think about it. I told you I was prepared to do anything to bring her back. But you've got to give me some time to prepare myself.'

'Agreed.'

Dian Cecht bowed and left the room, almost unable to contain his triumphal air. Hunter continued to sit with his thoughts for a long while. He had done many bad things in his life, bad things that had brought about a good end, and bad things he was told would bring about a good end, but which appeared to have no discernible impact. But saving Laura's life was clearly a good thing, for him personally and for life in general, and so it justified the use of any means necessary.

With that thought in his head, he set out to explore the court. Word had already filtered out of his impending sacrifice. Wherever he went, he was met with the impassivity reserved for someone already dead. No longer a threat, he was allowed to come and go as he pleased.

In the depths of the court, he saw the abattoir halls where living creatures – many of them blinking, befuddled humans – were broken down into their smallest parts by whirling blades and silver drills, and other implements that he couldn't comprehend. The screams hurt his ears, and the rich, coppery smell of blood filled the air as it gushed through the network of channels cut into the marble floor.

He witnessed the impressive discoveries that had resulted from the Tuatha Dé Danann's investigations into the nature of Existence: three-dimensional maps of reality, doors that opened into other times, other worlds, goggles that could see to infinity or just as far within. He spoke to people who had been given strange, troubling powers by the Tuatha Dé Danann's alterations.

And then he made his way to an enormous underground bunker filled with weapons developed as a by-product of Dian Cecht's questing. Many were beyond his ability to comprehend; some had sickening biological components that squirmed and spoke when he approached. But for someone whose business was killing, others were clear in their function.

And finally he found his way to a room of silver and glass where Laura was lying on a slab. It looked as if she was only sleeping, and perhaps she was, for around Dian Cecht the truth was as elusive as the Pendragon Spirit. Hunter's options, though, were limited.

Dian Cecht found him there, deep in thought, his eyes never leaving Laura's face, but his focus deep within himself. The god was accompanied by six others in crimson robes, masks and skullcaps, the bright colour only emphasising the deadness in their eyes.

'The time has come,' Dian Cecht said, with barely restrained eagerness.

'I reckon it has,' Hunter replied.

As one of the Tuatha Dé Danann approached him, he turned and plunged his hand through the god's chest and out of his back. Those unfeeling eyes recognised a moment's shock, and then the body exploded in a flurry of golden moths.

As the moths soared up through the ceiling, the other Tuatha Dé Danann remained rooted. It was only when Hunter had destroyed the next god that Dian Cecht exclaimed, 'The Balor Claw!'

Hunter wore an elaborate gauntlet with silver scales around the wrist and on the back of the hand, edging into brass talons. He had recognised its potential in the weapons hall and had forced one of the attendants to describe how it had been constructed from a shard of the essence of Balor, the one-eyed god of death of the Fomorii, the race enemies of the Tuatha Dé Danann.

Another god fell. Dian Cecht fled, but the others were too slow. The clouds of golden moths became a storm.

Hunter had planned his strategy carefully and followed it to the letter. The security of the Court of the Final Word demanded only one entrance, with the worst of its atrocities taking place in the impregnable far reaches of the compound. He jammed the lock of the door, and with no other exit available proceeded to run his quarry to ground.

Moving relentlessly through the court, he sought out every member of the Tuatha Dé Danann and despatched them mercilessly. Gods cowering in the corners of gleaming rooms. Others, oblivious, as they flushed gallons of blood into the sewers or worked silently on some screaming subject. Some saw the Balor Claw and knew what it meant, giving in to their fate with a sense of bewilderment that could only be mustered by those who thought they would never die. Many ran, and Hunter let them, knowing it wouldn't be long until he felled them. He took his time, searching and herding and slaughtering dispassionately.

He lost count at two hundred and seventy-seven, but he took the time to commit every face to memory before it exploded into shimmering wings. He only paused when he came to the final, extensive killing room, where half-dismembered victims still writhed on the tables in front of the two hundred or more Tuatha Dé Danann packed against the rear wall in shocked disbelief.

He took his time locking the door and then let his gaze wander slowly over the faces. He guessed they could swamp him eventually if they all attacked at once. Mortality, however, and the fear it brought, were new sensations that paralysed them.

Hunter moved forward.

When he was finished, only Dian Cecht remained.

'What you have done this day is an abomination,' the god declared.

'Well, it kind of is, and it kind of isn't.' Hunter examined the gauntlet. 'Nice bit of kit, this. You must be very proud you invented it.' He stretched. 'After all that hard work I'm looking forward to some r 'n' r. Good wine, bit of sex, know what I mean? But first, we've got one more bit of business to sort out.'

Hunter herded Dian Cecht back to the glass and silver room. 'No more double-speak. No more "there's a price to pay". Wake her up. Any malarkey and you'll be spitting moths.'

Seething, Dian Cecht went to work. Hunter had no idea what happened in the room. Afterwards he remembered light and distant chimes, glimpsed the wriggling movement of a silver thing, but all he really recalled was Dian Cecht standing back with hateful eyes and announcing, 'It is done.'

Hunter leaned over Laura to feel the warm blush of her breath on his cheek. Her breasts rose and fell. Her eyelids fluttered.

'What you have done this day will not be forgotten or forgiven,' Dian Cecht said. 'You will be hunted down and made to pay.'

'I know. That's usually how it goes. Which is why I never leave any loose ends.'

Hunter punched the Balor Claw into Dian Cecht's chest. And within a few seconds, for the first time in its history, there was silence in the Court of the Final Word.

9

Laura came round quickly. She remembered lying on her back in long grass, and then she was looking up into Hunter's face.

'No, don't worry,' he said. 'You're not in heaven.'

'Can you put me back under?'

'I've just saved your life. A bit of gratitude wouldn't go amiss.'

'Big deal. We're in and out of death so many times they've fitted revolving doors especially for us. So what did you do? Give me the kiss of life? Fan me? Hold my hand really, really nicely?'

Hunter laughed, long and loud.

'All right,' she said. 'What's the joke?'

10

On the blasted heath beyond the Court of the Final Word, above the river of blood, they made love with a degree of tenderness that surprised them both. Afterwards, Hunter traced his finger down between Laura's breasts to her navel, but there wasn't even a hint of a scar.

'So have we worked out exactly what you are?' he said.

'Fabulous, and that's the end of it.' She rolled over and grabbed her cloak.

'We could run away together,' Hunter said. 'I'd water you twice a day.'

'Do you really think it would work?'

'I'm just being charitable. Who else would have you?'

She surprised him with a passionate kiss, then pushed him away. 'Could you really deprive the world of men of this body . . . these brains . . . this wit and intelligence? Hunter, dude, you'd be Public Enemy Number One.' She held his gaze for a moment, then turned away to dress. 'Besides, we've got work to do.'

'I had a horrible feeling you were going to bring that up.'

'I know you, soldier-boy. You were giving me the chance to say it before you had to.'

He didn't reply.

'The way I see it,' she continued, 'we can both head back to our world, but that leaves the A-team a bit mob-handed. Now, I'm not one to denigrate the power of womanhood, but Mallory could use a little old-fashioned, thick-headed male brutality on his side. And let's face it, you might as well trademark that description.'

'We split up.'

'Not for ever. I still haven't completely sucked the life out of you yet.'

Hunter realised she was dressing slowly so he couldn't see her face.

'Just till this whole thing is over,' she said.

The sentence hung for a while, but its weight was too great.

'Fair enough.' He tried to keep the bitterness out of his voice; he was sick of responsibility and obligation, sicker still because she was right. 'But you'd better not try to skip out on me, 'cause I'll only have to track you down. In our world, or this, or any other you care to mention.'

And then she did glance back, her gaze challenging, teasing and blasé all wrapped into one. 'Looks like we've got ourselves a deal.'

11

'Where are we?'

After what felt like a walk through an icy, refreshing waterfall, Mallory stood in a long, stone corridor lit by torches with doors at irregular intervals. Beside him was a window that looked out onto a dark space lit occasionally by distant flares, like stars coming to life and dying in an instant.

'The Watchtower between the worlds,' Rhiannon said quietly. 'Few come here.'

Turning away from the window, Decebalus spat. 'I can see why. I do not like it.'

Responding to the subtle atmosphere of unease that permeated the Watchtower, Jerzy scampered close on Mallory's heels.

The nearest door was locked, but as Mallory let go of the handle there was a sound of scuffling within, as if someone had leaped to their feet in anticipation.

'Come on then, you tosspots. Where's my grub?' The earthy Birmingham accent was incongruous in the Otherworldly surroundings.

Decebalus's severe expression broke into a puzzled but hopeful beam. 'Ronnie?'

A moment of silence, then, dismally, 'Don't tell me they got you, too.'

Between Decebalus's straining sinews and Mallory's sword, the lock was soon shattered. In the dark chamber stood a young man in the field uniform of a British soldier from the Great War. He was stubbled and pale from his imprisonment, but grinning broadly. Decebalus and the soldier threw their arms around each other.

'All right, you big old bastard! It had to be you, didn't it?' Ronnie said.

Decebalus thrust Ronnie towards Mallory. 'One of us.'

Ronnie's eyes gleamed. 'Ronald Kelly, Second Army, Thirtieth Division. And a Brother of Dragons.'

'You're one of those Church pulled out of time to save you from Veitch?' Mallory realised.

'Yes, sir. That bastard – excuse my French, sir, but he is – he killed a lot of our kind. And we're all just waiting for a chance to get back at him.' His expression grew flinty. 'But first we need to sort out that witch who threw us in here. Traitorous bitch.'

Jerzy tugged at Mallory's sleeve. 'We should hurry, good friend. The queen's guard may be here soon to feed the prisoners.'

'I'm surprised she didn't just kill you,' Mallory said.

'Oh, no,' Ronnie replied. 'She's scared of us. Or rather what we stand for. Better to lock us up than risk waking something she can't control.'

'It's already woken,' Mallory said.

'That's what I hoped, sir.' Ronnie stepped into the corridor and got his bearings. 'I know where they keep the keys. Shall we free the others?'

12

Along the endless corridors they moved, flinging open doors to reveal pale faces, blinking eyes, hope rekindled: women in dirty flapper dresses; men in sharp suits with slicked-back hair; a Spitfire pilot still wearing his leather flight jacket, goggles pushed back on top of his head; a hard-faced woman in rough, rural dress from some time at the end of the nineteenth century. And more, scores of them, from different eras, dressed in different styles, but the Pendragon Spirit clear and strong in all.

And when they found Aula, Decebalus crushed her to his chest and wept tears of joy. The Roman woman cursed and spat and forced her way free before giving him the briefest of revealing smiles.

Finally they climbed a set of stone steps to another corridor that was sealed by a newly installed iron gate. Breaking through it, they found that all the doors were treble-locked and marked with sigils that Rhiannon said were ancient spells of imprisonment. The Brothers and Sisters of Dragons shattered the doors to reveal the missing Tuatha Dé Danann, who emerged into the corridor with the expressions of people who still couldn't comprehend how their world had been upturned. Math the sorcerer was bound with chains, his head sheathed in an iron mask. Another chamber was filled with an impenetrable darkness that persisted even when torches were brought to the door. Two red eyes glowed from the depths. All concerned left the Morrigan to emerge in her own time.

Lugh, the great warrior and god of light, was one of the last rescued. He hugged Rhiannon silently for several moments. When he turned to Mallory, his eyes were wet. 'You have my thanks, Brother of Dragons, and those of all my people. A terrible blow has been struck against the Golden Ones, one from which we shall not easily recover. To be betrayed by one of our own, to be imprisoned and tortured, it strikes to the very heart of who we are.' He drew a deep breath. 'To be betrayed by my own sister.'

Rhiannon comforted him with a gentle hug.

'From this day on, we will never forget what the Brothers and Sisters of Dragons have done for the Golden Ones,' he continued. 'This is the start of a new age, when Fragile Creatures will take their place alongside my people at the heart of Existence. We stand with you now, Brother of Dragons, and always.'

'Then gather your people and get ready,' Mallory said. 'We're taking this fight back to the Court of the Soaring Spirit. It's war.'

chapter thirteen

waking up in the
sleepless city

1

The night was warm as summer reached its end. Frank Sinatra crooned 'Fly Me to the Moon' and the middle-aged Irish guys around the radio joined in as if they were on stage at the Sands. In their beer-fuelled exuberance there was a sense of good times just around the corner.

In the backroom of McSorley's Old Ale House on East Seventh Street, a nude woman with a parrot looked down on the proceedings. Church, Shavi and Tom sat near the old fireplace under the motto *Be good or be gone*, blending into the background amongst the collection of weirdos, loners and curious tourists. They had spent three days searching the city without any luck. Halfway down his fourth glass of beer, Church was desperately trying not to behave like some lachrymose old drunk, but was unable to shake the memory of the last time he had heard the song performed with such abandon, in a pub on Dartmoor, with Ruth.

He gained some comfort from the bar's long, rich history and the knowledge that he was drinking in the shadow of Abraham Lincoln, John Lennon and Woody Guthrie. Faces stared from the old black-and-white photos lining the walls, reminding him of the turn of events, large and small, and how the world was shaped.

'Ruth is staying with Ryan to prevent him from doing any more terrible things,' Shavi insisted quietly.

Tom had been oblivious to their conversation as he soaked up the surroundings, overjoyed to be back in the country he loved most.

'It's more complex than that,' Church replied. 'I could see it in her face. She wanted to be with him.'

295

'We are all so close, bound by the Pendragon Spirit, that our feelings are often confused and distorted. Under stress, thrown into close proximity with him for so long, perhaps she does not even know herself what she really feels. And then there is whatever spell Veitch has cast over the three of you—'

'Will both of you shut up!' Tom snapped. 'It's only love. Anybody would think you were fretting about something important.'

'Haven't you ever been in love?' Church responded sharply.

'Why, yes. I fell in love with the queen of the Court of the Yearning Heart. She kidnapped me from my home and had me torn apart and rebuilt by that bastard Dian Cecht. I think that's what you call a metaphor. Never again.'

Church sighed. 'All right, beats me.' He pushed his empty glass towards Tom. 'Make yourself useful. And have a small sherry yourself while you're at it.'

Muttering and grumbling, Tom went to the bar.

'I'm not going to give up on Ruth,' Church said to Shavi. 'I crossed two thousand years to get back to her. This won't stop me.'

'That is good.'

'There's something else.' Ever since he had arrived in New York, he hadn't been able to bring himself even to think about the devastating revelation that had emerged in the Forbidden City, but it loomed darkly over everything he did, and everything they planned. 'In Beijing, while you were off with Tom, I was given a vision of my future. There's no easy way to say this: the Libertarian is me. I become him, sometime in the future, because of how I feel about Ruth. Everything falls apart because of me, because of my failure. I become that sick killer working for the Void.'

Outside in the street, police sirens blared past.

'All that slaughter he carried out as he moved through time – how could I do that? It's all got to be inside me, somewhere. Is the Pendragon Spirit just a lie?'

'Nothing is written, Church. You know that. Time does not exist. Reality is not fixed. These concepts are all just illusions we create so our poor human brains can cope with what is out there. Remember, reality changes, like the globe that Dian Cecht showed you in the Court of the Final Word. Put pressure on one point and another part shifts to accommodate it.'

Another police car sped by.

'Matter cannot be destroyed,' Shavi continued. 'Nor can energy, which is why no one ever really dies. It all just reforms in endless new shapes. Whatever you were shown, you can change it.'

'I wish I could have your faith.'

'I told you – that is why I am here, so you do not have to.' Shavi followed Church's gaze to Tom at the bar. 'Why did you wait until Tom had gone to tell me about the Libertarian?'

'He's getting back his old flashes of the future. Why didn't he say anything about me becoming the Libertarian?'

'Because he is protecting you as he always has, from the moment you met. He is the best friend you could ever hope for.'

Church watched Tom wind his way back through the drinkers, just another sixties burn-out mourning Jerry Garcia, no sign of all the scars he kept assiduously hidden away.

'Yeah, I'm a useless friend, aren't I? One day I'll get over this whole self-obsessed thing.'

'I think we are all allowed one flaw.'

Church took his drink from Tom and raised his glass. 'Here we go, then: no happy endings!'

They all drank to it.

2

'It's a big city. How are we supposed to find the Second Key before Veitch?' Church stood outside McSorley's looking uptown. 'He could already have him.'

'I think we would know,' Tom replied. 'Probably from the hell-fire raining all around.'

'No luck with the ring?'

Tom twisted the gold ring around his finger, bitterness darkening his expression. 'Next to useless here. I think it's because we're not exactly sure what our heart's desire is,' he added pointedly. 'Is it me or is it cold?'

'It's you. You're old.'

Shavi returned from the alley where he had been attempting to meditate. His frustrated expression gave away his failure. 'This is the most un-spiritual city on Earth. Even with the power of the Blue Fire at its height, I am finding it near-impossible to tap into anything.'

'We're lucky it didn't spit us out of the Blue on the city limits,' Church said, enjoying the feeling of being slightly drunk.

'We could always petition whatever gods we have awakened in this Great Dominion,' Shavi said.

'I'd steer clear of that lot wherever possible,' Tom warned.

Not too far away, the police sirens had congregated. The drone made

Church's head ache. 'I wish this Mundane Spell would shatter once and for all.'

'It's the disguise the Void wears,' Tom said. 'It'll hold on to it until there's no hope of maintaining the illusion.'

'And then?'

'Then the Army of the Ten Billion Spiders will come out and take everything apart so they can start all over again.'

Shavi tugged on Church's sleeve. 'Look at that.'

Amongst the tall buildings, the *Morvren* swooped as if with one mind.

'A portent,' Church said. 'Bad times ahead. As if we didn't know.'

'No,' Shavi insisted. 'They are moving differently this time. Do you see?'

The birds always appeared to have an eerie intelligence, but now they were acting with an out-of-character singular purpose. Fleeting shapes appeared in the apparently random pattern of their flight. After a moment, Church began to see them more clearly.

'Is that a key?' Shavi said.

'And an arrow,' Tom added.

'They are trying to guide us,' Shavi exclaimed.

'I don't get it,' Church said. 'They've never done anything like this before. Why now?'

Despite his doubts, Church allowed himself to be persuaded by Shavi and Tom, who both argued that they had no other lead. They made their way towards the Bowery. The police sirens had died but there was still activity all around, cars driving too fast, people running, glancing over their shoulders, others talking intensely into mobile phones.

High above the cityscape, Church got a fleeting impression of a burning figure in the sky, but it was lost to the lights and the looming buildings. Before he had time to consider what he had seen, tyres screeched as a Lexus swerved across the road and mounted the kerb next to them. Two men in casual suits were out before the engine had died. Both had guns. One held out a police badge. He had an acne-pitted face and thin ginger hair.

'Stay where you are.' He identified Church as the main threat. 'These the ones?' he asked his partner.

An African-American, almost too tall to fit in the car, checked his BlackBerry, glancing up and down a couple of times before grunting, 'Sure looks like it.'

'Whatever you think we've done—' Church began.

'You just opened your mouth,' the ginger-haired one said with faux incredulity. 'I wouldn't do it again. Turn around.'

As handcuffs were snapped on, the other detective radioed for support and ended his conversation with a hearty, 'No shit!'

Turning to his partner, he said, 'Eddie, you are not going to believe this.'

'I believe everything you say, Detective Brinks. You're my mom, my priest and Superman, all rolled into one.'

'Deakins ran their faces through SEISINT. Got a match with Homeland Security. Two of these squirrels—' he indicated Church and Shavi '—are on Global Red Status from British Intelligence.'

Eddie looked Church up and down. 'Now isn't that something. They're going to have to build a whole new wing to keep you guys safe. Terrorists *and* cannibals.'

3

The holding cell was starkly lit and smelled of ammonia. Church felt like a gorilla in a zoo as various men and women in suits cast a cursory, puzzled eye over him before moving away, deep in hushed conversation. Every protest, every request, every comment he made was ignored. His visitors gave no sign that they even heard him speaking.

After three hours he was led to an interview room with a single table, two chairs and a mirror along one wall. The two detectives waited for him in shirtsleeves. Church was shown to a seat with a politeness that somehow managed to infer incipient menace.

'Detectives Nelson and Brinks interviewing suspect Jack Churchill,' the ginger-haired one announced for the recording. Nelson sat at the table. Brinks remained standing, like a big cat ready to pounce.

Brinks grinned broadly. 'Tombstone, they call me. I haven't decided if that's an unfortunate slur on my size and the colour of my skin, or the destination of the people who annoy me.'

'Good cop, bad cop is a bit of a cliché,' Church said.

'You see, you don't get to be smart,' Nelson said calmly. 'You don't get to be wry. Or aloof. Or British. You don't get to pretend you're a normal person. We're extending you the courtesy of treating you like one, but we all know you're not.'

'Anyway,' Tombstone noted with a slow nod, 'we're bad cop, worse cop. And we have a competition to see how bad we can really get.'

'Funny,' Church said.

'Says the man carrying a sword strapped to his back,' Nelson said. 'At

299

least, we *think* it's a sword. Seems to be some debate in the Evidence Room. Care to enlighten us?'

'No.'

Nelson flipped open a plastic folder. 'Okay, let's review. This afternoon we responded to a nine-one-one on Delancey. Blood leaking through a light fitting into the apartment below. We found two deceased – one white male, one Chinese-American female. Look familiar?'

He tossed Church a handful of crime-scene photographs. The bodies were in such a gruesome state that Church gave them only half a glance before handing them back. 'I don't know these people. I've never been to that apartment. I didn't kill them. Categoric enough for you?'

'Take another look. You'll see that the bodies are missing several organs. Let me draw your attention to the close-up of the male torso. You see the jagged edges of the wounds? The crime lab tells me those are teeth marks.'

'I'm sorry for these people, but I had nothing to do with their deaths.'

Nelson glanced at his partner. 'Detective Brinks?'

Tombstone threw another file on the table. 'Crime scene number two. Partially eaten victim in a Dumpster at the back of the Happy Chicken fast-food joint on Houston. Time of death around ten p.m. About a half-hour before we picked you up.'

'We were in McSorley's half an hour before. There were witnesses.'

'We got witnesses, too, haven't we, Detective Nelson? Ours don't lie or have random memory failure.'

Nelson opened his laptop and spun it towards Church. Grainy CCTV footage played out above a time-code. Three people feasted on a body next to a Dumpster. One by one they glanced up at the camera. It was unmistakably Shavi, Tom and Church.

'It's a fake!'

Nelson shook his head firmly. 'The digital signature holds up. Anything you want to tell us now?'

Church wrestled with the images he'd just been shown. Some kind of set-up by the spider-controlled elements of the NYPD? Why go to so much trouble?

'We'll get you a lawyer,' Nelson began.

'No point. There won't be time.'

Nelson and Tombstone exchanged worried glances. 'You've got some-thing else planned? Bomb?'

'I'm not a terrorist, either.'

'No, you're a freedom fighter.' Nelson was uneasy now. 'Let's get the Homeland Security guys.'

Church only had to wait in the holding cell for ten minutes before the uniformed police officer watching him left quietly. The Homeland Security representative entered a moment later sporting a government-issue haircut and the kind of focused but frozen expression that always reminded Church of an Action Man doll.

'Where is he?' Church said.

The Action Man shifted uncomfortably.

'He's preparing another theatrical entrance, isn't he?'

A fearful, fixed look grew in the Action Man's eyes. Church had seen it before when the victim's mind was in conflict with the controlling spider.

'Oh, stop tormenting him.'

The Libertarian sauntered in. He was still wearing sunglasses to hide his red eyes, but this time his outfit was a smart charcoal suit and a white shirt. 'I thought a formal approach would be appropriate in these circumstances, don't you agree? Good for funerals, too.'

Church shivered involuntarily, bleak horror overcoming him as he looked the Libertarian up and down, seeing for the first time the familiar body language, the gait, the bone structure. 'How did I get to be you?' he said, sickened.

The Libertarian was mildly surprised. 'Oh, a revelation. I never thought you'd see it myself. Convinced you're the big, big hero – you could never believe you were working towards becoming something like me.' He held Church's stare for a long moment, enjoying what he saw there, then turned to the Homeland Security representative. 'Get out, Oakes. You irritate me. Go and urinate in the coffee or something.'

Sweating, Oakes left.

The Libertarian sighed. 'Alone again, me and my shadow. I have to say, you'll have much more fun as me than you've ever had as yourself. All that pain from the woman who spurns your feelings for your arch-rival. And poor Niamh – all those years as a love-sick puppy and you not even noticing. She's a wild woman in bed. You really missed out there.'

'At least I know you can't kill me.'

'A little pain never hurt anyone, though. But business first. I have to ask – what has possessed you? Killing and eating people? Not that I don't admire the artistry, and not that you won't be doing it on a regular basis very shortly, but . . . somewhat out of character, shall we say?'

'Very funny.'

'What do you mean?' The Libertarian looked honestly puzzled.

'Slight overkill. The terrorist charge was enough to keep me locked up till you get what you want.'

'You're suggesting I had something to do with this?'

'You didn't?'

'I saw the recording . . .' The Libertarian paused, annoyed. 'Now, who would be playing games at this late stage in the proceedings?'

Church registered an odd note in the Libertarian's tone. 'Proceedings?'

The Libertarian smiled.

'You've been manipulating events.'

'I learned a great deal from the Tuatha Dé Danann when I was you. This is all about alchemy. You need to be shaped by events so you can transmute into the gold that is me.'

The Libertarian was consciously echoing Hal's words of guidance; both sides trying to see him transformed so he could be a force for either Light or Dark.

'Of course, it's not all about that. I have to ensure you don't end up with the two Keys. That would be very bad. Thankfully, that terminal failure Veitch already has his hands on one of them.'

'If only you knew where the other was,' Church taunted.

'Enjoy your stay. I hear the New York Police can be quite rough with terrorists. Oh, and cannibalistic serial killers.'

He waved flamboyantly and left, but there was an uneasiness behind the gesture that both pleased and troubled Church.

5

Church was being led out of his cell for another round of questioning when a loud crashing of glass was followed by a thunderous cacophony punctuated by shouts. His escort ran Church into the open-plan detectives' office only to be brought up sharp by a whirlwind of black wings. The *Morvren* had burst through one window and were flocking around the room in a dense mass. Detectives pressed themselves against the floor to avoid beaks and talons.

In the birds' movements, Church once again saw strange patterns take shape, but this time they remained enigmatic; yet some single intelligence was clearly directing them.

Amidst the chaos, Church glimpsed a figure flitting across the office, barely more than a shadow, and though it approximated a human shape there was something avian about it, too. It disappeared into the mass of feathers, and a moment later the *Morvren* funnelled out through the shattered window into the night.

'What in the name of Alfred Hitchcock was that all about?' Tombstone levered his huge frame upright.

'I tell you, it's the pollution,' someone said. 'Gets into the rain, birds drink it, this is what you get.'

Nelson brushed himself down, then coolly summoned Church over. 'Homeland Security handed you back to us. Lucky you.'

'Hey! What's going on?' Brow furrowed, Tombstone stared at his laptop. Nelson joined him, and for several minutes they pored over whatever was on-screen, casting occasional glances towards Church. Finally, they brought the computer over and ran the CCTV footage from the back of the fast-food restaurant. Church, Shavi and Tom were no longer there. Instead, a man with wild, black hair was hunched over the body. When he was done he loped away without showing his face.

'Explain that,' Nelson said.

'I couldn't explain what you had the first time. Maybe this is what really happened.'

'Shit,' Tombstone hissed. 'This is fucked-up. The digital signature was right before and it still is now.'

Neither Nelson nor Tombstone was prepared to voice the questions running through their heads.

'He's still a terrorist, right?' Tombstone said eventually.

'Except Homeland Security don't want him. Tried to pull the files, but all the intelligence community are tied up with whatever's going on in China.'

'What about that sword? We can hold him on hidden weapons—'

'Bit big to hide,' Church said. 'It's a sword.'

'Don't get smart.' Nelson studied Church. 'You're involved in all this. The sword, the birds, the homicides – it's all too much of a coincidence.'

'There aren't any coincidences,' Church said.

Tombstone answered a ringing phone, and when he was done he said to Nelson, 'Another one. In a car outside the Guggenheim. Throat torn out, only partially eaten, perp was probably disturbed. Guess that clears him.' He nodded towards Church.

Nelson slipped on his jacket. 'We'll take him with us. He's involved. I want him knee-deep in it, see how he reacts.'

Church protested, acutely aware of being dragged further and further away from the hunt for the Second Key. But at least out of the precinct he might have a chance to escape and double back to free Shavi and Tom. 'Okay. I'll do what I can to help.'

As Nelson and Tombstone led Church out of the room, he saw a detective with a sly face talking hastily to Oakes, the Homeland Security Action Man. A moment later Oakes had summoned Nelson over and was forcefully questioning him.

'Oakes is coming with us,' Nelson said when he returned.

'He doesn't trust us?' Tombstone said. 'I thought Homeland Security had walked away from this.'

'Reckons he's the only one who can keep an eye on sword-boy.' He turned to Church. 'He's going to be on you like slime on a toad. Me, I reckon you were better off with us.'

6

Frank Lloyd Wright's distinctive inverted ziggurat that housed the Guggenheim Museum loomed up pure and white in the darkness. In front of it, a car was surrounded by yellow police tape, the doors flung open so that it resembled a bird about to take flight. Crime lab cameras flashed, the white glare turning the arterial spray across the windscreen into a Rorschach blot that haunted Church with hidden meaning.

As the traffic rolled by feet away, Nelson escorted Church to see the victim. It was a man, early thirties, long blond hair, tattoos.

'Know him?'

Church shook his head, the iron smell of the blood and the exposed flesh making him queasy. He felt the looming presence of Oakes at his back and the psychological pressure of the spiders.

Oakes grabbed Church roughly by the shoulders. 'What have you got to do with this?'

Church threw him off. 'You and your little spider-buddies don't like it when you don't know what's going on, do you?'

Rage bloomed in Oakes's face, and Nelson was forced to intervene. 'Leave him.' He held Oakes's gaze, underlining who now had the authority.

Tombstone approached, examining his BlackBerry. 'The CMU downloaded the feed from the camera.' He nodded towards a red light high up a lamp post across the street. 'We've got him leaving the vehicle, but still no ID. This is what disturbed him.'

The BlackBerry's screen showed a car swerving to avoid the victim's fishtailed vehicle, slowing as it passed, and a teenage boy leaning out of the rear window to shout abuse. Instantly, the wild-haired killer leaped out of the passenger side of the victim's car and chased the disappearing vehicle until he moved out of range of the camera.

'Got a short fuse if the kid pissed him off,' Tombstone noted.

'What kid?' Oakes said.

'The one hanging out the back window.'

'I didn't see a kid.'

Tombstone patiently rewound the footage and indicated the boy.

'What are you talking about?' Oakes said. 'I don't see any kid.'

Tombstone and Nelson eyed him with an expression reserved for complete idiots. Uncomfortable, Oakes shuffled off to talk to the members of the crime lab. Tombstone whistled. Nelson tapped his foot. They shared a quick conspiratorial grin.

Church was turning back to the car when a realisation struck him with astonishing lucidity. Oakes really didn't see the boy on the CCTV footage. There were only two people in the world that the Void and its servants the spiders couldn't see: the two Keys.

'Show me again,' he said, unable to hide his eagerness.

Nelson's eyes narrowed, but he nodded to Tombstone to replay the footage. The boy had blond hair and a strong, honest face. The car was being driven by a large man with a wide-brimmed hat, but Church couldn't make out his features, and there was somebody else in the back. But those two didn't matter. The boy was the Key.

'Can you trace that car?' he asked.

'Why would we want to trace the car?' Nelson said.

'I think it might be something to do with the homicide.'

Tombstone tapped his head. 'That's, what, intuition? Or is the word . . . insanity?'

Nelson didn't respond. 'Jude Law here knows something.'

Tombstone shrugged, and returned to the footage to get the licence plate number.

7

Accompanied by the constant crackle of the police radio, they drove south, past steaming manhole covers turning the after-hours people into ghosts, surrounded by the slow, constant movement of the sleepless city.

At one point, Nelson's phone bleeped with an incoming text. Tombstone eyed him with weary sympathy. 'Gina?'

'Yeah. Guess I'll have some time on my hands this weekend.' Church sensed sadness, but Nelson's face gave nothing away. 'You got a girl, Jude Law?'

'Yeah . . .' The hesitancy in Church's voice was as clear to Nelson as it was to him.

'I know how it is.' Nelson looked out of the side window thoughtfully. 'I know how it is.'

They ended their journey near Washington Square Park in the Village. The smart buildings of New York University surrounded the large open space, the arch in the centre glowing spectrally in the gloom. Oakes pulled up behind them, watching every movement with an unblinking stare.

The owner of the car from the CCTV footage was a twenty-one-year-old Latino with an asymmetric haircut wearing sunglasses despite the hour. He was thin and small and clearly not the person who had been driving the car.

A hint of unease troubling his usually implacable face, Nelson returned after questioning him and two others from the video store where he worked. 'Guy says the car hasn't been out tonight. Engine's cold. Confirmed by two witnesses.'

'Lying?' Tombstone asked hopefully.

'Don't think so.'

Church instantly knew the recording on Tombstone's BlackBerry would no longer show the car, or the boy hanging out of the rear window. The notion struck Nelson and Tombstone at the same time.

'Getting a little creeped-out now, Jude Law,' Nelson said. 'Time to start putting my mind at rest.'

'I can't,' Church said.

'Don't talk to him,' Oakes interjected. 'He'll only lie.'

'Agent Oakes, do you have a take on this?' Nelson asked pointedly.

'There's some glitch in the system, that's all. Recordings don't change. Just focus on the crime, Detective. You have a serial killer. Catch him.'

'A serial killer who doesn't fit any FBI profile. Three random homicides in rapid succession by a cannibalistic sociopath. Doesn't happen.'

'So it's a first. Make a name for yourself.'

'Don't listen to him,' Church said. 'He isn't who you think he is.'

'Shut up,' Oakes snarled, sweat beading on his forehead. He noticed that Nelson and Tombstone were no longer trying to hide their suspicions. 'I'm taking him back,' he said. 'You two can keep pretending you're in Fairyland for as long as you like.' Oakes tried to drag Church towards the car.

'Now hang on . . .' Tombstone began.

Oakes shrieked. A raven bigger than any Church had ever seen was clinging onto Oakes's head as it pecked furiously at his eyes.

Church saw his moment. With Nelson and Tombstone gripped by the bizarre sight, he raced through the slow-moving traffic into a side street. He heard Tombstone yell, the threat that he would be shot, but as he anticipated, there was no gunfire. When Nelson and Tombstone dropped out of direct sight, he ducked into a convenience store. The Korean owner watched him suspiciously as he made his way to the back amongst the frozen goods and the day's special offer.

He wasn't alone. A tall, big-boned man with long, wiry hair and beard, once black, now turning grey and white, loaded staple goods into his basket: a two-gallon carton of milk, two loaves of bread, several cans of beans. He had the florid face and burst capillaries of a heavy drinker, but it was the wide-brimmed hat that struck Church. There could have been thousands like it in the city, but he was acutely aware of the pile-up of coincidences; he was sure it was the same hat he had seen on the man driving the car in the CCTV footage.

Church pretended to inspect a box of Froot Loops. From outside, he heard loud voices and running feet as Tombstone, Nelson and a lumbering Oakes passed by.

Anxiously, he watched as the man in the hat paid for his goods and left. Church followed him across the road and down another street until he entered a door next to a club where punks and goths congregated on the sidewalk, smelling of patchouli, hair-dye and make-up. After a moment, Church followed him inside.

The building was a former commercial premises and appeared close to being condemned: broken floorboards, graffiti, the stink of damp and mould. Yet it was clearly occupied: Church could smell fried food and dope smoke. His quarry's footsteps echoed on the stairs.

Church passed several rooms all missing doors, obviously squats with bedrolls laid out on the bare floors. He came to the floor where he estimated the man in the hat had ended his journey. There were three closed doors.

As he approached the first door, he heard movement in the shadows behind him just before a knife was pressed beneath his right eye.

'One move and I take it out.' It was a girl's voice, with the perfect, clipped vowels of an expensive English private education.

'I'm not moving.'

'Why are you following Crowther?'

'I'm looking for someone. A teenage boy, blond hair—'

'What are you? Immigration? Social Services? Police?'

'Nothing like that. I'm trying to help you. There are people looking for you who might want to hurt you—'

The knife dug deeper. Blood dripped down Church's face.

'Is it Creed? Is it?' she shouted.

'No!'

'I'm not joining his little gang!' She put her hand around the base of Church's head and smashed his forehead against the wall.

'Jack! Prof!'

Church rolled onto his back, purple flashes darting across his vision. The girl was no older than sixteen, black, her features hard.

From a door further along the corridor emerged the man in the wide-brimmed hat and the boy, maybe a year older than the girl. He had the most piercing eyes Church had ever seen.

'Good Lord!' Crowther exclaimed. 'Can't I leave you alone for one minute? Who have you attacked this time?'

'He was following you.' She gave Crowther a surly stare for emphasis.

'I'm trying to help,' Church protested. 'There are people after Jack.'

The boy came over to study Church. He had a strong, honest face with a touch of innocence. Church wondered how he would be able to tell the boy that he carried a force for destruction inside him. 'My name's Jack, too.'

'Is that supposed to create a bond or something?' the girl sneered.

'Mahalia,' the boy cautioned. 'Why would anyone want to come after me?' he asked Church. 'I just want a quiet life. I'm no trouble to anyone.'

'Frankly,' Crowther said, 'we've found that the best way to survive is not to trust anyone.'

A deep, low moan rose up somewhere nearby, slowly becoming a chilling howl. It sounded like a word, but all Church heard was the 'oooo' that ended it. They all fell silent, unnerved.

'Was that an animal?' Mahalia said, spooked.

From the bottom of the stairs came the sound of the front door being thrown open. Tombstone's voice drifted up: 'That kid definitely said he came in here.'

'Okay, Jude Law!' Nelson called. 'This is Detective Nelson! Get your ass out where I can see you!'

'Cops!' Mahalia said. 'He led them here!'

'They're after me, not you!' Church said.

'It looks like we need to find a new home,' Crowther said. 'Let's try to get out of here with a little more alacrity, shall we?'

Crowther disappeared back into the room, but Jack waited for Mahalia to catch up with him; Church noted the tenderness of the boy's expression when he looked at her.

As Church made to get up to follow, Mahalia planted her boot forcefully in his gut, then ran with Jack after Crowther. Gasping, Church managed to scramble into the room as the detectives thundered up the stairs.

The apartment was clean and orderly, but empty. In the final room, a ragged hole in the wall gave way to a crawl space and a ladder to the floor below. Church followed the sound of disappearing footsteps down and through two other apartments to a makeshift hatch that gave access to a large, dark industrial space, which appeared to be an old warehouse. It was a maze of vast, echoing rooms and low-ceilinged corridors with peeling, lime-washed walls.

Distorted echoes made it almost impossible to tell who was pursuer and who pursued. As someone approached, Church slipped into a space behind a heavy door that had been jammed open. It was Oakes, talking quietly on his mobile phone.

'I've lost him for now,' he said. 'It's only a matter of time. Kill the other two – we can't risk any contact with the Key. And get someone to dump that sword in the river.'

He pocketed the phone and moved cautiously down the corridor, gun drawn. Church's heart pounded. He had to get back to help Shavi and Tom, but that would mean losing whatever tenuous lead he had on Jack. In a city of nearly twenty-two million people, what chance would he have of finding the boy again? There was no choice. He had to trust Shavi and Tom to look after themselves.

For the next ten minutes he roamed the labyrinthine area, hiding whenever the echoes of voices or footsteps drew closer, but the exit proved elusive. Either the building was bigger than he thought, or whatever force was at play in the city was attempting to keep him trapped.

The animalistic howling rose up again, unmistakable but so low it could have been the wind blowing through an empty room. It was in the building with him.

As he rounded a corner into another long corridor, he was stunned to see Ruth at the far end, her head bowed as she worked the lock of a door. She got it open and peeked inside the room, excited by what she saw there. Was it Jack? he wondered.

Church couldn't risk calling out to her, but as she prepared to enter the room, she glanced round and saw him. Her smile lit up her face. She beckoned to him eagerly and then went through the door.

Church raced to catch up. The door had closed behind her. His fingers were already on the handle when a shiver of doubt ran through him. Instinctively, he felt something was wrong. Why hadn't Ruth waited for him, or left the door open?

He removed his fingers from the handle and listened. All was silent on the other side of the door. He shivered. It could have been his imagination, but he had the impression that something was waiting for him, listening for the moment when he would open the door. A chill ran through him.

Telling himself he was foolish, he gripped the handle again and began to turn it, but this time warnings shrieked in his head. He paused again, and in that instant he heard a barely audible sound on the other side, little more than an exhalation, but it filled him with unaccountable dread. As he released the handle and ran, he could feel on his back the weight of that door and whatever lay behind it.

Finally he came to a large echoing space where water dripped from a broken pipe high up in the shadows. As he made his way across it, the smell of fresh blood reached him. In an area illuminated by a shaft of streetlight coming through a dirty window lay Oakes. His stomach had been torn open, the pool of blood around him looking like a sea. Not all of him was there.

The brutality of the scene held Church in its gravity. He wasn't aware of the approach until the gun was placed at his head.

'Jesus H. Christ.' Tombstone couldn't tear his gaze from Oakes's body.

Nelson bumped the gun barrel against Church's temple. 'You saw who did this?'

'No,' Church replied. 'But you've got to get back to the precinct. Someone's going to try to kill my friends. I heard Oakes order it—'

'Shut up and lie down on the floor.'

8

'Stand up. You're coming with me.' The policeman at the door of Shavi's holding cell was not the guard who had been watching him for the last four hours. This one reminded him of an older Brad Pitt, good-looking in his youth but now starting to turn to fat from too long at a desk.

'Is this more questioning? I have told you all I can.'

'Shut up.'

He escorted Shavi past the interview room where he had spent an unpleasant twenty minutes with the detectives earlier that night, but when he bypassed the main detectives' room and entered a deserted stairwell that took them two storeys below street level, Shavi's unease grew. At that time of night, they encountered no other people.

'Where are you taking me?' Shavi pressed.

His guard didn't answer. Eventually they came to a small room cluttered with filing cabinets, where Tom was slumped in a chair, dried blood around a bruised cut on his forehead. The policeman locked the door behind them before taking out a gun that was not police issue. He proceeded to fit it with a silencer.

'If you haven't guessed by now, he's one of the spider people,' Tom said.

Shavi glanced around for a weapon.

'Don't bother,' Tom said, 'unless you want to give him a lethal paper cut.' He added ruefully, 'I never thought you would be the Brother of Dragons to die.'

'You know we will lose one of our own?'

'I've known for a long time that one of you will go very soon. It was just a flash . . . more an impression . . . a blue flame being extinguished.' He shrugged. 'No point making a meal of it. It wouldn't have helped matters to have everyone worrying about their mortality.'

'It must be difficult for you to continue with that knowledge . . . with all the other knowledge of future suffering you must have.'

'It's not been a holiday in the sun. Not that I'll have to worry about it any more now.' Tom appeared almost to be welcoming his impending death.

The policeman levelled his gun at Shavi. 'On your knees.'

'I am not afraid to die,' Shavi said, getting down. 'I have lived a good life, filled with experience. I have known love and friendship. I have attempted to do something worthwhile with the time I have been granted here.' He smiled at the guard. 'And this is not the end.'

Sweat stood out on the policeman's forehead, but he couldn't resist the compulsion to tighten his finger on the trigger.

Behind him, a pot plant on a filing cabinet began to waver as if caught in a breeze. The leaves shivered, grew larger and then erupted in an explosion of greenery that lashed around the policeman's head. His hand jerked as he pulled the trigger and the bullet whipped by a half-inch from Shavi's head. The leaves continued to sprout rapidly, wrapping around the policeman's face faster than he could tear them free. They forced their way into his mouth and nose, and he crashed to the floor, unconscious.

Shavi wrenched the door open to reveal Laura, hands on hips. 'Three cheers for Chlorophyll Kid,' she said.

Shavi threw his arms around her and lifted her off her feet. 'I knew you would have a use sooner or later,' he teased.

'Takes it out of you, the whole growing plants thing. But I'm getting better at it.'

'I was sure you were going to be the one to die,' Tom muttered as he pushed past her.

'The world needs me as a balance to miserable old bastards like you.' She prised herself free from Shavi's hug.

'How did you find us?' Shavi asked.

'I remember crossing over and then . . .' Laura struggled to recall. 'Somebody was there, grinning at me. That's all that comes back, the grin.'

'The Puck,' Tom said. 'He likes to guide, but not interfere.'

'So.' Laura grinned. 'New York. Hedonism capital of the Western world. Tell me we've got time to hit a bar, a club, get off our faces—'

'Of course,' Tom replied. 'Pamper yourself. Meanwhile, Shavi and I will get the sword, rescue Church, find the Key and save the world.'

9

'Thank you,' Nelson said into the radio before turning to Tombstone. 'That's a confirmed sighting of our three runaways – in the vicinity of Grand Central Terminal.'

'This is a fucked-up world,' Tombstone said as he pulled into traffic. He was still queasy from the shock of seeing the spider Church had pointed out, embedded in Oakes's body, shortly before it freed itself and attempted to scurry away. Nelson's shoe had ended its run. 'The Army of the Ten Billion Spiders? What is that, like the Jesus Army but with extra legs?'

'All that matters is that they're mind-control agents,' Church said.

'Don't think for a minute that I believe any of this,' Nelson said. 'All I know is that things don't fit and until they do, I'm keeping you near.'

'My friends—'

'Still no sign of them.'

'And why are you so important, Jude Law? British Secret Service? Or just an asshole with paranoid delusions?'

'I can't say.'

'Course you can't.'

They drove up Park Avenue to East Forty-Second Street and Vanderbilt Avenue where the imposing Beaux Arts facade of Grand Central

Terminal presented itself to them. The first hint of dawn was visible in the sky, but it would be a while before the trains started running.

'Don't go for another jog,' Nelson cautioned as they got out onto the deserted street. 'This time I will shoot. Only to wound, but it hurts like hell, believe me.'

'If they're trying to skip town we'll need to call for back-up to cover all the gates,' Tombstone said.

As a newspaper delivery truck passed, its rumble merged with the chilling low, moaning cry, this time clearer: *Weeen . . . deeg . . .* Another truck cut off its ending.

Some underlying quality of the sound chilled them all. It conjured up images of wintry wastes, and frigid skies, and blood on snow, as though a stream of information was encoded in a precise combination of notes and timbre.

Nelson considered what he had heard. 'It's saying a word,' he concluded.

'Yeah? It's not in my dictionary,' Tombstone replied.

' "Wen-dig," ' Nelson repeated.

'The last syllable is "oh",' Church said.

Tombstone consulted his BlackBerry, 'Okay, Google. Wendigo. "A traditional belief of various Algonquian-speaking tribes, particularly the Ojibwa/Saulteaux, the Cree, and the Innu/Naskapi/Montagnais".' He struggled over the pronunciations. ' "A malevolent spirit that can possess humans or take on a life of its own. A ravenous beast with a hunger for human flesh that can never be sated. It consumes the victims down to the last bone and drop of blood. It carries a feeling of winter famine with it. Icy blizzards rise up around it, trees crack, water freezes, snow clouds form." '

'So our killer thinks he's a mythical beast,' Nelson said.

Church knew the truth but kept it to himself.

Tombstone glanced towards the station entrance. 'Sounded like it came from inside.'

They raced through the columned entrance to the stairs that swept down into the cavernous main concourse. The four-faced clock above the information booth ticked away the seconds. Overhead the ceiling was painted with an astronomical design, but all the constellations were back-wards: a reflection of reality.

'Is it me or is it cold in here?' Tombstone said.

A cleaner trundled a yellow trolley across the floor. After he had passed, Church registered some quality in the sly glance the cleaner had given him

– it reminded him of the detective who had warned Oakes at the precinct. He hurried down the steps, but the cleaner was nowhere to be seen.

The Wendigo cry drifted over the empty concourse.

'Shit. I wish he'd stop doing that,' Tombstone growled.

The sound of running feet made them all whirl. A shout followed. Jack, Mahalia and Crowther ran through one of the platform entrances, to the annoyance of a rail employee who was now barking into his radio and running after them. Tombstone, Nelson and Church sprinted in pursuit, through the entrance, down steps and into a brightly lit tunnel.

The temperature dropped drastically as they ran. Frost glistened on the walls. Small drifts of snow appeared here and there.

Rounding a corner, they nearly fell over another dismembered body. The railway employee was missing his upper half. Blood formed a garish crescent across the frozen floor ending in a Jackson Pollock spray up both walls.

'*Weeen-dee-gooh!*' The sound of hungry birds over Arctic wastes, loud, nearby.

Tombstone backed against Nelson, gun raised. Church saw in their eyes that they were beginning to grasp the truth.

At the end of the corridor, he glimpsed Jack. He'd barely run a few paces towards him when the raging sound of wings heralded the arrival of the ravens flooding into the corridor. Church threw himself onto his back to avoid them. They swirled to block his path.

When they finally retreated, the corridor reverberated with the rumble of the first train of the day entering the station.

Tombstone dragged Church to his feet. 'What the hell's going on?' he yelled with anger born of incomprehension.

Church looked along the corridor to where he had glimpsed the Jack that he now realised was *not* Jack, and from where the *Morvren* had emerged. 'I'm starting to get an idea,' he replied.

Screams drew them onto the platform. Snow encrusted the roof of the newly arrived train and the windows were covered with an impenetrable hoar-frost, apart from the driver's cab which was splattered on the inside with blood. Crashing and rending boomed within as a terrible force tore through the carriages.

Further down the platform, Jack, Mahalia and Crowther were rooted with fear. This time Church knew they were real.

As Church ran towards them, a door exploded out from a carriage halfway between Church and the detectives. From the frozen interior emerged something that had the form of a man but moved with the loping gait of a beast. Wild, black hair framed a skull-like face, the bottom half of which was smeared red with blood. It was larger than any man, with powerful, sinewy limbs that ended in broken, red-stained nails. As it moved, it appeared to alter shape briefly, becoming all beast with thick, grey fur and yellow-green eyes, before reverting back to its original form.

Shot after shot from the detectives' guns crashed into the Wendigo. It roared with annoyance at Nelson and Tombstone before continuing to prowl towards Church and the others.

'Why won't it die?' Jack said.

Nelson and Tombstone reloaded and continued to fire.

Church could smell it now, meat and wet fur and a heavy animal musk. The cold grew more intense the nearer it came.

'Oh, God,' Crowther whispered.

Just as the Wendigo was about to leap, Church turned his back on it and shouted, 'Stop this now! I'm not going to play the game any more! See, I'm walking away!'

The Wendigo's breath rasped on the back of his neck, but it didn't attack. Church walked past Mahalia, Jack and Crowther towards the end of the platform.

Ahead of him the air shimmered and two shadowy shapes appeared as if emerging from a heat-haze. They launched themselves at each other, rolling and punching and clawing as they fought fiercely. The indistinct figures became a raven and a coyote, both trying to rip out each other's eyes, and then two young men: one had jet-black hair, yellow eyes and pointed features, the other long brown hair and green eyes with a broader, flatter nose. They continued to roll around the platform like brawling children, snapping and snarling.

Church got between them and threw them apart. 'Stop fighting!'

The two men crouched on opposite sides of the platform, glaring at each other.

'You cheated!' the one with brown hair said. 'There was to be no involvement in the game.'

'You cheated!' the other one said furiously.

'Game?' Church interjected angrily. 'People have died.'

'Well, they're only human,' the brown-haired one said slyly.

'Who are you?' Church asked.

The brown-haired one bowed. 'Your people like to call me Coyote or Akba-Atatdia, or First Scolder. I am the cleverest and the trickiest and no one can ever beat me.'

'Except me.' The other bowed, too. 'Your people like to call me Raven. Or KwekWaxa'we. Or Chulyen, Hemaskas, or a score of other names.

And I am the cleverest and the trickiest.' He sighed. 'Though it is always he who plays tricks on me.'

'So you set loose the Wendigo—'

'He did that,' Raven pointed at Coyote.

'—and all those people were slaughtered for some kind of stupid competition?'

Raven looked sheepish. 'But that is why I chose you, Brother of Dragons, to prevent the mayhem this fool unleashed. And because I was selected as your totem, and you already have the *Morvren* at your disposal. I helped you every step of the way, and he hindered you.'

Church looked from one to the other with contempt. 'Some day humans are going to move up the ladder, and then we're going to put all you gods out of business.'

'Surely not,' Coyote said. 'Then what will you do for fun?'

Drained, Church turned to walk back up the platform. The Wendigo was gone. But so were Jack, Mahalia and Crowther. Nelson and Tombstone stood in a trance, guns hanging limply.

Coyote and Raven leaped alongside Church. 'The boy is gone. That was always the end of our competition,' Raven said.

'He is too dangerous to exist in our Great Dominion,' Coyote added. 'He will always attract trouble.'

'Where is he?'

Coyote and Raven both pointed up.

'Apoyan-Tachi, Sky Father God, has taken him,' Coyote replied.

'If you wish to find him again, you must first find your way through the Sky Maze,' Raven stated. 'Take a step off the highest point of any of the highest buildings in this city and perhaps you will find yourself standing on the invisible path.'

'Or perhaps not,' Coyote added.

chapter fourteen

clutchinG at straws

1

New York was awake. From Battery Park to Harlem, the streets were already beginning to gridlock under the bright, silvery gleam of the dawn sky. In the diners, the cooks were preparing for the onslaught of morning customers, filling the air with steam from the coffee machines, loading trays of bagels and croissants, opening boxes of eggs. The chatter of life started low, the words not yet apparent.

Church sat on the sidewalk at Fifth Avenue and Thirty-Fourth Street, bone-weary from the night's exertions, knowing the worst was yet to come. The Lexus pulled up next to him at speed and Laura lurched angrily out of the back seat.

'God, the smell in there was disgusting. Ham. And shit.'

Nelson climbed out of the passenger seat. 'You sure you want her back? I think we've got due cause to put her away – for being in possession of a dangerous mouth and a lethal personality.'

Exchanging a silent, knowing look with Nelson, Church hugged Laura as Tom emerged from the car carrying a long package wrapped loosely in pages from the *New York Post*. He handed Caledfwlch to Church.

Bad-tempered, Tombstone threw open the driver's door. 'More weird shit.' The police radio was continually interrupted by bursts of loud static, within which Church could just make out a single repeated word: Croatoan. On Tombstone's BlackBerry, random emails blinked in, quoting the same word.

'Multiple streams of information transmitting the same message,' Shavi said. 'It is starting.'

'Then we'd better get moving.' Church unwrapped Caledfwlch and slipped it into the scabbard on his back.

'We're giving you one chance here,' Nelson said.

'That's all I need.'

Nelson glanced at Tombstone, unsure. 'You think we've been infected with stupidtron particles?'

'Oh, yeah. You, me and the rest of the world.'

'My girlfriend's always going on about shit like this,' Nelson confided. A flicker of doubt crossed his face. "The world is an illusion. We're all tricked into believing a lie. The evidence is there if you look close enough." She always thought it was funny – me, a detective with ten years' service, couldn't see the evidence. I used to laugh at her.' He tapped his head. 'Last week she tried to kill herself. Nearly did it, too. Now she won't talk to me.'

'Don't start with all that maudlin shit again,' Tombstone said. 'She'll come round, I told ya. Give her time.' He grinned, but he couldn't keep his true thoughts from his eyes.

Nelson looked up to the summit of the Empire State Building at Church's back. 'I still think you're crazy.'

'Main observatory is on the eighty-sixth floor, another on the one hundred and second,' Tombstone said. 'You can see eighty miles on a clear day. They say.'

'You've not been up?' Nelson asked.

'Don't like heights.'

'That's not high enough.' Shielding his eyes, Church tried to see to the top of the one-hundred-and-two-storey structure. 'Can you get me out at the very top?'

After Nelson and Tombstone spoke to security, they returned to the car as Church and the others took the elevator as high as it would go. Steel steps led to a small, circular, windowed observation area with a ladder leading up to a hatch that gave access to the dirigible mooring mast.

Pressing her face to the glass, Laura looked out over the city. 'Church-dude, it's not often I agree with the Filth, but that detective is right. You are seriously fucked in the head if you're going out there.'

With his alien eye, Shavi searched for some sign of the invisible maze, but found nothing.

'What if those gods were just ragging on you?' Laura continued. 'There's nothing out there. One step, one thousand four hundred feet to the pavement. My friend Church, a fine red mist.'

'That's it – give him a pep talk,' Tom said.

'I've come prepared. To a point.' Steeling himself, Church stepped onto the ladder. 'We don't have a choice. We need the Second Key now.

If you listen carefully you can hear the city talking, repeating one word over and over again, everywhere. The Void isn't going to take any chances. It's going to pull the plug.'

'I can go,' Shavi said.

Church smiled unconvincingly. 'You get to have the second go.'

They all fell silent. Church nodded once, then climbed the ladder and went through the metal hatch.

'Idiot or hero, you decide.' Laura glanced back out at the dizzying drop. 'I think I'm going to vomit. Look away.'

The rattle of feet on steel made them think Church was returning until a low sound like a badly tuned radio set their teeth on edge. Veitch stepped into the room, the black flames of his sword casting odd shadows.

'Here we are again,' he said. 'All together one last time.' Behind him, Ruth looked uncomfortable and Miller kept his eyes down self-consciously.

'How did you find us, you tattooed fuck-head?' Laura said.

'Me and Church are like brothers these days, didn't you know? Even more than we were in the old days.' He began to climb the ladder to the hatch. 'Time to finish this.'

2

Back on Summer-side, the rain still sheeted down and ran in torrents along the winding, cobbled streets. The Court of the Soaring Spirit cowered in the face of the storm. Mallory led a small army towards the Palace of Glorious Light, just a hulk lurking in the darkness.

Axe in hand and ready for battle, Decebalus strode beside him, and at their backs were the Brothers and Sisters of Dragons plucked from hundreds of years of Earth's history. They were still coming to terms with their freedom, but Mallory could tell the Pendragon Spirit was alive in their hearts.

With Lugh and Rhiannon at their head, the Tuatha Dé Danann were grim-faced. They, too, were trying to come to terms with the new status quo, but their task was more difficult. Their race was built upon the mythology that they were special, perfect, above all other creatures. To be told their survival depended on fighting and defeating one of their own destroyed the very foundations of their existence.

Lightning flaring overhead, Mallory brought them to a halt on the approach to the palace. 'Go back to the Hunter's Moon and look after

Virginia,' he told Jerzy. 'If we don't survive, get her out of the city. Try to find Church. Just keep her safe.'

The Mocker grasped Mallory's hand fervently. 'I see you are a great man, as great as my good friend Jack Churchill. My life has been better for having known you.'

'Just get the drinks in. And look after yourself.'

When Jerzy had scampered away, Mallory turned to Lugh. 'Are you ready?'

'It is my sister.' Lugh's voice trembled, though his face remained emotionless. 'I am not ready. I will never be ready.'

'That place is a fortress,' Mallory said. 'Our only option is a frontal assault. If we can take Niamh by surprise—'

'She will be ready for us,' Rhiannon said. 'She already knows that the Watchtower has been breached and that the prisoners are free.'

'You should go back with Jerzy . . .' Mallory began until he saw her affronted expression.

She held up her stump. 'One missing hand does not make me lesser. It does not amount to one fraction of the scars I have borne throughout all my time.'

'Of course. I'm sorry.'

'Your instinct is to protect. I understand that. It is why you make a good battle leader.'

'I just want to finish the job here and get back to my life.'

'And I will say again,' Lugh began, 'this is a turning point in the relationship between Golden Ones and Fragile Creatures. Now there is hope for my people – because of you. We will not forget that.'

Mallory looked out over the wet rooftops of the jumbled city, rolling down towards the main gate.

'What do you seek?' Rhiannon asked.

'I thought Sophie would be here. That old Craft business usually makes her sensitive to what's going on.' He shrugged. 'She'll probably be along when we need her most, just like the cavalry.'

'You should speak to our troops,' Rhiannon said.

'They're not my troops.'

'Do it. They expect it. They deserve it.'

Reluctantly, Mallory climbed onto the crumbling stone base of a rune-carved obelisk and looked out over the ranks. Concentrated in one place, he could finally see what the Pendragon Spirit meant. The Brothers and Sisters of Dragons had the rough faces of country stock and the educated features of city dwellers, the formalised styling of the Reformation and the austerity of the nineteen-fifties; their expressions revealed their fears and bravery, doubts and arrogance; but all of them to a person exuded a quality of hope and a strength of character that suggested they would do what was right, whatever the personal cost.

Mallory drew Llyrwyn. The blue flames licked hungrily towards the looming, oppressive figure of the Burning Man. Everyone fell silent, watching him.

'You don't know me,' he began, 'and that's probably how it should be. I'm a nobody. But I'm one of you. And that's what it means to be a Brother or Sister of Dragons. Individually, we're a mess. We're filled with doubts and flaws and guilt and shame and personal failures. We can barely get through our own lives. But when we come together, when we support each other and contribute our strengths to one single, good end – watch out. Because that's when we work magic.

'This flame, this blazing Blue Fire, gives us our strength. But it also symbolises who we are when we unite. A beacon in the dark. A light that will never be extinguished.

'Some of you haven't had the chance to discover who you are, or what you're capable of. You're going to get that chance now. It'll be scary and tough. But you'll always have a Brother or Sister beside you, picking you up when you fall, protecting you when your guard is down, carrying you when you're too tired to take another step. You'll never be alone. Let's enter this fight not as individuals, but as Brothers and Sisters of Dragons. And let's come out of it winners.'

For one moment there was only the sound of the wind and the lashing rain, and then a cheer rose up. Mallory shivered at what he heard in that sound. Surprised that he had found the words to express his feelings, he stepped down; Decebalus clapped him on the back, and even the Tuatha Dé Danann regarded him with respect.

'Let's go,' he said.

Under cover of the storm, they approached along the narrow street that led to the square in front of the palace. Mallory still held out hope that they would be able to gain access undetected. But as they crossed the square, roaring oil fires ignited along the ramparts and on the towers, and the gloomy building was instantly transformed into a hellish fortress.

The gates were closed, and although they had not been designed to resist a major assault, Mallory could see it would take a long time to batter them down.

Yet as they surged around the base of the palace, a cry rose up. Running furiously and determinedly from the narrow street were many of the strange characters from the Hunter's Moon, with more of the court's residents joining them by the second. Living in fear of Niamh's secret brutality and the enforcement of her guard, they now felt empowered.

Shadow John, tall and thin in his stovepipe hat and black suit, was transformed from his urbane geniality into a terrible sight, eyes ablaze with fury. He leaped to the gate and with one sweep of his long fingers tore open the lock.

With the doors flung open, the ragtag army surged into the suffocating maze of long, low corridors and tiny rooms. The lower ranks of Niamh's guard rushed from secret passages in guerrilla strikes or attempted to hold the winding staircases leading to the upper floors. At first, Lugh, Rhiannon and the other Tuatha Dé Danann were hesitant at attacking their own, but when they saw the guards' uncaring ferocity, they began to respond in kind. Soon the small passageways were filled with clouds of fluttering golden moths from both sides. As Mallory fought his way through to the upper floors, he caught sight of Lugh, his face grim and now wet with tears. Every blow he struck left him shaking.

While the battle raged below, Mallory, Decebalus and one of the new Brothers of Dragons, a sallow-faced Victorian wearing a long, black coat, moved swiftly through the upper floors.

'What's your name?' Mallory asked the newcomer.

'Charles Granger.' He carried a short sword awkwardly. 'I wish I had a good pistol.'

'Okay, Charlie, you drop back and keep your eyes open for anything we miss. They're sly bastards and they won't be averse to popping out and stabbing us in the back.'

'Let them try it,' Decebalus growled. 'I'll have their heads from their shoulders before they've even taken a step.'

They came to a long, low corridor leading to the main staircase to the next floor. Heavy tapestries lined both walls and the only light came from a solitary torch at the far end.

'I'd have thought we'd have encountered the elite guard by now,' Mallory said.

'You are right,' Decebalus acknowledged. 'Something is amiss.'

'I do hope we get through this without too much fuss,' Charles noted. 'I'm looking forward to spending some time with my girl.'

'You and me both.' Cautiously, Mallory moved along the corridor, keeping his eyes fixed on the opening to the staircase. The silence was broken by a faint, brief sound behind them, like air escaping from a pipe.

Mallory halted. 'What was that?'

'I know not.' Decebalus scanned the corridor.

'Probably nothing. Let's keep going,' Charles prompted.

'Everything's something in this place. That's the rule.' Mallory edged forward.

Another burst of air, still behind them but louder than the last.

'Again!' Decebalus said with irritation.

'From the ceiling.' Mallory indicated a series of holes barely visible in the gloom.

Behind them, Charles began to cough. The coughing soon became choking, and they turned to see him clutching at his throat.

'He can't breathe!' Mallory caught him as he fell to his knees. The panic in Charles's face became horrified realisation as blood oozed from the corners of his eyes, nose, ears and mouth. Blisters erupted all over his skin, bursting to reveal thick yellow pus that turned to blood as it dripped away. Within seconds, he pitched forward, dead.

'Witchcraft!' Decebalus exclaimed.

'Poison, more like.' Mallory felt a pang of grief and turned it on its axis into cold rage. 'Poor bastard. She's going to pay for this.'

'She will pay,' Decebalus agreed. 'Threefold. Pain upon suffering upon hell on Earth.'

Mallory tore a tapestry off the wall and held it aloft so Decebalus could get under it. Shielded from the blasts of poisonous air, they ran down the corridor.

At the stairwell, they threw the tapestry off and prepared to climb to the next floor until what sounded like the roars of jungle beasts rose up beneath them. Feet thundered up the stairs from the floor below, accompanied by an abattoir stink.

Rounding a turn in the stairs came a score or more of squat, brutish Redcaps clothed in the remnants of their human victims. Mallory braced himself for the fight, but Decebalus said firmly, 'Go. I will hold them off.'

'You can't. They're killing machines.'

'Go!' Decebalus roared. 'If we both fall here, there will be no one to avenge our dead. Besides, I fight better alone.'

Mallory hesitated for only a second before he clapped the barbarian on the shoulder. 'You're a hero. I'm not going to forget this.'

'Then you buy all the ale when next we meet in the Hunter's Moon.'

Mallory ran up the stairs. Glancing back, he saw Decebalus crash his axe into the skull of the first Redcap and then kick the body back down onto the ravening horde. His insane laughter boomed up the stairwell. 'To hell!'

Mallory sprinted up the stairs to the very top of the palace where he knew Niamh would be preparing her defence, or her escape. In the annexe that led into the queen's suite of state rooms, he found Evgen and five members of the elite guard dressed in black and silver armour and full helmets. They brandished broad, curved swords.

'One Brother of Dragons,' Evgen sneered. 'How disappointing. Pray to your God. You will be with him soon.'

'I don't have a god,' Mallory replied. 'This is what I believe in.'

He swung Llyrwyn and as he attacked, the Blue Fire became an inferno, fed by his Pendragon Spirit and feeding it in turn. The first two guards exploded into moths before they had even taken a step. The third was more of a challenge, but Mallory would not be contained. The Blue Fire filled him until there was no Mallory, just a righteous weapon that struck with all the strength and skill he had learned as a Knight Templar.

Another guard fell, then another, until Evgen faced him, alone. The captain threw back the mask of his helmet, revealing an expression of incomprehension.

'You can leave,' Mallory said.

'My duty is to my queen. I have neither will nor desire beyond that.'

Mallory felt briefly sorry for him. But then Evgen raised his sword and for five minutes they battled ferociously until Evgen misjudged a strike and Mallory ran through his open defence.

Dropping his weapon, Evgen crashed back against the wall. 'How can Fragile Creatures defeat the Golden Ones?' he said in disbelief.

'This is a new age.'

Once the moths had dissipated, Mallory entered the reception hall. The stifling heat made him choke. The fire in the great hearth roared as if driven by bellows, and all around the room braziers glowed. There was no other light source, and a claustrophobic gloom clustered in the corners.

Niamh stood before the fire. She wore tight-fitting ebony armour etched with silver filigree and a black ceremonial headdress with six horns that resembled the arms of Shiva.

'Dressed for a funeral?' Mallory said.

Niamh smiled. 'Dressed for victory.'

The flames of Llyrwyn licked towards her hungrily. 'What happened to you? Church told us how you—'

'How I loved him? Jack Churchill taught me many things. He ignited a fire inside me, and then chose the love of another. A Fragile Creature,' she added contemptuously.

'You can't always get what you want. So is that it – you've caused all this misery just because of a broken heart?'

Niamh laughed. 'How dismissive you are of the signifying quality of Fragile Creatures! Everything you do is because of love! I have observed your kind for an age. If you seek money or power, it is in a pitiful attempt to fill the gap left by an absence of love. Adult lives are corrupted and distorted by the search for love denied them as children. Love drives Fragile Creatures to achieve astonishing things, and love lies behind murder and betrayal and cruelty. Love destroys confidence and creates doubt and self-loathing. Love turns Fragile Creatures into gods. It is all and everything. To dismiss it so only shows your ignorance.'

'So now you've signed up with the Void because you didn't get the kisses you wanted.'

'This is the twilight of the gods, foretold in all your stories since your first days. The old ways are passing, for every living being. I choose my path accordingly.'

'It makes no sense. How can you give in to control? To a universe that denies freedom, belief, magic? You had that spider removed to escape control—'

She laughed. 'Yes, I had the spider removed.' She raised her arms wide. 'And then I chose to be filled with spiders.'

Under her skin, lumps of varying sizes began to move across her hands, her face, distorting her features. She opened her mouth wide and the spiders swarmed out and over her body.

Mallory had hoped he could talk her into giving up. Now he saw there was no hope. He raised Llyrwyn and prepared to attack.

A ferocious wind blasted from a corner of the room, throwing him hard against the wall. Niamh hadn't moved. The spiders still crawled over her, but now she wore a cruel smile.

From out of the shadows walked another woman in the same black armour and headdress as Niamh. It was Sophie, her cheeks wet with tears. 'You bastard. You betrayed me,' she said with devastating bitterness.

Mallory gaped. 'What's happened to you?'

'This.' She gestured and the wind rushed around the room. From the corner behind her came Caitlin, strapped to a wooden frame with barbed wire, barely conscious, badly beaten and bleeding from numerous wounds. Sophie raised her hand and the torture frame floated forward, a foot above the floor.

'What have you done?' Mallory could barely believe what he was seeing.

'She paid the price for being a duplicitous bitch.'

'You did that to her?'

Sophie shifted uneasily. There was a faint glassy quality to her eyes that gave him some hope. 'Of course not! I don't agree with it—'

'But you didn't stop it—'

'She deserved it! You and her – behind my back!'

'What? Caitlin and me? That's ridiculous.'

'I saw you!' The wind raged, tossing Mallory across the room.

His head ringing, Mallory struggled to his feet. The wind continued to rush around Sophie and there was lightning in her eyes. He'd had no idea she was capable of wielding such power, and it scared him.

He approached her cautiously, but couldn't help glancing at Caitlin.

'See?' Sophie snapped. 'You care about her.'

'Of course I do – she's hurt. Anybody with any compassion would care.'

His words stung her. She allowed her anger to rise up so she could ignore them. 'I'm sick of being betrayed by everybody I ever trust!'

'I'm not going to betray you.'

'Shut up!' The wind whisked around him, but this time didn't punish him. Tears filled her eyes. 'My mother and father betrayed me, and now you. The only people I've ever loved.'

'I don't understand.'

'They killed themselves when I was nine. A suicide pact. They said they loved me and they left me all alone.'

'You never told me that—'

'Didn't you ever wonder?' she sneered. 'The Pendragon Spirit only comes alive in us when we've experienced death. Didn't you think to ask who'd died around me?'

Mallory saw her desperate hurt and suddenly so many things about her became clear. 'I'm sorry.'

She looked away, her tears running freely.

Niamh watched with detached amusement.

'You manipulated her,' Mallory accused. If she had been close enough he would have killed her in an instant.

'I only allowed what was in her to take form,' Niamh said. 'Now she has chosen to be with me. I will not betray her.'

'Soph, don't fall for this,' he pleaded.

Sophie tore at her hair. The wind around her rushed wildly in random directions. A brazier crashed over, the glowing coals igniting a tapestry. Flames rushed up the wall.

'Soph, this isn't you!'

Tormented, Sophie threw her head back and screamed till her throat was raw. In the face of the gale, Mallory couldn't even get to his feet.

'Look at that woman!' Niamh pointed towards Caitlin. 'She didn't care about you. She is made of lies and deceit. She doesn't deserve your friendship.'

'Sophie!' Mallory called. 'She's trying to get you to do something you'll regret for the rest of your life. She's trying to damn you.'

'She deserves to be eradicated!' Niamh's voice rose above the gale.

Sophie cast a pitiful look at Mallory. 'Why couldn't you have saved me?'

'Hold him back,' Niamh insisted.

'You can kill her,' Mallory said, 'but she'll come back. That's what we do. Death can't hold us.'

'This is beyond death,' Niamh said. 'The Devourer of All Things has allowed the universe to create a handful of weapons of power that can strike at the very heart of Existence. They are scattered, unknown, lost. They can be used only once, because of their power.' She smiled sweetly. 'They can wipe a being out of Existence. Not just so they are dead, but so they never existed in the first place. No one will remember them ever having been. Their words, their gestures, their caresses, their kisses – all forgotten, because they never happened. Removed from the cycle of rebirth. It is worse than the worst thing you could ever imagine for yourself, for it means that you amounted to nothing.' From her pocket, she removed a crystal in the shape of a snowflake. It spun slowly of its own accord an inch above her palm. 'And I have such a weapon here.'

She held her hand higher and the snowflake spun faster. Shards of light blinked off it.

'Stop her!' Mallory shouted at Sophie. 'Caitlin's one of us!'

Sophie closed her eyes, sobbing silently. The wind continued to pin Mallory against the floor.

The snowflake pulsed. Like all the other objects of power Mallory had witnessed, he knew he was not seeing its true shape. He had the sense of some enormous machine grinding into life behind the illusion of the world he saw before him. Caitlin lolled on the torture frame, defenceless, broken.

And then the wind dropped and all was still. Mallory only had a second to register this before he heard a small voice.

'You should have saved me.'

A dagger of white light burst from the spinning snowflake towards Caitlin. Before it reached her, Sophie took the full force of the weapon in her breast, a halo of white light burning around her.

For a second, Mallory felt as if the weapon had hit him and he had winked out of existence. Desperate to hold on to the last of her, he scrambled to where Sophie had sunk to the ground.

The white light sparked and fizzed around her as it unstitched her from reality. Her skin was freezing to the touch, as though she had lain in the snow for hours, as though she was already dead.

Mallory tried to say something, but the words died in his throat.

Sophie smiled weakly, already a ghost of the smile he remembered. 'I'm sorry,' she said. 'I've made a real mess of things.'

'It wasn't true . . . about Caitlin and me. I'd never do anything like that.'

She looked into his face and saw it was true.

'I love you.' He gripped her hands tightly. 'You saved me. I was worthless before, and . . . and—'

'Ssh. Don't say it.' The light gave her skin a translucent quality. 'I love you, too.'

Her eyes flickered and closed.

Mallory closed his own eyes and thought hard. The pub in Salisbury where he had first seen her came to mind as clearly as if he was there. Sophie, with her traveller friends, wearing a faded hippie dress beneath a pink mohair sweater, a clutter of beads and necklaces around her neck, her sharp, questioning intelligence, the knowing quality around her eyes that he instantly found deeply sexy. Though he hadn't realised it until much later, that first moment was when she had trapped him in her gravity.

He recalled the first time they kissed, every detail of the surroundings, the temperature of the air, the smell of her hair. He recalled the first time they made love. Watching her in the dealers' room of Steelguard Securities, when he knew she was special even though the context had been stolen from him.

So many memories, every sensation, every word spoken, mundane and unique. He wanted them all, but there were too many. Desperately, he tried to hold on to her.

Then, from somewhere far away, a cold wind blew and she was gone. His hands clutched thin air. Broken, he sagged until his forehead touched the floor.

Niamh had moved to a window that had been hidden behind one of the tapestries, now flung wide open to the night. From outside came the sound of wings.

Mallory turned to her, filled with a residual hatred that was fading fast. In a second she went from the woman he would have travelled to the ends of Existence to destroy to just another enemy. There would be no revenge.

He saw in her face some kind of secret knowledge that pleased her, and then there was movement behind her. Standing on the back of a flying, bat-winged beast was the Libertarian. He held out his hand for Niamh to join him.

Grasping Llyrwyn, Mallory ran to the window, but he was too late. The beast was already moving away. The Libertarian had his arms around Niamh's shoulders, like old lovers reunited.

'Your new life is yours to enjoy,' Niamh said sardonically, 'in what little time remains.'

The leathery wings beat faster and the creature turned towards the Burning Man, soaring on thermals, out of the court and away.

Mallory raced back to where Caitlin hung on the torture frame. Her wounds were all superficial and already healing. As he cut through the barbed wire, her eyes flickered open.

'Oh,' she said weakly. 'Why are you crying?'

Mallory touched his damp cheek. 'I don't know,' he replied.

3

In the bright, fresh hour after dawn, the Court of the Soaring Spirit took on a new mood. In the streets – no longer dark, no longer claustrophobic – people turned their faces to the sky for the first time in many days. Music rang from the open doors and windows of the Hunter's Moon.

In the airy, sun-drenched corridors and rooms of the Palace of Glorious Light, the old was swept out. As Mallory watched over Caitlin, asleep now and recovering from her wounds, a dark mood came over the room. He had thrown open all the curtains to allow some light into the place, yet an area of darkness was growing in the centre of the room and spreading out to drive the light back. Fearing another attack from Niamh, Mallory drew his sword, but even its flames were dimmed.

In the heart of the darkness, Mallory glimpsed piercing eyes. A potent sense of threat pervaded everything, yet it was also sexually charged. Mallory had felt it before in the Watchtower. 'The Morrigan,' he said.

The darkness swept towards Caitlin and disappeared inside her like smoke being sucked into a fan. Caitlin's eyes snapped open, and in them Mallory could see no sign of the woman he knew, nor did she even appear conscious. She floated an inch or two above the surface of the bed.

'She's back with us now.' The fearful voice came from Caitlin's lips, but Mallory recognised the tone of Briony's persona.

'Leave her,' Mallory said.

'The Dark Sister has a bond with this one. They know each other, and benefit from each other's strengths.'

'What does the Morrigan want with Caitlin?'

'Revenge. For the indignities heaped upon her in the Watchtower by the queen of this court. She will ride this Sister until the debt has been paid, in blood. And it will be paid in full soon.'

Caitlin floated back to the bed, sleeping peacefully once more. No response came to Mallory's further questions, and there was no sign that the Morrigan waited inside his friend.

Troubled, he returned to the charred royal reception hall. Open windows along one wall now flooded the room with sunlight. He felt a strange connection to the place as he looked out over the shimmering rooftops, yet also inexplicably sad.

Decebalus boomed a greeting. He was covered in cuts and a jagged, badly stitched wound now ran diagonally across his face, but he was in high spirits.

'You have a visitor,' he said.

The barbarian gestured towards the door behind him and Hunter entered, looking around curiously. 'I like what you've done with the place.'

'I thought you'd walked out on us.'

'I'm nothing if not capricious.'

'The Brothers and Sisters of Dragons are resting after the battle,' Decebalus said, 'but to a man and a woman they are ready to take the war to the Enemy.'

'We'd just be sending them to their deaths. I was tasked with finding the Extinction Shears – that's the only thing that'll stop the Void,' Mallory said. 'And we're no closer to achieving that.'

Flopping into a chair, Hunter draped his legs over one arm. 'Don't worry. You've got me now.'

'Is that supposed to encourage me?'

'You haven't heard my plan yet.'

'All right. First we need to get you a sword.'

Hunter grinned. 'Oh, I've already got a weapon.'

'Then it's the three of us – you, me and Caitlin.' Mallory was suddenly overcome with a devastating pang of loneliness. He turned back to the bright, new day, searching for an answer he would never find.

4

The high winds gusting along the chasms of New York City threatened to tear Church from the few square feet on top of the Empire State Building.

Clutching onto the mooring mast to save himself, the world spun far below.

Don't look down, he repeated like a mantra, and focused instead on the blue sky of a new day. But he couldn't help himself. His stomach churned and his head whirled, and he dropped to his knees, fighting to keep control. The wind continued to pull him back and forth.

This is insane, he told himself. An invisible maze up in the clouds, where one wrong step meant plummeting to the ground far below?

Crawling to the edge of the platform, he peered around. There was no sign of where the maze began. Leaning out, eyes screwed shut, he flailed about but felt only thin air.

From his jacket, he pulled the can of spray paint he had bought in a convenience store on the way from Grand Central Terminal. He had no idea if it would work. Reaching out again, he sprayed a small amount. The paint particles were caught by the wind.

Edging along the platform, he tried again. When he was near the end of the second side, some paint remained, frozen in the air. With relief, he sprayed a strip extending out from the platform. The first steps of the maze were revealed.

That was the easy part. Steeling himself, Church stood up and stepped into the gulf. His heart flipped and his knees buckled, but the maze held his weight.

Away from the platform, the vertigo was even more debilitating. He felt as if he was suspended in the air, with nothing beneath his feet but the street far below. An overwhelming sensation of falling made him spasm from side to side, or pitch forward. Only his willpower stopped him going over the edge. Every step he had to steady himself, shut his eyes and fight the rushing fear that threatened to paralyse him, and, he thought, drive him mad. Gradually, he established a kind of control by keeping his eyes fixed as much as possible on the horizon or the sticky paint at his feet.

He discovered the maze was barely two feet wide. He sprayed a section, edged forward, desperately holding on to his stomach, and then sprayed some more. But the paint wouldn't last for ever, and if the maze was extensive, what would he do then?

Thirty feet out the wind blew even more fiercely. It came in intermittent high gusts, and each time he had to crouch down and brace himself to resist being blown off. It felt like only a matter of time until a gust took him unawares.

Every now and then he would stop and close his eyes, and breathe deeply, pretending he was on solid ground. And that was when he heard the sound of clapping. Wobbling as he looked over his shoulder, he saw Veitch sitting on the platform at the top of the Empire State Building.

Rage exploded in Church with a ferocity that shocked him. He thought of all the Brothers and Sisters of Dragons Veitch had slaughtered over the years, the agonising wound he had inflicted on Church in Beijing, the spell that had sucked at Church's Pendragon Spirit and driven a wedge between him and the woman he loved. But most of all he thought about how Veitch had stolen Ruth from him.

'You're expecting me to risk my neck out here just so you can steal the Key when I get back?' Church said.

'Something like that.'

Veitch's nonchalance made the blood thunder in Church's head even more.

'Actually, I was just having a little bet with myself,' Veitch continued. 'How long before the path turned left and you went right, or before you leaned a bit too far to one side and went over the edge. But carry on, mate – don't let me stop you.'

Consumed with anger, Church drew his sword. 'We end this here and now,' he shouted, marching back along the precarious path.

His own anger sparking viciously, Veitch drew his sword and stepped hesitantly onto the path. Church could see him cursing under his breath as he walked out over the void, but soon his rage made him forget where he was, and he focused solely on Church.

'We've come a long way, you and me,' Veitch said, 'from strangers to friends – until you abandoned me.'

'Don't give me any of your pathetic whining. You can't blame me for what happened to you. You can't blame anyone, not even yourself. You got a raw deal, and that's just the way it was. But everything that's happened since – that's all you, through and through.'

Veitch's face darkened. 'You know what pisses me off about you? You give me that look my dad used to give me when I was a kid – that I *disappoint* you. I wish you'd just go at me with that sword, because nothing's worse than that look.'

Church levelled Caledfwlch, instantly feeling Veitch's own sword sucking at the power it contained. 'Made sure you got your equaliser in place before you faced me properly.'

'If you want to chicken out, mate . . . The truth is, we're tied together on some level you don't understand, and if you were smart enough, you could suck all the nasty, black misery out of me and make yourself stronger. Only maybe you're just not as smart as you make out.'

'I don't want to pollute myself with what you've got.'

'You're not smart, or you'd get the fact that we're the same. Or maybe not exactly that – different sides of the same coin, perhaps. We'd each benefit from a little bit of the other.'

'Been doing some thinking, have you?'

'Yeah, I have.'

'Think harder.'

Church attacked forcefully, oblivious to the gulf on either side. As Veitch blocked the blow, blue and black lightning flashed across the sky.

They moved back and forth along the narrow path amidst the furious storm of energy discharges, a whirlwind of swords, both fixed intently on the other, the world, the stakes they had both striven for, all of it forgotten.

The wind caught droplets of blood from Veitch's arm, and from Church's cheek. They were evenly matched in skill and motivation.

Occasionally, Church would duck a blow and come sharply up against the precariousness of his position as he teetered on the edge of the path, fighting to regain his balance, the world rushing beneath him. Veitch didn't give him a second to recover. Returning his attack, Church drove Veitch back, trusting his own instinct to keep him in the centre of the path.

'What are the pair of you doing?' Ruth's desperate cry interrupted them. Fearfully, she clung to the mast.

Veitch was distracted. Unable to stop carrying through with his thrust, Church sliced Veitch's upper arm. In his pain, he lost his footing and went over the edge.

Ruth shrieked.

At the last, Veitch's silver hand crashed against the edge of the path and clung on. The strain was clear on his face.

'Go on, then. Let me die,' he shouted. 'You get your girl back. I pay the bill for all the shit I've done. You win.'

Veitch was right – everything would be simpler if Church just let him fall. For a moment, he even considered it, but then he saw the Libertarian's grinning, cruel face in his mind, and wondered if this was the turning point on his path to becoming that twisted mass murderer: one death for his own benefit could easily become two, become many. In the end, wasn't Veitch right? They were both capable of the same thing, given the right circumstances. Veitch had slaughtered in the past and Church would do so in the future. The seeds were inside them, two brothers from the same stock. How could he judge?

He grabbed Veitch's forearm and hauled him back onto the path.

'You're so bleedin' noble, you make me sick,' Veitch said.

'You're welcome.'

'Don't get all girly and think just 'cause you saved my life it's going to be all smiles. All you've done is help balance things out a bit.'

'Ryan, we're more than a thousand feet above a messy death. This isn't the place.'

Veitch glanced back at Ruth, who was tearing herself apart with concern. 'All right. But I'm coming with you.'

'So you can stab me in the back and take the Key?'

'You're going to have to take a punt, aren't you, 'cause you haven't got a choice.'

Now that his anger had subsided, Church could see Veitch was right. Creeping to the edge of the path, he began to spray.

'Just like old times,' he heard Veitch say sarcastically.

Church kept one eye on Veitch, fearing that if he dropped his guard he would be pitched off the path to his death, but Veitch followed sullenly, keeping several feet back. Progress was slow. The path dog-legged, twisted, turned back on itself and ran in long, straight lines until they were well out over the city and the Empire State Building and Ruth were far behind. And that was when the paint ran out.

'Now what?' Veitch said.

'We can't go back.' Church pondered the point, swaying uneasily in the wind. 'We'll just have to feel around and do it without any help.'

'You're nuts.'

'We don't have a choice.'

Bracing his right foot, Church felt out with his left. Slowly, they edged onwards. Their progress was even more gut-churning without the meagre comfort of the sticky paint path beneath their feet. It felt as if they were floating in thin air.

'If I throw up, don't look back,' Veitch said.

At that moment, the path took a sudden turn to the left and Church's foot skidded over the edge. His weight carried him over after it. He saw the streets spinning far below, the air rushing into his lungs.

Veitch caught him by the back of his jacket and held him there. Church could tell Veitch was weighing whether to let him drop.

After a moment, Veitch pulled him back. They exchanged one look, and then continued on their way in silence.

Half an hour later, Church came up hard against what appeared to be a wall in the air, though he could see straight through it.

'Maybe the path goes round the edge,' Veitch suggested.

Church tested. 'No, this is it. Dead end.'

'That'd be plain stupid. All this way to a dead end.' Veitch thought. 'A door?'

Church felt around and something gave beneath his fingers. The door opened into a small room that was unmistakably floating in the air, but the walls, floor and ceiling had a translucent quality that gave it some solidity.

Inside sat Jack, Mahalia and Crowther, in a trance. Church immediately sensed another, invisible presence.

'Where are you?' he said.

'All around you, Brother of Dragons. I am Apoyan-Tachi, Sky Father God, and this is my home.'

From the corner of his eye, Church saw Veitch's hand moving towards his sword. Church signalled for him to stop and Veitch paused, but remained wary.

'I've come for these three Fragile Creatures, Sky Father God,' Church said.

'One is too dangerous to remain in this Great Dominion. He will only draw unwanted attention.'

'I won't let him stay here. We're going to the Far Lands. He will help us defeat the Devourer of All Things.'

'Too late.' There was a sound like the sighing of the wind through branches. 'The Devourer of All Things has closed all the doorways to the Far Lands. It knows your plans, and it wishes to keep you trapped here in the Fixed Lands where you are forever limited.'

'That's it, then?' Veitch said. 'It's all been for nothing?'

'No, it's not been for nothing,' Church said firmly.

'I've always admired your optimism.' For the first time there was no sarcasm in Veitch's voice.

'Sky Father God, let me take these three and I promise they will be removed from this Great Dominion.'

Another moment of whispering wind. 'You have made your way across my ritual path, and so you are worthy, Brother of Dragons. But know this: the moment the One is in your hands, the Devourer of All Things will rise up. Your End-Time will be close.'

'I'll take that risk. And thank you.'

'Hurry, Brother of Dragons. The path back will not remain in place long. Hurry!'

Veitch muttered under his breath, 'I don't bleedin' like the sound of that.'

When Church opened the door, the invisible path now sparkled as if it was sprinkled with gold dust. Veitch led the way, followed by Jack, Mahalia and Crowther tramping like sleepwalkers. Church brought up the rear and kept a close eye on them in case they woke suddenly and fell.

Halfway along the return journey, Church glanced behind him and saw the sparkling dust drifting down towards the grimy streets. The path was falling away.

'Ryan, you have to move faster!' he called out.

Veitch saw the reason for Church's anxiety and increased his pace, though the danger of slipping increased with it. Church herded the other three along as fast as he dared, but the disappearing edge of the path was racing towards his heels.

A loud noise, like a heavy, metal object being dragged, echoed all around.

'What the bleedin' hell is that?' Veitch called out.

'Don't think about it now,' Church said. 'Just get a move on!'

The edge of the path was only a few feet behind him, and he was jostling against Crowther's back. The wind gusted stronger, and on the horizon storm-clouds gathered rapidly; there was something unnatural about the speed with which they were rolling together.

The Empire State Building appeared in the gathering gloom ahead. Church could see Ruth still gripping the mooring mast, the wind whipping her hair. At the window, just below, the others watched anxiously.

'Ryan, you're going to have to run or I'm dead!' Church shouted.

Veitch held Church's gaze for a moment, thoughts racing across his face, and then he ran, only his innate balance keeping him from falling. The others followed somnolently.

Thin air sucked voraciously only inches from Church's heels.

The metallic grinding echoed again, even louder, setting Church's teeth on edge.

Veitch leaped for the platform and dragged Jack, Mahalia and Crowther onto it behind him. Church was a second too late. The path disappeared beneath his feet, but then four arms pulled him to safety. He fell in a heap with Veitch and Ruth. Her hand gripped his back and gave it a squeeze that told him all he needed to know, for now.

'That was mental!' Laura said when they were back inside. 'Church-dude, you are a mad bastard and no mistake.'

Shavi hugged him tightly.

'Enough of all that homoerotic stuff,' Laura continued. 'Can we toss the traitor off the top of the building now?' She fixed a cold eye on Veitch. 'I haven't forgotten that knife you stuck in my chest in London.'

'I knew you wouldn't die.'

'Yeah, but what about the agony, you tosser?'

Church searched Veitch's face as his own doubts twisted inside him. 'Are we going to fight?'

'Up to you.'

'I need both Keys, Ryan. I'm going to destroy the Void. Nothing else matters.'

Incomprehension flooded Veitch's face. As it gradually cleared, it was replaced by an instant of revelation. 'All right. I'm coming with you.'

'You have got to be kidding!' Laura exclaimed. 'He's murdered God knows how many of us, and now he wants to be friends!'

'I didn't say anything about that!' A crack of emotion broke in Veitch's voice.

'Ryan's done some awful things,' Ruth began hesitantly. 'He's made a lot of mistakes, and we're not going to forget that.'

'Damn straight,' Laura interjected.

'But he can help us. We need to be Five again – we need to have all our strength if we're going to face what lies ahead.'

'You're vouching for him?' Church asked.

Ruth bit her lip, nodded.

Laura cursed loudly, but Shavi interrupted, indicating outside where the storm-clouds had made the city as dark as night.

Mahalia emerged from her daze. 'What the hell's going on? Who are you losers?'

'Oh, look – a little Laura,' Ruth said.

Mahalia slapped off Miller who was trying to comfort her, and he turned his attention to the awakening Jack and Crowther.

The metallic noise began to boom with a regular beat, and beneath it was a rustling whisper, growing louder.

'What the hell is that?' Laura asked quietly.

'The people,' Shavi replied, 'speaking with one voice.'

As the sound grew, they could make out the words: *Croatoan, Croatoan*, repeated constantly.

Shavi drew their attention to the outline of buildings against the storm-clouds, now blurred with movement. 'The spiders are coming,' he said in awe.

Amidst a mounting sense of doom, they made their way to the sidewalk where Nelson and Tombstone waited in disbelief. The spiders swarmed across the sides of skyscrapers and surged up from the sewers.

'Ten Billion, huh?' Laura said.

'I am starting to think that was a slight underestimation,' Shavi replied.

Church grabbed Nelson. 'We need to get back to Grand Central Terminal.' Nelson nodded, dazed, and ordered Tombstone to commandeer a taxi.

Veitch pulled Church to one side. 'What's the point?' he said quietly.

'You heard that Sky God say all the gates to the Otherworld are closed. We're stuck here.'

'I'm not giving up, Ryan.'

Veitch shook his head, but as they raced as fast as they could through now-seething streets in two packed cars, he kept glancing at Church, his confused emotions playing out on his face.

All around people stood in a trance, faces turned to the boiling storm clouds, each of them quietly chanting, 'Croatoan, Croatoan,' in a pre-programmed ritual of release. Over it all, the flaming outline of the Burning Man was now clearly visible in the sky.

A small number of people who had seen through the Void's spell and had spent their days living outsider lives now ran in horror, searching for some escape that they would never find.

'This world is coming to an end,' Tom said. 'The Mundane Spell has been shattered once and for all, and you have become a threat to the Void's rule. It's shutting the planet down and starting again.'

'All those people,' Ruth said desperately.

'There's still hope for them. Nothing dies,' Church replied. 'It's up to us now.'

At the entrance to Grand Central Terminal, Church asked the detectives to come with them. Nelson shook his head. 'Somebody I've got to see.' He looked out across the blackened, churning city. 'She shouldn't have to face this on her own.'

'I'll drive,' Tombstone said with bright fatalism.

Church led the others down the sweeping steps and across the main concourse to the tracks.

'You're planning to catch a train?' Laura said incredulously. 'You've lost it!'

'We're going to the Far Lands.'

Veitch prodded Mahalia to keep moving and she glared at him murderously. 'What are you planning?' he asked.

At the end of the platform, Church sliced his arm with Caledfwlch and sent blood spraying across the rails. Within moments, the Last Train rumbled into the station in a cloud of steam and smoke. The doors slid open to reveal Ahken, smiling obsequiously, a cruel glint in his eyes.

'I was expecting you for one last journey,' he said.

'Can you take us to the Far Lands?' Church asked.

'Of course. That is our next and final destination. We have always been travelling towards this time, towards that place. The end of the journey is near now.'

He stepped aside to let everyone on board. Church, Ruth and Veitch remained in the open doorway as clouds of steam gushed across the platform from the starting engines. They watched as a wave of scurrying black washed down over the platform. Everywhere they looked was black and seething. The city, the world, was being taken apart by the spiders.

The train pulled out of the station slowly, gathering speed.

'It's going,' Ruth said. 'It's all going.'

'The Blue Fire's still out there,' Church said. 'And we're not beaten. We're stronger than ever.'

Veitch watched the spiders at work, his deep thoughts unreadable. 'From now on, it's war,' he said, almost to himself.

They let the door close and took their seats with the others. Silence filled the carriage as they all pondered what they were leaving behind, and the weight of the responsibility that now lay on their shoulders.

Then Church drew Caledfwlch and said to Veitch, 'Draw your sword.'

Puzzled, Veitch took out his blade. As the two great swords were slowly brought together, the black flames and the blue flames jumped towards each other, danced, mingled. Church winced at the touch of the cold as the fire around Caledfwlch grew a shade darker. But Veitch was wide-eyed with wonder as small blue flames shimmered amongst the black fire around his sword for the first time.

'We're ready for the fight,' Church said, and seeing the confidence and hope shining in the faces of his Brothers and Sisters, he knew they all agreed. For the first time in a long while, they were all together, drawing from each other's strengths. He felt a surge of pride and the belief that anything was possible.

The train moved out from the gathering darkness towards an uncertain future. The old age had passed. A new one lay ahead.

endwords

If you wish to find out more about the many mysteries and secrets hidden in The Kingdom of the Serpent, please read:

- The Age of Misrule sequence – *World's End, Darkest Hour, Always Forever*
- The Dark Age sequence – *The Devil in Green, The Queen of Sinister, The Hounds of Avalon*

It is not necessary to have read these books to understand the Kingdom of the Serpent sequence, but they will add a deeper appreciation of the overarching tale.

The hidden mysteries of this story are also regularly discussed on the forum at www.markchadbourn.net, where you will also be able to find out more about the author and his work, and sign up for a regular newsletter offering exclusive extracts, information and rare items.

More information is also available at www.myspace.com/markchadbourn.